DON'T FORGET ME, LITTLE BESSIE

Also by James Lee Burke

JAMES LEE BURKE

DON'T FORGET ME, LITTLE BESSIE

A NOVEL

Atlantic Monthly Press
New York

FIRST EDITION

Published simultaneously in Canada
Printed in the United States of America

Text design by Norman E. Tuttle at Alpha Design & Composition.
This book was set in 13-pt. Spectrum MT with Albertina MT
by Alpha Design & Composition of Pittsfield, NH.

First Grove Atlantic hardcover edition: June 2025

Library of Congress Cataloging-in-Publication data is available for this title.

ISBN 978-0-8021-6452-0
eISBN 978-0-8021-6453-7

Atlantic Monthly Press
an imprint of Grove Atlantic
154 West 14th Street
New York, NY 10011

Distributed by Publishers Group West

groveatlantic.com

25 26 27 28   10 9 8 7 6 5 4 3 2 1

In memory of my mother, Frances Benbow Burke

BOOK ONE

BOOK ONE

Chapter One

The first time I saw a spirit, I was fourteen years old, going down the furrow behind a single-tree plow and a mule named Lancelot, the baked ground folding over the point of the plowshare, my dress little more than cheesecloth, blowing in the dust and wrapping around my thighs, with nothing more than lonely thoughts in my head.

The colored lady who pulled me out of the womb was named Aint Minnie and said she knew I was special as soon as my eyes popped open. She said I had a haint and directly I would see the Other World. Now I knew what she meant.

The spirit had a face the shape of an ax, and was leaning against a pine trunk, paring his nails with a penknife, the way soldiers leaned against street lamps in town. He had greasy bronze hair that was combed up in a pompadour, and never lifted his eyes. "Come talk to me, little girl," he said.

"You have goat's feet," I replied. "I don't talk to goats."

"I was born with little feet. I ain't no goat."

"Even though you have hooves?"

"Those are my shoes. They're Buster Browns. Have you seen Buster Browns on an animal lately?" He lifted one foot and brightened his shoe on the back of his leg.

"You'd better git before my father comes out," I said.

"That surrey tied up at your veranda is owned by a certain woman who don't spend a lot of time at church. I think your daddy has his hands full right now, if you get my meaning."

"No, I do not get your meaning."

The spirit, if that's what he was, folded his penknife against his palm and placed it in his pocket. Then he lifted up his face and let his eyes crawl all over my body. My skin was cold and pale as last week's milk. He walked toward me, his teeth showing at the corner of his mouth, like his jawbone was broken. The sky was stacked with black clouds, towering all the way to the heavens, crackling with electricity. With no warning, the spirit reached out to touch me. I had never been so afraid. I stepped backwards and almost fell down.

"You got hair like cotton candy, except a lot thicker and not sticky," he said, lowering his hand. "Are you part albino? You're mighty pretty. Walk me up to your house."

"That is the most obnoxious thing I have ever heard a human being say. Walk your own self."

He turned his back and began heading toward the paintless, two-story Victorian home in which I was born, now inhabited by only my brother Cody and me and a father who I loved but who in turn did not love me.

I did not know what to do with this spirit. So I wrapped the reins on the plow's handle and leaned it in the furrow and followed him to the house. He looked back at me, his expression playful. "What's your name, little thing?" he asked.

"Little *thing*?"

"I didn't mean no offense."

"Bessie Holland, if it's any of your business," I replied.

Why did I just do that, I asked myself, although I probably didn't want to know, because the fact was I didn't have many friends.

"That's quite a name," he said. "It bounces around. Like a jawbreaker."

"What's that supposed to mean?"

"Nothing. My name is Slick. But there's some that calls me 'Hit-it-and-git-it.'"

He laughed loudly, his mouth wide, like a funnel, just as a bolt of lightning split the sky. The windmill by the barn was spinning, the hogs grunting in their pen, grit flying, the air blooming with the smell of rain. That was Texas in the dry season. Oh Lordy, I wanted to float away on a cloud. My days were not happy. I longed for my dead mother and my other siblings who found their way to the cities and disappeared into the grind of the twentieth century.

The spirit had walked fast and left me behind. Now he was looking over his shoulder, smiling like a jack-o'-lantern. He hammered the door with the flat of his fist, all the time grinning at me.

"My father has been ill," I said.

"Yeah, he's ill, all right."

I looked at his feet again. His cuffs covered his shoes and I could not see his ankles or socks and the goat hair I believed I had seen on his ankles. "Be advised, sir," I said. "My father is one of the most critical, insulting people I have ever known."

The heavy wood door jerked open, and suddenly my father was in the doorway, all six foot six of him, in his suspenders and unironed clothes and his deep-creased, hand-tooled Mexican boots. "What are you doing on my property?" he said.

"A few friends of mine want to settle up with you, Hackberry," the spirit said. "Financial-wise. Get my drift?"

"You address me as Captain," my father said.

"I can certainly do that, even though you ain't exactly in the Texas Rangers no more. Is that lady on the couch who I think it is?"

A woman dressed in mourner's black with a scarlet silk blouse was sitting erectly in the gloom, one hand cupped on a gold-knobbed walking cane. She was in her forties, and had a small waist and a large bosom and skin that looked powdered with talcum and the hooked nose of a hawk and lilac eyes lined with a pencil. Her name was Bertha Lafleur. I didn't like her, and never knew what to call her. Her eyes could take you apart, like a ceramic doll that's been run over.

Behind her were shelves filled with ancient encyclopedias, the covers worn, the pages stained with whiskey rings, in no order, many of them published by different book companies. Papa read them every day. He also had guns on the wall and hidden in the furniture and in the tool shed and barn. He also kept cats in the house, with names like Dr. Medico, Rumper, and Fat Kitty. On occasion he let in the lambs or a chicken or two, and dared anybody to call him eccentric.

"Let my daughter in before I knock you down," Papa told the spirit.

"He didn't bother me, Papa," I said.

The spirit stepped aside and bowed like a musketeer as I walked inside, then followed me in without asking permission. My heart started beating like a drummer boy rolling on his snare drum. I didn't like this smart-aleck spirit, but I didn't like seeing people picked on either.

"Papa, did you hear me?" I said.

My father's eyes were riveted on the spirit. Papa had a profile like an Indian, and hands that hung like skillets from his shirt cuffs. The woman with the cane rose from the couch. In a voice as soft as a feather, she said, "Hack?"

No reaction from Papa, who looked like he was about to pop the spirit in the face.

"Do not put yourself on the level of white trash, Hack," she said.

The spirit knew he had stepped in it proper. His face was twisted out of shape, as though he couldn't find the expression he needed for the moment, scared he was going to excite Papa more and scared to show how scared he was. He raised his chin and rolled his head like he had a crick in the neck. "Trash?" he said. "You call me trash? That is not seemly or fair or deserved. Not in my opinion. No, sir!"

Good try. The woman was not fazed and gave the spirit no recognition. "Sit down with me, Hack," she said.

Papa came out of his daze and looked at me as though I had wandered in from a dream. His eyes were a washed-out blue, his cheeks flecked with broken blood vessels inside his whiskers. "Where's your coat, daughter?" he asked.

"I lost it," I said.

"Whereabouts?"

"Probably at church."

He looked into space. "Today is Thursday."

"No, sir, it's Friday," I said.

"Why aren't you at school?"

"I quit going three weeks ago."

He wiped his face, then stared again at the spirit. "Why are you standing there?"

"I got my job to do," the spirit said. "The people I work for has bought up all your paper."

"What paper?" Papa said.

The spirit made a coughing sound, like a piece of chewing gum was stuck in his windpipe. "Debts in three gambling houses. Also a shitload of back taxes on your ranch."

"So they sent a little-bitty moron who cain't button his britches?"

The spirit had walked in with his fly open and his shirt sticking through it. His face turned as red as a lamp. I did not like to watch what was happening. The Hollands were a violent family but they weren't bullies. Papa always said you don't pick a fight with a weakling; it's unseemly. His shoulders were like a pair of anvils. Before liquor got him, he was treated as a hero by the whole state. He was a friend of Susanna Dickinson, the only white survivor of the Alamo, and also a Texas Ranger who rodeoed with Tom Mix and was good to Mexicans and colored people.

Bertha Lafleur walked slowly behind him and placed her hand on his shoulder. "Sit down, Hack. This young man is fixing to leave. Aren't you, young man?"

"Yes, ma'am," the spirit said.

She paused and looked at the spirit in a kindly way. "I'm sorry I offended you, sir."

"No, ma'am, I ain't offended," he replied. "Not a-tall."

His teeth were still clicking.

"Then go quietly now," she said. "You've done your job. Tell your employers that the debts will be paid. They have my word."

The spirit was shaking so bad he could hardly speak, the kind of fear that makes people give up all caution, and I knew he was going to say something he would regret the rest of his life. The biggest fear of a coward is the knowledge that he's a coward. There was a knot in his throat as big as a doorknob. "I don't let nobody call me trash, though," he said. "It just don't set right. It's like a saw going across a sixteen-penny nail."

There was a long pause. "I obviously mistook you for someone else," Bertha Lafleur said. "I deeply regret my mistake."

"Well, that's mighty nice," the spirit said, gulping a mouth load of air, his eyes widening with relief. I doubted if Lazarus could have been happier.

"Did you want to say something else?" Bertha Lafleur said.

"No, ma'am, apology accepted," the spirit blurted. "Forgotten. Erased, all bad feelings down the honey hole."

But my father wasn't finished. The spirit had said something that would not go away. "The people you work for are fixing to take my ranch?" he said.

"I don't know nothing about that," the spirit said. "I just carry the message."

Papa's light-blue eyes looked painted on his face. He loved his ranch more than any material thing in his life. He looked at the Henry rifle that was mounted above the mantel. I shoved the spirit out the door and down the steps and on his face in the dirt. I was amazed at his weightlessness. Or how strong I was when I needed to be.

"Run!" I said. "Run and run and run and don't ever come back! If you do, my father may kill you."

But the lady in black had closed and locked the door behind us, and the spirit knew he had been spared. He got up and dusted himself off. However, instead of thanking me, he reconstructed the arrogant personality that could have gotten him flung into the hog pen. "You ain't seen the last of me, little girl. Like the expression 'A family that prays together, stays together.' I got big people behind me."

"Call me 'little girl' again and I will bash you in the mouth."

"You don't have to get violent about it," he said.

"Pull up your britches and show me your feet."

"I ain't no demon. That's all that matters."

"Do you know what your problem is?" I said. "It's not that you have bad manners. It's that you don't have any manners at all."

"Well, people has got different kinds of talents," he said. "You don't have to be personal about it."

My heavens, some people, I thought. I went back to plowing and continued my various discussions with Lancelot's rump.

Chapter Two

ody was two years older than I, but each of us was delivered by a different stork. I had one personality. Cody had a closet full of them, all of them taking turns hurting each other. He beat up Jubal Fowler, the tallest and roughest boy on the schoolyard, for peeking in the outhouse when I was in it, then the same day he kicked me in the knee where I had a boil. When I asked him why he did such a mean thing, he said, "You deliberately got Jubal Fowler interested in you and forced me to punch him in the nose. Now we'll never get rid of the Fowler family."

"I did *not* get him interested, and I certainly didn't ask him to watch me in the privy."

"Stop lying."

Maybe he was partly right, but he didn't have to be so ugly about it. "All right, I'll take care of my own self," I said. "I'll also tell people I'm not related to you. You hurt me real bad, Cody, inside and out."

I wished I didn't say any more. But I did and I also started crying. "I hope you die," I said.

He flinched at my words. See, that was the little boy in him. The only reason he could beat up an older and bigger boy like Jubal Fowler was because he knew how to box. Everybody knew it, too. Cody's fists were a blur. He sent off ten cents and a comic book coupon, then knocked out a professional fighter behind the Green Lantern Saloon in town.

Late the same day he kicked my boil, he came upstairs into my bedroom with a pallet and lay down on the floor, the moon shining on him. He looked like a corpse.

"What are you doing down there?" I said.

"Guarding you."

"No, thank you. There's a screech owl in the pecan tree. Why don't you guard him?"

"I'm sorry for hurting you, Bessie. Sometimes I ain't no good. Something just takes hold of me."

"Don't use bad grammar, Cody. You know better."

"I wake up feeling like there's no point in anything. Like every minute of the day is just gonna get worse. Papa doesn't fuss at me, but he doesn't say anything good, either."

"Mama used to say, 'A drunkard is full of love, and his biggest love is his liquor.' The only thing she got wrong is that Papa doesn't love even that. He hates his whiskey and what it does to him, but he drinks it anyway. He's not mad at you or me. He's mad at what he is."

"I beat up Jubal Fowler for more than one reason, Bessie. His uncle is a constable in San Antonio. He says Papa goes to a straddle house there."

"A what?"

"A whorehouse."

The rawness of the term, as least in its association with my father, was like a slap on the ear.

"That woman who was here in black clothes and carrying a cane is a madam, Bessie. Her name is Bertha Lafleur. She's a bohunk."

"I know who she is. What's a bohunk?"

"Somebody who is half Mexican and half Bohemian. Most of them are fence-post cutters. Like gypsies and such."

"I'm not going to talk about other people like that," I said, trying to change the subject.

The truth is I knew my father's weakness for women. He wasn't just a womanizer; he had them on the brain all the time, drunk or not, every race, thin as clothes hangers or fat women who ate Goo-Goo Cluster bars around the clock. He claimed God's only perfect creation was women and would say it in the middle of a full saloon or at the church, and either embarrass or enflame anyone within earshot.

By the way, Papa's father was Sam Morgan Holland, a violent man who rode the Chisholm Trail and shot and killed nine men and lost two thousand longhorns to dry lightning outside Wichita, Kansas, which he dealt with by staying drunk on his horse all the way back to San Antonio. After sitting many Sundays on the mourners' bench at the local Baptist church, his depression rose like ash lifting from a dead fire. Supposedly he became a saddle preacher and did good deeds for the Indians on the Staked Plains and visited the graves of the men he killed on the Chisholm Trail. But I have seen his photograph close-up, and since then have doubted I would enjoy one of his sermons.

Sometimes I wanted to flee my family and all their lunatical behavior and live like a normal person, but I have yet to learn what a normal person is. Papa's male friends spat tobacco constantly and drank their coffee from the saucer. Most of them still carried guns, whether they were still lawmen or not. Every one of them would go after a calf in a lightning storm, but had no remorse in taking human life if they considered it legal. That gave me considerable concern.

"I have nightmares all the time," Cody said.

I rolled on my side and looked down at him. He had curly black hair, thick locks of it, and clear skin and plump arms and a chest shaped like a turkey's. He was wearing the cotton gown Aint Minnie gave him for his birthday, because Papa never remembered birthdays, not even his own.

"Nightmares about what?" I asked.

"Us all burning up. The house, everything. The horses running in the barn and you and me trying to get blankets over their heads."

"A dream cain't hurt you," I said.

"I saw lights out in the woods tonight."

"What kind of lights?"

"People chanting and walking in circles."

My stomach turned to water. "Go to sleep."

He had brought a blanket with the quilt he used for a pallet. He pulled it to his chin, his face suddenly quiet, the way a baby's face can turn quiet. I knew that one day he would be a ladies' man. Not because he was a fraud or a predator, because no matter how violent the Holland men were, down inside they were always looking for the nipple. At least that's what Mama said. He stared at me for a long time, with the same light-blue eyes as Papa, then they clicked shut, like a doll's, his hands curled into balls of white dough on the blanket's edge.

I went to the window and looked at the woods by the dirt road that led to town, and thought I heard a cowbell clanking. A few years ago that would not have been unusual. We had over one hundred head of Brahman. Now, thanks to my father's gambling and financial recklessness, we had virtually nothing.

A rain cloud moved across the moon, dropping the woods into darkness, like a great shaggy animal falling asleep. Then I saw a man wearing a flop hat ignite a lantern and raise it over his head in the middle of the dirt road. My heart stopped. Was it the man self-named Slick? His eyes were aglow under the brim of his hat. Then he spun into the ground and his lantern went out. I wet my underwear and could not get out of bed. I trembled under the blanket until sunrise, ashamed of my fear and too scared to do anything about it. I never wanted my father so much, except the night my mother died in childbirth.

In the morning I decided to go back to school. Why? Because of my English teacher Miz Ida Banks. She was a spinster and a Yankee and stood out like Queen Victoria in a cattle herd. Our textbooks were used and tattered and smeared with food and half-erased pencil marks and contained little literary merit, so she brought her classics to the school and perched her bottom on her desk and her glasses on her nose and read and read and read, especially the works of Hawthorne and Homer and Keats. But the boys were interested only in stories about the Alamo and the War between the States, and the girls wanted something that dealt with their first period.

She said little about her political beliefs, but there were rumors she had been a suffragette, which made our local politicians uncomfortable, particularly after a San Antonio newspaper published an editorial about "filth" being taught in Texas schools. The editorialist did not mention Miz Banks's name, but he said "a Northern, unmarried female teacher" was sexually corrupting the young women of our county. How was she doing that? Why, teaching the poems of Emily Dickinson.

Poor Miz Banks. The other teachers started avoiding her. The principal pretended he didn't know her in public, and the janitor tried to ask her out in front of her students.

The other reason I went back to school was the walk. It was almost a mile, but I loved the freshness of the morning and the smell of the wildflowers that bloomed in the spring. Have you ever seen a Texas prairie blanketed with bluebonnets and Indian paintbrush? After Mama died and Papa got drunk again, I was angry with God and I wanted to ask Him about all those innocent people who died on those endless Texas prairies and were buried without a gravestone or a shade tree, under an empty and endless sky that took no notice of their travail.

But He gave me no answer. Thousands slept under the wildflowers. White infants murdered by Comanche Indians, Indian babies murdered in kind by white people, the Tonkawa Indians exterminated by Texas Rangers, the Sutton-Taylor feud that extended the

Civil War into the 1890s and left many a cowboy facedown down among the tumbleweeds.

Mama said the frontier wasn't a new territory waiting to be discovered. She said it was a necropolis already groaning with the dead.

I sometimes talked to the flowers and pretended the people down below could hear me. When the grass was tall in the summer and the wind blowing from the Gulf of Mexico, I could hear a tinny musical sound, like the strings of a lyre being played with invisible fingers. I wondered if the wildflowers and the grass were showing the dead another way to heaven, because none of them expected to die where they did.

Cody had been skipping school, too, but this morning I made him go with me.

"Cain't Miz Banks fight her own fights?" he said.

"Some bad people are spreading rumors about her, Cody."

"How are we supposed to change that?"

"You can stand up for her, cain't you?"

"What if the rumors are true?" he said.

"Then we should stand up for her even more."

"You're gonna get us killed," he said.

"Fail your friends and you'll never have any peace," I said. "Now pack your lunch and stop being a worrywart."

I should have borrowed Papa's watch and arrived right before the principal clanged his cowbell and watched everyone file into the old church house that served as our school, one with a small bell tower that had bats in it. Instead, we were twenty minutes early, and Jubal and his cousins and his friends were on the back of the playground. Jubal was shooting a slingshot at an abandoned boxcar that tramps sometimes slept in.

The Fowlers were what we called "po' white trash," but of a different kind. They had more money than ordinary trash. They usually stole it, but they had it. It didn't change either their state of mind or their outlook on the world. The men always walked in front of their women, spat every chance they had, forced colored people to step off the sidewalk, and beat their children and thought themselves good Baptists. Back then there was no town in the South that didn't have them. Papa said that's because toadstools grow around outhouses.

Jubal Fowler's face lighted up like a lampshade when he saw us, then he and his gang headed across the playground, all the other children getting out of their way. I saw Miz Banks looking out a window, her face puffed, as though she had been crying. Then she was gone. I had no idea what was happening.

"Go home, Cody," I said. "Now. Please."

"I'm not going anywhere without you," he said.

He pulled off his belt, one that had a big buckle, and wrapped it around his hand. "Hey, Jubal," he said. "You need another ass-beating?"

Jubal was fifteen and somehow always grew faster and more mature than the rest of us. He knew about our private fears and how to insult us about the changes in our bodies. He knew about our secret loneliness and the failings of our parents, particularly the ones who had no power and instilled low self-esteem in their children.

That was the big irony. If Jubal wanted, he could have been a hero. His chest and stomach were plated with muscle, as though his whole body was as flat as a plank from his chest down into his jeans, and I sometimes felt guilty about the thoughts I had when I looked at him. And he had long brown hair that he washed and kept clean and let hang in his eyes like a little boy's. Sometimes I couldn't sleep when I thought about these things, and they made me feel guilty and I didn't know why.

Secretly I said prayers for Jubal. But I didn't have much faith in my prayers. Jubal had eyes I didn't like to think about. They were as colorless as water and would brighten with a thought he was having or turn as gray as lead, but whatever he was thinking never escaped his lips. Supposedly his father whipped him with a belt when he was two years old. I guess that's why I could never get mad at Jubal. It was hard to believe any parent could be that cruel, but that's why we called white trash white trash.

Well, anyway, that spring morning I wasn't thinking about Jubal's background. His teeth were gritted with pleasure, the thoughts in his eyes like a beehive someone had thrown a rock at. "Hear the news about Miz Banks?" he said. "She just got her Yankee twat kicked north of the Mason-Dixon."

"What for?" I said.

"What do you think, twerp?" he replied. "She's a hermaphrodite. Hey, Cody, look at me."

"What for?" Cody said.

"How do you like my nigger-shooter?"

"Neat," Cody replied. "Why don't you shoot yourself with it? Or cram it up your ass?"

"Then I couldn't do this."

Jubal pulled back the strips of rubber on his slingshot and fired a marble right into Cody's eye.

That was on a March day in 1914. I do not remember the exact date, but for me that day the world changed forever. I thought I was smart and understood the people around me, the good ones and the bad ones, and was confident I could take whatever the world threw at me. But I had been fooling myself.

Cody and I had to walk home by ourselves, him with a handkerchief wadded in his eye. Not one person stood up for us or even offered a kind word. They were all scared of Jubal Fowler and his peckerwood family. My feet hurt because I hadn't had time to rest after walking almost a mile earlier. I also had to go to the bathroom, and now the wind was blowing cold out of the north, and the sky was full of yellow dust clouds, and water was leaking out of the heel of my brother's eye, even with the heel of his hand pressed to it.

"Don't worry," I said. "Papa will take us to the hospital in the buggy. Then he'll have something to say to the principal and the sheriff."

"People don't care what Papa says, Bessie. He's a drunk and makes a fool of himself every time he goes to town."

"Don't talk about him like that, Cody. He's sick, just like somebody who has pneumonia or measles. You wouldn't call them to task, would you?"

"My eye is throbbing," he said. "I got to sit down. I'm gonna kill Jubal Fowler."

I felt miserable. I had forced Cody to return to the school, when I could have left well enough alone and saved all this trouble and the effects it would have on Cody's life. Cody had his faults, but if Mama hadn't died the best things in him would have flowered and choked out the bad seed in him, namely the Holland family rage and violence we passed down generation after generation, going back to a chain gang in Louisiana in 1835. Now because of me Cody was talking about killing a teenage boy. Worse, I knew he meant it.

Up ahead was a wood bridge over a creek that had water running in it most year-round, swelling and wobbling over the pebbles, a cool tannic smell rising from it in the shade. The creek led into a woods where two outlaws were hanged and their bodies degraded in a way I don't want to describe and left to be picked to pieces by birds. Some people still believed the year-long presence of the water in the creek was an acknowledgment of a little girl's kidnapping ordeal and death. Her body was never found, but the natural world gave her a home. Sometimes I tossed flowers off the bridge onto the riffle and watched my reflection float with the petals into the woods, and felt a chill I couldn't explain.

I was just about to say something to Cody about his threat to kill Jubal Fowler, but I didn't have the chance. Up ahead a figure was leaning against the rail on the bridge. It was the man who called himself Slick or Hit-it-and-git-it.

"What the hell happened to *him*?" he said.

"None of your dadburn business," I said.

"I have two chairs down by the creek. Y'all are welcome to sit down. In fact, I insist."

I had never wanted to put my bottom in a chair so bad. My back and feet were aching, and my eyes were like sandpaper from lack of sleep. But if you give an inch to a man who calls himself Hit-it-and-git-it, he'll take a mile. "I told you I do not seek company with billy goats, or nanny goats either."

"And I told you I ain't no goat." He pulled up his britches. "See, my Buster Browns and my clean socks and my white ankles are winking at you. If you like, I'll take off my Buster Browns and my socks and you can examine my feet and toenails."

"I'll take your word," I said.

"I'm awful dizzy, Bessie," Cody said.

I got his arm over my shoulder and walked him down to the creek among the trees, and eased him into a slat chair. The other chair was split through the middle, but I sat down on it anyway. The creek side was colder and damper in the shade, but the water in the creek was rippling over the pebbles like green Jell-O and so relaxing I wanted to go to sleep there and stay for a hundred years, even though the chair hurt my bottom something fierce.

"What are you doing here, Mr. Slick?" I said.

"Mr. Slick?" he said. "That has a nice bounce to it. In answer to your question, I camp here sometimes and study nature in all its manifestations."

"The devil has many devices," I said. "You have not quite convinced me you're all flesh and blood, so don't go sticking your nose in the air."

"Is that a lunch sack you have?" he asked.

"The last time I looked."

"I could sure use a bite."

"Mr. Slick, you must have had a special kind of upbringing."

"You're wrong about that. I didn't have no upbringing."

I sat down and watched him eat almost everything in our lunch sack, except one crust of bread with mustard smeared on it. He looked as though he had forgotten something and needed to concentrate on what it was. He squeezed his eyes shut, then opened them. "Excuse me, y'all want some of this?"

"Oh, no, go right ahead, Mr. Slick. We always fix lunch so we can find somebody on a dirt road and give it to him."

He sucked the mustard off his fingers, then wiped his fingers on his britches. "I'm sorry I went banging on your door about your daddy's debts. I just don't have much choice about my vocation."

"I'll lend you my Bible. In case you're not aware of its subject matter, it's called redemption."

He tore a strip of paper off my lunch sack and twisted a hard point on it so he could pick his teeth. "I hate to tell you this, but you were part right about my spiritual composition. There's people that ain't bad enough to go to the hot place but ain't good enough to get in Upstairs. I ain't no goat. But I ain't no reg'lar person, either."

"You're dead?"

He stared into the woods. When the wind puffed the canopy and straightened the air vines, the shadows seemed to leap from tree limb to tree limb, like bears bouncing through last winter's leaves. "Put it this way," he said. "I ain't alone. I got lots of company. People just cain't see them."

"I doubt that."

"Pardon?" he said.

"I don't think you have friends. Your hair is dirty. You smell bad and do your dental cleansing in front of others. What is the matter with you?"

"What do you expect from someone with no education?"

"Why don't you stop feeling sorry for yourself?"

"I feel like throwing you in the creek," he said.

"Try it and see what happens."

"I thought we would have a decent discussion," he said. "I was even gonna tell you a few things about the land under your feet."

"The land under my feet looks like dirt and grass," I said.

"There's a big war coming in Europe. A lot of money is gonna be made. There ain't gonna be no tax on it, either. You just have to know where to put the drill at. Are you hearing me?"

"Yes, and I don't like the notion of making money from a war. Neither does my father."

"He don't seem bothered about losing his money to gamblers and liquor and girls of the night while his children go without."

I had no defense for his words, as though he had found a bruise on my soul where he could sink his thumb. Cody looked at me, then at Mr. Slick, and removed the wadded handkerchief from his eye. The white in it had turned into a blood-red clot; a single, long tear streamed down his cheek. "I'll get you for talking that way about my father," he said.

"You got a mouth," Mr. Slick said. "I cain't blame you. My daddy was no good, either."

I heard a mechanical sound that was like the music of the spheres. I told you earlier I felt the whole world had forsaken Cody and me. Now a machine made in 1910 was coming up the road with a sound like the oiled wheels and clogs turning with the deliberation and exactitude in a clock. It came over a rise and descended into its own dust, the driver's face barely visible under her large, wide-brimmed hat, her chin tilted upward so she could see over the wheel.

Thank You, Lord, I said to myself. *I will never leave You as long as there is still one person on earth like Miz Banks, because as long as she is here, so are You.*

She veered off the road and almost tipped her Model T Ford into the creek. Her vehicle had only a windshield and no other glass. The top was canvas. She climbed out of the seat backwards, her rump swaying back and forth, then waved a handkerchief in front of her face until the dust settled. She wore a plum-colored shirt and a long, pleated beige dress that touched her shoes, an ivory brooch on her bosom, and had a pug nose and a face that was as round as a cake pan and curly hair the color and tint of polished mahogany. No matter how Miz Banks dressed, her clothes looked like they belonged on a child. But I loved her and wanted to be like her and to have her knowledge and manners. She smelled like a pineapple cake with vanilla icing on it.

"I am so sorry, children, for what has happened to you this morning," she said.

"Did they fire you, Miz Banks?" I said.

"Yes, they did, but I should not have let it bother me," she replied. Then she saw Cody's face. "Oh, goodness, get in the car. We need to get you to the hospital."

"A hospital cain't fix an eye, Miz Banks," Cody said.

"Is your father home?" she said. I know she started to add "Or somebody?" But she didn't.

"Yes, ma'am, my father is resting at home," Cody said.

"Well, we'll see what your father has to say," she said. "But one way or another, you're going to see a doctor, Cody. You're a good boy, but don't argue with your friends when they try to help you. I'm not always going to be around here."

"You're not going back up North, are you?" I said.

Her eyes began to mist. Then she put her arms around me. "I don't rightly know," she said. "I just hate to leave you."

"Can you give Mr. Slick a ride?" I asked.

"Who?"

"Over yonder, in the shade," I replied. "He puts on like he's a bad fella. But I think he's more afraid than bad. I have to warn you, though. He might be a spirit."

She stared into the shade, quizzically, then gazed at me. "You children have had a very stressful morning and carry a burden that should not be yours," she said. "Now hop in. One way or another, we'll make this a better day. And no talk about spirits."

Chapter Three

When we reached the ranch my father, unshaved and hung over and dressed in his long underwear and his canvas britches and floppy, colorless boots and sweat-ringed, battered Stetson hat, was carrying buckets of water in both hands from the windmill to the tub in the barn with the fire burning under it. To this day, I cannot believe the degree to which he punished his body and still managed to do the physical labor of an elephant. I always had the feeling he nursed his pain in order to absolve himself of the great harm he had done his family, particularly my mother, who bore him one child after another until she died in a wagon trying to make the hospital.

Miz Banks drove straight to the barn and got down and told him what had happened to Cody. He stood stock-still, an empty bucket in each hand, a column of sunlight striking the gin roses in his face.

"Is that what happened, Cody?" he said. "You didn't hit the Fowler boy first?"

"No, sir, I didn't," Cody said.

"Where's the boy now?" he said.

"If I were you, Mr. Holland, I'd concentrate on us getting Cody to a doctor," Miz Banks said.

My father dropped the buckets to the ground, then squatted down and cupped his hands on the points of Cody's shoulders. "Do you feel flashes of light inside your head?" he asked.

"No, sir."

"Don't lie."

"Yes, sir, like stained glass broken out of a window."

My father stood up and looked out the barn door at the sky and a huge balloon of yellow dust blowing behind a row of poplar trees. I could smell the heat in his body. His right hand opened and closed on the side of his thigh. "Does Mr. Fowler still work at the slaughterhouse?" he asked me.

"What are you thinking about, Papa?" I said.

"Getting Cody to the doctor, like Miz Banks said," he replied. "First things first."

Oh, Lord, don't let him open the top drawer in his bedroom, I thought. *Please. Please. Please.*

I knew my father's capabilities. At fifteen he was flying hell-for-breakfast across the Cimarron, Indian arrows stuck in the mail bags tied to his cantle. As a Texas Ranger he dared Deacon Jim Miller to draw on him, and later complimented Miller as the most religious, well-dressed bucket of pig flop he ever knew. In 1897 he danced with Etta Place, the Sundance Kid's mistress, at the Brown Palace in Denver; told Longabaugh (Sundance) he had no legal authority in Colorado; but suggested Longabaugh find a rat hole before he got blown out of his socks. People at our church said Papa might be a sinner, but he couldn't be accused of mediocrity.

He wet down the fire in the steel plates under the tub and went into the house to get his long coat, at least that was what he said, and got in the back seat of Miz Banks's Model T and shut the door and put his arm over Cody's shoulders. "We'll get you fixed, son," he said. "Yessiree."

But we all knew better. The eye doctor surely did. He cut right to it. "I wish we were in Switzerland, except we're not," he said. "Change the bandage and come see me in a week. In the meantime stay away from white trash."

"What do I owe you, doc?" Papa said.

"Nothing," the doctor replied. "Just keep in mind this is the twentieth century. Do you get my message, Mr. Holland?"

"Yes, sir, I do," Papa said. "Which door is the way out, doc? I always get confused in this place."

Outside, the wind had kicked up and was blowing the dust from our dirt streets high above the two rows of brick businesses that constituted our business district, newspaper and empty cardboard and apple boxes bouncing and scudding along our elevated sidewalks, the kind that still contained tethering rings, the grit so dense it could knock a squirrel out of a tree, the dust so high the sun was a pink wafer. Only last week a traveling tent preacher was picked up by a tornado and dropped outside Goliad without a mark on him. Supposedly he preached three days straight before he passed out. I think this is why William Sherman said if he owned Texas and hell, he would rent Texas and live in hell. I also think William Sherman helped starve the Indians and made Southerners blame the Negroes for their grief.

Papa helped Cody into the back seat of the Model T and tipped his Stetson to Miz Banks.

"Thank you, ma'am," he said. "I have some business to do here in town. I would appreciate you taking my children back home."

Miz Banks leaned sideways so she could see past me into Papa's face, the dust vibrating on the hood, sliding off the fenders. I knew Miz Banks. She was incapable of ignoring the plight of others, and that included all creatures, either in the ocean or the air or slithering in a bog. She buried a bird that broke its neck on her classroom window, and got the children to say a prayer over it, which caused them to be late for gym class and earned her a lecture from the principal, who believed the universe was created in seven days.

"You need to get in my vehicle, Mr. Holland," she said.

He lifted his hat, his long coat whipping in the wind, and made no reply. As I mentioned, Papa respected all women, but particularly Miz Banks, and would take a bullet rather than offend her. But he walked away, just like that, not saying a word, and that scared me to death. Papa had been an admirer of Wild Bill Hickok and Wyatt Earp because they lived by the same credo of all good lawmen: don't speak, don't blink, and don't miss.

"You listen here, Mr. Holland!" she called out. "You will not leave these children alone!"

I put my hand in Miz Banks's. It was a forward thing to do for a girl my age, but I hated to see her drawn into all the trouble I started over Jubal Fowler. "Just take Cody home," I said. "I'll stay here and watch out for Papa and be along directly."

"No, you will not," she replied.

But this was one time I had to go my own way. I jumped out on the road, feeling empty and disloyal, wanting a tornado to suck me up its funnel the way it did the preacher. "They had no right to fire you, Miz Banks," I said. "You're the best teacher any of us ever had. I'll always love you."

"Bessie, your father is a violent man. Do not let him take you down with him."

"I won't," I said. "I promise."

I hurried after my father, although I had no fix for him or Miz Banks or finally anything. Ambrose Bierce called pacifists dead Quakers. We say we're a peaceful people, but does anyone really believe that? It was hard being a child back then. Work and pain were the norm, and often there was no mercy for the weak. Is it a surprise our churches were full?

I followed him past the hardware store, one that sold guns and ammunition; a clothing store that contained no clothes but a Sears, Roebuck catalog you ordered from; a decrepit, two-story brick jail where a black man bashed his head against the bars and walls until his brains came out his nose and he lost his ability to speak; a mortuary; a loan and bondsman's office; a grocery and a bakery; an all-night café that caught the railroad clientele from the train station, the biggest building in the county; and finally the saloon, one that had batwing doors and had been open since 1870. This was the town where the Chisholm Trail began.

The concrete sidewalks were darkened by the balconies overhead and gave shelter to the local drunkards and loafers perched on their chairs below. Papa knew every one of them and always acknowledged their greetings and treated them with goodwill. Not this day, however. He walked stone-faced past them, his long coat swirling, his Stetson pulled down on his eyebrows, the first drops of a real frog-stringer pattering on the felt.

"Papa!" I cried out. But he heeded me no more than he did the loafers who were now looking at his back in confusion.

To my mind, the slaughterhouse was a physical obscenity and a disgrace, not just because of its long, black, windowless walls and the offal stink from its chimney, but because its presence contradicts the Book of Genesis, particularly the description of the Fourth Day of Creation and Yahweh's words about the critters and fish and birds we are supposed to take care of. I know preachers and deacons whose Bible I would like to take from their hands and pound them in the head with.

"Papa!" I yelled again. "Maybe I started it all! Maybe I made Jubal Fowler have some bad thoughts!"

He stopped in the entrance of the slaughterhouse, frozen, his back to me. The doors were gigantic and slid back into the walls, so that the interior of the building resembled an empty mouth. He pinched the back of his neck and turned around.

"Wait for me at the drugstore, Bessie," he said, and took a buffalo nickel from his watch pocket and flipped it at me with his thumb. "Get yourself a soda. I won't be long."

I let his nickel bounce off my chest. Then he smiled, the way he used to when he was a sober and loving father. "You're like your mama," he said. "You never cut bait."

"I cain't lose you, Papa," I said.

"Learn it now or learn it later, Bessie. The only difference between a Fowler and a Gila monster is a Gila monster turns its prey loose at sunset."

Chapter Four

I followed him through the gloom and a pair of swinging doors that for me was the closest place I had ever gotten to hell. The stalls were piled with congealed woodchips and sawdust, the planks in the floor blackened with blood of every kind—pigs, cattle, lambs, chickens, and turkeys. Their squeals and cawing, the bolt guns thudding on bone, the ripping sounds of viscera torn from a hanging carcass, the hooves sliding in the gore before an escaping animal was slammed to the planks, the steam rising from the scalding pots, the raw feces streaked on the walls, the rubber aprons and gloves and goggles on the workers greasy with feathers and hair and brains; it was a symphony of pain and terror.

I suddenly lost my reserve about the fate of Jubal Fowler's father, whose first name was Winthrop, who, like most white trash, had a grandiose name.

Papa cornered him in front of a stall where three lambs were tied together by their necks. "Your son shot a marble in my boy's eye this morning," he said. "You have a comment on that?"

Mr. Fowler was not tall but had shoulders as rectangular as a door and arms that looked as hard and dark as oak and stained even darker with purple and blue ink and rippling, green-blood veins that ran from his wrists to his armpits. He worked off his goggles and honked his nose in a handkerchief. "Cody made up a story about my Jubal looking into the privy while your daughter was doing her business. If that wasn't enough, he hit Jubal with a board."

He finished wiping his nose and put away his handkerchief.

"That's a goddamn lie," Papa said.

"Ask the other children."

"I was one of the other children, Mr. Fowler," I said. "Cody fought with his fists, not a board."

Mr. Fowler laughed under his breath, nodding his head. "Yes, Jubal has told me all about you. Looks like you've kicked into season, Missy."

"What did you say?" Papa asked. Then he said it again. "*What* did you say?"

"It don't matter the species, rutting time is the nemesis of us all," Mr. Fowler said. "Now stop pretending about what went on. I'm willing to call it even. We done here?"

I will never be sure about the events that followed. For years the images have been like pieces of broken glass from a pictorial scene in a medieval church window. The more I try to push the pieces together, the more I cut my fingers. I saw Mr. Fowler reach under his rubber apron, a smile on his face. Then almost simultaneous I saw my father push back his long coat and reach behind his back for the .38 Special I knew he had taken from his bedroom drawer at the house. I also knew what Papa planned to do. He was an admirer of Wyatt Earp, who had put many a gunman or drunk cowboy in jail by clubbing him across the head without firing a shot. But Wyatt Earp was not a drunkard, and my father was.

Last night's whiskey was not done with him. His coat had a heavy silk lining, one that he had torn and not repaired. The gun barrel caught in the rip and dropped to the plank floor. Mr. Fowler's face split with a grin. "I think you have finally fired your grits, Mr. Holland," he said.

Oh, Papa, what have you done? I thought.

But I was thinking only of the fool he had made of himself, and the shame he would feel every time he saw the Fowlers and the employees of the slaughterhouse and the saloon crowd to whom he was a Texas Ranger and a hero. He looked sick, his face suddenly old and helpless. He had twisted his knee, and his right leg was about to cave. I thought he was having a seizure.

"What is it, Papa?"

He reached out toward me. "Go home! Now!"

Mr. Fowler's hand was inside his apron. He had taken something from either his belt or his vest.

"Gun bolt!" Papa said.

I had forgotten the tool the butchers used to stun the animals before they cut their throats. Mr. Fowler lifted a cylindrical, dark object from under his apron. "Want a little of this?" he said, an iniquitous light in his eyes.

I picked up the .38 Special. It was heavy because of the fat rounds in the chambers. But when I swung the iron sight at Mr. Fowler, the frame and checkered grips and the coldness of the steel were like helium, as though the pistol wanted to float up to the ceiling and not do what I wanted it to, or maybe I had taken on a physical strength I didn't know I had possessed.

I pulled the trigger twice. The .38 jumped in my palm, the flame leaping from the barrel, while the lambs squealed. The first round struck a spot between Mr. Fowler's neck and shoulder, and slung a strip of blood on a post behind him. The second round clipped a piece of scalp and bone out of his head, just above his ear. He looked frozen in midair, like a puppet tangled in its own strings, a grin painted on its face. Mr. Fowler was holding a tightly packed, dark-leaf cigar in his right hand, pointed at me, as though he wanted me to take it.

I had just shot an unarmed man.

Chapter Five

For three days the skies stayed dark and the rain pounded down on our small town while I sat in the same cell where a man of color had left his blood and hair on the bars. The cell was in the basement, where the windows were half size and gave a prisoner a view of the world that was cut off above the waist. When the sun broke, I could hear people's voices, but what I could see of their bodies did not coincide with their conversations or their tonality. I learned a lot about people from their navels down to their feet:

A businessman jingling the coins in his pocket while talking to someone in a three-piece suit. A colored lady stepping aside so a white man could pass. Raggedy kids trailing behind an ice wagon. A man in overalls without socks wearing shoes that must have filed the skin off his feet. A deputy sheriff talking through a car window, pressing one hand to his loins. A preacher known for his fire-next-time sermons and his pointy, spit-shined boots, a spur on one heel, the rowel clotted with hair and a speck of blood.

Miz Banks said her favorite British novelist was Charles Dickens because he saw the world from the bottom up. I now had a much better understanding of what she meant.

Mr. Fowler didn't die, but he wasn't going to get well any time soon either. Maybe some of his motors were damaged. The doctors didn't know. He drooled and couldn't control his speech, and walked lopsided when he was taken to pee, which was not helping Papa's attempts to get my bail set. The country judge and sheriff were not my father's friends. The judge called him a drunken embarrassment to the community, and the sheriff denounced him for throwing a Klansman off a bridge in the dry season.

Miz Banks and Papa both visited me and brought me clean clothes and a package of fruit and some warm tamales wrapped in corn shucks and a bottle of Hires root beer. I was glad to have the soda, because my faucet water was brown and had orange rust in it, but I couldn't get the food down, no matter how good it was.

I hated Mr. Fowler and everything he represented; however, I wasn't up to shooting people. I'll tell you something about shooting a person. The guilt and fear in the aftermath are not because you shot somebody; your real worry is why you did it. You start searching the inside of your head and learn all kinds of things about yourself, almost all of it bad. You learn it doesn't take a big person to pull a trigger.

Mr. Fowler made fun of me. He and his son probably laughed about his son peeping in the privy. Why? I was holding my dress up so it didn't touch the streaks around the honey hole. If there was a single reason I shot Mr. Fowler, it was pride or shame and the sound of boys laughing at me. Nobody knows how much that hurts a girl.

"I know what you're thinking," Papa said on one of his visits. "You're blaming yourself for busting a cap on a fellow human being. Get those thoughts out of your head. Mr. Fowler is not a fellow anything. His kind are not born but are defecated into the world. Number two, I hollered 'bolt gun.' That was my order for you to drop him. You were doing what I told you. It was a done deal as soon as the words left my mouth."

"I could have shot low."

"Believe me, daughter, if Fowler had a bolt gun, either you or I would be dead or crippled or blinded. Why do you think he works in a slaughterhouse? He enjoys it. Don't let your gentle side hurt you."

This was Papa without the alcohol. His mantra was "Be fair, firm, and flexible." He was a good man inside a ferocious body. A lawman who never took advantage, and never looked back. I prayed every night he would never drink again.

"You reckon the judge is going to set a bail we can afford?" I asked.

He was sitting in a wood chair just outside the cell door, the dried blood of the colored man on the bars just above his head. He gazed down the corridor and rubbed his hands idly, his calluses as rough as a board. A line of buckets overflowing with feces stood in a shiny silhouette outside the cells, like a military tribute to a degenerate world. "I've made us 'land-poor,'" he said. "I told myself God wasn't making any more dirt. Now the oil under other people's property is going to eat us alive. I hate those sons of bitches."

Two hours later I had another visitor, this one cutting across the courthouse lawn, ignoring the sign warning not to walk on the grass, not even glancing at the statue of Sam Houston on horseback at the Battle of San Jacinto. Yes, you guessed it, it was my friendly spirit, Mr. Slick, his oily, bronze-colored hair freshly barbered, his face shaved, his clothes pressed and his shoes shined. Why is it that when you're in trouble, only troubled people come to see you, and usually to see how they can capitalize on your trouble?

Then he walked out of my vision. And remained out of my vision. Since I was locked in the jail, I could tell when people came and left, because the acoustics were like a bowling alley. But five minutes passed and I heard nothing. Then suddenly he was standing in front of my cell, like one of those buckets lined up down the corridor.

"How did you get in here?"

"I got my ways," he said. "I need to warn you."

"About what?"

"You're fixing to get used," he said. "All the ciphering is over my head, but I know it's big. And I mean 'big,' like shit-hogs oinking in a bathtub full of slop."

"I am not going to talk with you unless you tell me how you got in this building."

"The woods I was camping in has been taken over by some private dicks. Same ones that are after your daddy. So I just drifted into town with the morning fog, and now here I am. Miss Bessie, the truth is, I ain't got no home."

"Mr. Slick, I have an awful lot of worries right now. I sure don't need any more."

"Well, that's why I'm here. I can he'p. That San Antonio brothel woman, Miz Lafleur, is on her way," he said. (He pronounced the word "woman" as "woe-mon.")

"To see me?" I asked.

"The people I was working for was no good. You can put a word in with Miz Lafleur, cain't you?"

"I don't know anything about her, and I don't want to."

"She's got power, the horizontal kind and the kind you carry to the bank. When you got them things, you ain't got to worry about power."

"I don't like that kind of talk, Mr. Slick."

He looked at his feet, sniffing wetly. "I'm not educated, Miss Bessie. I thought you'd understand. Children know how the world works. If they didn't, they wouldn't survive. It's adults who are the liars, and their biggest lies are the ones they tell themselves."

"I didn't mean to hurt your feelings, Mr. Slick," I said.

"You didn't," he said. "I just get weary sometimes."

"Is it hard being a spirit?"

"There's worse things," he replied. "Some people die and just stay dead. Them kinds of thoughts gives me the willies."

Then, like a puff of smoke, he disappeared.

That evening a deputy escorted Bertha Lafleur down the corridor and held the chair while she sat down, then walked away. She wore an emerald-green satin dress that looked like skin on a snake.

Her ebony cane was gripped tightly in her hand, each knuckle as white as bone. I never saw a more rigid person in my life. I didn't know if she was afraid of the jail or me or experiencing some bad memories.

"I can get you out of this," she said.

"I'm pretty much used up, ma'am," I replied. "I don't need to hear somebody's tales, either."

"Don't underestimate me, girl. I'll slap your face."

I took my tin cup from my bunk and raked it across the bars. "There's a woman down who needs to leave!" I shouted.

"The deputy will not be back. Have you heard of Goree Farm?"

"No."

"The older women will have you on your knees, and not to scrub the floor."

"They'll have to do it after I'm dead," I replied.

The sun was a dull red through the barred window at the end of the corridor, like an ember cooling in its ash. She stared at it. "At age fifteen I wore leg chains and cut cane on the Brazos. I had no one to help me. Want me to describe what they did? When they were finished, I dreamed about snakes all the time and the way their tongues slither."

I felt my knees weakening, the backs of my thighs shaking. "I shot Mr. Fowler, Miss Lafleur. That won't change."

She lowered her voice. "Just say he touched you. I'll handle it from there."

"But he *didn't*."

"It doesn't matter. Two of my girls will swear he groped them. He did it in back of a saloon in San Antonio."

"Does my father know you're doing this?"

"No."

"Are you going to tell him?" I asked.

"No."

"Then I'm not going to cooperate."

She stood up from her chair. "You have a problem with pride, Bessie. You're going to ruin your father's life because you want to feel good about yourself. It's a corrupt world out there. Get your head right, girl. Don't let people like Winthrop Fowler write your destiny."

"How did Papa get mixed up with someone like you?"

"You'd like to know, would you? Here, I'll show you."

She propped her walking cane against the bars and with both hands grabbed the tops of her purple jacket and her white blouse and ripped them down to her navel. "On a late evening, just south of the Rio Grande, seven men roped me by my heels and dragged me through the cactus and branded my chest. Then I heard your father yelling and his horse's feet clacking on the stones and the water thrashing around his horse and your father riding high in the saddle, the reins in his teeth, firing with both hands."

Papa had never told me any of this. "What happened then?" I said.

"He shot and killed six of them. I watched them float around a bend in a canyon, their clothes puffed with air. The sun was just as it is now, turning orange, against a purple sky, with no heat."

"Where did the other man go?"

"He ran away. But someday I'll find him."

She pulled her blouse and jacket across her scars.

"This was when my father was a Ranger?" I said.

She nodded, her eyes going somewhere else, a picture of what-might-have-been disappearing.

"You didn't stay with him?" I said.

"He bathed my wounds and took me to a doctor, then rented a carriage and bought me a dish of ice cream in Terlingua. It had cinnamon on it. I had never eaten ice cream."

I heard someone scratch a bucket across the concrete, then begin peeing in it. Miss Lafleur reached through the bars of my cell and stroked my hair. "You're such a pretty young girl," she said. "So soft."

Chapter Six

Papa was at my cell door two days early. He had not taken off his hat, something he always did, even in a jail. He motioned for me to approach him. "Did Bertha Lafleur tell you to lie to the prosecutor?"

"She didn't put it that way."

He was breathing through his mouth. He smelled of fried eggs and potatoes and meat and tomato sauce but not alcohol.

"What did she ask you to say?"

"That Winthrop Fowler put his hand on me."

"Whereabouts on you?"

"I won't talk about this anymore, Papa."

"Were you fixing to lie or not? These people are trying to put you on a prison farm for twenty years."

My eyes started to water. "If I go to prison, you'll get drunk again."

"I'm not the goddamn issue here. Just tell me the truth."

"I told every one of them—the judge, the district attorney, and the sheriff—to flat go to hell. I told them I'm sorry I shot Mr. Fowler, but shot him I did. He's a cruel, awful man who kills animals and beats his family, and everybody knows it. I hope they got their fill of it."

"You said that to them, did you?"

"Yes, sir."

He nodded his head. His eyes were blue and clear with no tiny red veins or the pinkness around the rims that drunkards wear daily.

"I'm proud of you, Bessie," he said. "That's my daughter. These people don't care about Winthrop Fowler. They aim to own this whole county and turn it into the Grand Canyon."

"What are we going to do, Papa?"

"We don't have to do anything," he replied. "You know that little fella, what's-his-name, calls himself Slick? He walked into the sheriff's office and told him he was in the slaughterhouse when Fowler was shot and that Fowler was carrying a pistol and had pushed it under the straw after he got hit. The sheriff went to the stall with him, and there it was, right under the straw. Don't tell me the Good Lord doesn't have a sense of humor."

Miz Banks picked us up in her Model T and drove us out to the ranch. She had tried to visit me at the jail, but was told she was not a relative or an attorney and was turned away. I didn't know if the deputies were lying or not. Mr. Slick didn't have any trouble getting in. Of course, I wasn't sure if Mr. Slick was flesh and blood. Anyway, we had a grand trip out to the ranch, bouncing in the seats, a rainy mist blowing in the sunlight, the bluebonnets and Indian paintbrush peeking out of glorious fields of green grass. Miz Banks had fixed fried chicken and potato salad and had put it on the back seat, where Papa was sitting happily with his arm resting on the basket. I was starting to think of Miz Banks as a possible substitute for Mama.

Except as we got closer and closer to the ranch, the sky began to cloud and the air turned cold and Miz Banks's forehead began to furrow, like a tooth was bothering her. We rumbled across the cattle guard onto the hardness of the ground. Our mule Lancelot was nowhere in sight. Neither were any of the Mexicans who worked for us. The windmill was ginning, the lock chain clanging, the stock tank overflowing. Miz Banks pulled up to the veranda and cut the engine. Before she could speak, I ran inside. The house was empty. I walked back outside.

"Where is Cody?" I asked.

Miz Banks squeezed her temples. "He's not inside?" she said.

"No, ma'am," I said.

"Then I guess he's chosen to go," Miz Banks said.

Papa was climbing out of the back with the picnic basket. He set it down on the steps. "Did I hear y'all right?"

"I came out here earlier to give you a ride to town," Miz Banks said. "Cody and that strange man you call Mr. Slick were on the porch. Cody had a suitcase and said he was leaving home. He was wearing a leather patch on his eye."

Papa looked like a pile of leaves about to be blown away. "Leave for where?" he said.

"That's what I asked him," she replied. "He said, 'New York City, where all the big money is.' I told him that was foolishness. So did Mr. Slick."

"Why didn't you tell me?" Papa said.

"Boys don't put on knickers and shined shoes and a cap and long socks and a tie and dress shirt to walk two thousand miles," Miz Banks said. "I thought he just wanted to welcome his sister home."

Papa looked into the distance where the train ran through a piney wood every morning, going no more than ten miles an hour, the boxcars empty and rocking on the rails.

"You said he made a choice," Papa said. "That means you knew what he was thinking and you didn't say anything about it."

Miz Banks's jaw tightened. "Maybe I should have," she replied. "But you haven't treated that boy right, Mr. Holland."

"I did my best," Papa said.

"And where did it get you?" she said. "I am sorry for any harm I have caused your family."

"What was that character 'Slick' doing here?"

"Waiting to welcome your daughter home, I suspect. He also gave your son three dried apples and a piece of bread and his penknife. I think those apples and bread were Mr. Slick's lunch. Good day to you, sir."

Then she drove away, the dust drifting into our faces and settling on the picnic basket she had prepared.

I do not like to tell this part of my story, but perhaps age has softened Cody's description of the events that occurred after he left our impoverished home. It was 1923, and we were sitting by a barrelhead in the storeroom of a shoreline Galveston nightclub, one that contained roulette wheels and dice tables and women whose evening dresses shone like pink champagne poured on their skin.

I could hear the waves slapping under our feet. Cody's hair was parted in the middle, the prohibition whiskey on his breath as cold as the grave, the tuxedo and boiled-white shirt and boutonniere immaculately at odds with the clutter and dusk of the room. A tommy gun with a drum magazine was propped against his thigh, his patch still on his eye, perhaps as a warning to others or as a reminder of the debt he owed the Fowlers.

But he asked for me to come to Galveston for other reasons. He wanted to confess a heinous deed he had never confided to anyone, a deed that sat like an ogre on his chest every night of his life.

On the day Mr. Slick gave him three dried apples and a piece of bread and a penknife, he climbed abroad a boxcar wobbling down the tracks on the north side of our property, then rode into the freight yard in Houston, where he jumped off and outran a yard bull, his suitcase hitting his legs, his lungs bursting, and climbed on a flat-wheeler, a boxcar with no springs, that was already picking up speed, and barely pulled his feet inside before they were cut off by a highball stanchion next to the track.

He looked back as the yard bull shrunk smaller and smaller in the distance, the black smoke from the locomotive curling with the train, lines of grain quivering on the floor from the vibration of the wheels. He straightened the patch on his eye and rested his back against the wall of the car, then gradually fell asleep in the clacking of the rails. He paid no attention to the two hoboes humped like gargoyles in the corner.

When he awoke one of them was peeing out the door, his urine flashing against a red sun. Outside the door was a great swamp of cypress trees that seemed to bleed into the Gulf of Mexico. The wheels suddenly went over a steel bridge, shaking the car. The man in the doorway stepped back and buttoned his fly and wiped his palms on his jeans, which were faded and tight on his body and stiff with dirt. He seemed to pay no attention to Cody as he returned to his corner and his companion.

"How y'all doin'?" Cody said.

The two men sat side by side, their knees pulled up, covered with burlap. He could barely make out their faces. The one who had peed out the door was much taller than the other. Neither of them answered.

"You know where this train is going?" Cody said.

"Out of Texas," the shorter man said. "That back yonder is the Sabine River, boy."

"I don't like people calling me 'boy,' even if they don't mean anything by it," Cody said.

"Well, then, we'll call you 'Mr. Boy,'" said the shorter man.

"I'm not looking for trouble," Cody said.

The tall man's face was creased and sunbrowned, like old leather; his eyeballs misshaped, like sunken raisins; his mouth a slit. "Come on over here, kid," he said.

Cody pretended not to hear him. "Are we in Louisiana?" he said.

"Home of Angola Pen," the tall man said. He patted the planks next to him. His teeth were yellow. "Come on, sit with me. It's drafty in here. I ain't gonna bite you."

"In Angola they got a levee full of dead men," the other man said. "The ground glows at night." He paused. "You think I'm lying, boy?"

Cody didn't move. The engineer had started to highball, picking up speed, the rails clicking louder and louder, the great mouth of the Calcasieu River and hundreds of half-submerged cypress trees etched against a blood-red sun.

"Y'all hungry?" he said.

"Depends on what you got," the tall man said.

"Apples and a piece of stale bread," Cody said.

"You going where the cigarette trees and the lemonade springs are?" the tall man said.

"I don't know what that means," Cody said.

"Where'd you get the eye patch?" the tall man asked.

"An accident."

"What kind of accident?"

"One not worth talking about," Cody said.

"He's cute, isn't he?" the shorter man said.

"Oh, yeah, they're all cute. Yes, indeed," the tall man replied, his face tightening. "Yeah, 'Cute' is the word."

Cody unwrapped the bandana from the apples and extended them to the men, the floor of the boxcar wobbling under his feet. "I haven't tried them, but I suspect they're all right."

"You gonna keep the bread for yourself?" the shorter man said.

"Not if you want it," Cody replied.

"He's a smart boy," said the tall man. "He's got money for nice clothes. He knows better than to eat spoiled food. What are you doin' in a boxcar, son?"

"I'm the son of only one person," Cody said. "And you aren't him."

The tall man looked into empty space, thinking, putting his tongue in his cheek. He got to his feet, the burlap sliding from his loins. He took the biggest apple from Cody's bandana and bit into it, chewing loudly, the juice running from the corner of his mouth.

"You mind saying grace for us?" he said.

"Grace?" Cody said.

The short man was grinning. "You need to do that on your knees."

"What are y'all talking about?"

"Everybody gets turned out, kid," the tall man said. "Jail. Chain gang. The Boys' Home. It don't matter. 'Riding the rods' has got lots of connotations."

The short man rose from his feet and locked his arms around Cody's ribs, then flung him to the floor.

Cody wasn't religious. But he told me he saw Mama standing in the doorway, her blond hair and white gown blowing in the wind, the sun molten on the Gulf of Mexico. She pointed at the watch pocket of his knickers, where he carried the penknife given to him by Mr. Slick. The hoboes were kicking and stomping him, finding places where it hurt the most, knocking him back down when he was almost up.

"I'm done. Don't hit me anymore," he said on his hands and knees, a string of blood hanging from his mouth.

"Good boy," the short man said. "Now drop them drawers."

They stepped back from him, their legs like prison bars. Cody stared at the floor, the lines of wheat chaff shaking and shaping and reshaping themselves on the planks, like a design in another universe. He worked his thumb into his watch pocket.

"Did you hear what I said?" the shorter man asked. "Spread them cheeks."

Cody opened the blade of his penknife, and gripped the case and let the blade protrude from his fist, then came straight up off his feet and slashed the blade across the shorter man's windpipe.

Before the tall man realized what had happened, Cody jabbed him repeatedly in the throat and the carotids until the tall man was spurting blood all over his shirt, his knees caving.

Both men were on the floor now, the short man's face already turning blue, one hand gripped over the hole in his windpipe, as though he were trying to strangle himself. The tall man lay on his back, his expression like an air bladder ripped from a basketball.

Cody rode with the dead men until dark, when the train began to slow north of Baton Rouge and go clicking through a community of poor people. The dead men were vibrating facedown on the floor, as though they wanted to get up. The sky was filled with stars, like powdered ice, the fields lit with stubble fires, brightening, then fading, as the wind gusted and died. He jumped from the boxcar with his suitcase and ran across the gravel without losing his balance, then ran at least a mile through more farm country and stole clothes off a wash line and food scraps that had been left by a hog pen. He washed in a rain puddle and put on the stolen clothes, and at dawn woke in a culvert he occupied with a possum, then waded a swamp and dragged his suitcase up a levee and found himself looking at the Mississippi River.

He had never seen a body of water so big, miles of it flowing down to the Gulf, the trees shuddering with birds, the rain clouds like spun glass in the sunlight. There was a ferry moored on the bank, and on the far side of the river a parked freight train pointed north. It was the legendary train that black people called the Yellow Dog, and he wondered if somehow a miracle was taking place in front of him, one that perhaps Mama had arranged. Why not? The earth was a magnificent place. Why should Mama's children not share in its bounty? The men he had killed were evil, and would never again hurt a child or a woman or an old person, upon whom they obviously preyed.

He knelt in the midst of a freshly plowed field that smelled of manure and thanked Whoever Was Up There for sparing him from the fate he had just escaped, and for opening the door to a kingdom where the touch of a sword on your shoulder could never be taken from you.

The next day he was riding the spine of a boxcar loaded with ice and strawberries, headed not only to Chicago but to New York City and a life he could have never guessed at. As he looked over his shoulder through his good eye, he saw the melted ice whipping from the cars, wetting the tracks, the locomotive undaunted by curves or tunnels or bridges. This was the power of the twentieth century at work, offering every kind of reward for the brave at heart. He knew his time had come.

Chapter Seven

The Great War began at the end of summer. The oil people came to town and bought and leased every inch of dirt they could get their hands on. Anybody with a flatbed truck and some pipe and a scrapped car engine became a driller. Test wells were everywhere, most of them dusters. But I learned quickly that failure in the oil business is not what it seems. The oil and natural gas are down there; you just have to punch into a dome. The issue is, how far down do you have to go? The second issue is control of the spigot, not the drilling itself. Thirdly, the government allowed the oil companies to suck a reserve dry, and to claim it as a loss. How many American businesses were given an opportunity like that?

It was great theater. Unless you were a stubborn man like my father. I'll never forget the day he went over a rise in the buggy and saw the loggers and dynamiters and workmen attacking the woods where the two outlaws were decapitated for the rape and murder of the thirteen-year-old girl. Apparently they enjoyed tearing it to pieces. They had blown stumps and century-old root systems into toothpicks; the craters looked like the newsreels of no-man's-land in Europe; what they couldn't chop up, they burned. The creek that threaded itself through the trees with the radiance of green Jell-O was now clogged with mud and bare of all shade under a blistering sun.

I thought a lot about the murdered girl. Her body was never found. Most people believed it was buried in the woods. The men who killed her denied their guilt unto their deaths, and took their secrets with them. I did not know how her family lived with such a grievous weight on their shoulders.

Papa was furious at the damage the workmen had done, and stopped the buggy and got down and told a man driving a steam contraption to shut down his machine. Papa might as well have been a tree stump. He picked up a clod and hit the machine operator between the shoulders. This time Papa got his attention. The operator was a big man and wore strap overalls and a train engineer's cap and had a black beard and swaths of black hair on his arms. But he wasn't angry. Actually, he was smiling.

"What's the trouble?" he said.

"Who gave you permission to do this?" Papa said.

"The State of Texas."

"My goddamn ass," Papa said.

"I know what's bothering you, mister. It's a shame what's happening here. But one month ago I was making twenty cents an hour. Now I get a half dollar. If you was me, what would you do?"

Papa didn't have an answer. He had always been on the side of working people, and paid his help as much as he could afford. "There's other ways of doing it, aren't there? You don't have to rip the place apart."

"I don't make the rules," the operator said. "Step back. I don't want to hit you with my machine." He tipped his hat at me and climbed back on his contraption.

Papa seemed in a daze. We got back in the buggy. "Don't feel bad," I said. "You tried."

"There were still Indians here when I was a little boy," he said. "It was like a fairyland. We used to run kites through the fields." He picked up the reins but didn't pop them.

"What are you waiting on, Papa?" I said.

"I don't know," he replied. "This happened in two days. Think what they'll do in two months."

Papa got moody. Not just that day but all week. He started spending more time with Bertha Lafleur. It was embarrassing because most people hereabouts knew what she did for a living. No, not just a living. What she did to get rich. She owned a Victorian home outside San Antonio and a summer retreat on the Comal River in New Braunfels.

"I don't think you should be friends with that lady anymore," I said one morning.

Papa was drinking coffee at the kitchen table. The sun was pink in the east, a half dozen cows under the windmill. "Which lady is that?" he asked.

"The one Mama would not want you consorting with."

"That's not a nice thing to say."

"She runs a straddle house," I said.

"Where did you hear that term?"

"Cody used it."

He looked blankly at a photo of himself and Mama on the wall. She was wearing a bonnet tied under her chin. She was fifteen. He unbuttoned his shirt pocket and pulled out a postcard. He had folded it longways, cracking the face of the Statue of Liberty. "This came from Cody yesterday," he said. He pushed the postcard across the table.

"Why did you bend it, Papa?"

"I guess I didn't think first."

He had been sober several weeks, and I didn't want to give him an excuse to be otherwise. I flattened and smoothed the Statue of Liberty and turned the postcard over.

There was no salutation or date or return address. It read, *I have a job at a gym and am treated fine. I'm sorry I didn't say goodbye. I'm doing o.k. I hope you are too.*

The words were written in pencil. He signed the bottom with the letter "C."

Then he added a PS: *Papa, don't let them drag you down in Mexico again.*

Nothing Cody wrote was said directly to me.

Papa read my mind. "Cody thinks the world of you," he said. "But he's a loner. My father was the same way and passed it on to me, and I passed it on to Cody and messed y'all up proper."

"You don't have to make up excuses for me, Papa," I said. "What did he mean about Mexico?"

"Mercenaries are making good money on the border," he replied. "Most of the killers in the Johnson County War up in Wyoming came from right around here. The same bunch are still at it, meaner than spit. They hung a woman named Cattle Kate Watson, just for cussing them out."

"You're not going with them, are you?"

"I cain't rightly say. We're about to lose our home, but you don't want Bertha Lafleur to he'p us. You also don't like the thought of me going down to Mexico. So where does that leave us?"

"Let the oil company drill," I replied. "What's to lose?"

"Those Rockefeller gunmen in Colorado used armored cars and machine guns to kill innocent people. Is that what you want, daughter? Men who'd wipe out a family for a bottle of tequila and a two-dollar whore?"

I knew better than to say more.

I tried to stay away from the Fowlers. I'd see Mr. Fowler in his wheelchair outside the pool room at the end of Main, and head for the grocery or the movie house that was just starting up or the ice cream parlor that sold a scoop in a dish for ten cents. He would always holler at me and get up on his crutches, grinning from ear to ear, like a broken spider web hanging in a doorway. He'd yell something cordial, such as "I declare, you look good enough to eat, little lady."

I wished more and more I had killed him, and feared I was more like the Hollands than I'd admit.

Jubal Fowler was a different matter. Maybe I was a hypocrite. He had deliberately shot my brother in the eye, but I couldn't help looking at him when I saw him on the sidewalk dressed up for the evening or standing without his shirt on top of logs on their way to the sawmill. My body was changing and I guess his was, too. But I didn't have anyone to talk with about it, and would get lonely in the middle of the night.

It was late summer now, and because I didn't plan on returning to school, I started taking my lessons from Miz Banks. She would not allow me to pay her, so I helped her do things I was good at: growing garden vegetables, laundering delicate clothes, butchering and plucking chickens, hiving bees, putting up preserves, cleaning out the grease trap, fixing fancy side dishes with simple things like eggplant and okra. I could bust firewood, too; each time I swung the ax, I felt my body getting strong and stronger.

Then out of nowhere Miz Banks wanted to give me driving lessons.

"Thank you, but aren't I supposed to be older?" I said.

"Not in Texas," she said. "A horse could legally drive if it knew how."

She said she wanted me to run errands for her because she needed more time to work on the book she was writing about Emily Dickinson. I had my doubts, however. I had heard her fussing with somebody over the telephone a couple of times. Whoever the other party was had a nasty voice. On the day before Halloween I was carving a pumpkin in the kitchen when the telephone rang on the wall. Back then each person on a party line was assigned a certain number of rings. I could see her counting the rings, her breath rising with each ring, one, two, three, four, five. She picked up the earpiece from the hook and placed it on the side of her head. "Yes?" she said.

She listened but did not speak, her eyes brimming. She stood there a long time, then replaced the earpiece on the hook and cleared her throat and wiped under her eyes with a handkerchief. "A friend is sick and needs to come over, Bessie. Take my car to your home and return with it tomorrow. I'll finish the pumpkin."

"Is there anything I can do, Miz Banks?"

"No, no, everything will be fine. My friend just needs a little care for a short time."

I believed nothing she said. Her face seemed filled with an irrevocable loss, the kind like I felt when Papa left us to go on a drunk, or like the emptiness in my chest when I knew I would never see my mother again, or the betrayal that made me feel I was nothing when Cody left me to struggle on my own, with not a soul in the world to cling to. Those feelings were so bad sometimes I didn't want to live anymore, and I wondered why only women seem to have those experiences.

I put my hand on Miz Banks's arm, as a sister would. She immediately stepped away from me.

"No, you mustn't do that, Bessie."

"Do what?"

"Touch an older person," she said. Her bottom lip was trembling.

"I don't understand."

"The world is a cruel place. Please take my car and go home now. My friend will be here any minute." She was hugging her own body, as though she were freezing. Then her voice sharpened. "Please, Bessie, do what I say."

She went down a dark hallway to her bedroom and shut the door. I could hear her weeping as though she were holding a pillow to her face. I didn't know what to do. I went outside and started the car and drove perhaps a hundred yards, then stopped and shut down the engine and stared at the house for over an hour. Nobody showed up at the house, nor did I see Miz Banks return to the kitchen to use the telephone. In the west the sky was ribbed with purple rain clouds, the sun buried like a red coal inside them.

I drove the Model T home and sat on the steps and watched the fireflies and listened to the cicadas in the waning of the day. Guess who came to see me? He was wearing starched overalls and shined cavalry-surplus boots and a clean gray shirt buttoned at the wrists. Isn't it strange how sometimes the most peculiar people you've ever met turn out to be the best friends you've ever had?

"Hi, Mr. Slick," I said.

The house was lit inside. Mr. Slick stretched his head one way, then the other, trying to see inside the living room.

"Don't be afraid," I said. "Papa considers us in your debt, Mr. Slick. If you hadn't told the sheriff Mr. Fowler's gun was in the slaughterhouse stall, I'd be in the pen."

"Actually I had to go get it from Fowler's house."

"Pardon?" I said.

He stuck a stick of chewing gum in his mouth and worked on it. "There's two kinds of truth, see? The kind that *is* and the kind that *should be*. I turned 'should be' into 'is.'"

"Your thinking skills seem a mite confused, Mr. Slick."

"Don't call me 'mister.' Not one more time."

"I'm not going to give up my manners, Mr. Slick. It's the way I was brought up."

He blew out his breath. "Can I sit down next to you?"

"Of course."

"Your daddy is not gonna knock me into the next county with a broom?"

"Will you stop acting like this?"

"I just got something awful bothering me, Miss Bessie. That little girl who was murdered by them outlaws don't have a home no more."

"Please don't start bringing up things like that again, Mr. Slick. I'm plumb wore out thinking about all the grief in the world."

"I saw her two or three times before the woods was torn up by them oil people. I saw her again this evening. She looks like you."

"Me?" I said, my stomach dropping.

"Exactly like you."

"Don't be telling me this. I don't want to hear it," I said.

"Can I stay in your barn tonight?"

I cupped my hands on my forehead. "You're going to drive me crazy."

"You're my only friend, Miss Bessie."

Papa stepped out on the porch, backlit, the sleeves of his flannel shirt rolled over his biceps, the hair on his skin glowing. There was a long pause. His shadow seemed to swallow poor Mr. Slick.

"I'm going, sir," Mr. Slick said.

Papa shook his head. "Come in, son."

"Sir?" Mr. Slick said.

"You drink coffee?"

"Yes, sir, you betcha," Mr. Slick said. "I was just fixing to invite y'all for a cup down at the highway café."

Chapter Eight

The next day I returned Miz Banks's Model T and pretended that her upset over the telephone call of yesterday had not occurred. I also pretended she had not told me to keep my hands off her person.

"It's such a fine day," she said. "Let's go shopping at the dry-goods store in town. I think you need a new pair of shoes. Don't argue, now."

"You don't have to do that, Miz Banks," I said.

Her hand hovered in the air, then she pressed it against her cheek, as though a mosquito had bitten it. "Let's be on our way, shall we?" she said.

The dry-goods store was a happy place, with a balcony on the second story and an elevated sidewalk and high windows and big doors that rang when you opened them. It smelled good, too, with stacks of rugged clothing for men and fine dresses and hats for women, with posters on the walls that showed what people in San Francisco and Denver and even New York were wearing.

It had just rained, and the brick-paved street was pooled with water and the sun was shining on the bricks and the rain was still feathering off the roofs of the buildings; there was a glassy, damp brightness in the air that made you feel the world was a wonderful place after all.

But that did not last long.

The owner had gone to lunch, and Jubal Fowler and his gang of hoodlums came inside and spread out among the display tables, fingering whatever they felt like, making remarks to the high school girls who had been trying on a new getup in front of the mirrors, grinding out their cigarettes on the floor. Many of Jubal's friends had been in the reformatory at Gatesville, and nobody said a word when they were around. Their hair hung like straw over their ears, and their clothes were as loose as rags on their bodies, which were supple and smooth, the way a garter snake's is. Every one of them had tattoos, done with the same color ink, the same ugly designs.

Jubal saw me from across the room and walked straight at me. "Hey," he said.

"Hey," I said.

"You shopping here today?"

"Just helping Miz Banks."

"You quit school altogether?"

"I got into the home-lessons program."

He looked over his shoulder at his friends. They were all watching him. "Bessie, I got no bad feelings about you shooting my old man. My old man is a shit."

I let my eyes go empty. I didn't want to be piling on Mr. Fowler, or giving Jubal's friends any reason to gossip about me.

"You hear from Cody?" he asked.

"From time to time."

"I'm sorry for what I did with my slingshot."

He didn't say "nigger-shooters," which most of the boys called their slingshots. "I have Cody's address, if you'd like to write him."

"You think he'd like that?"

"Sure."

He looked at his friends. They were getting bored, picking at themselves, scanning the interior of the store, as though it owed them something. "I'll get his address later. I got to ride herd on these guys," he said.

"Whatever you want, Jubal."

"Come on, don't be like that," he said. "Say?"

"What?" I said, my heart rising.

"That new movie house is gonna be opening up in a couple of weeks. Want to go?"

"You need to tell my brother you're sorry."

"Or you won't go to the movie house?"

"I didn't say that," I said.

"Yeah, but that's what you meant. Okay, maybe I can do that."

I got a piece of paper and a pencil out of my purse. Then I dropped the pencil. He started to reach for it, then his friends started laughing. One of them had pushed out his stomach and was marching inches behind a fat colored woman.

"I got to go," Jubal said.

"Leave them alone. Stay here. You're smarter than they are. Don't ruin your life for them."

"They're my buddies, Bessie. They depend on me."

He rejoined his friends, then the whole gang floated over to a glass case filled with ornamental items reminiscent of the Old West: oversized chrome-plated roweled spurs, Bowie knives, gold pocket watches, and a gold-and-silver belt buckle embossed with the head of a longhorn that had tiny red emeralds for eyes. To this day I still think about how different our lives could have been had I agreed to go with him to the movies.

Jubal's friends formed a curtain around him while he unlatched and slid open the door on the glass counter. Just then, the owner, Mr. Hennigar, returned from lunch. Kids called him Quasimodo because his body looked like a bag of rocks. He grabbed Jubal behind the neck and mashed the side of his face on the counter. I thought the glass was going to break and cut off his head. A rope of spittle was draining out of his mouth.

"You want to steal from me, smart-boy?" Mr. Hennigar said.

Miz Banks fished in her purse and hurried down the aisle. She pounded with her chubby fist on Mr. Hennigar's back.

"I told him to get the buckle for me, Mr. Hennigar!" she said. "Please don't hurt him! Here, I'll show you the twenty-dollar bill. I was about to give it to him."

Mr. Hennigar released Jubal, whose neck looked like it had been stung by a jellyfish. "This boy is no good, Miz Banks."

"I'll take responsibility for him," she said. "You're a nice man, Mr. Hennigar. Here's the money. I'll send the buckle to a friend in Boston. I'm going to take him with me now. Is that all right?"

"If you want," he said.

"Thank you, sir. You're very kind," she said.

Jubal rubbed the side of his face, his eyes wet, his hand slick with saliva. Then he saw me watching him. And his friends. And everyone in the store watching.

"Hey!" Jubal said. "I boosted the buckle! I don't need a dyke making up lies for me! And you, Quasimodo, go brush your teeth! You got borscht breath!"

His friends' faces lit up like light bulbs. "Fuckin' A!" one of them yelled. Mr. Hennigar grabbed Jubal by the neck again and the back of his pants and marched him down the sidewalk to the constable's office and threw him headlong into the furniture.

Jubal was charged with shoplifting, his fifth time in three years. Two weeks later he was sent to Gatesville, one of the most infamous reformatories in the United States.

All of this because of pride.

Late in November the days were golden and the nights chilly, and fires were burning in the woods where the oil companies planned to drill more test wells. Every morning, Papa drank coffee at the general store and read the news about the war in Europe and said that Wilson was against the working man and was an elitist son of a bitch and would get us into a war. The owner was likable, but most of the customers at the general store were not fond of my father's politics. Nor were they happy with his sometime companion, Bertha Lafleur.

Occasionally she stayed over, although she never came to his bedroom. Papa had strange relationships, including multiple wives. He thought he was wanted for bigamy in Old Mexico, but couldn't be sure if the warrants were issued there or while he was prospecting in Argentina, because the pulque he drank erased about six months of his memory. He had a son named Ishmael I never knew, and said he would eventually find him somewhere inside the United States Army. How about that for exemplary fatherhood?

"Miss Bertha shouldn't be here, Papa," I said one night after she had settled herself in the back bedroom.

"I'll say this once and only once," he replied. "I never crossed the line with this lady."

"She runs a brothel. Isn't that enough?"

"Susanna Dickinson was barely an adult and carrying an infant when the Alamo was overrun. She saw the Mexicans pitch James Bowie in the air with their bayonets in the chapel, and saw her husband killed while trying to blow up the magazine. After the peace, the legislature denied her a pension, so she and her baby had to live in a brothel. God works in funny ways."

"Are you going to leave me, Papa?"

"What?"

"You never stay put. Your whole life. You always have an excuse."

We didn't have electricity then, only oil lamps. He was sitting in his favorite chair, a wash-faded cloth cover with a rose design stretched on it. His face looked furrowed and yellow in the light. "I wouldn't hurt you for the world, Bessie."

"But to how many children have you told that, Papa? How many, indeed?"

I saw the hurt in his eyes. The kind that hangs in the memory, the kind you cain't take back. He pinched his mouth with his hand and stared into space. Then said, "Stay here a minute."

He walked to the back of the house, then returned with a tote sack we usually kept onions in. He unfolded a newspaper and spread it on the floor, then tumbled the contents on the paper. The bills were bound with rubber bands in thick stacks, dozens of them, the denominations in twenties and fifties.

"How much is that?" I said.

"I haven't counted it."

"Is it stolen?"

"No."

"She loaned it to you?"

"She gave it to us."

I was speechless. I had never seen so much money in my life, not even when I saw the vault open in our local bank. I was breathing hard through my nose, my heart seizing, but I didn't know why.

"You're going to keep it, Papa?"

"For the time being."

"It's dirty," I said.

"One kind of money is as dirty as the next."

"That's a lie, Papa. You know it, too."

He turned down the wick inside the lamp, the light dying on his face. "I'll see you in the morning. No matter what the day holds, it's a gift."

But gift of what? He certainly didn't say, and I didn't ask, and because I didn't ask I knew that money had germs all over it.

Chapter Nine

Early the next morning, frost was on the ground and Bertha Lafleur's new car was gone, the tracks leading in two long black stripes to our cattle guard. I put on a wrap and went to the smokehouse and cut a slab of bacon and went back in the kitchen and fired the kindling in the woodstove and started Papa's and my breakfast, although I would not eat any of the meat. There were dark blue clouds of fog all across the countryside, as though the sun had dropped off the edge of the earth. I kept listening for Papa's noises, because he was always an early riser, but the only sound I heard in the house was the eaves creaking in the wind.

"Papa!" I hollered up the stairs. "Better get down here before I throw it out!"

No answer.

I went upstairs and then through all the rooms downstairs, even in the cellar. There was no sign of him, nor his footprints in the frost, unless he went away with Bertha Lafleur or left before she did. Nothing was making any sense.

Then I realized the Henry above the mantle was gone. He treasured that rifle. It was a long-barrel, lever-action .44 and used the same caliber ammunition as his Colt revolver. With just those two weapons he tore up a gang of bank robbers down near Nogales that was going to bury him alive in an anthill if they got their hands on him.

With just my slippers on my feet, I put on my beat-up flop hat and tied it under my chin with a bandana and walked out to the barn and the hog pen and out to our biggest field, one that was rattling with dead cornstalks, the ground itself frozen as hard as iron. Papa was nowhere. The only sounds were the chickens cackling and the hogs snuffing and a piece of tin banging on the barn roof. Plus a sound like a woodpecker knocking on a telegraph pole, which they sometimes did, but not when it was this cold.

Then I thought I heard Papa's voice, as thin as a bobby pin twanging in the wind.

"Papa?" I called out.

There was no answer. I called again and again. But still nothing. I started back home, then the wind shifted and I heard his voice from the woods on the north end of our property. I started running and yelling "Papa! Papa! Papa!" The dirt clods were as hard as rocks under my feet.

I could see him sitting just inside the woods, his legs splayed, a steel trap locked on his ankle, the teeth buried in the flesh and the cloth of his britches, his rifle out of his reach, the chain on the trap spiked into a thick oak root. The blood was drained from his face, with either shock or the cold or both. He had one hand gripped on the trap's chain, and probably had been knocking it on a stump in hopes someone would hear him.

We kept no traps, and did not allow anyone else to bring them on our property, even though we had cougars. I had no idea how the trap got there.

"Good morning, daughter," he said. "I hope you have breakfast ready."

They didn't grow many like Papa. "What happened?" I said, kneeling down beside him.

"I saw somebody with a lantern or battery light out in the cornfield. Then I saw a couple more in the barn. Watch your step. They may have salted the whole place."

"Who did this?"

"Probably the Fowlers. It has their kind of stink. Call the sheriff's office. Neither of us can get this thing off my leg without leaving half of it on the ground."

"I can try if you tell me how."

"Bessie, for once in your life, please listen to me."

"Papa, I don't think Mr. Fowler is up to dragging bear traps around. What are you hiding?"

"I'm not hiding anything. There's an army of Fowlers around here, each one of those sons of bitches worse than the other, if that's possible."

"I know you, Papa. There's something you're not saying."

"I got a look at one of them through my scope. He looked like an Indian with greased-down hair. Or a Chinaman."

"An outlaw Chinaman? The kind who own laundries?"

"I feel like a bear has his teeth locked on my ankle and is about to swallow it. Will you please get your butt up to the house and ring the operator and tell her we have a problem here? If you don't mind."

The only reason for my delay was fear that someone would attack Papa while I was gone. I put the Henry in Papa's hands and ran as fast as I could, hating the evil that men do, and the thieves who break in and steal.

The sheriff took us to the hospital in Victoria, then drove us back home. As I mentioned earlier, the sheriff was not a friend of the Hollands, in large part because he had in-laws amongst the Fowler family, who were now our enemies forever. It seemed like half the county was related to them. There are places in the South like that. There's one county full of inbred people like that in Mississippi. Most of them are born with six fingers or toes. That's a true story.

The sheriff was a tall, mean drink-of-water named Slim Millard who couldn't put on his britches without a diagram, or at least that's what Papa always said. Colored people crossed the street when they saw him. The preacher in our church unconsciously rubbed his hand on his trousers after shaking hands with him. The president of our bank loved him. Does that say it all? I had made a bed downstairs for Papa and was standing in the living room with the sheriff while he was filling out a form he wanted me to sign.

"What have you written there?" I asked.

"Just sign it."

"I'll sign it after I read it. If I sign it at all."

"Suit yourself."

I looked at it ten seconds and handed it back to him. "You wrote 'accident' down there."

"I wrote 'accident' with a question mark behind it."

"Someone deliberately set a trap or traps on our property. Go find who did it," I said.

"I can shut this investigation down for 'failure to cooperate,' little girl."

"Is there anybody in your family who has six toes or fingers?" I replied.

"*What?*"

"You should see a doctor about your stomach," I said. "It's called distention. You have a sack of viscera hanging over your belt. I am trying not to be unkind. Eventually you will have to undergo surgery and wear a girdle on yourself."

"Maybe you need a bar of soap in the mouth," he replied.

That night I built a fire under the tub in the barn and helped Papa bathe, then dried him off and put a robe on him and got him back in the house and cleaned his wounds with antiseptic and bound them with gauze and surgical tape, then I fed him a bowl of stew that could make a body get out of the grave. His pajama top was unbuttoned, and I could see the bullet and knife and arrow and barbed-wire scars that had been carved into his chest. Mama used to say he was the best and bravest man on the Rio Grande, if only he didn't drink. She would say that with mist in her eyes.

But Papa didn't just drink. He did all the bad things that went with it. Except one. He never said a critical word about Mama, not when she was living, not when she was dead. Even when she cussed him or beat her fists on his chest, he'd let her finish, then he'd say, "I love the name Alafair."

"What's on your mind, daughter?" he said.

"You're going to run out of luck one day," I answered.

"Everybody gets to the same barn. It's how you get there that matters."

"What does that mean for Cody and me?"

"People my age belong in the last century. We cain't change who we are. If Cody were here, he'd tell you that."

"You did everything but run him off, Papa. What you just said really makes me mad."

I hit him hard in the face with the pillow and walked out of the room.

"Come back, Bessie!" he called through the doorway. "I shouldn't have said that!"

But I kept going, through the kitchen and out the mudroom and into the night, with no coat or hat. I plunged a bucket into the stock tank and carried it into the barn and threw it on the coals under the bathtub, even though they were already drenched. Then I picked up a mattock and broke Papa's mirror on the wood post where he shaved above the tub, and smashed his bath salts and shaving items and hair tonic and beeswax and tweezers and hairbrush, then threw the mattock through the glass window at the end of the stalls.

Finally I sat down in the middle of the barn and cried. When I was done with that, I dropped a canvas tarp over my head, like a monk's hood, and went out of the barn toward the house, the sky black as India ink, the stars cold and distant in the heavens, the woods puffing with fog. I heard a tinkling sound from the cornfield.

"Who is that?" I said.

"Just me," Mr. Slick said.

"What are you doing with that cowbell around your neck?"

"So people won't be taking shots at me."

"You are surely an unusual spirit, Mr. Slick."

"I ain't got full spirit credentials, Miss Bessie. Besides, there's some full-bred humans that's eviler than demons. I know a mess of them."

"Mr. Slick, why are you roaming around out here in the dark? Are you trying to break your neck or just pester people to death?"

"Miss Bessie, you and your daddy are being drug into something y'all don't have no experience with. I know that bohunk woman Miss Lafleur give y'all a chamber pot of money, but it's not what you think it is."

"*What* are you talking about?"

"It ain't hers. It was supposed to be paid to some people in Galveston. For certain commodities."

"Mr. Slick, you are a nice man. Or spirit. But I am flat worn out. Let me go inside my house and go to sleep. Or you can go to sleep in either the barn or the house. But I don't want to hear any more of your crazy talk."

"Go in the barn with me. I got to show you something."

"No!"

"Then I'll dig it up my own self and throw it on your porch."

"Dig up what?"

The mattock was lying below the broken glass window I had thrown it through. He picked it up and hefted the handle onto his shoulder. He made me think of a medieval serf, one wearing an iron collar, except he was wearing a bell.

"Ain't nobody ever treated me the way you have, Miss Bessie. You're good from your hairline down to your feet. You're one of them people who don't know how to act bad. So spirits like me has got to take care of you."

I hated the thought. But if Mr. Slick had not planted false evidence after I shot Mr. Fowler, I would be on the women's prison farm.

"You have been a good friend, Mr. Slick," I said. "I will always be in your debt."

He took the mattock off his shoulder and pumped it above his head, snapping gum in his jaw. "Follow me," he said. "Watch my smoke. I'm fixing to sling some dirt."

I went inside the barn with him and watched him swing the mattock in an empty stall, its weight more than he could handle. He gasped for air and lost his balance and for fifteen minutes staggered and stumbled and started banging the sides of the stalls.

"Maybe you should rest for a while, Mr. Slick," I said.

"I'm just getting warmed up," he replied, his voice so weak I could barely hear him. He rolled his shoulders and his neck, and spat out his gum and put a fresh stick in his mouth, then started in again.

"I'm pretty tired, Mr. Slick," I said. "I'm going up to the house. I have to sleep."

"Do go nowhere, Miss Bessie. It's here."

"Good night, Mr. Slick."

I was almost to the back door at the house when I heard him running, his thin chest heaving.

"I found it," he said.

"You found what? I don't even know what we're looking for."

"It ain't good. But you got to know about it."

He got down on one knee in the stall and reached into the three-foot hole he had dug and inserted his fingers inside a rope loop that served as a handle and pulled out a wooden US Army cavalry ammunition box.

"What is it?" I said.

"It come all the way from China. Or one of them places."

"How did you know it was here?"

"Some bad women who work for Bertha Lafleur told me. She and her colored driver hid it here."

I pulled the mattock from his hands and drove the sharp end into the box, then prized one of the boards away. The box was lined with tinfoil packets the size of a hot dog.

"Don't open them," Mr. Slick said.

I split the first one I could dig the mattock into. The contents were brown and black and moist looking, like compressed deer excretions.

"This smells like vinegar," I said.

"It's tar."

"Tar?"

"Heroin or opium. I wish you hadn't busted the box up, Miss Bessie."

"Why not? This is evil."

"It don't belong to Bertha Lafleur. I wanted the people who own it to dig it up and be gone. I could have made that happen, Miss Bessie."

He remolded the tinfoil and tried to replace the pieces of the board I had splintered, then shoved the dirt on top of the box.

"Don't be afraid, Mr. Slick," I said. "We had some prowlers. My father got a good look at one of them."

He waited for me to go on.

"Papa said this one fella had greased-down hair. Maybe he was an Indian or a Chinaman."

Mr. Slick looked like he had swallowed a dead frog. "That ain't no Chinaman. That's Indian Charlie. And he ain't no Indian, either. He *kills* Indians and colored people. He's the man who stuck a hot iron on Bertha Lafleur's chest. I cain't think about what we have done."

Chapter Ten

In the morning I fixed Papa breakfast and carried it to his bed. "You've got a glare in your face, daughter," he said. "You hit me with a pillow last night. I hope you're not going to do the same with the bedpan."

"There's a box of opium or whatever buried in the barn," I said. "Or maybe it's called tar."

His face became deadly still, his eyes never blinking, never disengaging from mine. "If it's buried, how do you know it's there?"

"I dug it up with Mr. Slick. He says the money Miss Lafleur gave you was supposed to pay for whatever it is. He says the man you think is a Chinaman is named Indian Charlie."

He looked away from me. I could hear his breathing, even smell it, like he was lighting a match to a pipe. "Take the tray," he said.

"You're not going to eat?"

He didn't even bother to answer. He twisted on the mattress and hung his legs over the side of the bed. "What else did Slick say about Indian Charlie?"

"He kills Indians and people of color."

"If that's all he does to them," he replied.

"What are you going to do with the money Bertha Lafleur gave you, Papa?"

"I got to think about it," he replied.

"Don't you say that."

"Maybe this is more complicated than we know."

"Don't you dare say 'we.'"

"I saved Bertha's life from Indian Charlie. She'd do anything for me. Give her a chance, Bessie. You're too hard on people."

"I'll give her a chance to run before I put some birdshot in her twat," I said.

"Of all my children, you're the one who could restart the Civil War. You're fourteen years old."

"Look around you, Papa. Only a fourteen-year-old is willing to stay with you. Does that say something?"

I didn't know I was capable of being that cruel. But I was. He sat for a long time on the side of the bed, his hands folded between his thighs, staring at the floor, his bandage hanging like a snake half off his ankle.

Papa was a private man, and shared few of his thoughts. As a lawman he bore no animus toward others. He told me that anger blurred the bead on your gunsight. However, those who abused women or children or the elderly knew better than to get near him. That said, he himself was irresponsible with family obligations, profligate with money and women, and dangerous when someone stepped across a line only he saw. His great weakness, though, was his inability to accept the passage of time.

I would see it in his face. A frown on his brow, an angry moment in his eyes, as though the Great Plains and its God-given contents were being replaced unfairly by the mechanized culture of the Industrial Age. To him the shutting down of the West was a personal betrayal. I don't know how he lived through the 1890s. The Indians were mass-murdered or starved onto the reservations; Frank James and Cole Younger became carnival performers; the Hole-in-the-Wall

Gang discovered they couldn't outrun a telegraph or an automobile; and Fannie Porter's cathouse in San Antonio was purchased by the Carmelite Sisters for a daycare center.

He spent long hours on the porch staring at the dust in the sky, as though a great herd of longhorns were moving toward the cattle pens in Kansas, when in reality the land was simply eroding away. Sometimes he said he heard the tinkling of a piano in a saloon, then began talking about dancehall girls pulling up their dresses on a balcony and the time Wild Bill Hickok bought him a bottle of Vernon's Ginger Ale in an Abilene ice cream parlor. He loved his Colt .45 revolver and slept with it under his pillow.

But Papa had a greater enemy now than just the passage of time. He would walk out on the porch after sunset and see the irrevocable change taking place in the countryside. There was a stench in the air like rotten eggs, a monotonous clanking of oil derricks, and a sky dark with soot, the fields lit with thousands of tiny tin flames that resembled rose petals. Two or three oil men from the Atlas Oil Company came to our door and offered to lease Papa's land and make him rich. They spoke to him as they would a child. When they left, it was a wonder they didn't burst their tires bouncing across the cattle guard.

There was a difference between us, though. He had lived most of his life the way he wanted. I had not. I was also sickened at the notion of a brothel owner paying our bills. Plus, the notion of criminals hiding their opium in our barn made me mad. That was the place where our animals lived, and all of them were like our mule Lancelot—gentle and loving and dependent on us to care for them, just as they cared for us. I think animals are holy. To this day, I have thought myself capable of killing anyone who abuses them.

How could my father bring the culture of needles and opium pipes into our lives?

"Bessie!" he called from upstairs.

"What?" I shouted back.

"Help me get my boots on."

This was just after he had told me to take away his tray, with the fine breakfast I had fixed him uneaten.

"Put them on yourself!" I shouted.

"We're going to San Antonio on the train," he yelled back.

"What for?"

"To get us out of this damn trouble!"

"Why didn't you say so?"

Then he mumbled something.

"Say that again!" I yelled.

"I said I swear to God I'm going to have a heart attack," he replied.

"Maybe you deserve it," I said, more calmly now.

Then I went about my business for the next twenty minutes. Finally I went upstairs, dragging his empty suitcase. He was sitting in a chair by the window, dressed in his best suit, with a vest and tie and starched white shirt and a boot on his left foot. In the distance I could see a dust devil spinning across an empty field.

"I need a fresh bandage," he said.

"I'll get the medicine kit. You can put it on yourself."

"Night and day, remorse has become my companion, Bessie. Can you not see that? Do you wish to add to it? Tell me."

I had to look away from his eyes. "You make me mad, Papa. I found the address where Cody is living. Can I borrow the money I need to send him a telegram?"

"You're my daughter and the love of my life. The day I make you borrow money or anything is the day I stop living. Now help me with my goddamn foot, would you, please?"

"Don't use God's name in vain," I said.

I didn't have much more to say until it was time for us to board the train.

★   ★   ★

We stepped off the passenger car in San Antonio at three that afternoon, the steam white and hissing from under the locomotive. Papa
hired a jitney and gave the driver Bertha Lafleur's address. The driver
looked at us curiously in the rearview mirror. A small crucifix was
hanging under it.

"Something wrong?" Papa said.

The driver turned around and looked at me, then at Papa. "You
sure you got the right address?"

"Yes, I'm sure," Papa said.

The driver scratched the back of his neck, then swung into
the traffic and remained silent until we reached our destination, a
part of town called Dignowity Hill, at one time a neighborhood of
Victorian wealth, now threatened by commerce and factories and
the grime of immigrants and the working class. Bertha Lafleur's
home made me think of a freshly iced wedding cake couched in
greenery and flowers, unable to escape its fate.

Papa had the driver carry his suitcase up the porch while he
labored up the flagstones on his crutches. "What's your name?"
Papa asked.

"Robert," the driver said.

"I'd like for you to come back in an hour, Robert."

"I usually don't service this house."

"You're not servicing it. You're picking up me and my daughter."

"Yes, sir. I'll be here in an hour."

Papa watched the driver walk out to the street, then twisted
the bell. "Everything is going to be all right, Bessie."

"I don't want to be here."

"Why not?"

"The person who owns these surroundings tried to make
them like the Garden of Eden. She's a hypocrite, Papa. Don't let
her fool you."

He shook his head. "We'll go to the Alamo later. We'll stay at the St. Anthony. It's brand-new. We'll have a grand time. Cain't you smile a little bit?"

That was Papa, spending money we didn't have, pretending the rules of existence didn't apply to him. I could hear someone with heavy shoes walking toward the door. My heart was thumping. Papa took off his Stetson and combed his hair with his fingernails. Then I realized he was actually raking his scalp.

"Are you all right, Papa?" I said.

He took a deep breath and let it out and straightened his shoulders and squeezed the grips on his crutches. "I shouldn't have brought you here, Bessie. You're my little pal, the one person in the world who has never let me down."

I wanted to cry.

A trim, flat-chested man in a lavender shirt and a black tie and gray britches with a shiny, thin leather belt opened the door. He wore a shoulder holster with a blue-black revolver in it. But his features didn't go with his body. His head was shaped like a cider jug and his expression never changed, as though it were painted on his face, a twisted leer you see on stupid and violent white men down South. "You're Mr. Holland?" he said.

"That is correct," Papa said.

The gunman looked past us down the flagstones and at the gate and at the hedge.

"Come in," he said.

I dragged our suitcase across the threshold, and Papa followed. The gunman closed the door, shutting out the sunlight in the room. It smelled like a mausoleum. The curtains were dark blue and made of velvet, the walls hung with paintings of people who had faces that looked like toadstools. "Leave the suitcase by the door," the gunman said.

"Say that again?" Papa said.

"Leave your things and follow me," the gunman replied. "Miss Lafleur is in the gazebo."

He led us through the kitchen onto the back porch. It was elevated and columned and made of bricks and hung with wood-bladed electric fans. "Wait here," he said.

"We can find our way," Papa said.

"No. You wait here. Understood?"

Papa's eyes dulled over.

"I didn't get your reply," the gunman said.

"I didn't give you one," Papa said.

Bertha Lafleur rose from behind the trellises of clematis on the gazebo and waved at us.

Papa smiled at her, then turned to the gunman. "In a little bit I'll need you to fetch my suitcase. In the meantime, you keep yourself outside of earshot. I'm not trying to demean you. But you should treat your elders with respect."

The gunman looked like someone had struck a match on his face. He was about to speak when Papa went out the French doors on his own and stumped across the lawn on his crutches, grinning at Bertha Lafleur as though he were twenty-five years old and the world was his.

Instead of funereal clothes, Miz Lafleur was wearing a white dress printed with pink camellias, a wide red belt clamped tightly around her narrow waist, her breasts bulging, her face happy and small inside her thick black hair, one hand gripped on her cane.

"It's so good of you to come here, Hackberry," she said. "And you, too, Bessie. I've fixed sandwiches and tea. Please sit with me."

The gunman had positioned himself perhaps twenty yards away, inside the shade of the trees. Another man joined him, this one short and stout as a stump, with an expression like a smoked ham. He wore a derby hat and a suit that hung on him like cardboard, and looked straight at us, his coat open, his shoulder holster visible. In it was a German "broomhandle" pistol. The colored soldiers who captured Kettle Hill took them off the dead bodies of the Spaniards and sold them to the pawn shops on Congress Street in Houston. A bunch of the colored soldiers got hanged, too. It's a bad story, and I don't like to think about it.

"Aren't you going to say something, Bessie?" Miss Lafleur said.

"Why do those two men have to be here?" I replied.

"They're security personnel," she said.

"They look like embalmers," I said.

She tried to laugh. We were already seated at the table. We should have just walked across the lawn, gone through the house, and left the property forever. I felt that each second there was the equivalent of sinking in quicksand.

Papa covered my hand with his. "You're a generous lady, Bertha," he said. "But I've thought things over and have realized I need to make some choices. Could you ask your man to fetch my suitcase?"

"Your suitcase?"

"Yes, it's in your living room."

The autumnal sunlight was spangled on her face. She tried to smile. "What are you saying, Hackberry?"

"I guess I'll have to show you," Papa replied.

He rose from the table and pointed at the two gunmen. "One of you or both y'all get my suitcase. No, don't look at each other. Just do it."

Both men were motionless in the silence, waiting for Bertha Lafleur to speak.

"Fletcher, would you be so kind as to bring Mr. Holland his suitcase?" she said.

While he went back into the house, she paced up and down on the gazebo, using her cane, opening and closing her free hand, the sunlight brittle, like gold coins sliding across her skin. I tried to eat my sandwich, then set it down and stared into empty space, my heart thudding. The man with the German pistol shoved the suitcase onto the gazebo, his eyes on Papa, his Irish mouth like someone sucking a soda straw, his face warped out of shape. He walked back into the shade and fixed his glare on us.

"I do not understand you, Hack," Miss Lafleur said, although I think she understood everything about him, in particular how to manipulate him.

Papa clicked open the latches on the suitcase. "There's not much to understand, Bertha. I cain't take your money. It's not because of its origins, either. It belongs to you, and it belongs to the women who he'ped you earn it. I respect you and I respect them. That's the end of the story." He began placing the rubber-banded bundles of twenty- and fifty-dollar bills on the table.

"You saved me from the hands of Indian Charlie," Miss Lafleur said. "Now that I've tried to repay you, you've decided to become a moral example for others. At perhaps the expense of my life."

"I think you're leaving something out, Bertha," Papa said. "That pile of grief buried in my barn belongs to Indian Charlie, doesn't it?"

She sat back down and put both her hands on top of his forearm. "You've never allowed me to come into your life. Never. When I could have been good to you and kept you from drinking and squandering your wealth."

"I think maybe we shouldn't talk about this anymore," he said.

She let her hands slide back in her lap. Oddly she looked smaller and thinner and actually beautiful in that moment, maybe because she was truly bereft and unable to conceal her emotions, her face suddenly sculpted by a lifetime of pain and rejection. Papa always said never to condemn the poor prostitute on the street or in the crib, and now I knew why. It's the prostitute who pays the price, not her customer.

"Why are you looking at me like that?" she said.

"I didn't mean to stare," I said.

"I visited you at the jail and told you I would do everything in my power to keep you out of prison, didn't I?"

"Yes, ma'am, you did," I replied.

Her eyes were starting to water. "Then why don't you speak to your father and tell him to come to his senses?"

"I appreciated what you tried to do for me, Miss Lafleur," I said.

"Let her be, Bertha," Papa said.

"How about me, Hackberry? What happens to me?"

"Indian Charlie knows better than to come around here," Papa said.

"Liar," she said.

"I wish you wouldn't talk to me like that," he said.

"You've broken my heart, Hackberry. I never thought you would do something like this."

The wind had shifted, blowing her words toward the two gunmen in the shade. They began walking toward us. "Want us to escort the gentleman to the front entrance, Miss Bertha?" asked the man with a broomhandle pistol.

She stared at him silently, her face disjointed, like it had been sawed down the middle and stitched back incorrectly. Then she scratched the top of her wrist, her eyes veiled. "No, he can find his way, Fletcher. Would you get me some more tea, please? It's such a nice afternoon. Also, see if the Empire is open tonight, and call the masseuse as well. Suddenly I have a terrible pain in my lower back."

Before we left town, I sent Cody a telegram. It read: HELP.

I didn't even sign it.

Chapter Eleven

The fire came four nights later. I had my bedroom window opened an inch to let in the clean smell of a storm blowing off the Gulf of Mexico. Then I had a dream, or I thought it was a dream. I saw lightning flickering in the clouds and heard the windmill clanking and ginning and cows herding up in a dry irrigation ditch. Then I sneezed and woke up and smelled kerosene burning and a stench like someone cooking chitlins. When I sat up I could see smoke and flames spiraling in the sky.

I went barefoot to the window, the hardwood floor so cold and hard I had to squinch my toes. At least three men were running from the barn. They had opened the doors on both ends so the wind could suck the fire through the hay bales stacked in the loft and cave the roof. They were good at what they did. The whole building was alight.

"Fire, Papa!" I yelled into his room, then ran downstairs and into the night, still barefoot and in my nightgown.

Someone had punched the wood plug through the hole on the stock tank, draining most of it, and broken the shaft and cogged wheels in the windmill, disallowing the transfer of wind power from the spinning of the blades. The roof on the chicken run was attached to the barn and the chickens didn't have anywhere to go.

Most of the horses and mules had taken off, but I could see Lancelot through a window, his eyes full of glassy light, wide as doorknobs, running back and forth.

For just a moment I saw a man outside stripped to the waist, his fists raised at the sky, his head shaped like a darning sock, hair that was like shiny black paint, pumping his loins, his voice roaring with animal sounds, the shadows and the lights of the fire streaming like leaves on his skin. In a blink he was gone.

I ran into the barn. It was like the inside of a furnace. I saw a rope on the ground and ran to get it, and Lancelot almost knocked me down when I was picking it up. I got it around his neck and screamed and made him run in circles and got him more scared of me than the fire until he charged out the door, and all the time I was stepping on embers and watching holes burn in my nightgown, like a helpless witch tied to a stake.

Then I heard Papa yelling at me in the smoke, and saw him on one crutch, his long underwear and socks sprinkled with soot and ash that was still glowing, the sweat on his face as bright as Christmas morning.

He let the crutch fall from his armpit and picked me up on his shoulder as though I were a leaf and wrapped the rope I had tied on Lancelot around his wrist and took all of us out the door.

But he didn't stop. He kept going until he was to the front porch and could seat me on the steps and release Lancelot and wipe his eyes on his arm and smell himself. In the background we heard the roof of the barn crash on itself.

"They leave their mark, don't they?" he said.

"Yes, sir," I replied.

"Did you get a good look at anyone?"

"A man howling at the moon."

He stared at the stars and at the animals who were still criss-crossing the fields.

"Let's have some breakfast," he said.

We went inside and washed with the handpump in the kitchen, then put on clean clothes and watched the sunrise and fixed breakfast for two neighbors and three Mexican workers and Aint Minnie, the colored woman who had been with us before I was born, and her daughter Snowball.

It's funny how the simple people you grow up with on a stretch of land are always with you, no matter what happens. You miss them when you leave home, and you see them in your dreams when you're old. The community you share with them has no borders nor does it have a beginning or an end, no more than the deed in the courthouse has governance over the rising of the sun or its passing across the sky into the west, nor the lightning that dances silently on the horizon and the dust devils gliding across the plains, nor the ticking of a clock that human hands cannot stop.

Those early friends are always with us, always kind, sharers in a common heart, their old photographs hovering on a nightstand.

Chapter Twelve

Cody didn't answer my telegram for three weeks, and did so by mail. But I did not take him to task. He had just turned sixteen, and was living in a place called the Bowery, cleaning spit buckets at a gym and sleeping in a flophouse to save money. He said he had lied about his age and was applying for admission to an open-door college where the students were mostly immigrant Jews who worked all day in the garment district with their parents and went to school at night. He had made friends with a little Jewish boy named Lansky and another little boy named Benny and a man named Mr. Madden. They liked Cody and showed him around the city, and told him he could either keep cleaning spit buckets or get rich, because the Statue of Liberty means the liberty to choose one or the other, and if you're smart you won't let a rich man put his foot on the back of your neck.

Why would little boys know things like this, I asked myself, but Cody said Texas wasn't any different, except we believed the lies we were taught in school and helped rich people squish us down in the mud. He asked if I would like to come on up. I wrote him back and said, "Thank you, can I have my own spit bucket to clean?"

Actually it was a temptation. But I couldn't leave Papa. He had stopped drinking and the effect on him had been dramatic, as though a disease had left his organs and his skin. You have probably guessed by now that alcohol is the bane of my family. I hope I will never turn out to be what many of my kin are. They give the product of their labor to saloons and gambling houses, and orphan their children and often lie in unmarked graves on the prairie or a potter's field. And they do it all with their eyes open, raining tragedy on the people they love the most. I sometimes feel a bitterness that I fear will make me a spinster.

All in all it was a lonely time. In those days the late fall could be unkind, with the frost on the ground and the dust and corn stubble and tumbleweed blowing in the fields. The fading light itself gave me a shiver.

I visited Miz Banks often and helped her start up a library in the town's old firehouse. I couldn't figure out why she kept at it. Teenagers broke her windows and sniggered behind her back, and women looked askance when they passed her on the street. Even I got dirty looks because I was at her side. Know why small towns are small? They're small.

That's why I was so happy when I saw my favorite spirit, Mr. Slick, walking up the path to our front porch, whistling and wearing a starched high collar with a gold pin and a suit and high-heeled shoes with cloth tops.

"Well, howdy-do, Mr. Slick. Join me on the swing," I said. "What brings you by?"

"I have been doing various investigations regarding the fire," he replied, and flexed his teeth. "Actually I have started up my own agency." He inhaled somberly and gazed at the horizon. "I have pretty much nailed down the crew that burned your barn and why they did it."

"Mr. Slick, that didn't take a lot of guessing," I said.

He sat down beside me and tapped on his knees. "Indian Charlie and his people dug up the tar before they burned the barn, but they're telling people y'all kept it."

"That's the kind of thing they would do, Mr. Slick. Horseshoes don't float on the water. Frogs don't marry princesses."

My metaphor did not get through.

"Miss Bessie, bad people are gonna come after you for what y'all ain't got," he said.

"Well, I thank you for telling me that."

How do you talk to a man or spirit like Mr. Slick? Even though he had a good heart, he probably couldn't put on his socks with a map.

"You're just not listening," he said. "There's all kinds of going-ons happening now."

Have you ever heard grammar like that in your life?

"I cain't put it all together," he continued. "It makes my head hurt. But them oil people is after you, and so are the Fowlers and the sheriff and Indian Charlie."

"Why are the oil companies after us?"

"It has to do with the woods where I was living. Where the little girl was raped and murdered and never found. They've torn it all up. There's sludge pits as far as you can see. They squish under your feet."

The pain in his face made me think of bumblebees closed up inside a fruit jar.

"I'm sorry, Mr. Slick, I don't understand what you're trying to tell me."

"I think I found her bones. I don't know what to do with them."

I placed my hand on top of his. "Don't blame these things on yourself, Mr. Slick. You're a good spirit or good fella or whatever you are. Now, I'm going inside and get us both a piece of pie."

"I think they're yours," he said.

"What's mine?"

"The bones. Before I met you plowing with the mule, I saw a glow in the middle of the woods, then a little girl standing on a sunken grave. It was you, Miss Bessie."

"I won't listen to that kind of talk, Mr. Slick."

"Two nights ago at almost the same spot, I saw the bones on the edge of a sludge pit."

I got up from the swing. "Stop it!" I said.

"Ain't none of us is what we think we are," he said. "That's how come the world is messed up. Ain't none of it real. You got to listen to me."

Papa opened the door and looked at both of us. The evening sun was pink inside the dust in the west, and a solitary tumbleweed was bouncing across the hardpan. "A Texas Ranger just called and said Jubal Fowler decided he had rabbit blood in him and took off from Gatesville. His bunkies said he couldn't stop talking about you, Bessie."

I didn't pay it any mind. Why should I? I never as much as touched Jubal Fowler, although I sent him a short letter at the reformatory telling him I hoped things worked out for him and that I wished we had gone to the movie house in town and had a soda at the drugstore and maybe worked together at the library Miz Banks and I were building at the old firehouse. Mama always said children don't get to vote on which womb they're coming out of.

I have to say, an awful lot was stacking up on me. One evening I walked down to the sludge pit where Mr. Slick said he saw the bones, but I didn't see any such thing, just miles of derricks and pumps clanking like broken arms and a quivering glow on the surface of the sludge. What was I expecting? Mr. Slick was not the most ordinary of people or creatures. Then on the way home I saw a whole flock of white pigeons flying over the wells and circling like they couldn't find their home. What was puzzling was the fact we didn't have pigeons of that kind. These were the times when I missed Mama the most. I sometimes got mad at God about this. When you're little and by yourself, you feel like the whole world has shut you out, and it seems like only bad people come into your life. When I had thoughts like these, I'd reenact shooting Jubal Fowler's father.

I went to bed by kerosene lamplight and read *The Adventures of Tom Sawyer*. That was my third reading of it. The chapter I liked the most contains the account of Tom convincing his friends to pay him to paint Aint Polly's fence. If that doesn't capture human beings, blue jays don't get drunk in mulberry trees. I think Mark Twain should have been president of the United States.

But no matter what books I read or the strolls I took or the arguments I had with myself, I couldn't get the sunlight back into my life. Papa was good to me, but I knew his pattern. The past was always calling him, like specters on horseback beckoning in the distance. No one else saw them, no matter what the surroundings were. He could be standing in a room full of people, then he would suddenly stare out a window as though someone had clapped his hands and told him to put away whatever he was doing and swing into the saddle and ride into eternity.

I closed my book, extinguished the wick in the lamp, and pulled the covers over my head. A minute later a pebble hit the glass in my window. I walked barefooted to the window, my breath fogging the pane, and looked down in the side yard. My heart swelled the size of a football. It was Jubal Fowler.

I put on my coat and went out the back door into the dark. Jubal was thinner, his hair uncut, sifting like straw in the wind. He wore a coat that was too small for him, with only a strap undershirt beneath.

"You must be freezing," I said.

"Yeah, I reckoned I'd sleep in your barn. What happened to it?"

"Some drug traffickers burned it down."

"What are drug traffickers doing here?"

"Causing trouble."

He gripped his arms, compressing them against his body. "You got a blanket?"

"I'll get you one," I said.

But he wasn't looking for a blanket. He looked at the house, like a dog that's been shut out in the yard with snow on the ground. "I'd appreciate something to eat, too," he said.

What was I supposed to do? "Come inside," I said.

We went through the back door and into the kitchen. It was cold and full of moonlight, and every board seemed to creak under our feet. I lit a lamp and put some kindling in the woodstove and got a pan with some leftover grits and sausage from the cool box and set the pan on the lid burner. Jubal was sitting at the table and starting to drift off. His strap undershirt was full of holes. I could see red stripes on his chest.

"Did somebody whip you, Jubal?"

"I sassed an instructor. But that's not much compared to what the older boys do."

He held his eyes on me. I knew where he was going. I had heard about Gatesville and didn't want to talk about it. "I have a dollar and thirty-six cents in my piggy bank."

He stared at nothing, like he was speaking to somebody from a different planet. "I'm looking at two years in Eastham. I got to get across the Rio Grande. I was thinking—"

I took the pan of grits and sausage off the lid and emptied it into a plate and stuck a spoon in it, even though it was still cold. "Here," I said. "Eat it."

"Don't get short with me, Bessie," he said. "You mean a lot to me. I'd lay at night at Gatesville and hear what was going on in the latrine and stuff my fingers in my ears so hard I made them bleed."

"Well, you're not there now, Jubal, so don't have to talk about it. Understand?"

I guess I was being mean, but I cannot stand people who talk about all the evil that's in the world. I think they want it that way so they don't have to take care of themselves. You ever see a Judas goat at work? Leading his fellow animals up the slaughter chute, then ducking out himself?

"I heard Cody is doing okay in New York," he said. "You ever think about going up there?"

"I have Papa to take care of."

"He can take care of himself, if you ask me."

"Well, I'm not asking *you*. So stop minding other people's business."

A board squeaked in the ceiling. Jubal looked up at it. "You're better than me, Bessie. So is Cody. I did hateful things because I was jealous of people like y'all and Miz Banks. If you'll go away with me, I won't ever let you down. I'll work hard and go to trade school or whatever it takes."

The ceiling creaked again.

"You have to go," I said. My eyes were getting wet and my forehead hot. "Take the blanket and the food."

"Just like that?"

"I'm just fourteen years old, Jubal. I'll get the money from my piggy bank."

He stood up and let the blanket slip off his knees. His eyes looked like he was staring a hole in the wall. "It's been nice. Thanks for the food."

"I don't know what else to do," I said. "I cain't make the right things happen for you. I've got my father to look out for."

"I understand," he replied. "Just don't forget me, Bessie. In your heart, always save a little place for me."

He smiled and went out the door, into the dark, his shoulders hunched against the wind and the grit that was blowing against the windowpanes. Then a square of light from an oil lamp upstairs fell on the ground, right next to his feet. He picked up a piece of pipe from the junk around the windmill and flung it through Papa's window, then cupped his left hand on his right bicep and jerked his fist upward. "Here's the Italian salute for you, Mr. Holland!" he said. "I'll be back, and I'll piss in your mouth or on your grave!"

Chapter Thirteen

Three days later the sun rose inside black clouds that were roiling with flames and smelled like the new refineries down at Texas City. Papa had left early in hopes of borrowing money from a bank in a small town down on the Pecos River, which showed how desperate he was. In many ways I felt responsible for the financial plight we were in. I had emotionally battered him into giving back the money the brothel lady Bertha Lafleur had lent him, which left us with clean consciences and empty pockets and bill collectors knocking at our door. Many preachers will tell you a clean conscience is a wonderful possession. Unfortunately you cain't spend it at the grocery store.

That particular morning I had just finished eating two inches of pork rind and a half bowl of grits for breakfast, when I saw Mr. Slick ride up bareback on a horse with a ribcage that made me think of the Four Horses of the Apocalypse. I had gone to bed with about the same amount of food I had for breakfast, and was a little light-headed and not up to Mr. Slick's grammar that was like a box of broken soda crackers. However, I had to admit his heart was sincere and his intentions good, and you cain't run that kind of person from your door, lest you run Jesus out of town also, although I don't know if that's in Scripture or not.

I stepped out on the porch without my coat and said, "Good morning, Mr. Slick. I have exactly three tablespoons of coffee in the cupboard I would like to share with you. My father is not home, but he would certainly want to invite you in if he were here."

Mr. Slick was wearing a derby hat with a hole in it and a yellow vest and checkered britches and a bushy coat that looked like it had been torn off a bear while it was asleep. He peered at the horizon like he had robbed a bank. "Anybody been by here, Miss Bessie?"

"Not to my knowledge."

"No activity of any kind?"

"I noticed all that smoke that has stunk up the countryside and the tumbleweed you see bouncing across the yard."

"That ain't just those sludge pits burning out there. Somebody used explosives to blow up a couple of wells last night. Them oil men is flat browning their britches, I mean dancing up and down, I mean spotifying their drawers like a cupful of birdshot."

"I think I got the picture, Mr. Slick. Come in."

"I found the horse wandering round by the slaughterhouse. Can I put her in your shed?"

"Of course," I said.

"You got a little feed?"

"Sure, Mr. Slick." I smiled at him. How could I not?

I got the coffee started, then Mr. Slick came inside and took off his hat and sat in a chair close to the stove, blowing on his hands, his face ruddy from the wind. Or that's what I thought.

"Is there something you want to tell me?" I asked.

"You don't believe me about certain things I inform you of, Miss Bessie, but this time you got to listen. You also got to tell me the truth about yourself and that woods they tore up. Them woods was haunted, and it's got something to do with you."

"That's silly."

"No, ma'am, it is not."

"I've been truthful with you, Mr. Slick. Now stop carrying on."

His stuck his nose up. "Hiding the truth is the same as a lie."

"You know what St. Augustine said about that, don't you? 'Do not use the truth to injure.'"

"I don't know who that is or what a city in Florida has to do with anything, but four or five people said they saw a girl who looks just like you prowling around the wells that got blowed up."

"They used my name?"

"One fella did."

"Who?"

"Indian Charlie. He's working as a security man for Atlas Oil Company now."

"I cain't believe that, Mr. Slick. He's a murderer. He burned Bertha Lafleur with a cattle iron."

"That was in Mexico. That don't count here. Oh, Miss Bessie, I am afraid of what them people is gonna do to you. It just frets me something awful."

I used a hot pad to pour our coffee in two metal cups on the drainboard. The tip of the pot was clinking against the cups. He got up from the chair and took the pot from my hand. "I didn't want to upset you. But somebody had to tell you."

"It's all right, Mr. Slick," I said. "I told you you're my favorite spirit, didn't I?"

"There's something I left out. Jubal Fowler is here."

"I know. He broke my father's window."

"He's not just here. He's working for Atlas. With Indian Charlie. The Fowler family has got some connections in Austin."

"I'm glad to know that," I said. "Maybe this will change his ways."

"You're about to fall down, Miss Bessie. Here."

He was right. The room was spinning. He walked me to the breakfast table and sat me down, his eyes peering from under his derby hat like a cat looking out of a garbage can. "Don't cry," he said.

"I'm not crying. I just have strange feelings today. I cain't close my hands. I had dreams all night, but I cain't remember what they are." Then I said, "It's my birthday."

That was a mistake. "Your daddy left you alone on your birthday?" he said.

"It was an emergency."

He knew better. Papa could have invited me to go with him to the bank, but he didn't. Mr. Slick's face was a study in woe.

"Mr. Slick, you mean well, but pitying people can be an insult."

I went to pat his hand, but my fingers went right through his skin and the skeletal outline inside the skin until my fingers touched the table. "What's happening, Mr. Slick?"

"I don't know," he replied. "The woods and creek is gone. That little girl blowing up the wells is gonna start killing people. You ain't her, Miss Bessie?"

Then I was alone in the room. I looked out all the first-floor windows and could see nothing but tumbleweeds rolling in the wind and dust devils and clouds that a hundred years ago could have been created by bison thundering across the plains. There was no Mr. Slick, nor his emaciated horse. I don't think I ever felt so alone.

I breathed hard through my mouth, in and out, and went upstairs, then realized I had forgotten to make my bed. I picked up my pillows and fluffed and straightened them, then saw an envelope on the sheet. I pulled out a piece of lavender stationery that had come from a box my mother had bought on a trip to New Orleans. It read:

Happy birthday, little pal, friend of mine. The Lord doesn't make them any better than you.

                                                              Love,
                                                              Papa

Tucked in the corner of the envelope was a silver dollar. I sat on the side of the bed, the large coin clenched in one hand, pushing the dampness out of my eyes with the other.

Poor Papa didn't get the loan, but he came home without getting drunk or blaming other people for his problems. The latter was a virtue in Papa. He used to say, "You cain't get rid of your shadow." He fixed the window Jubal had broken and didn't fuss at me for letting him in the house, and didn't report him to the sheriff's office, either, although that might have been for a slightly different reason: namely, he couldn't stand the sight of the sheriff and said he wasn't worth the water it would take to flush him down the courthouse toilet.

Papa had brought home a birthday dinner for me, six tamales wrapped in corn shucks, still warm. After we ate, I told him that Jubal and Indian Charlie were working as security men for the Atlas Oil Company. I don't know if I mentioned that Papa's eyes never changed their expression. In fact they had no expression. It was his eyebrows you had to watch. They were bluish-gray and trim and stiff as wire, and they either went up or down or crooked or didn't move at all. When they remained stationary, you needed to get out of his way.

"Really?" he said, fiddling with a piece of food behind a tooth.

"You're not bothered?" I asked.

"Crab lice find their level," he said. "End of story."

But I *was* bothered. Papa had lived in an era when duels were fought on Alamo Plaza, sometimes on horseback, and were considered honorable and not under the governance of the judiciary, even when the dead man was stirrup-drug on a dirt street for everybody to see on Sunday morning. Also I had become fifteen years old. I know that sounds funny. But at some point I had to announce my adulthood or remain a child.

You probably don't understand. Rights didn't come to girls or women on a particular day. Did eighteen make me grown? How about twenty-one? No matter what my age, I couldn't vote. There were states where I couldn't own property. If I had the romantic inclinations of Miz Banks, I could probably be stoned to death without a big commotion being made. Why should I allow people to tell lies about me because I was only fifteen? I was blowing up oil wells? Who could think up something like that?

I'll tell you who. The loafers and drunkards and white trash who spent their time at the Green Lantern Saloon on the main street of our county seat. A big piece of white canvas hung from the balcony above the front doors that read, ALL NATIONS WELCOME EXCEPT CARRIE. Since most of the patrons did not read newspapers, they probably were not aware she had died three years ago.

When Papa and our Mexican hands were cleaning up the burnt remains of our barn, I went down into the basement and from a trunk dug out an old cap-and-ball revolver that had been converted for brass cartridges. The steel was dull-colored and pitted, the barrel long with a ramrod underneath, the edge of one walnut handle notched with a tiny file. A cracked leather holster and a box of ammunition lay next to it. I suspected the gun had belonged to my grandfather, Sam Morgan Holland, although he had killed nine men, not three.

I loaded five bullets in the cylinder, and set the hammer on the empty chamber, then slipped the barrel and frame into the leather. The weight, the coldness of the steel, and the dark, oily grain of the walnut handles seemed like an old friend. I knew I shouldn't have felt that way, but it was not I who was threatening a fifteen-year-old girl, or destroying the woods and the creek where a little girl had been molested and murdered whose only solace had been the Edenic place where her body had been buried and never found.

I hitched up Lancelot and told Papa I needed some things in town and would not be long. I loved Lancelot. I loved his name. I think he and I always had the same attitudes. Camelot was out there. On a rainy day or in the early morning mists. Yes, Avalon awaited us all, not in our eventual deaths but in the dreamworld of all those who can hear the jingle of the armor and the ringing of the swords and hold eternity to their breasts and not fear it.

I carried the pistol and a jolly umbrella, one that was painted with pink and orange and purple flowers. And I was glad I had brought it, too, because it snowed before Lancelot and I entered the town limits, Lancelot and I, crossing the moat and drawbridge, unafraid, the snow as cool on my skin as chicken feathers in the wind.

I tethered Lancelot to one of the iron rings in the elevated sidewalk in front of the saloon and started inside.

"Child!" a woman's voice shouted. "What are you doing?"

I couldn't believe it. Miz Banks, coming fast across the brick-paved street. At the wrong place and the wrong time, her skirts swishing through the pools of water and mud.

"I'm taking care of some business," I said. "Please do not be concerned."

"I certainly am concerned. Does your father know where you are? If he does, I'm going to give him a good swat."

I believed Miz Banks was taking on some characteristics I had not seen in her before. "Please take care of Lancelot for me, will you?" I said. "I'll be back in just a minute."

Then I opened the saloon door and went inside, my umbrella over my head. Every man at the bar turned around and stared as though they were in a photograph. Every one of them was mustached and unshaved and wearing a three-piece suit that could have been peeled off a corpse. The door slammed shut behind me, the bell tinkling overhead. I almost gagged at the density of smoke and the smell of their cigars and expectorated chewing tobacco. I couldn't imagine these men having wives.

"Wrong door, girlie," the bartender said.

"What is your name?" I said.

"*My* name?"

"Yes," I said. "I assume you know your name."

Someone in back snickered. Behind me the door opened softly and closed again. I smelled the soap and perfume and cleanliness of Miz Banks. I could almost hear her heart beating.

"Women aren't allowed in here," said the bartender.

"How about the poor tarts you keep upstairs?" Miz Banks said.

God bless Miz Banks, I said, because truth be told I was scared to death.

"My name is Bessie Holland," I said. "When you gentlemen finish spitting in the cuspidors and splattering one another's britches, would you please pass on a message for me to your friends Indian Charlie and the other security employees of the Atlas Oil Company? I did not blow up an oil well. I will sue the person who claims I did. Also, if any of Atlas's hired criminals come on our land again, I will shoot them."

The bartender lifted a flyswatter from under the bar. "I'm about to run the pair of y'all out in the street," he said.

I folded up my umbrella and handed it to Miz Banks and opened my coat and exposed my grandfather's holstered revolver that I had buckled from my shoulder to the opposite waist. "Will one of you other gentlemen get the sheriff and tell him that a child of fifteen is being threatened by a grown man at the Green Lantern and that I am about to shoot him and perhaps several of his friends."

There was not a sound in the room. A calliope was playing outside. A couple of women had come out of the bedrooms upstairs, their dresses as tight as sealskins. They were smoking cigarettes and letting the ashes fall over the handrail, their lipstick as bright as cherries.

"Take your complaint to Indian Charlie," the bartender said. "Now—"

I cocked the revolver. It was heavy, a .44, I think. I wasn't even sure if it would fire. I raised it over my head with both hands and pointed it at the ceiling and pulled the trigger. The report was deafening, like my head was inside a giant bell. The bullet punched a hole through the stamped tin on the ceiling, and a stream of termite sawdust streamed down on the bar like sand in an hourglass.

"Thank you for your time, gentlemen," I said. "I hope I haven't disturbed your day."

All the men at the bar had ducked when I pulled the trigger. After I holstered the .44, they straightened up slowly and several laughed and an old man clapped. Then they went back to their beer and hard-boiled eggs and pickled hog's feet, their boots cocked on the brass rail, as though Miz Banks and I had never been there.

I had the feeling Texas would not change for a very long time.

Chapter Fourteen

"Why did you do it, daughter?" Papa said that night, standing in front of the fireplace.

"People were telling lies about me," I replied.

He was leaning with both arms against the mantel, the fire flickering on his face. "But you borrowed trouble from people who have nothing to do with the problem. Secondly, you broke a cardinal rule when you deal with criminals like Indian Charlie: you never let them know what you're thinking."

"I'm sorry, Papa."

"That said, you've probably scared the lights out of those damn oil people. What I cain't figure is why they're telling this tale about a little girl blowing up their drilling rigs."

One of his favorite cats was a big, fat orange tabby named Dr. Medico who always sat in the windowsill, even when the glass was cold. I picked him up and cradled him in my arms and snugged his head on my cheek and looked at the north end of our property and the woods that bled into the oil field where the little girl had probably been buried.

"Did you hear me?" Papa said.

"I don't know why they have the little girl on their minds, Papa," I replied. "Guilt and misery usually find the right people. I hope they go to hell for what they're doing."

"Say that again?" he replied.

*   *   *

Christmas came and went, and I stopped thinking about Indian
Charlie and Jubal Fowler and my performance at the Green Lantern
Saloon. Oddly I thought more about the news stories regarding the
German submarines that were sinking ships along the British coast
and drowning noncombatants. I had nightmares after I saw a photograph of civilians in life jackets floating in a black wave, walleyed,
their faces burned and slick with oil. In the daylight I would hear the
clanking of the oil pumps in what used to be the little girl's resting
ground, and wonder if the great companies of the world cared about
the poor souls who slipped like ants off the hulls of torpedoed ships
or whose bones were pulverized by an iron dredge.

Papa picked up some money as a guard on the Katy and the Santa
Fe mail car, although the job did not sit well with him, which I couldn't
understand. At first I thought it was pride. He had been a city marshal
or a Texas Ranger for over thirty years, and had once slapped Harvey
Logan across the head with his Colt six-shooter. Now he babysat a safe
that usually contained little more than the engineer's lunch.

"Why don't you be a little humble, Papa?" I said when he made
a remark about riding in a hay-fever wagon on the Katy.

"The railroads stole every other section along the track," he
replied. "And lawmen like me he'ped them do it. I hate the thought
of it."

Then I knew where things were going to go. Mexico had become
an outdoor mental asylum, and every mercenary and misfit and
weapons salesman in Texas could splash across the Rio Grande and
be drunk in Monterrey by sunset. Papa's body was hard, his vision
free of cataracts, his chest corded with veins when he picked up a
heavy weight, his ability with horses and guns the envy of rodeo
performers. He was also possessed of an element that was not so
fine. A wanton streak for the ladies. You could see it flicker in his
eye, even on the occasions he attended church.

I wanted to confront him. I wanted him to think of me and not always himself. I wanted him to be my father.

On a cold morning in January, I got up early and fired the stove and heated the kitchen and fixed biscuits and bacon and milk gravy, then set the table when I heard him come down the stairs.

"You're not speaking this morning?" he said.

"I didn't get much sleep last night," I said.

"Why not?"

"You were banging around. Maybe with problems of conscience. Like you're going somewhere."

"Have you fed the cats?"

The rule in our house was: you feed the animals before you feed yourself. "I cain't recall," I said.

Doctor Medico and five other cats were either staring up at us or milling around.

"What's got into you, Bessie?"

"You're going to take off on me."

"I am not." He got the cat scraps from the cool box and began feeding them.

"I see it in your eye, Papa. That's why you got mixed up with Bertha Lafleur. She represents the past."

"I am what I am. I don't apologize for it."

"No, you're my father and I'm your daughter."

"That's right. And that won't change. So stop trying to mess up the morning."

He sat down and dipped a biscuit in a bowl of gravy and put it in his mouth, his eyes out of focus.

I left the table. I couldn't let him see my face.

I had seven dollars and thirty-eight cents in my piggy bank now, most of it earned by doing odd jobs for Miz Banks. I was thinking about running off, getting as far as Chicago at least, then getting onto the palm of God so He could set me down in New York City, maybe at Cody's door.

I had reached a time in my life when I knew I would always be different. I fought with it at first, then gradually realized that whether I liked it or not, for good or bad, I would always be the odd one in a bag of carrots or a dozen eggs. That notion scared me, as though someone had suddenly placed me by myself inside a bare room without windows; then I thought about an elderly, blind spinster who used to make candles for a living outside town. This is the story she told me about an event in her life in the spring of 1836.

In the early morning twenty-two men, all of them armed with long rifles, rode into their farm, led by a man in buckskin who said they were on their way to Bexar, which is what people called San Antonio back then. He asked if they could have breakfast, provided they paid for it. The father of the family told the riders he didn't have a great amount of food but he and his wife and their eight-year-old daughter would cook breakfast for them on an open pit in the backyard. While the father built a fire and laid strips of meat on a grill, his daughter became fascinated by the leader of the armed men and his youthful, almost effeminate looks.

"Excuse me, little girl, but do you not know that it is impolite to stare at your elders?" he asked.

"Well, we don't get to see many people who wear dead animals on their heads," she said.

"Back in Tennessee a cap like this is considered right smart fashion."

"Smelly deerskins are smart fashion, too?" she replied.

"I'll tell you what, little girl," the man said. "When you're an old lady, you can tell your grandchildren you fixed breakfast for Davy Crockett and his Tennesseans on their way to the Alamo to give ole Santa Ana the fight of his life."

I believed that story because the event changed the little girl's life. She had a quiet dignity about her, the same way Miz Banks did.

Both of them read John Donne and talked about no man being an island, entire of itself. I wanted to be different the way they were different. And that meant I couldn't stay home and simply await the day Papa would place me with a relative, then saddle up and ride across the Rio Grande.

What I mean is the little girl who fixed breakfast for Davy Crockett wasn't just a footnote in history. She was part of it. The rest of her life she seemed to see through a hole in time, as though she were watching Crockett as he vainly tried to invert his rifle and use it as a club as he was shot dead against a stucco wall, while the hordes of Mexican soldiers around him were so thick in the smoke and chaos they shot each other. The little girl from our town was never afraid, and never judgmental, as though she saw actors around her no one else saw. But what her story really taught me was not to become a spectator in my own life. I didn't have the right words to say that, but that's what I felt. I was determined that I would stand in front of a train before I let that happen.

On the Sunday after I confronted Papa about his mercenary temptations, I went with Miz Banks in her car to the Free Will Baptist Church, way down the road, almost to the border. The day was sunny and both cool and warm, and there was a hint of green in the rolling landscape, clutches of palms and banana fronds, a breath of Mexico in the wind. The pastor was a woman. At the end of the service, I felt like becoming a missionary and heading down into Mexico myself.

"You seem so happy," Miz Banks said. She was wearing goggles to keep the dust out of her eyes, and a maroon wool jacket that made her bosom look like a robin's.

"It's just that kind of day, Miz Banks," I replied.

"I hope you don't mind, but I packed us a lunch and thought we might have a picnic down by the river."

"I would enjoy that," I replied. "Actually, I would like to drive and drive and not stop. There're hills and a gorge down there, aren't there?"

"Yes, but sometimes bad people go through there."

The road was the color of mustard. We banged over the potholes and went around a corner where a house had been burned and an old stucco wall jutted out of some pines with the word VIVA! painted on it. The rest of the wall had been obliterated. I stuck my head out the window to see the wall and house better, then saw in the outside mirror a funnel of yellow dust behind us, and inside the dust a black automobile with headlights the size of garbage-can lids. And four men with bandanas on their faces and the couched posture of unfed canines.

Chapter Fifteen

They came up close on our bumper, then tried to swing wide and get in front of us, but Miz Banks straddled the road and, for one mile, with the help of the trees and old fence posts, kept them from passing. The consequence was a huge amount of yellow dirt in the faces of our pursuers and I suspect a growing anger and self-justification for what they were planning to do.

"Do you have a gun?" I said.

"No!" she said. Her hands looked small and round and soft on the steering wheel. "Take my purse!"

The left front tire hit a hole that was as hard as a rock and shook the frame and pitched me against the door. "Get my purse, Bessie! I have a knitting needle in it!"

We came out of the shadows and into the open, where the road was winding, with swales on the shoulders that could allow cars and wagons to pass easily. There were no houses anywhere, just rotted fences and loading pens from the days of the Chisholm Trail and the long, empty roll of the land as it dipped down toward the Rio Grande. Miz Banks was whipping her Model T back and forth, but it made the men in the black automobile even more angry and dedicated. One man was half out the passenger window, yelling, shaking his fist. My heart had sunk into my stomach. I took the steel knitting needle from Miz Banks's purse. It had a wood handle, with a knob on it. It felt as helpful as a soda straw.

Then Miz Banks swerved off the road, almost throwing me out of the Model T, and headed toward a series of hills and farther on a gorge that dropped into the river.

"What are you doing?" I said.

"There's a lepers' ranch in those hills. They won't follow us there."

"I never heard of a leper ranch around here."

"They don't announce themselves."

The ground was hard, and pieces of chert as sharp as knives were clattering like hammers under the frame of the car, the tires pinging under the fenders. I looked in the outside mirror and saw the black automobile carving its way in and out of our dust, two men sitting up on the windows, clinging to the roof, yodeling like turkeys.

"I don't see any ranch, Miz Banks," I said.

"It's there. Believe me."

The black car smashed into our back bumper, knocking me into the dashboard. "Who are they?" I said.

"Evil men," she said.

The black automobile dropped back, then accelerated and hit us again. I didn't know what kind it was. I knew it was big and heavy. And I knew the person driving it had crossed a line in his head, and would leave no witness to the crime he and the others were about to commit. I looked through the front window. The hills were sun-baked, too hard to abide grass, spiked with cactus and splintered trees that had been dead for decades. When the Indians crossed this same place during great droughts, they put pebbles under their tongues to cause their mouths to salivate.

Did Miz Banks believe we could ward off these men with a knitting needle?

"Why did you give me this needle, Miz Banks?" I asked.

She looked at me, caked with yellow dust. Then she looked straight ahead without speaking.

"Did you hear me, Miz Banks?" I shouted.

"Do what you will. No matter what happens, you will remain greater than they."

The right front tire exploded and we spun sideways like a pinwheel and came to a dead stop, the dust drifting over us, our pursuers making a wide circle to ensure we had no weapons before they got out of their vehicle.

Miz Banks had hit her forehead on the steering wheel and a rivulet of blood was sliding out of her hairline. My door was jammed and I couldn't get out, my mouth so dry with fear I couldn't swallow. Two men, the lower halves of their faces still wrapped with bandanas, were pulling Miz Banks from behind the steering wheel. She tried to hang on to the wheel, but they beat her hands with their fists and jerked her hair and peeled back her fingers until she slid off the seat. The shock and pain of her ordeal had transformed her sweet, round face from one of goodness into the expression on a rag doll.

I got my door open and was thrown to the ground, and when I tried to get up, a fist exploded on my face. I had never been hit so hard. Then I realized I wasn't hit by a fist. It was a sock, one filled with dirt and tied with a knot. The blow was like the sting of a scorpion inside my nose. My nose was running; my eyes felt as wet and big as raw oysters; the ringing in my face would not stop.

I was on my knees, but I could see what the men on the other side of the Model T were doing to Miz Banks. They stretched her over the fender and pulled up her dress and ripped off her undergarments. I heard her say, "No-no-no-no-no," then, "Please don't do this. Please."

There was a pause, and I thought these men might show mercy. Then Miz Banks screamed. Long and hard, as though glass was working its way through her entrails. I thought it would stop, as all pain was supposed to do. Instead, it was prolonged and grew worse and made me see images that seemed unrelated to what was happening to her. In my mind's eye I saw a red-hot poker, a medieval figure with a leather hood tightening a wooden screw, a girl crying out inside an envelope of flame, saying, "Oh, Jesus. Oh, Jesus. Oh, Jesus."

I tried to get up and was knocked down again, this time on all fours. But it may have been a blessing, I told myself. My right hand was pressed flat on the knitting needle. One of the men was standing inches from me. I picked up the needle with both hands and plunged it through the top of his foot.

"Goddamn it!" he yelled.

I jumped to my feet and ran and made about ten yards in front of the Model T before the fourth man tackled my thighs and dragged me down and would not let go. He lay parallel with me, behind my back, his arm locked under my chin, his loins pressed against me. There was no way I could get away from him. In the meantime I could see everything the other two men were doing to Miz Banks. They had pulled her arms so tight her feet were off the ground, and the man behind her had dropped his britches and let them collapse on his ankles. I couldn't see his features with any clarity, but I could see his profile. It reminded me of a spoon. Or a darning sock. Like the man I saw framed in the firelight when our barn went up in flames.

I struggled with the man who had me pinned against him. He hadn't spoken. Nor had he tried to violate me. Nor did he fight when I kicked his shins. Actually he had loosened his grip on my throat. He also pulled his bandana farther up his face, and I could see his nostrils pumping and sucking air against the cloth.

"Let me go," I said. "I won't run away again."

He made a wet shushing sound in my ear.

"What?" I said.

He shushed me again. I tried to turn my head. He clamped his fingers on the back of my skull and kept my vision pointed straight

ahead. Miz Banks was crumpled on the ground, hiccupping and
incoherent and shivering, like Jell-O shaking in a bowl. Her assailant
pulled up his britches and buttoned his fly and pulled the point of his
belt through the buckle, his shoulders hunched with his concentra-
tion, his knees bent like springs. "Sloppy seconds, anyone?" he said.

"Better go," one of them said.

"Even if you don't like that piece of pie over there, we still got
work to do," the chief assailant said. "Understand?"

And I knew what he meant. Miz Banks and I were going to die.

"That's just fine," said the man I drilled with the knitting
needle. "But I'd still like a piece of pie."

The wind had dropped and I could hear my heart drumming
in my ears. The man who'd been holding me got up slowly, one
hand pushed hard in the middle of my back as he rose to his feet.
He walked to the chief assailant, obviously the man in charge, and
said something, then pointed at a lavender rain cloud pulsing with
electricity above a green hilltop. Two riders were silhouetted on the
crest of the hill, like black specks jotted on a canvas.

"All right, let's roll it up," the leader said.

"Just like that?" said the man I stabbed with the needle. "You
get the fun? I get to soak my foot in a public toilet bowl?"

The man in charge nodded his head in an understanding fashion. "They got a picnic basket," he said. "It's yours. Eat up."

"That ain't funny," said the man I hobbled.

Then they drove away, leaving two lives changed forever, perhaps one ruined for good, passing around a bottle of mezcal with
a fat worm in the bottom, eating the sandwiches Miz Banks had
made. I knew that my dreams would never be the same.

Chapter Sixteen

The two riders on the hilltop turned out to be Hebrews who lived and worked at the leper community and looked not simply unusual but struck by lightning. They were obviously twins, dressed in black, with long, shredded beards, faces sunbrowned and as wrinkled as a discarded leather glove, and eyes that contained an inner fire a cautious person would probably not probe. They introduced themselves as Ezra and Ezekiel, but gave no last name. They put Miz Banks gingerly in the back seat of the Model T, unsaddled their horses, and sent them home with a pop, then drove us to a decayed stucco hospital that had been a United States Cavalry post in 1891, when the Indian Wars were formally ended at Wounded Knee.

One hour later the sheriff arrived. He must have weighed three hundred pounds, but it was gristle, not fat. His upper half looked like an inverted triangle of concrete stuffed in a tweed coat, the shape you see on a rodeo rider who will break a horse's bones first bounce out of a bucking chute. His silver shirt and customized boots and tall-crown Stetson and chrome-plated Peacemaker with a gold trigger were probably more expensive than an ordinary sheriff's salary would allow. He carried a notebook full of carbon-paper receipts and loose pages strung with cursive that could pass for hieroglyphics. His dark britches were freshly ironed and his fingernails manicured.

But like most Southern sheriffs, he sent a message to those who might think he was a dandy and gentle in his ways. His mustache looked like wire and moved as he breathed, and his cheeks were aflame with either hypertension or this morning's bucket of beer.

The Hebrews stayed with us, in the waiting area, just outside the cubicle Miz Banks was in. I was glad. They carried no weapons, but I would take their side in a gunfight with or without a gun. The sheriff was standing by the bed, his pencil hovering over his notebook. "So they just run up on y'all, without no reason, just out of nowhere?" he said.

"That is correct," I said.

"Without no license plate?"

"None that I could see," I replied.

He wrote on his pad. "And you don't know what kind of automobile it was, except that it was big?"

"It was black," I said.

He wrote on the same page again. Then stopped and stared at it, his eyebrows crawling up on his forehead. He put a piece of chewing gum in his mouth. "Is this lady the one who writes articles supporting those coal union people in Colorado?"

"If you mean the miners who were murdered in Ludlow, yes, she is their supporter."

He chewed on his gum. "You say you put a hole in a man's foot?"

"Yes, after he threw me on the ground."

"You didn't try to pull down his bandana?"

"It was rather hard to do while I was on my hands and knees."

He leaned over a wastebasket and spit his gum in it. "You say one of your attackers looked familiar? A fella who burned down your barn?"

"Yes, his physique and the shape of his head."

"You saw all this in the firelight? I mean at the barn? Physiques and such?"

"That's what I said. It's not a complicated idea."

"So maybe this bunch was following you around?"

"I didn't say that."

He let out a slight burp. "But that's what you meant?"

"I think we're talking about a man named Indian Charlie," I said. "He's a security man for Atlas Oil."

His expression took pause. Then he resumed whatever he was thinking about. "Were the other three men from Atlas Oil?"

I was beginning to tire. I had been standing a long time, and both of my feet felt like I had rocks in my shoes. "Why are you talking to me like this, Sheriff? We're asking for your help. But I do not feel that is forthcoming."

"I know who you are, little lady. You shot a man in a slaughterhouse and got away with it, most probably because your father is a former Texas Ranger. We don't do things that way down here. I'll see what your friend has to say after she comes out of the ether, but right now there's a lot more questions being asked than is being answered."

"Sir, excuse me, but you talk like an idiot," I said.

"I'll tell you what I got on my hands, little lady. Armies of wetbacks and Chinamen coming across the border. Pancho Villa and Germans fixing to start a war, and leper people who look like they come from Mars. That includes them two out yonder who remind me of vultures. Then you waltz in and claim y'all came down here to attend a church you've never been in, and for no reason someone chases you almost to the border in broad daylight, and to get away you drive out on the hardpan where it's guaranteed you will blow out your tires. When that happens, your friend, who certainly is not Helen of Troy, gets raped while you more or less are let alone. Does that make sense to you, little lady?"

I didn't answer. The silence in the room creaked in my ears, as though I were in the bottom of a deep pool, my head about to be crushed. A nurse came in with a bedpan and a stack of bandages and two folded white towels and a bottle of alcohol. "Y'all will have to go outside for a few minutes," she said.

Miz Banks made a sound like she had been pinched when the nurse turned her on her side. Her eyes were half shut, the lids bruised; one nostril of her nose was clotted with blood; her bottom lip was split, exposing all her teeth on one side of her mouth. I wanted to kill someone.

I had forgotten about the Hebrews. They had driven the Model T because I was not a good driver. Now they had no way to get home. The sheriff went to his office and made no offer of transportation for either them or Miz Banks or me. I sent Papa a telegram because we had no telephone, but so far he hadn't called the hospital, which I had asked him to do. Now the sun was a huge red wafer on the horizon, and the men who had attacked us were gone, a blip inside the dust. The doctor said Miz Banks should stay in the hospital two or three days because she was bleeding inside and her psychological problems might be even more serious.

"How can you know that, Doctor?" I asked.

"She asked for morphine," he said. He was a slight man, like someone who played badminton, with a clipped gray haircut and calm face and smokey-blue eyes that probably hid the life he was forced to live. "When I was out of the room, she tried to pay the nurse to give her more. Did you see the attack?"

"Some of it."

"I won't repeat what she told me, not unless I'm in a courtroom. The world has done your friend a great injury, Miss Holland, but her ordeal is probably just beginning. Do you understand what I'm saying?"

"I'm not sure," I replied.

"This isn't a random crime. The men who did this are evil incarnate."

I could hear myself breathing. I didn't know what to say, and I didn't want to believe him. "Sir, I'm only fifteen. Are you telling me I'm deliberately putting myself in jeopardy?"

"No, I'm telling you the men who did this exist in greater numbers than you think."

His face was absolutely motionless, his gaze unblinking. Then he walked away. My hands were shaking, and I didn't know why. I heard a phlegmy sound come from Miz Banks's throat.

"Miz Banks?" I said.

"Come here," she whispered.

I lowered my ear to her mouth. Her breath was like the tip of a cat's tail teasing my skin. "Can you hear me?" she said.

"Yes, what is it?"

"We must go home. We have our library work to do. Did we have an accident? Who are all these strange people walking around? Oh, dear, I hope nothing bad has happened."

A short time later Papa called the hospital and said he was on the way with Aint Minnie and her daughter Snowball, colored people who were as much members of our family as I was. We couldn't have had better helpers. There was no task Aint Minnie couldn't master. She was also fearless. When she was working for my uncle in Houston, a white man tried to burglarize the apartment. She hit him in the head with a skillet full of hot onions and threw him down a fire escape. Unless you lived down South in that era, you cannot imagine the courage it took for a woman of color to do that.

I still didn't know what to do about the Hebrews. Neither Miz Banks nor I could drive them home, and nobody in the hospital or the sheriff's department seemed to be in a volunteering mood, which wasn't a big surprise considering the references to leprosy in the Bible, which was on a level with the garbage dump at Gehenna. Also, the waiting room was uncomfortable, with a hard bench to sit on, not to mention that nobody had entered the room since the Hebrew brothers. They made me think of a pair of bookends with no books to prop up.

"Y'all have sure been nice to us," I said. "I am very sorry to have taken you away from your work."

"It's no bother," the brother named Ezekiel said. He was maybe an inch taller than his brother, which was the only difference I could tell between the two. Their faces were oblong, their noses hanging like sausages, like Devil Anse Hatfield. Did you ever see his photo? You'll see what I mean.

"Y'all are Levites, aren't you?"

"What makes you think that?" Ezra asked.

"I have read the Book of Leviticus several times. You seek what's proper in people so they can remain holy in their service to God. You're also known for your charity."

They both smiled.

"But the Levites also messed around with animal sacrifice," I said. "I think that kind of thing should get pitched out of Scripture. In Genesis chapter 1, verses 19 to 31, God protects the animals and the fowl and the fish from unnecessary death and gives Man the green fruit and seed as the designated food for all Creation."

I was about to put them to sleep. "What I mean is, y'all are righteous people. Like John Brown, although I hope you don't get hanged."

I did not say anything about Devil Anse Hatfield, and I could see they knew nothing about John Brown and Bloody Kansas. Knowledge of history can sometimes be isolating.

"Men such as yourself probably know a whole lot more about Scripture than I do," I said.

They smiled again.

"What I wanted to say is, y'all have been mighty good to us," I said. "I'd like for y'all to meet my father."

"We have to go now," Ezekiel said.

Their lips were dry, their eyes dulling over, like heat leaving charcoal. I knew their fatigue had caught up with them, and I also knew I was acting selfishly. I couldn't help it. I didn't want to be alone.

"If y'all go without meeting my father, he will never forgive me," I said. "Please. It's been a mighty hard day."

They looked at each other. Through the window we could see a Mexican café with lights on, white curds puffing from its chimney in the moonlight, the stars blinking in the cold. They nodded and rose from the bench and let me walk out the door first.

Chapter Seventeen

I n the weeks that followed, Aint Minnie babysat Miz Banks at Miz Banks's home, and I tried to wake in the morning without my dreams trailing me into the daylight. It was hard to do, but I made up my mind that, hard or not, I wasn't going to allow a collection of white trash to rob me of who I was, and by that I mean the person God made me, and by that I mean the lines in Genesis that say I was made in His image.

How about that, White Trash of the World?

Also, Papa was acting like a father and no longer like a drunkard. We went to movies and ate out and played checkers on Old Folks Night at the Baptist Church, which meant cheering up people who couldn't tell the difference between a checker and the cap on a soda bottle. He also brought home some friends who were of a breed I've known all my life and who make my stomach flop when I get too close to them. They were all lawmen, from Texas and Louisiana, with accents like fence wire twanging, all with the same rural backgrounds, the same certainty about everything, the same quiet, mean-spirited humor in their eyes. They had a stink on them, too. They came out of the womb with it. It was feral and not like sweat, either. It came from somewhere else. Think I'm kidding? You didn't grow up in the South. In 1934 three of them would be part of the ambush that ended the lives of Bonnie and Clyde. The mortician who worked on the bodies described them as "wet rags" and said there were so many holes in them their bodies couldn't hold the embalming fluid.

One night, after his friends had left, I helped Papa clean up the dining table.

"You don't care for my friends, do you?" he said.

I picked up another dirty steak plate with a toothpick floating in the juice. "I try not to judge."

"They risk their lives for the rest of us."

"They may risk their lives. But it's not for us."

"You're probably right. I got to ask you something. About the man who held you to the ground."

"I don't want to talk about it, Papa."

"He was trying to keep the other men from you?"

"I don't know what he was trying to do."

"But the head man reminded you of Indian Charlie? A head like a darning sock and black paint for hair?"

"We've been through this, Papa."

"Indian Charlie works for Atlas Oil. So does Jubal Fowler."

"It wasn't Jubal," I said.

"How do you know?"

"I'm not going to talk about this anymore." I stacked up several more dishes and cups and headed for the kitchen. "Oh, I forgot. I saw a new invention in the drugstore called dental floss. Next time your friends are over, we could put it by their plates."

I didn't blame Papa for his attitudes. He was doing the best he could. Back then not many rape charges were filed, not unless the crime involved a colored man. In those instances, the colored man had no chance at defending himself. All a white woman had to do was say he touched her or perhaps even looked at her, and the colored man would be placed in jail and not allowed bail. If he denied the charges in court, he would be verbally scalded for calling a white woman a liar. Lynchings of colored men, and sometimes boys, were common. That's when I began to believe there are depraved people among us. I saw three hangings, the kind that were left over from Jim Crow, and I saw what was done to the bodies afterwards. The people below took pictures of each other, grinning like it was Independence Day, the dead men hanging as straight as railroad spikes, nothing left of their clothes.

I helped Miz Banks whatever way I could, and read Jack London's and Stephen Crane's stories to her (she particularly liked "The Bride Comes to Yellow Sky"), and created a sunroom on the south side of the house where we could paint with watercolors and start some perennials in a few window boxes and bell jars. She would have a wisp of a smile on her face, then go silent and drop her head on her chest and sleep for a half hour until she lost control of herself and water dripped from the cushion on the straw chair she sat in.

During this period Mr. Slick remained my loyal friend and was kind to Miz Banks as well. What a history he and I had. He had come to our home as a bill collector, obnoxious and corrupt, and ended up a bumbling bearer of charity and goodwill, like a guardian angel who was always tripping down the staircase. I'm convinced God has a sense of humor.

On that subject, I was experiencing some problems of faith. When people are in trouble, they believe what they need to believe. There was no doubt I wanted a friend with supernatural powers. Maybe I had made up Mr. Slick. One afternoon he and I were splitting firewood behind Miz Banks's house, and I told him to take off his Buster Browns and even his socks so we could settle the question of his spiritual status once and for all.

"Why do you keep bothering me about my feet?" he said.

"Because I need to see them," I replied. "So just do it!"

I guess you could call that a lapse of faith. At least that's what he thought. He answered my demand by running through the neighbor's cornfield and leaving me to finish the woodpile with a blister on my right hand. I was starting to wonder if Mr. Slick was just slick.

Two days later he tapped on Miz Banks's back door, his derby hat held against his chest. He was wearing a yellow-and-black check-ered coat and a pair of puffy purple britches I know I saw on a scare-crow. Parked by the woodpile was a handsome car with a canvas top and all-around glass windows and in back an elevated, padded leather seat for passengers.

I wanted to fuss at him for running off, but I couldn't. It was late afternoon in February, a gaseous sun guttering on the earth's rim, a wintry bitterness in the air.

"Who is it?" Miz Banks asked.

"Mr. Slick," I replied.

"Why, that's not possible, child. Mr. Slick is dead," she said.

Her face had the color of pie dough, her brown eyes lidless.

He came inside and nodded to both of us, his face meek, his hands chafed. But he spoke only to me. "I'm sorry I run off, Miss Bessie."

"That's all right, Mr. Slick." I kept the blister on my hand out of sight. "Where did you get the automobile?"

"I'm working at the movie house now. The owner don't mind if I drive it for errands and good deeds and such."

"I know the owner of the movie house well, Mr. Slick," I said. "He's so tight he squeaks and doesn't care if Noah's Flood drowns all of Texas."

"I made a movie."

"With William Hart?"

"I borrowed the camera and the projector from the movie house."

"Along with the car?"

"This ain't a joke, Miss Bessie. Can I bring in the projector or not?"

I didn't know how far to take this. Miz Banks was walking with canes and getting a little better, at least physically, and I didn't want to upset her. Mr. Slick was not only unpredictable but perhaps not from this world. "What's your movie about?" I asked.

"You won't believe it till you see it."

"You have to be honest with me, Mr. Slick. Miz Banks has been hurt awful bad. You're a good fella. You should know that."

His face was downcast, his eyes hollow. "I don't know what to say or do. I'm fixing to give up," he said.

Then Aint Minnie walked into the room. She was over six feet and must have weighed two hundred pounds and had breasts the size of watermelons. "How'd this man get in here?" she asked.

"He's a friend of ours, Aint Minnie. Don't be talking to him like that."

"This man's a haint, Miss Bessie. He ain't *carrying* a haint. He *is* a haint."

"How do you know this?" I said.

"He's been around here a long time, Miss Bessie. My mother was a slave and lived in the Quarters of the Jordan Plantation. She told me about him."

"I don't believe that, Aint Minnie."

"Believe what you want," she said.

"I'm going," Mr. Slick said.

He went through the kitchen and out the door, slamming the screen, the cats scattering.

"I wish you wouldn't have done that," I said.

"You're too kind," Aint Minnie said. "Ask other colored people. That man give up his soul a long time ago in the woods."

"Which woods?"

"The one where the oil wells is at now."

I looked out the window and could see the automobile Mr. Slick had come in but no Mr. Slick. Then I heard Aint Minnie's daughter

Snowball running down the stairs and through the house and into the sunroom wearing a white pinafore and pink ribbons in her braids. Snowball was the jolliest little girl I ever knew.

"A man in the yard took off his shoes and was walking around on his hands and making faces at me upside down," she said. "That ain't all, either. He's got hair on the bottom of his feet."

I went outside and found Mr. Slick in the side yard. The wind was cold, the sunlight almost gone. Mr. Slick's face was covered with shadow. "Bring your equipment inside," I said.

He set up a hand-crank projector in the kitchen with the lens pointed at a clear place on the wall, and closed the curtains on the windows. I asked Aint Minnie and Snowball to stay with Miz Banks in the sunroom. "Bessie?" Aint Minnie said.

She didn't address me as "Miss." When she left out the "Miss," it was for a reason. She was talking to me like I was her daughter.

"What is it, Aint Minnie?" I said.

"There's evil in the country. We ain't dealt with it yet. It's been waiting its time. The Surrender never set us free. The war's fixing to come around again."

Mr. Slick began cranking the projector.

"Stop!" I said. "Tell me where this was filmed."

"At the woods that's dug up and destroyed and clanking with oil pumps. But that ain't what you're gonna see, Miss Bessie."

I felt my lungs constrict, as though my windpipe had been pinched, and said nothing else. Mr. Slick began rotating the crank again. The lighting was like the night scenes in *Birth of a Nation*, the characters macabre, marbled with shadow and the reflection of burning torches inside a clearing where two booted and coatless men, their hands bound behind them, stood as somber and motionless as stakes driven into the ground. A man dressed like a preacher threw two ropes over a limb above their heads.

"Mr. Slick, these could be actors," I said. "Secondly, I don't know if I want to see this."

He paused the film, the image I described still on the wall. "The colored lady told you bad things about me. I don't hold it against her. It ain't right what's been done to the darkies. But this ain't about them. It's about you."

"I'm not mixed up with the woods or the oil field of any of this craziness."

"Yes, ma'am, you are," he said.

He began rotating the crank again, faster and faster, the figures in the film brightening, the characters as tall as we were, like they were going to step off the wall onto the floor.

"Don't go any farther with this, Mr. Slick," I said. "Please."

"You got to keep your eyes on what you're about to see, Miss Bessie. Ain't nobody else gonna show you who and what you are."

"What do you mean about who and what I am? I know what I am! Don't you dare talk to me like that!"

I didn't believe I could get so mad at Mr. Slick. But unfortunately I also knew the people we get maddest at are the ones who tell us the truth about ourselves.

His shoulder and arm and hand were working furiously, as though he were in a fever. And it was not due to physical stress. He was crying. "Don't look away, Miss Bessie!" he said. "Just see it this once and you'll never have to look at it again."

And that's what I did. I gave up. I watched a half dozen men separate themselves from the crowd and take hold of the ropes and pull them tight on the limb, then keep walking with the ropes over their shoulders until the two men in nooses were lifted into the air a few inches at a time, their mouths agape, like their jawbones were broken, their tongues curling up in their mouths, their feet kicking as though they could find a ladder. The man who looked like a preacher grabbed them around their knees and dragged them down with his full weight and broke their necks.

I thought I would pass out. But not just because of the two lynched men and the snapping sound I heard before they died. There was a little girl at the edge of the crowd, her face turned upward, as though she were in a religious grotto. No one seemed to see her, even though there was a glow in her face, a strangeness that was less ethereal than mystified, as though she could not understand what had become of her.

I was the little girl. I could not deny what I was looking at or what I just witnessed. I picked up Mr. Slick's projector and threw it against the wall and stamped all the glass in it and the film on the two reels. When I turned around, I looked straight into the face of Miz Banks. She was standing without her canes, a smile on her lips.

"My," she said. "What a pretty little girl. She looks so much like you, Bessie. Who is she?"

Chapter Eighteen

I went home in a daze, not remembering if I was driven home by Mr. Slick or in Aint Minnie's buggy. I cried and cried in the kitchen while Papa tried to calm me down and got me to repeat what I had seen, but each time I told him every detail I have told you, he would raise his hands in desperation and tell me to start over. Finally I couldn't talk anymore. I was bent over in the chair, hiccupping like a hysterical child, unable to breathe. His face and eyes looked thirty years older.

He still had a limp from the bear trap someone set on our property, and the aches and pains of other wounds he had acquired in a lifetime of splashing across the Cimarron with Indians on his tail or going up against men like Harvey Logan and the Sundance Kid, who he said didn't know how to breathe except through his mouth. I hated to add to his burden. He went to the cookstove and poured warm water from a tea kettle into a towel, then folded the towel and wiped my eyes and forehead and cheeks, then tried to smile and raise my spirits. That was a mighty hard job to take on.

"You're the best little gal I've ever known, Bessie," he said. "I don't know what you saw on that film, or how it got there, but I can tell you a few things that happened years ago nobody wants to talk about. That's how small towns operate. Do you understand what I'm saying?"

"I'm not sure."

"Back then people did what they had to, usually at night, then erased all their memories before sunrise," he said. "That doesn't make it right, but you cain't look at the nineteenth century with modern-day eyes." He smoothed back my hair with the towel and winked. "I suspect that's why we ended up with the holy-rollers. Their consciences had them writhing on the floor. You understand now?"

"Maybe," I said. "At least some of it."

"Okay, it was 1881, down in the fall, with an orange moon so big it seemed to touch the treetops. There was a Dutch family that owned a pecan orchard about ten miles from here. The father was a preacher. They had a little girl named Heidi who was one of the prettiest and sweetest children I ever knew. She went out to gather some pecans to bring to school the next day, but she didn't come back. A colored man said he saw some riders on the road. He said they had pistols and rifles tied to their saddles, and looked like mean hombres.

"Heidi's parents and neighbors started out with lanterns in what they used to call 'widening the circle.' That meant starting at one spot and enlarging the search area until you found what you were looking for. Except there was no sign of that little girl, and no sign of her foot tracks, just a pink ribbon hung on a thornbush."

My hands were knotted in my lap, my nails cutting into the skin, my thighs squeezed together. I was already seeing images of the little girl's captivity in the hands of men like these, and my eyes began welling up again.

"I know what you're doing, Bessie," Papa said. "You making up pictures in your head that are plumb awful. Don't do it. For the next year the girl's family did the same thing. It drove them crazy. The mother took to laudanum. The father was worse, except he didn't get drunk. He brooded and brooded and refused to give the homily at his church and scared away most of his congregation. That's how evil steals away the few years we get. The lesson is you have to let the world break its fists on your face sometimes."

"Stop talking down to me, Papa! Just tell me what happened!"

"Get mad all you want," he said. "I cain't blame you. What I'm saying is, don't give power to people who are probably going to hell, if there's such a thing. About six weeks after Heidi disappeared, two drunk men got thrown out of a Mexican hot-pillow joint. One of them had a pink ribbon tied onto his watch fob. It didn't take much for the story to get back here. Some of our neighbors broke the two drunkards out of jail and brought them back here in the woods and evidently really laid it on.

"From what I heard, the two drunkards were pathetic creatures who couldn't win a knife fight with a howitzer on their side, although they claimed to have ridden with William Quantrill. They were beaten until blood was coming out of every orifice in their bodies. The problem was if they confessed they'd get hung for sure, and if they didn't confess they'd be marmalade by morning. I don't like to give you all that ugly information, so maybe we ought to quit here."

"No. Tell me what happened."

"In that film you said there was a preacher?"

"Yes, he wore a black suit and hat and a white shirt. He had a pencil mustache. He looked like he was made of whipcord."

"That sounds like Heidi's father, all right. You say in the film he pulled on the bodies of the two who were strung up?"

"Yes, sir."

Papa started to speak, but couldn't. He wet his lips, then cleared his throat. "The story is the Dutchman almost tore their heads loose. How did this Mr. Slick get these things on film? I think he might be some kind of confidence man."

"I saw their necks break," I said. "It was real. And I was in the film."

"No, that cain't be," he said. "Don't say that. You're *here*. You're my daughter. Stop saying crazy things."

"I know what I saw. I was dead. The others in the film couldn't see me. The preacher couldn't see me. How could he kill the men without finding where my body was buried? How could he wrap his arms around the thighs of the men who raped and murdered his daughter? What kind of man was he?"

"I don't know," he said.

"Yes, you do. He cared more about vengeance than Heidi or me."

Papa stared at the cookstove, the firelight flickering under the steel lids. The towel he had used to wipe my face was on the floor. He looked like he had not slept in weeks.

In the next six weeks I learned a different kind of loneliness. I slept little and in the daytime I was listless and irritable and unable to concentrate, as though the external world had no bearing on my inner life. I talked to myself and sometimes to Lancelot, who would rest his forehead on my chest, as horses and mules often do when they know you're troubled or in mourning. I worked in the dry-goods store in town, and at our movie house, and with Miz Banks, and at the end of the week made about fifteen dollars. However, the size of my growing piggy bank was poor consolation for the life I was living.

I confided in no one, and in the back of my mind saw the lynching in the woods over and over again. I also could not forget the attack on Miz Banks and me down by the border. Even worse than the attack was the indifference to it on the part of our legal system, which I do not think was different from others, not then, not now. My phone calls to the local sheriff and his colleague by the border went unanswered. Rumors began to spread, namely that Miz Banks and I had brought the assault on ourselves, that Miz Banks was a lesbian and had insulted the wife of one of the supposed attackers, and that I carried a weapon and provoked the encounter, just as I had when I shot Jubal Fowler's father. There were people in town who crossed the street when they saw Miz Banks or me coming, as though we possessed a contagion. I was let go by the dry-goods store and the movie house.

Papa did what he could. He had an increase in hours and a raise in pay on the Katy and Santa Fe, and he called his friends of yesteryear regarding what could be done about Indian Charlie. One or two came up with suggestions that made me shiver and of which I wanted no part. In the long run, neither did Papa, who seemed to be more and more concentrated on the stories in the San Antonio and Houston newspapers about German intrigue and Huerta's Jackals and the idealism of Emiliano Zapata. I felt like I was in a tug-of-war with forces I could not see.

Then on an April day, when the bluebonnets and Indian paint-brushes were blooming, and the grass green denting in the wind, I knew our family's greatest enemy had descended on our poor, decayed Victorian home once again. I had returned with groceries from the general store at the crossroads, and was putting them on the porch, wondering where Papa was, because he always helped me unload when I went for things, more to show he missed me than out of concern about my lifting a box of crackers. Then I saw through the living room window into the kitchen. He was pump-ing water into the sink and palming it into his mouth and gargling and spitting it out.

I quit unloading and went straight to the kitchen. "What are you doing, Papa?"

"Just getting a drink of water," he replied. "Get everything we needed?"

"Why don't you come and see?"

"I trust you." He tried to grin.

"Why do you do it?"

"Do what?"

I pulled open the cabinet under the sink, where we kept the garbage we eventually buried out back. An empty bottle with no label was pushed down in it. Inside the neck was the remnant of a liquid that looked like stale milk. "You're drinking pulque?" I said.

"I found it in the basement. I took a little sip."

"Damn you, Papa," I said. "Damn, damn, damn you!"

"I'm your father. You will not swear at me like that."

"You ruin life for all of us, Papa. Your wife and all of your children. I want to beat you to a pulp."

"Well, I guess I cain't blame you."

"Do you know how mealy-mouth that sounds," I said. "If you talk to me like that again, I will flat hit you in the face. And I will not allow you to drag more misery into our lives, either."

"Then I'll get out of your way."

"Going to Mexico?"

He didn't answer. The silence was awful. I felt my own words eating through the bottom of my stomach.

I left the groceries on the porch and drove the buggy to Miz Banks's house and asked her if I could sleep on her couch.

The dreams I had that night were terrible, the kind you cain't detach from or prove unreal, no matter how long you walk the floor. In the dreams I believed the world was ending, a red sun descending into a horizon that looked made of coal dust, both animals and people dying at a river that was fringed with bones already picked bare.

In the morning my hands were shaking so hard Miz Banks had to hold them in hers. "One day we'll get the men who hurt us, child," she said. "They'll be on their knees."

I was surprised at her clarity, and wondered if a change was taking place inside her. She pressed my head against her bosom and stroked my hair, then drew me in so tightly I could hear her breathing and the beating of her heart. As with Aint Minnie, I felt my mother had somehow taken residence inside Miz Banks. Her blood made a sound like a river humming under its bank. She kissed the top of my head. "You poor child," she said.

I knew it was time to go. There is no harder mantle to carry than the pity of others.

I went back home, only to find Papa gone. I knew the pattern. He took one drink and headed to either the saloon in town or the Mexican cantinas down by the border, where he would drink enough busthead whiskey to convince himself the year was 1885. I sometimes wondered if I would like that kind of life myself. The guitars, the dancing girls, the mounted revolutionaries with their big hats and their German rifles raised above their heads, the smell of coffee and tortillas on warm stone at sunrise, the mountains like piled igneous rock dropping away into eternity. That was the world Papa longed for. Maybe at one time or another, we all do. A life spent whittling a stick or knitting on the porch can be a hard sell.

I put on a pair of blue jeans and two pairs of socks so Papa's old work boots would fit me, and plowed and hoed weeds all day and told Lancelot that he and I were done with the grief and the carrying on of others, and if people didn't believe us, they had better watch out.

When I finished talking to myself, I would swear that Lancelot said, *That's the way to tell them.*

Chapter Nineteen

Papa came back to the house two days later, sick and unshaved and unwashed and in such physical and emotional pain he couldn't hold a cup of coffee to his mouth. I told him if he wanted to haul water from the windmill to the iron bathtub, which stood in the middle of the big black smudge that used to be our barn, I would help with perhaps one or two buckets; otherwise, I would be headed to town and taking care of business.

I didn't tell him what kind of business, in part because I wasn't sure myself. But I had learned a lesson from my brother Cody. You don't have to keep the cards you were dealt at birth. If you decide to be something else, you can click a switch inside you and start a new life. Just don't tell anybody about it. In my case, I didn't have much to lose. The law certainly wasn't on our side. I had no job. My father was ensuring himself an alcoholic death, and I ached every night for my mother. All these things were worse than anything Indian Charlie could do to me. Or at least that was what I thought.

I drove the buggy into town and told the men who had fired me that they were cowards and hypocrites and defamers of an innocent schoolteacher and a fifteen-year-old girl and I was ashamed that I had set my foot on their property. I also told them they would probably go to hell and suggested they read Timothy 11 by Saint Paul and what he said about the Lord rewarding a slimy character named Alexander the coppersmith. They had stupid looks on their faces. The owner of the movie house asked if I knew where Mr. Slick was. When I asked him why, he said Mr. Slick had borrowed his projector and smashed it up. I told him Mr. Slick didn't smash it up, I had done the smashing, and then left him with his stupid look.

Then I went to the remodeled, two-story brick building with a wood-roofed porch that had become the headquarters for the Atlas Oil Company, and asked where I might find Indian Charlie.

A big man in a gray uniform behind a metal desk said, "We have no employee by that name."

"You most certainly do," I replied. "If you take your feet off your desk, maybe you can ask somebody where he is."

He wore a city marshal's badge and had knuckles the size of quarters.

"There's a Charles Swan who works security for us. He might have a nickname like that. But he works odd hours, mostly the night shift, and is a hard man to catch. Anything else you want?"

"I believe he raped a friend of mine, and wanted to rape me," I said. "I'd like to talk to him."

"He did what?"

"Indian Charlie also tortured and killed numerous women south of the border," I said. "Thank you for your time. Did you know you have a hole in your shoe?"

I heard his feet drop to the floor behind me.

I went straight across the street to the Green Lantern Saloon. Why wind down when you can show liars what they are? It was still morning, the inside of the building deep in shadow, the stamped tin ceiling as dull as an old nickel, a couple of customers at the bar, another at a table knocking back shots with a private bottle, some elderly men playing dominoes. A colored man was wiping out the cuspidors while squatted on a wood stool, his spine rounded, his eyes half lidded, like a racist curb ornament used to tether horses.

A bartender with slicked-down hair parted through the middle was eating a hard-boiled egg and drinking a Dr Pepper and reading the newspaper. "He'p you?" he said, wiping at his mouth.

"I'm looking for Indian Charlie," I said.

"I'm a little vague on some of the patrons here."

"Some call him Charles Swan."

"Nope. Want a Dr Pepper?"

"No, I want to talk to Indian Charlie."

He leaned forward, creating a V shape with his newspaper, momentarily obstructing the line of sight between us and others. "You don't belong in here, little lady. And you sure as hell don't belong around the guy you're looking for."

"Thank you for your protective attitude, sir. I can take care of myself."

"You're the one who put the bullet hole in the ceiling, aren't you?"

"I prefer not to comment on that."

"I bet," he answered.

"Sir, you look like a good judge of people. Do I look like I'm going to just walk away?"

He folded his newspaper and dipped his hand into an ice cooler and pulled out a Dr Pepper and wiped off the ice chips and snapped off the cap on the side of the box. I could hear the cap bounce on the duckboards. He leaned close to me again. "Take it with you, kid. Don't get mixed up with these fellas," he said.

"What's your name?"

"Carlo."

"I think you're a nice man, Mr. Carlo. Could I have one of those pickles?"

He blew out his breath and raised his hands as though in surrender. Out of the corner of my eye, I saw the man with the shot glass and private bottle staring at me, his gaze as palpable as a spider crawling up my cheek. Through the window I swore I saw Mr.

Slick, whom I had not seen since I destroyed his film projector. The man with the bottle limped to the men's room, then returned to his table and before sitting down gave me a dirty look, the kind a mean-spirited simpleton gives people when he's mad.

"Come back here, kid," the bartender said.

"Thanks, Mr. Carlo," I said. "My name is Bessie Mae Holland. I'm pleased to meet you."

"I think I'm gonna get into a different line of work," he said.

I took my Dr Pepper and my pickle to the table of the simpleton. He poured his shot glass to the brim, his eyes flat. The laws about alcohol in Texas were always strange. Beer could be sold on any day except Sunday mornings, but what were called "the blue laws" could be used to shut down soda fountains. Whiskey could not be sold in bars, but the bottle could be brought into the bar as long as the patron paid for the mix that went into the whiskey, even if the "mix" was only water. Think that's odd? Check the history of dancing on the campus at Baylor University.

All of this supposedly had something to do with Jesus.

"You want something?" said the man at the table. He was playing solitaire with one hand, thumbing the cards one at a time on the table, his hat sitting crown-down next to his cards. He had a profile like a turtle, and a waxed yellow scalp that had dents in it, as though someone had tapped it softly with a ball-peen hammer.

"What's your name?" I said.

"My friends call me Tater," he replied. "Or 'Tater Dog' because I like fried taters and hot dogs."

"May I sit down, Mr. Dog?"

"What for?"

"To find out why you've been staring at me."

He lifted his shot glass to his mouth, his eyes green the way a viscous liquid is green, his cheeks pitted, probably by scarlet fever. He rolled the whiskey over his tongue and grinned confidently. "You on the stroll?" he said.

"I've shot one man. I don't mind making it two," I said, and sat down.

"Bartender, I got a problem here," he said, lifting a curved finger in the air, pointing it down at me.

But my friend Mr. Carlo began sweeping out the back and paid him no mind.

"You're lucky you didn't get tetanus," I said. "That was a steel object I drove through your foot. A touch of rust could have given you lockjaw."

"Don't know what you're talking about, girlie. Now get out of here, please." He drank his shot glass dry and rotated it on the table with the ends of his fingers.

"You were in the big black car with Indian Charlie. His real name is Charles Swan. He works for Atlas Oil and has told a number of people about y'all's relationship. I think he's going to talk the two of you onto a chain gang."

"What do you know about Indian Charlie?"

"I know he's not going to Huntsville Pen when he can send you there instead. Did you know he was a dope smuggler and arsonist? Or maybe you were with him when he burned our barn. As we speak, some Texas Rangers are investigating the pair of you. You've heard of Frank Hamer, haven't you?"

The name Frank Hamer hit home. Frank Hamer eventually killed over fifty men. Maybe as many as seventy, and also Bonnie and Clyde. Tater Dog's mouth was moving but no sound came out of it.

"You have dents in your head and scars like birdshot all over your face," I said. "Do you know who else does?"

"No," he said.

"The fella whose foot I put a knitting needle through. I got a good look at you when you were jumping around holding your foot."

This was a lie, of course. But people who knock back shots in the morning usually cain't tie their shoes, much less cipher through a conversation that can put them in Huntsville. He tilted up his chin, one eye squinted, his defenses gone. "I ain't gonna listen to none of this."

Then I had a revelation of sorts. I was tired of dealing with evil people. Fooling them, taking them over the hurdles, whatever you want to call it. Cruelty is cruelty; theft is theft; murder is murder. And what's almost always behind it? Money, just like the Bible says.

I scraped back the chair and stood up. "Please listen to me, Mr. Dog. I have no weapon upon my person, but if you open your mouth before I'm through, I will arm myself and come back here and shoot you. You and your friends did a terrible deed to two women who never did anything to you. How do you explain that to yourself? What would your father or mother say, particularly your mother? Don't just look at me with that stupid expression. I'm really tired of people with stupid expressions."

He started to speak, but I didn't let him. I slapped his playing cards out of his hand. "Think of all the people you have hurt. I suspect that most of them were defenseless. You and Indian Charlie seem to carry the same badge of dishonor. He uses a branding iron. Look at me. I'm going to get every one of you. Those oil people won't be able to save you. You tell that to Indian Charlie."

I don't know why I said all those things. I didn't plan them. Some other men had come in; one of the house girls was watching me from the balcony; the bartender Carlo had stopped sweeping and was looking at me as though he had entered a church unexpectedly. Everyone in the building was silent and staring at me, as though they were listening to an echo from the childhood they had lost or had always longed for.

It made me feel that nothing in the world was a constant. It made me feel that I knew everything or I knew nothing at all. To this day I do not like revisiting my experience with Mr. Dog, or the fate that eventually befell him.

Chapter Twenty

I had not mentioned to Mr. Dog the man who held me down on the ground while Miz Banks was being raped, in pretense that he was restraining me when in reality he had become my protector. I was almost sure the man who kept shushing me was not a man but a teenage boy who kept his loins from touching me, and the teenage boy's name was Jubal Fowler. In short, I felt like a hypocrite.

Mr. Slick came from the side of the saloon and asked if he could get in my buggy.

"Of course, Mr. Slick," I said.

He had a smile like a half-moon slit in a muskmelon. "You just earned a star in your crown, Miss Bessie!" he said.

"Star for what?" I said.

"You flat gave it to that ole boy in the saloon! And them other people was listening up, too! You betcha Buster Browns!"

I snapped the reins gently on my eight-year-old blue roan that Papa named Traveler, in honor of General Lee's horse, although our Traveler would sometimes kick the daylights out of anyone who walked behind him without keeping a hand on his rump, or sometimes just kick somebody because he was in an ornery mood.

"Can I take you somewhere, Mr. Slick?"

He started combing his hair, then frowned at what he was doing and stuck his comb in his pocket. "Combing your hair in front of people is impolite, ain't it?" he said. "Like blowing your nose at the table and that kind of thing?"

"Mr. Slick, would you please stop your mumbling and tell me what you want?"

"I was kind of hoping you'd carry me out to your place and give me a job. I know the film I showed you was pretty hard to live with. You know, the hanging and the little girl that's your looka-like watching them murderers dangle from the limb, their tongues sticking out and spit running from their mouths, till the preacher snapped their necks and pert' near tore their heads off. That could upset a person."

"Could you be more detailed?" I said.

"Pardon?"

"We don't have a place for you to sleep, Mr. Slick, and we're also strapped for money and cain't afford another hand. Right now, the Mexicans are working on shares, and our shares are mighty thin."

"I got a tent and I don't need no money. Just a home. Like in that song 'Wayfaring Stranger.' Like going over Jordan. Except I done been over Jordan."

"Mr. Slick, I think one day you may eventually destroy the English language."

"You're hiring me?"

"I guess we wayfaring strangers have to take care of each other. You vex a person, but you have a kind heart. Welcome to our family, Mr. Slick."

"I think that's the nicest thing anybody has ever said to me," he said.

We picked up his duffle bag and a folded-up canvas tent where he had stored them in a big pipe under the dirt road that led south of town, then I turned us toward home and Papa and the confrontations I would have with him and the explanations for my conduct in town, because I had not only rolled the dice for me, I had done so for him as well.

He was sitting on the couch in the living room when I told him of everything I had done that day, his light-blue eyes staring out the window at Mr. Slick putting up his tent by the windmill.

When I finished, he said, "Are you out of your mind?"

"Mr. Slick doesn't have anywhere else to go, Papa," I replied.

"This character you call Mr. Slick is not the issue. You tipped your hand to the oil people. We won the Revolutionary War because we learned to fight from the Indians. You shoot from behind a tree. You don't go running up a hill into a cannon."

One of his encyclopedias was open on the coffee table. I could see what he had been reading. "It's a nice time of year in Mexico, isn't it?" I said.

"Frank Hamer called me."

"That's funny. I was talking about Mr. Hamer to Mr. Dog in the saloon. Mr. Dog looked like he swallowed a carpet tack. Maybe that has something to do with the dozens of people Mr. Hamer has killed."

"Quit changing the subject. Frank says I can get my badge back. This fella Carranza wants to provoke us into a war and maybe take back the Southwest. The plan is to burn American ranches along the Rio."

"That's their business," I said.

"No, it's the country's business."

"No, you're just looking for a reason to leave, Papa. So go ahead and do it. Tonight or tomorrow or any day of the week. Just go, Papa. Don't let your children get in the way."

To this day I am ashamed for my cruelty to my father. I deliberately hurt him. He tried to hide the injury, to stare out the window at the gold and purple clouds in the west, to check the time on his pocket watch, to look at an Easter card he had bought, probably for me. Papa wasn't a good actor. His lips trembled and there was a pink shine in the whites of his eyes. He gave up his defenses and looked me straight in the face.

"For years I clouded my brains with pulque and whiskey and sometimes with cactus buttons or an opium pipe," he said. "I don't know how many children or wives I've had, or even the number of men I've killed. Too many of the latter, I suspect. But when I count my blessings, the biggest one is you, just like God leaned down with you one day and set you at the table and said, 'Here, this is the best I've got.'"

I could feel the backs of my knees giving way. "I have to face-down Jubal Fowler, Papa."

"Facedown him for what?"

"I think he was with Indian Charlie when Miz Banks and I were attacked. I think he saved me, but that doesn't matter. He was there, and he has to own up to it."

"I think it's more complicated than that. I think you fell in love with Jubal Fowler the first time you saw him. He's no good, Bessie, but you will never accept that from me. So go your way, and I'll be there for you when it's over."

He went upstairs, one slow step at a time. If he wanted to get even with his daughter, he had succeeded.

I went down in the basement and wrapped Papa's converted revolver and box of shells in a piece of butcher paper and exited through the storm door and got back in the buggy and swung it around in the front yard, breaking a pot full of carnations. Mr. Slick saw me and ran alongside the buggy and jumped inside.

"Where we going?" he said.

"To make Christians out of people who probably belong in hell."

"Sure you want us to be doing that?" he said.

"There is no 'us' in this, Mr. Slick. Do you understand?"

"Well, I——"

"Please just say yes or no."

"I ain't one to argue," he replied. "No, ma'am, that's not my way. Where at is this gonna happen?"

I refused to say any more to Mr. Slick.

"You sure like to keep things lively, Miss Bessie."

I still refused.

"Miss Bessie?"

"*What?*" I replied, ready to scream.

"There ain't gonna be no repercussions after this activity you got planned, is there? I don't like to butt in too deep where it ain't my bidness."

I gave him a look that made his face jerk.

The Fowlers lived in a sinkhole outside of town called "the Bog." The houses were not houses but shacks, with no plumbing or electricity, and not an inch of paint, blackened by dry rot and smoke from stubble and garbage fires. The yards had no grass, but were scattered with junk in place of birdbaths, statues of saints, or children's toys. Many of the families who lived there, such as the Fowlers, had the money to get out but preferred to live in a community that was a giant, living scab, a home to police officers and petty criminals, a place that had a welcome sign nailed to a telegraph pole painted with the message THIS IS THE BOG, NIGGER. DON'T LET THE SUN SET ON YOUR HEAD.

I turned into the winding dirt road where Jubal lived. Behind his home, up an incline, was an artificial lake dug in the nineteenth century to water thirsty longhorns that had been driven up from Mexico, many of them rustled. After the Chisholm Train was shut down by tick fever, the maintenance on the lake was abandoned and left to stagnate and seep through the compacted dirt walls of the reservoir into the neighborhood, oftentimes releasing an odor like rotten eggs, which some people believed might be oil or natural gas, a prospect that delighted him. The following was their motto: "Maybe our community stinks like shit to you, but it smells like bread and butter to me."

Every time I think of that statement, I remember Miz Banks's admonition that the Founding Fathers never intended for everyone to vote.

"Miss Bessie, is that the Fowler place up there?" Mr. Slick asked.

It was almost dusk. The sky in the west was orange and streaked with purple clouds on the horizon, and I had still not told him our destination. "Yes, how did you know that was the Fowler home?"

"I just seen Jubal's father walk out of the privy. Jesus Christ, Miss Bessie, you should have told me."

"Would you not have come with me?"

"I don't know. Right now I'm fixing to wet my pants."

"You want to get down here?"

"No, of course not."

"Then what do you want me to do?"

His feet were clattering on the floor, his fists thumping his knees. "Mr. Fowler has probably figured out I planted his pistol in the slaughterhouse after you shot him. He's about the meanest man I've ever knowed, Miss Bessie."

"I'll park the buggy and go up to his door myself. It's all right, Mr. Slick."

He was shaking all over. "No, I just ain't no good at going up against mean people. I been hiding from them all my life. I'm ashamed of myself. I ain't got no backbone."

The temperature must have been seventy-five degrees. He was trembling like it was below zero.

"You're the bravest spirit I've ever known, Mr. Slick," I said. "Whether you have goat's feet or not."

A single tear slid down his cheek. "What you're saying ain't true, Miss Bessie, but I sure like to hear it, anyway."

Growing up in Texas could surely be a challenge, I told myself. Maybe other places were no different, but I doubted that. Almost everybody coming to early Texas was running from somewhere else. That's why they were called GTTs, meaning "gone to Texas." It also meant they had probably robbed their local bank.

I pulled into the yard just as Winthrop Fowler stepped out on the porch. The passage of time had not made him a better man.

Chapter Twenty-One

I knew I was entering what you might call the Edge, one of the moments when you step out on thin air and pray that God will hold you in His palm. I had come geographically to the most dangerous place on earth I could be. And for what purpose? And how did it all begin?

The answers to my questions were not reassuring. All of this was about money, not a fight between Jubal and my brother Cody because Jubal peeped at me through the slats of the schoolyard outhouse. Bertha Lafleur sent her people to steal opium tar from Indian Charlie to get even for branding her chest and killing her prostitute friends, then lent Papa the money she was supposed to pay Indian Charlie. Then Papa gave her back her money, and she responded by keeping it and letting Papa take the blame. What a friend.

And now I had brought Mr. Slick and myself into a place where colored people refused to enter, night or day.

Mr. Fowler was propped up on a pair of canes. "What do you want, girl?" he said.

"I need to see Jubal," I replied.

The bullets I had fired into Mr. Fowler's body had surely achieved their purpose. The slice of bone that had been taken from above one ear was now a welt of gray tissue that resembled a bicycle patch; the round that had shattered his collarbone made his shoulder droop like half of a coat hanger. His mouth could have been made of rubber, grinning one second, twisting another. "You come here to get your cunny fixed, girl?"

"What did he say?" Mr. Slick said, not believing what he heard.

"Hush, Mr. Slick," I said.

I rested the reins in my lap, my knuckles as shiny as bone, the tips of my fingers quivering, and gave Mr. Fowler my meanest look. "I'm sorry that you have the life that you do, sir. But you got what you deserved. Now take your filthy language and dirty mind to the devil."

I let out my breath, my heart as big as a drum.

He looked over his shoulder and shouted through the door, "Jubal! Get out here! Wait till you see who's here!"

Jubal pushed open the screen door, barefoot, in strap overalls, a piece of fried chicken in one hand. A solitary ray of sunlight shone on his face, and I saw him swallow. He stepped out on the porch gingerly, more afraid of me, I think, than of the splinters he might get in his feet, and I knew he had been with Indian Charlie when Miz Banks was raped.

"What are you doing here, Bessie?" he said.

"You need to face up, Jubal."

His eyes went sideways. "Face up for what?"

"You know for what."

He flipped the drumstick into the side yard. A cat ran after it. He tried to hold his gaze on the cat. "The Bog is a different world," he said. "It ain't your kind of place. Go home, Bessie."

"Because your father is ignorant and mean-spirited doesn't mean you have to be the same."

"Tell her who's back yonder, Jubal," Mr. Fowler said.

"She's leaving, Daddy," Jubal said. "We don't need no more trouble."

Mr. Fowler's twisted features were lit with pleasure, but I didn't know why. "Mr. Fowler?" I said.

"What?" he said.

"Your son saved me from being raped, maybe even killed by Indian Charlie. But he was not entirely innocent, either. So it's time for him to own up and be the good boy he was when we first started elementary school."

Mr. Fowler laughed out loud, balancing himself with one cane, lifting his other hand to push the spittle from the corner of his mouth. "You and that little pimp with you sure walked into it," he said. Then he shouted, "Charlie! You won't believe this! Get your ass out here!"

I heard Mr. Slick fishing under the buggy seat, but I had no time to look at what he was doing. Indian Charlie came out on the porch, dressed in black, the slacks and the boots and the silk shirt. His body was as lithe as a quirt, his skin yellow, his hair greased down, his eyebrows as thin as pencil marks. No, his hair wasn't just greased down. It looked like black paint that had dried on his scalp.

"What do we got here?" he said. "The little girl that's spreading lies about me all over town? And lookee here at our little buddy Slick, scared as a turd about to drop in the honey hole. How you doin', fart blossom?"

"Don't you dare speak to him like that!" I said. "You burned our barn with our animals and chickens in it. You raped Miz Banks and put her in pain every day of her life. You don't deserve to live."

"Tell another lie about me, and I'll put you over my knee and whop you blind, girl," Indian Charlie said.

"Stop all this," Jubal said, holding up his hands.

I heard something clunk in the bottom of the buggy and felt Mr. Slick groping around my feet and ankles. I knew our situation was unraveling by the second and I was responsible. I also knew that something else was taking place inside me, a sudden recognition, perhaps a partial explanation for all the strange things that had happened in the woods by our ranch, the bones that glowed in the oil field, the little girl who could have been my twin looking up at the two outlaws hanging from the tree limb, her father the preacher clenching and weighting their bodies with his own in order to crack their necks and end the madness he had become part of.

I felt the barrel and iron sight and the hammer of Papa's converted revolver against my thigh. Mr. Slick was working his palm around the grips and his index finger through the trigger guard. *Oh dear Jesus, don't let this happen,* I prayed, and at the same time pushed the revolver under the cushion on the buggy's seat while Mr. Slick tried to free it.

Jubal had not moved. "Look at your horse, Bessie!" he said.

"My horse?" I said.

"His left front foot. He's lame."

I leaned sideways so I could see past Traveler's rump. Jubal was right. Traveler had half thrown a shoe, and the nails and the shoe were twisted under the coffin bone, the ankle as swollen as a baseball. I was amazed Traveler hadn't gone down with the pain, the way horses founder when they have laminitis.

"I got some shoes in the shed," Jubal said. "Just hang on and I'll get my rasp and hammer and we'll get him fixed. Everybody hear that? We got some fried chicken in the kitchen. We don't need all this bad talk out here. That's right, ain't it, Daddy?"

For the first time since we were little, I was truly proud of Jubal.

"Y'all do as you please," Mr. Fowler said. "I'm gonna have a drink. How about it, Charlie?"

"That's the way you run your household?" Indian Charlie said. "You let the girl who shot you sass your guests and talk to you like you're white trash?"

"Everything in its time," Mr. Fowler said.

"If you ask me, that's a coward's way," Indian Charlie said.

"Them oil people don't like publicity, Charlie," Mr. Fowler said. "You've got you a good job. Why lose it? You can end up a rich man."

Mr. Fowler's words could have been confetti blowing in Indian Charlie's face. He looked at his nails, then picked at them, his face impossible to read. I slowly pulled the revolver from Mr. Slick's hand and lowered it to the floor of the buggy and eased it as far as I could under the seat, then got down from the buggy and helped Jubal release Traveler from his bridle and straps and snaffle. Jubal was good with animals, particularly with horses, and I knew he would do all the right things with Traveler, no matter what happened to Mr. Slick and me. In fact, I felt we were out of the storm.

Mr. Fowler started toward the porch. Mr. Slick was staring into space; Jubal was pulling nails from Traveler's foot with his grippers; the wind was warm, blowing away the stench that was like rotten eggs from the Bog. I stroked Traveler's head and kissed his nose, the same way I kissed Lancelot.

But Indian Charlie had not moved or spoken, as though he had gone to a private place inside himself. Then he tilted his head one way and the other, then straightened himself and smiled.

"Me and your father got a history together," he said. "Down in Old Mexico."

I pretended I didn't know what he was talking about.

"Your father killed a bunch of my best friends. Boys that was hardly men. Good boys."

"No, they were neither boys nor good," I said. "They were torturers and murderers and they got outgunned by a solitary Texas Ranger."

"No, they surrendered and your father lined them up to see how many he could kill with one bullet. That's the kind of man Hackberry Holland is."

"You're a liar," I said.

I had done it again. But my insult didn't seem to bother him.

"I cain't fault you for defending your father," he said. "That puny asswipe up there in the buggy is a different deal."

He stared straight into Mr. Slick's face. "Don't look away from me, boy. You sold me out. I vouched for you, and got you a job as a collector for some powerful men. You repaid the favor by running straight to Hackberry Holland. I've thought about staking you out Indian style, and stripping off your skin one lick at a time. But you ain't worth the time it would take to do that. So I'm gonna cut you some slack. Stick out your nose."

Mr. Slick was frozen. I had pushed Papa's revolver so far under the seat he could not reach it. Also, I now knew why Indian Charlie spoke with such confidence. I could see the pearl-and-chrome butt of a derringer tucked in his belt. Mr. Slick was unarmed and helpless. Indian Charlie curled his index and middle fingers into a V-shape so he could twist Mr. Slick's nose into a bloody, weeping mess and forever rob him of his self-respect.

Don't do it, Mr. Slick. Don't do it, don't do it, don't do it.

"I know what you're thinking, girl," Indian Charlie said. "You can forget it. He's gonna do what I tell him, or I'm gonna do something to you that'll make you wish you wasn't born."

"Ease off, Charlie," Jubal said behind him.

"They know I'm just playing," Indian Charlie said. "And that means Slick is gonna stick out his nose, and this little cunt is gonna watch it and not say a goddamn word. Nor you either, boy."

I thought about shooting him. But I had always been a good Baptist, and good Baptists are not supposed to shoot other people. Unless they are completely out of control or threatening and you have to shoot them to protect yourself, which is what my grandfather the saddle preacher was forced to do on nine occasions.

That last statement bothers me a little bit.

Truth was, I had never felt so sad, except the night Mama died. I had put Mr. Slick in a terrible situation. He would never be able to hold up his head, never have a girlfriend, never have children, that is, if spirits have children. I hated myself for what I had done, because it was all about me and nobody else.

Then, God bless him, Mr. Slick proved to me once again that people are better than we think.

"You ain't no good," he said to Indian Charlie. "You prey on the weak. You never call a man out on the street. Shoot me if you want. I ain't afraid of you."

Then he spat in Indian Charlie's face.

Other things were happening, too. Indian Charlie had no knowledge of Traveler's neurotic nature, namely that no one walked behind Traveler without keeping his hand on Traveler's rump.

Traveler gave it to Indian Charlie with both back feet and flat kicked him all over the yard, sun-fishing, flinging his hindquarters at a forty-five-degree angle, hammering his iron shoes every place he could club Indian Charlie, creating a vortex of dust that was like a separate universe.

Jubal got a rope around Traveler's neck, but not before Traveler kicked Indian Charlie in the privates and trampled his chest and face and at least one kneecap and then ran from the yard, the rope stringing from his neck.

When the dust drifted away, Indian Charlie looked like he had been run over by a truck, then dragged around the block on concrete.

Mr. Fowler came back out on the porch, stupefied. "What the hell?" he said.

"Charlie started it, Daddy," Jubal said.

"No, what started it is that girl right yonder," his father said. "You hear me, girl? You ain't got no idea what's coming."

Chapter Twenty-Two

I t wasn't fair, I thought. I was barely fifteen. I shouldn't have to pay and pay for sins I wasn't responsible for. Mr. Slick and I went back to the ranch and in the living room I told Papa everything that had happened. He sat for a long time in silence, then widened his eyes and said, "I never dry-gulched a man, but in an earlier time that's what we did."

"I don't know what you're saying, Papa."

"You've given the high ground to our enemy, Bessie. He *will* come after us. But the place and the time will be of his choosing. He will know where we are, but we will not know where he is. He will also have his choice of weapons. Or explosives. Or poisons. That's why I would like to load my Henry and drop him from one hundred yards and go home and eat dinner."

"You want me to leave?" I said.

"I didn't say that."

"Yes, you did. You want me gone," I said. "And you keep saying it and saying it and saying, all the while pretending you're not. When I'm here, you cain't have what you want. And what you want is women and alcohol and to fight in a war that's not our business."

"That's a lie."

"Indian Charlie called me a liar, too. Thank you, Papa."

"Where you going?"

"I'm not sure. Somewhere else."

"There's a telegram for you."

"From whom?"

"Cody."

I pulled it out of his hand and went upstairs and stuffed some clean clothes in a pillowcase and came back downstairs. "Don't leave the lamp on," I said.

The sky was black, the stars white and cold, the oil wells clanking in the distance. There was a chill in the air, a star dropping in the west, like the edge of creation starting to slip away. I bridled Lancelot and slipped a blanket on his back, and rode the two miles to Aint Minnie's cabin, without having read the telegram, with no plan about anything. I don't think I was ever lonelier, not even the night Mama died.

"What we gonna do with you, child?" Aint Minnie said.

I had just come in and was sitting by the woodstove in the front room. She had only three lamps for the cabin—one for the front room, one for the kitchen, and one for the bedroom, where both she and Snowball slept. She scarcely got by, but she never complained, never asked for more, and was always there when I needed her. Whenever I wanted Mama, which was often, I went to see Aint Minnie.

"Is Mr. Hackberry drunk?" Aint Minnie said.

"He's fixing to be," I replied.

"What you ain't understanding is your father has got a big hole inside his chest he cain't fill. It's like a cannonball went through his chest, the same way you feel, a hurt that's so awful you cain't tell nobody about it, 'cause they ain't gonna understand. The difference between you and your father is he drove your mama to the grave, with all them children she had to bear, and all his drinking and gambling and the money he gave bad women. Your daddy's problem is he cain't forgive himself. That means he cain't forgive nobody else. You know what's on his mind, don't you?"

"To go to Mexico?"

"Mr. Hackberry wants to die, and you're keeping him from it."

I had never thought of Papa in that way. I suddenly felt angry at Aint Minnie. She knew it, too. "I ain't meant to hurt you, child."

"Stop calling me child."

She tried to smile. "What's in your pocket?" she said.

"A telegram."

"From Cody again?"

"Yes, but I haven't read it."

"This ain't a time to be taking advice from Cody, Bessie."

I got up from my chair. "I'm sorry I came here, Aint Minnie."

"Tell me what Cody says."

I took the yellow square of paper and the typed strips glued on it from my pocket, and read it in the firelight.

"What's Cody say?" she asked.

The words on the strips were typed with block-like capital letters: HAVE HEARD BAD STORIES. WILL SEND MONEY. COME HERE.

Papa was right about my giving up the high ground to our enemies. We were walking around blind, while Winthrop Fowler and Indian Charlie or their followers could leave their mark on us where and when and how they wanted to, and in the cruelest ways. We couldn't prove the source, either. The damage could be accidental in origin or the work of teenage hoodlums. Our two wind vanes were snapped off the peak of the roof, maybe by rifle fire or maybe by flying trash in a tornado that ripped through the county. Our rural mailbox was smashed, probably by a baseball bat. A dead turkey was stuffed down the chimney of a Mexican family who sharecropped with us.

The tires were slashed on a county utility truck that was supposed to incorporate us into the power grid; the same with the telephone company. We feared all strangers and trusted no one.

The worst of it was the cats. I had a hard time thinking about them even now. Someone put poison in their bowls and killed nine, including Dr. Medico and Rumper and Fat Kitty. Papa cried when he found their bodies, and went into the Green Lantern that night and used his Peacemaker to knock a man in the head he thought was a Fowler, but who turned out to be a Bible salesman.

When we finally got a telephone and electricity installed in our house, my first call was to the sheriff's office. By the way, I don't know if I described the sheriff, Slim Millard, adequately. He had the face of a prune and a voice that gargled like a rusty pipe, and had recently taken to wearing striped britches and long coats and stovepipe boots of the kind gunmen wore back in the nineteenth century. He was also spending a lot of time in the office of Atlas Oil.

"Someone killed most of our poultry," I said.

"How do you know it was people what done it?"

"They didn't commit suicide."

"There was a windstorm last night."

"They were in the brooder house."

"Coyotes love their midnight snacks," he said.

In the meantime the war in Europe was spreading by the day, and the first Mexican irregulars were starting trouble on the Rio Grande. Pancho Villa lost a battle and blamed Americans for giving searchlights to his enemies. Papa couldn't wait to get in the fray. Oh Lordy, what was I supposed to do? I've heard that dying soldiers cry out for their mothers. That's how I felt. Except I wasn't dying. I just felt that way. I took my piggy bank down to the train station and in the telegraph office smashed it all over the counter and picked out the coins I needed to send a telegram to New York, then went to the dry-goods store to buy the clothes I would need in a Northern city.

I said goodbye to Lancelot, and paid a Mexican boy twenty-five cents to return the buggy to Papa and bought a ticket to Chicago and crossed the Red River into Oklahoma at sunset, my window clouded by my breath, as cold as ice, my state and my father and Aint Minnie and Snowball and Mama's grave disappearing into the darkness.

BOOK TWO

Chapter Twenty-Three

I transferred at Chicago, and spent another day and half a night on a wood passenger seat that was not completely uncomfortable but bounced me twice on my rump in the aisle when I fell asleep. I walked two miles dead tired from Penn Station to the Lower East Side, carrying my clothes, both new and soiled, in my pillowcase, just as the sun was rising. I was sure I had turned a new page in my life.

I could see the Brooklyn Bridge and the five-story stone and brick buildings with pigeon coops on their roofs, and the vendors setting up their vegetable and fruit stands and ovens whose fires burned as brightly as rubies in the shadows. The farther I walked, the larger the street population grew. Every kind of person was there—the Irish and Italians and the East Europeans, rabbis and beggars and old women with cowls, and huge numbers of children, clotheslines strung with laundry from fire escape to fire escape high above their heads, the sidewalks and streets and gutters showered with rotted food that had been ground into the concrete, and newspapers and pamphlets blowing end over end, like the leftovers from a party, although the trash may have been there for weeks.

Then I saw a rusted sign on a stanchion at the entrance to a narrow alley paved with brick that had sunken in the middle, a green-blackish rivulet of water draining into the sunlight, the stoops already occupied by dirty children, some with rickets, a fat woman nursing her infant with her shirt open, her knees splayed, and mean-eyed hoodlums with a stick in their hand or a bocce ball that was not for bowling on the green.

I had to go all the way to the end of the alley to find Cody's building. It must have been a century old. The numbers were scratched into the door, probably with a nail, the screen torn, and broken glass was scattered on the concrete steps, along with a child's doll. I didn't want to put my hand on the doorknob.

"Lose your way, dollie?" said a man behind me.

I almost had a heart attack. He had on grease-smudged overalls that sewer workers wore, and a simian face and merry brown eyes that were a bit lunatical. The density of his breath was enough to make a person fall down. His accent was unmistakable.

"Good heavens, don't sneak up on someone like that," I said.

"You look like you're from County Galway," he said.

"Well, I'm not. I'm from Texas."

"I guess that's a forgivable sin. But you shouldn't be in this building, not unless you're coming here to fuck."

"What did you just say?"

"Be advised this is the kind of place you're about to enter."

"My brother lives here. His name is Cody Holland."

"Oh, I see." He took a bottle of whiskey from his pocket and drank from it.

"What do you mean 'you see'?" I said.

"The neighborhood is full of gutter rats. They call themselves boosters. You'll meet them. By the way, who was that odd-looking fella following you?"

"What odd fellow?"

"He was wearing button shoes, with hair growing out of them. Or at least I thought he did. I've been on the grog a couple of days."

Then he walked away. I couldn't believe what I was hearing. Had Mr. Slick followed me to New York? Or was I so fatigued I could

DON'T FORGET ME, LITTLE BESSIE   161

no longer trust my senses? I didn't come all this way just to be among people who call themselves Christians, but who are no different from the depraved souls who ran the Inquisition.

I opened the door of the building and stepped inside. Bags of garbage stood outside the doors in hallways, not unlike the buckets of feces outside cells in our county jail. The stairs zigzagged upward toward a skylight in the ceiling of the fourth floor. Babies seemed to be crying from everywhere. I began working my way up the stairs, and on the second flight had to stop and cup my hand over my nose and mouth. I thought the smell came from the garbage bags and the pails of diapers soaked with urine. But it was something else, like something that had been there a long time, something people had poured lye on and subdued and finally accepted.

On the third floor my legs gave out and I slid down on the wall and pulled up my knees and lay my forehead on my pillowcase and closed my eyes and fell instantly asleep. I didn't cry. But not because I was brave or strong or inured to the struggle of an imperfect world. I didn't cry because I was used up. There was no moisture in my eyes. They were like red tissue paper. I could see through them.

I was happy to lie down in darkness, in a cavern in the center of the earth. I didn't care if an airplane crashed on the roof of the tenement building or if the foundation collapsed and buried me alive. No one could be as tired as I was. Nor was anyone as forlorn. Then the world went black, and I could smell a musky odor and hear the clicking of claws inside the walls and squeaking and mewing sounds that were not plaintive but excited with the prospect of food.

Guess who found me? You've got it. Mr. Slick shook me awake and pulled me to my feet and propped me against the wall.

"How did you get here?" I asked.

"I got my ways. Come on, you got one more floor to go."

He took me by the arm and helped me up the next flight, then took a key from his pocket and stuck it in a door. "Your brother is at work. He gets off at eleven, then goes to classes at the city college."

"Where did you get the key?"

"Before I met you, I was a thief, Miss Bessie. You made me change my ways. Spirits make good thieves. Didn't you know that?"

"I don't believe this is happening."

He pushed open the door. The room was spotless, a window half open. That was Cody, always clean, always groomed and wanting to own uptown clothes.

"This ain't a good place, Miss Bessie. Your brother needs to get you out of here."

"Someone is going to hurt me?"

"Worse."

"You're talking about sexual things?"

"Bertha Lafleur would love it here. I got to go. Another thing, Cody's friends ain't regular little kids running around."

"An Irishman told me that."

"Oh, yeah, the drunk I saw you talking to. He smells like a corpse that's been soaked in a pickle barrel. The first time I met him, I thought my nose was gonna fall off."

"That's disgusting, Mr. Slick."

"Tell me about it," he said.

Then he went out the door. I thought I was losing my mind. Cody's "tenement" consisted of one room, a small bed, a picture of Jack Johnson on the wall, a cot, a cool box, a table, two chairs, wood pegs behind the door and on the wall, and no closet. There was a red blanket folded on the foot of the cot. I lay down on the cot, put my pillowcase with my clothes in it under my head, and pulled the blanket over me. I sent up a prayer of thanks for my safe arrival in New York and the fact that Mr. Slick had journeyed with me, although I was not quite convinced that I was of sound mind. Within five seconds I was back in my cavern and safe in my sleep.

*   *   *

Cody woke me gently at noon with a big smile. "It's so good to see you, Bessie," he said. "You're gonna love the city."

The skies were raining, the window completely lowered, water running down the glass. The odor I had smelled earlier in the halls and the stairway had returned. "What's that stink?" I asked.

"What stink?"

"Like a dead rat."

"Depends on who you talk to. Hundreds of thousands of Irish came here on the coffin ships. They were packed like smoked clams in buildings like this one. Then the gangs started killing each other and burying the bodies in the basements and the walls."

"You believe that?"

"The city is full of Irish gangsters," he said. "The Black Hand is scared shitless of them."

"Don't use that language, Cody. Don't make heroes out of criminals, either. What's the matter with you?"

"If I go back to Texas, I'm going back there rich. I get five dollars for going three rounds under a saloon. I never had to lay down once, either."

"What do you mean 'lay down'?"

"Throw the fight. Let's don't talk about this. I've met some important people. Owney Madden was gonna set me up for some big fights. Except he just got sent up."

"What?"

"Owney's a good guy. He was in the Gophers. That's an Irish gang here. He got sent up for manslaughter. I think he got a bad deal."

"I say puke on those kinds," I said.

"What do you call Jubal Fowler and his father and those oil people and Indian Charlie and those Texas Rangers who cain't wait to drop the hammer on somebody?"

"Can I stay here?" I asked.

"Sure. Where else would you want to stay?"

That was a good question. I had fled my home and the only world I knew: Miz Banks and Aint Minnie and Snowball and Lancelot and Traveler and the cats who were all over the house and finally Papa and all the bad things he couldn't keep from doing. I missed all of them. And now I was trapped in a place that seemed like a giant prison for the poor and the forgotten.

"Have you heard from Papa?" I said.

"Yesterday a policeman was asking about you."

"What did you tell him?"

"Nothing. That's how kids here deal with the police. This kid Benny says you turn DDD. That means Deaf, Dumb, and Don't Know."

"Who's Benny?"

"Benny Siegel," he said. He pushed at his left eye, the one Jubal had almost blinded. "He's ten years old and a good kid. All of them are. When you've been around here a while, you'll wise up."

"I don't like the way you're talking," I said.

Chapter Twenty-Four

I knew Papa had contacted the police, and I tried to stay away from Cody's tenement as much as I could. I bought food from the street vendors toward sunset, because that's when the prices were lowest, and sometimes watched a puppet show where the audience stood on the bricks in an alley or sat on garbage cans or looked down from the fire escapes overhead. The evening sunlight in the Lower East Side was always red. I don't know why.

For a short spell I worked half days at Cody's gym and was given forty-five cents an hour, but I didn't like either the hygiene of the gym or the people who hung around there. It smelled like mildewed towels and athletic supporters left in a locker. The men in suits who stayed in the background were fat and loud and smoked cigars but never got in the ring. They just made lots of noise. Cody said they were killers.

"They accidently sat on their wives?" I said.

I got into a typing class at New York City College. The streetcar was crowded almost all the way to Harlem, and none of the men gave up their seats. I told a couple of them they would love Texas, because it was filled with white trash such as themselves. They simply stared at me, as though they couldn't process what I was saying. Regardless, I joined the class without formally enrolling. I just sat down in front of one of the typewriters in a big room and said nothing. One day the instructor asked if I had been ill.

"A bit tired, but I think I'm all right now," I said. "Thank you for asking, though."

"What's your name again?" she said.

"Bessie Holland."

She looked perplexed. "Umm, I don't think I've gotten the complete role yet. Let me know if you need any help with the exercises you've missed."

I think she knew better but subscribed to St. Augustine's admonition not to use the truth to cause injury.

But regardless of her kindness and my opportunity to attend college for free and at my age, I missed our farm and the spiritual moments you share with farm animals: the cold, grassy smell on their breaths when they've drunk from the stock tank in the early morning, the steam rising from their bodies, and the way they nuzzle you and try to take a treat from your pocket or play an innocent trick. When Traveler was a colt he pulled off my hat and ran across the pasture and threw it in a palm tree. Lancelot ate one of my leather gloves. Fat Kitty slept on Papa's chest and one time sharpened her claws on his scrotum when he was drunk.

I believed a manger in the Bible had far greater meaning than Jesus's birthplace. If it's true that the Bible is God's word, He obviously meant for people to read it and think about the images in it. God told Noah and his sons to bring the animals and birds on board the Ark with them. The word is "with." Critters had the same importance as humans. So is it all right now to kill animals and birds and call it a sport? Sometimes I think we should have an open season on people, then ask them how they enjoyed it.

In Genesis God scoops us up from the clay and breathes His breath in our lungs. Does it make sense that we have wars and kill the very people in whom His breath still resides?

You have to pardon me. I got really depressed in New York. The person I missed most was Papa. I had deserted him. It was a rotten thing to do. You don't abandon your kin; you don't leave them with no knowledge of your whereabouts; you don't rip out their hearts and pretend you did nothing wrong. Desertion of your family is about the greatest emotional pain you can inflict on a human being, at least that has been my experience. What could be worse? That's why even today I believe kidnappers should be hanged. Even that fate is too good for them.

I'm sorry, Papa, I said inside my mind, wishing I could send my words to him on a passenger pigeon. But the passenger pigeons had been wiped out, never to return again, and for no reason at all. Is it any secret who has proved himself the earth's greatest enemy?

One Sunday I invited Cody's little friends to the Central Park Menagerie, but I did not include Cody.

"Why not?" he said.

"Because I want to talk to them," I said.

"About what?"

"Ruining their lives."

"When they're your friend, they'll do anything for you. They're tough, too. Their families work hard. What's wrong with that?"

"You said 'when they're your friend'?"

"In Five Points, friendship is a religion, Bessie."

"I think you're deceiving yourself, Cody."

"How about your feelings for Jubal Fowler? The kid who was probably there when Miz Banks was raped? Who's deceiving who?"

Only three kids showed up: Benny Siegel, Meyer Lansky, and a muscular boy named Frankie Carbo. They were handsome-looking boys, and always wore knickers and white shirts and ties and slug caps. In the Lower East Side, the poorer the family, the better they tried to dress. The boy I liked most was Benny, particularly when he smiled. It lit his face. He had the same light-blue eyes Papa had, in fact the purest blue I ever saw, without a dark thought in them. However, the lights in his face often did not coincide with his deeds.

I paid our streetcar fare, and we rode up to the park, on a gold-green day. Seeds and blossoms were floating out of the trees, and jugglers and mimes and clowns were performing along the walkways, and the wind was warm with the smell of candied apples and popcorn balls and the wild smell of the animals. We spread our picnic blanket, and Frankie Carbo walked on his hands for us, his shoulders bulging, all his blood rushing to his face, refusing to stop until I pushed him over.

I hated to break the subject that had been on my mind. The environment these boys lived in was one far more dangerous than the cages the birds and furry animals lived in. The Lower East Side was a scandal, inhuman, run by slumlords and the wealthiest people on earth. They paid no taxes and wore tuxedos on horseback in the park, while their footmen walked alongside them with silver ice buckets to keep their champagne cold. What right did I have to judge these boys or, more importantly, their parents, who had arrived at Ellis Island with little more than the clothes on their backs?

"Hey, fellas?" I said.

The three of them looked at me.

"I heard y'all had some trouble in a crap game," I said.

Their eyes quickly found other subjects to focus on. Meyer watched a bird in a tree; Frankie became intrigued by a unicyclist; Benny stretched his arms and breathed in a chest full of air. "Boy, smell that caramel popcorn," he said.

"Why were you boys at a crap game?" I said.

"We protect people," Frankie replied.

"Really? Why did Benny have a gun?"

They looked at each other, quizzical, as though they had never heard the word "gun."

"Did the Italians come down on you?" I said.

"I'm Italian, and I wasn't coming down on nobody, Miss Bessie," Frankie said. "Meyer and Benny and me were more or less doing oversight for the neighborhood, and some of the East Monk gang dropped in and it got kind of nasty, then these Irish cops came around the corner bouncing their batons on concrete. They scare the shit out of people."

"Watch your language, Frankie," Benny said.

"Don't worry about language," I said. "You had a gun, didn't you, Benny? Meyer took it away from you, otherwise you might be in a cell right now. Is that what happened or not? Don't fib to me, either."

"I don't remember it that way," Benny said.

"Do you have anything to say, Meyer?" I asked.

Meyer looked at the front of the animal cages where a clown was juggling wood balls painted red-white-and-blue. Meyer smiled, his gaze sleepy. "Nobody got hurt. It's very nice you have brought us out here today, Miss Holland. You're a nice lady."

"What did you do with the gun, Meyer?" I said.

He cupped his palm under his chin, then shut one eye and thought about it. "I think it got lost in a sewer."

"Yeah, that's exactly what happened," Frankie said. "I remember now."

I started to speak, but didn't get the chance. "Jesus Christ, look!" Benny said.

A young man, probably not more than twenty-two, in a dark, tailored suit and a tilted fedora, was coming down the walkway, everyone on the sidewalk turning to look. A strong gust of wind swirled leaves around him. He paused in front of a chimpanzee cage and removed his hat and picked the leaves off the brim one by one. His hair had just been clipped and there was a shine in it. His face was thin, his skin soft, his expression placid, as though he was unaware of the rest of the earth. Then he fitted on his hat again, with the same tilt over one eye. He could have been a movie star. "Who's that?" I asked.

"Anthony Vale," Benny said. "It's not his real name, but who cares about that?"

"He's a gangster?" I said.

Benny touched at his lips with one finger. "He's the kind of guy everybody likes. Know what I mean?"

"No."

Benny smiled. "They like him or else."

"That's not funny," I said.

Then I realized the man in the fedora was walking straight at me, his eyes merry. I felt like a hard wind was about to knock me down, but I didn't know why. I wanted to run.

Chapter Twenty-Five

"I've been wanting to meet you for a long time," he said, tipping his hat.

"Pardon?" I said.

"I've seen you from afar at the gym," he replied. "Up close you're everything people say you are."

I looked up and down the walkway, as though I were expecting someone. "I think you're talking about somebody else."

"I asked about you, but they said you quit. Your name is Bessie, right? Cody's Holland's sister?"

"Yes." My voice was hollow, my mouth dry.

"There's some people who say he's got a career. In the ring, I'm talking about."

"Which people?"

"Hey, what do I know?" he replied.

I was wearing a new pink-and-white dress. I had paid seven dollars for it, and now I felt strange and foolish inside it.

"What if I treat everybody to some ice cream cones?" he said.

"I already made a picnic basket."

He nodded, grinning. "I didn't mean to bother you. I bring my grandpa here on Sundays. Maybe see you around, huh?"

My heart was thudding. I felt a terrible itch on the side of my face, but didn't want to scratch myself. An eyelash caught on my lid and I had to wipe my eye socket, but I had nothing to do it with. I rubbed my eye with the back of my wrist, then the man named Anthony Vale gave me a folded, clean handkerchief scrolled with his initials. "An ice cream would be all right," I said.

"How about it, you mugs?" he said.

"Thanks, that's nice of you," Frankie said.

"What about you, Benny?"

"If Bessie is gonna have some, yeah, sure, Anthony," Benny said.

"Meyer?"

"I'm on a diet," Meyer said.

"You never surprise me, Meyer. Nobody will ever own you," Anthony said. "Tell you what, I know when I'm butting in. Here's two dollars." Then he looked at me and winked. "You know what the people at the gym said about you, Bessie? That you're beautiful and you're humble. See? You're already blushing."

I tried to clear my throat. "Sometimes flattery is impolite, sir," I said.

"You're right. But look in the mirror tonight. You're a special lady."

I think that's when Anthony Vale got inside my head.

The flowers arrived the next day. The card on it said:

I enjoyed meeting you. If you ever have a problem, put out the word. I'll be there,

Your admirer,
Tony

PS: I only let friends call me Tony.

Cody was looking over my shoulder. "Who's that from?"
I told him.
He raised his brows but said nothing.

"*What?*" I said.

"You're going out with him?"

"He just sent the flowers, that's all."

"Older guys shouldn't be sending flowers to girls your age."

"Every day you're with fight managers who are corrupt. When I say anything about them, you correct me. I didn't ask him to send the flowers. I cain't stop him from sending them. Just leave me alone, would you?"

"You got it all wrong, Bessie. New York is full of mobsters. But they got rules. They don't prey on underage girls, particularly the Irish and the Italians."

"Look me in the face and tell me you believe what you just said."

"Your man is breaking the rules."

The flowers were in a clay pot. I opened the window, picked up the pot, and sailed it over the fire escape and straight down into the alley. I heard it smack the bricks, then somebody yelling in Yiddish.

"Happy now?" I said.

Then Cody did something he had never done. He put his arms around me and buried his face in my shoulder. I could feel the wetness in his eyes. "We only have ourselves now, Bessie. There's no one else in the world who cares about us. We cain't be fighting."

"Papa cares."

"All Papa ever gave me was pain. We're Centurions, Bessie. We're loved by none and hated by all."

"How about Miz Banks and Aint Minnie and Snowball and all the animals?" I said, swallowing.

"That was then, not now. I dreamed last night I had blood all over me and couldn't wash it off. I saw the men I killed in the boxcar. I could smell their odor. They were shouting at me, but no sound came out of their mouths. Don't ever kill anybody, Bessie."

He sank into a chair, his head bent between his knees, his arms clenched across his chest.

The months passed, and in the middle of 1916, Pancho Villa began lighting up the American border. Mr. Slick came and went and sometimes perched himself on our fire escape. The police came, also, but we refused to answer the door, and finally they lost interest. Cody began to believe that Mr. Slick didn't exist. In fact, he said I created Mr. Slick because we had nobody to look after us. I told him he had seen Mr. Slick with his own eyes. He said he had just been fooling so I wouldn't get any crazier than I already was and end up in the asylum.

Thank you, Cody.

I worked in a newsstand, at a café, and for a janitorial service. I was beginning to believe that coming to New York was a mistake. Once a month a bouquet of flowers was left at our door. I threw them out the window, but without hitting anyone with a pot. I also pretended that the delivery was a nuisance. Except each time I read the card. The messages were always respectful, always happy. I tore them up and let the pieces flitter out the window with the flowers. Then I started tucking them in my dresser. Then I did worse than that.

A bestial creature on the first floor shoved me in the face after I tried to stop him from beating his dog. He genuinely frightened me, and I carried one of Anthony Vale's cards and its message in my dress, like a holy medal, because the neighbors said the creature on the first floor had damaged his wife's brain with his fists, and the beating had taken place in seconds and would leave her a cripple forever.

The message on the bouquet card was certainly a timely one: *You live among dangerous people, Bessie. Please contact me if anyone ever tries to hurt you. I will never let that occur.*

Then I took the situation a bit further. I knocked on this loath-some creature's door. When he opened it, the stink that surged in my face can only be described as a garbage can in which someone has vomited. "I'm the girl you shoved in the face. I came to check on your dog. If you've hurt him in any way, I'm going to cut off your toes."

"Who the fuck are you?"

"Your neighbor upstairs."

"Fuck you," he said, and slammed the door.

Two days passed. Cody was still at the gym. It was late in the day, the sun molten behind the tenements. I went downstairs and bought some food from the street vendors for our supper, then climbed back up the stairs, worn out, the bottoms of my feet hurt-ing. I put the key in the lock and my hand on the doorknob at the same time. My palm suddenly felt like it was coated with grease, but grease that was warm and thick and oozed between my fingers and smelled awful. I didn't want to touch myself. I pushed open the door with my body and stepped on a piece of paper bag that lay on the floor. The note on it was penciled in big block letters:

HERE'S SOME DOG SHIT TO WASH UP WITH.
ENJOY YOUR DINNER.
AND FUCK YOU TWICE.

I washed my hands and cleaned the doorknob, then sat in the gloom for almost an hour. I couldn't call the police because I was a runaway, and even if I could, it would do no good. There was no witness, and, worse, the police department was made up mostly of Irish pagans who didn't know the difference between a bathtub and a beer keg.

I went downstairs and tapped lightly on the dog beater's door. He opened it slowly, the chain lock still in place. He was wearing a filthy undershirt. In the background a woman who looked thirty years his senior was scrunched in a wood chair, her lopsided face full of fear.

"Look who's here," he said.

"Would you step out here, please?" I said.

"What for?"

"So we won't bother your wife."

"Go on with you and count your blessings, darlin'."

"I never got your name."

"Call me Mr. Fuck-You. Now stay out of other people's business."

I rolled Anthony Vale's card into a cone and passed it through the door and the jamb.

"What's this?" he said.

"Someone who sends me flowers wrote me a nice note a few days ago. He was worried about my safety. You can see his signature at the bottom of the card. He has very good penmanship. I think he went to Catholic school. He tells his friends to call him 'Tony' rather than Anthony Vale. You can keep this."

His face had already drained before I finished speaking. He wet his lips. "Listen——" he said.

"Is your wife all right?" I asked.

"Yeah," he said. "Look, sometimes there's misunderstandings. I probably shot off my mouth when I was drinking. That ain't gonna happen again. You need help with anything, call on me. Me and my wife try to be good neighbors."

"What about your dog?"

"Yeah, he's sleeping in the kitchen. He's doing fine."

I said nothing else and walked slowly upstairs. The building was as quiet as a tomb. I heard him ease the door back into the jamb and slip the bolt as quietly as possible.

One week later I received a letter from Papa. I knew that as long as he lived I would never know what to make of my father. This is what he wrote:

Dear Daughter,

I guess you were right. I was always yearning for Mexico and a way to relive the past. By the time you get this a bunch of us old Rangers are going to have some lively times with old Pancho Villa.

I just want to tell you a couple of things in case I cash out early. The greatest gift in my life has been you. You have all of your mother's virtues and none of your father's vices, which are many. You can be as tough as a mule in barbed wire, and five minutes later merciful to your enemies. In that spirit I hope you will forgive me for my failings and for crossing the Rio Grande one more time.

I'll try to write you from Mexico, but the whole country is an ammunition dump and I believe every bullet and cannon shell in it will be fired before there is any talk of peace. In fact, when the generals are done blowing up most of the population, they'll probably dig up each other and go at it with shovels. Most of them make me think of a shit-hog ear-deep in a slop bucket.

If you go back home, stay away from Indian Charlie. His kind always end in Huntsville or on a tree. If I get killed in Mexico, my will is on file at the county courthouse. I've paid the taxes on the land and left everything to you. Do not let go of the land, daughter. The price might not go up, but it won't go down, either. As Mama used to say, God isn't making new dirt.

Love,

Papa

I missed him something awful. Had he told me he was staying at the ranch and not going to Mexico, I would have gotten on the train that night. Instead, I sat in a little park full of hoboes in sight of the Statue of Liberty and watched the sun go down. Even though it was summer, the wind was cold blowing across the water and I couldn't get warm inside my sweater. I sat on the bench and listened to the drunks yelling at each other until the lights went on in the large buildings, then got up to walk home. One of the hoboes threw a rock at me for no reason and hit me between the shoulder blades. The blow felt like a ball-peen hammer wrapped with a piece of blanket cloth. The pain was dull, deep in the bone, the kind that stays with you a long time.

The following day another bouquet of flowers was delivered to our door. This time I contacted the flower store and left a message to be delivered to Anthony Vale.

It read, *The bouquets you sent me have been lovely. I would like to have lunch with you if you are so inclined.*

Chapter Twenty-Six

The next day Anthony Vale picked me up in front of the tenement in a chauffeured, electric-blue Buick automobile, one with a black canvas top. The children playing in the blast of water from the street's single fire hydrant began waving and shouting when they saw who was in the back seat.

For just a moment, in my best dress, I saw myself standing on the stoop like a princess. Anthony stepped up on the curb, in a white suit with a silver vest that had tiny purple fleur-de-lis on it. "You're beautiful," he said. Then he gave every boy in the street a one-dollar bill and helped me into the car.

"I would like to pay for the lunch," I said as we drove away.

"It's supposed to be the other way around, isn't it?" he said.

"I have a problem of conscience, Mr. Vale."

"Call me Tony. Hey, I got a secret for you. The people who worry about their consciences? They're not the problem. The ones who should be in cages don't have consciences."

He smiled and squeezed my hand. Something inside me melted.

The Italian restaurant was in the Financial District. The waiters wore white gloves and jackets and black trousers, and bottles of liquor of every kind crinkled in the light on the bar shelves. The businessmen on the terrace probably could have bought Central American countries by writing a check. My stipulation about paying for lunch had become an absurdity. I had another difficulty as well. Mr. Slick was lounging under an umbrella at a table on the terrace, one foot in a chair, digging a toothpick in the back of his mouth.

"Hey, tell me about your problem of conscience," he said.

"I made use of your name without permission."

His elbows were propped on the tablecloth, his fingers knitted together, his chin resting on them. "In what way?"

"A neighbor harassed me."

"Why would he do that?"

"He's cruel to animals. I told him not to do it. He put feces on my doorknob."

"So what did you do about it?"

"Gave him the card on which you promised to protect me if I felt threatened. He became very frightened."

"Who's the guy?"

"It doesn't matter now."

"Word to the wise. When you got an enemy, it's forever. Jesus forgives people. The rest of us get even."

"I think I'll just have a salad," I said.

He laughed to himself. "You're one in a million," he said.

I went to the ladies' room, my heart starting to pound with guilt and irresponsibility about the information I had given Mr. Vale. He sensed it when I returned to the table. As Mama always said, why borrow trouble? There were two glasses of white wine on the table now, although we had not ordered yet.

"Maybe I talked a little strong about enemies and watching your back," he said. "See, I grew up in Hell's Kitchen. My real name is Jimmie Adonis. But that sounds like a gangster's name. Also, it's a Greek name, of which there is none in our family. I lead a clean life. I just want you to know that."

"There are people who say you're too old for me."

"So tell me who these people are."

I glanced at the window. Mr. Slick had gotten up from his chair and pushed his face against the glass. Then he began making hand gestures at me. Mr. Vale glanced over his shoulder. "Somebody out there you know?"

"A friend from Texas."

He looked at the big glass window again. "Which table?"

Mr. Slick was standing right in front of the glass, but I said, "He must have left."

"I want to take you roller-skating later. Are you up for that?"

"Tony," I said, using his first name for the first time. "I need to clear up something. The obnoxious neighbor is not going to bother me or abuse his pet again. I'm sure of that."

He picked up a salad fork and set it back down. "You think I'm gonna hurt him?"

"No," I said, a piece of dry bread catching in my throat.

"Well, there's nothing to worry about." Then he smiled. "The guy's got my autograph? Like Babe Ruth?"

"I didn't think of it that way."

"It's the little things that eat up people's lives, Bessie. Come on, let's eat a decent meal. I didn't bring you here to eat rabbit food."

He took me to a roller rink, the first time I had ever seen one. The next night he took me to Coney Island, and the next evening on a carriage ride through Central Park, and the next Sunday to an outdoor concert in Long Island. The next morning I overslept and missed my business class at the college. I had never missed one class, and I felt ashamed for having done so, particularly when I knew the faculty and the administration had looked the other way on my age and my fees.

To punish myself, I went to the boxing gym and asked for a couple of extra hours. The owner said, "Sure, babe. Anything for you." He let me pour out the spit buckets and clean a dead rat out of a drainpipe.

At one o'clock I started home and collided into Benny Siegel and Frankie Carbo at the corner. They were wearing ties and white shirts and their slug caps.

"Hey, girl," Benny said.

"Don't be calling me 'girl,' Benny," I said.

"He don't mean anything," Frankie said.

"We're gonna buy you a knish," Benny said.

"Okay," I said.

"What's that smell?" Frankie asked.

"A rat I just pulled out of a pipe with my bare hands in the men's room at the gym."

They started to laugh, then stopped. "You're not kidding?" Benny said.

"It's on my clothes. Want a sniff?" I said.

"Jeez, you got to find another job," Benny said.

"Thanks for the tip, Benny," I said. "Will y'all tell me what this is about?"

Benny pointed to the café across the street. "All right," I said, and followed them. We ordered knishes and coffee in back. But I did not let them pay for it.

Benny looked around before he spoke. "You don't understand how things work here," he said.

"Really?" I said.

"Yeah, really," Frankie said, looking around, his face shaped like a perpendicular football. "Like double-really."

"What we're saying is, Tony Vale is a sensitive guy," Benny said. "He's good to kids and animals and old people. But, you know—"

"Benny, will you clean the knish out of your mouth?" I said.

"He's saying don't get fucked up, Miss Bessie," Frankie said.

"Thank you, Frankie. Do you speak like that in front of your mother?"

"We're trying to do a good deed here," he said.

"Tony is proud of his name, Miss Bessie," Benny said. "I'm talking about his real name—Jimmie Adonis. It hurt him to take another name. 'Vale' sounds better than 'Adonis.' So he made a sacrifice; so he doesn't want people messing with the name 'Adonis.' That's the culture in the Lower East Side."

"You're not making much sense, Benny."

"The guy has got some faults," he said. "I'm not saying anything else, except watch yourself."

"With Tony Vale?"

"It's been good having a knish," Benny said.

"Yeah, same here," Frankie said.

"Sit down, both of you," I said.

They paid no attention to me and went out the door, their faces pointed into the wind, as though the day were cold and they had to get home.

Four days later there were police in the building. In my vanity I thought they were after me. Then they walked up each flight and knocked on every door in the building. I was one of the last. The policeman was in uniform, not in a suit. He did not ask to come in nor did he remove his hat. "We're looking for a missing person, namely, your neighbor Mr. O'Reilly on the first floor," he said. He was chewing gum rapidly, snapping and sucking it between his teeth. "Do you know who I'm talking about?"

O'Reilly was the man who beat his animal and shoved me in the face. "Yes," I answered.

"Have you seen him hereabouts?"

"Not in a while," I answered.

"But you do know him?"

"I know he lives on the first floor."

"Do you know any of his associates?"

"No," I said. "Can you tell me why you're asking me these questions?"

"You know of any enemies he might have?"

"I don't know anything about him. Have you asked his wife? She's the one with the damaged brain."

"You're a little sharp at the tongue, aren't you, lassie?"

"Do you know how offensive it is to give other people pet names?"

He looked me up and down and gave me a lascivious wink. "Excuse me."

I could feel my chest tightening, a pressure band creeping along the left side of my scalp. "What's happened to him?"

He touched his hat. "We're not quite sure. Top of the day to you, baby girl."

I watched out the window while the police filed out the front door and walked down the alley. I went downstairs and did not see one person in the hallways. When I reached the first floor, I deliberately passed by the apartment of the wife-beater named O'Reilly. Through the door I could hear a woman weeping. I kept going out the front door and into the alley, into the gloaming of the day and the soft red glow of the sun on the bricks, the smell of ponded water and the smoke from the sidewalk food stores, all the beautiful things that were allowed the poor.

The alley was empty, the windowpanes a glassy black. Then Cody rounded the corner.

"What's happening?" I said. "It's like the last day on earth here."

"It's that character who bothered you," he replied. "Somebody beat him to death with a baseball bat. The cops didn't tell you?"

"No."

"I got a feeling they don't care about this guy. Stay away from these bastards."

*   *   *

The next day at the college, I borrowed the office phone of my typing and shorthand instructor, Miss Wilkes, and called Tony Vale's private number. Yes, I now called him "Tony" and not "Mr. Vale," and the informality of it made my scalp shrink. I had never realized that manners have more to do with self-protection rather than respect and that manners are often a substitute for morality.

"Can I meet you after lunch?" I said.

"You got it, kid," Tony said. "Can you tell me what for?"

"Some concerns that I have about a violent act in my neighborhood."

"You worry too much, Bessie."

"How do you know that if I haven't told you about my specific concern?"

"Where do you want to meet?" I said.

"In front of the Grand Theatre."

"We're going to a matinee and eat popcorn with the snooks?"

"One fifteen," I said. "Thank you for being there."

I lowered the earpiece softy on the candlestick phone. I had managed not to use the name Vale or Adonis or Anthony or Jimmie either formally or informally. But that was small solace considering my situation. He had kissed my hand twice and my cheek once. I knew the next time we went out, he would try to kiss me on the mouth. The image of that made me suppress a cough and long for Papa. It's not easy to be fifteen.

There was heavy traffic in front of the Grand, the sidewalks and the street littered with ticket stubs from the theater and confetti from a military parade. I saw Tony Vale's chauffeured blue Buick swing out of the rows of cars and trucks and buses, then cut off a vehicle that was trying to back into the only space at the curb. The other driver shifted gears and drove back into the traffic.

Tony pushed the back door open but didn't get out. "Hop in," he said. "We'll take a spin out to Long Island."

I got into the back and sat down. "No, we've got to get some things straight."

"What, the Statue of Liberty is taking a dump in the Bay?"

"There's a Baptist church two blocks from here. Ask your driver to take us there, please."

"To the Baptist church? You're serious?"

"Yes."

"What's in the paper sack?"

"The Bible."

"This is getting crazier by the minute."

"No, it isn't. We'll go down to the church and go inside and you can put your hand on it and swear you had nothing to do with the death of Mr. O'Reilly."

"Who the hell is Mr. O'Reilly?"

"My neighbor who was beaten to death. The one I gave your name to."

"This is nuts, Bessie. Don't do this. It's upsetting my head."

"You won't go to the church with me?"

"It's a Protestant church. I'm a Catholic. No offense."

I slipped the Bible out of the sack and placed it on his lap. "Put your hand on it."

He cupped it around the binding. "I swear to God I didn't have anything to do with hurting or killing this guy you're talking about."

Then he stuck it in my hand, almost into my stomach. "Satisfied?" he said.

"Yes."

"Are we still friends?"

"Why would I not be?"

He shook his head. "I've met my share of women, but none like you. I don't know if that's good or bad. I'm starting to get an ulcer."

"Can you take me home? I've got a new job at a café this evening."

"How about I give you a hundred-dollar bill instead and we say screw the job in the café?"

"Nope."

"Can I see you tomorrow?"

"I'd like to see the animals in the park again."

"You got it, beautiful," he said.

I have never learned much wisdom. I don't know that anyone does. Like most of us, I was raised to believe that if you got some education and worked hard and went to church, your life would be an outstanding one. But that was not the case for me or anyone I ever knew. For good or bad, my plans had no influence on my life. The good things that happened came out of nowhere. The same with the hardship and personal loss and the pain that seemed unjustified. My only conclusion was as follows: It's not the hand that fate deals you; it's how you deal with it. A rich man can drown with a money belt around his waist, and a virginal girl can discover you don't have to die to go to hell.

On a Saturday we went to Coney Island again. The sky was deep purple, the stars winking, the ocean wine-dark, the waves capping through the pilings, the lights on the Ferris wheel and the roller coaster printed against a sunset that looked like the world was on fire. We ate hot dogs and ice cream and caramel popcorn and shot air rifles at paper targets and watched the high-wire walkers teetering two hundred feet above us. It was the kind of evening that made you feel anything this beautiful must have an eternal source.

The fireworks began at ten o'clock. The rockets, the booming of the explosions, and the showers of sparks raining down on the water went on for twenty minutes. We were at the end of the pier, where the calliope was and where immigrant children ran back and forth in their excitement and happiness. It was a moment that made me proud of my country. Tony slipped his arm around my waist and put his face in my hair and kissed my neck and left his lips there for longer than should have been done in public. But I did nothing to discourage him.

We drove into the countryside, somewhere in New Jersey, where there were rolling, green pastures and I could smell cows and creek water and under the moon see silos and red barns and limestone walls. Then he pulled off the road onto a gravel driveway that meandered through an apple orchard to a large brick bungalow with a stone porch and walls that were crawling with English ivy. A single lamp burned in the living room.

"What's this?" I said.

"My private place. I come here to paint."

"You mean paint like an artist?"

"Yeah, I'll show you."

"I have to work tomorrow."

"It's already Saturday. I'll take care of any problem you have at work. Nothing spectacular, just a nice telephone call and a donation to whatever they do."

"I'm working at a laundry."

He stopped in front of the bungalow. "Your laundry days are over. If I have to create a job for you, I'll do that. But this janitorial and laundry stuff is over. Got it?"

"I'll think about it," I said.

"Jesus Christ, I've never seen anybody that stubborn. Is everybody in Texas like that?"

"You never know," I said.

"Here's the deal. Let's go inside. I've got a headache. I'll rest a little while, then we'll make some scrambled eggs and stay over or I'll drive you to the South Pole. Your choice."

I started to speak, but he touched his fingers to my mouth. "No, just give me fifteen minutes' sleep. I can't take this kind of stress. The British should use you as a secret weapon against the Germans. I'm not kidding. I am about to have a breakdown here."

He sounded like a comedian or one of those street-corner gangsters in Hell's Kitchen, innocent and self-mocking. I was sleepy; the backs of my eyelids were like pink rose petals; the air smelled of honeysuckle. I went into the bungalow with him and lay down on a black leather couch in the living room while he showed me a half dozen of his paintings. They resembled *The Scream* painted by Edvard Munch, except they were garish and imitative and ultimately ugly.

"What do you think?" he said.

"They're nice, Tony," I replied, slowly slipping into a dream.

"Nice? That's it?"

"I'm tired. I had a long day."

"You don't want any eggs?"

"I just want to sleep."

"So go to sleep."

He didn't have to tell me. I closed my eyes and drifted away. I felt him put a blanket over my body, from my shoulders down to my feet. I heard a train whistling in the distance and tree limbs rustling on the bungalow's eaves. Then I heard him say, "I must be losing my mind."

He seemed only a few feet away, but I didn't open my eyes. I was too tired. I felt like I was in a cocoon. Or maybe inside my mother's womb. I wanted to sleep for a hundred years.

"Get up," he said. Then he shook my shoulder and said it again, this time more sharply. "Get up!"

I had pulled the blanket over my face; it felt warm and comfortable and safe. "What's wrong?"

"You're treating me like a snook, that's what."

I took the blanket from my face. "What did I do? I don't know what you mean."

"Here, I'll show you," he said.

He jerked me to my feet. Then his fist exploded in my face. I fell over the coffee table and onto the floor.

"You want to be a grown-up woman?" he said. "Congratulations! You're about to be one."

Then he dragged me into the bedroom and locked the door and did not give me the key until sunrise.

Chapter Twenty-Seven

He dropped me off three blocks from my tenement and drove away without saying a word. I could hardly walk. My hair was tangled, my dress torn, my face bruised. Not one person paid any attention to me. I might as well have been invisible. I got up the four flights in the tenement by taking one stairstep at a time while pulling on the handrail. Cody was gone. I threw up in the toilet at the end of the hall and spent the next hour washing myself. I wanted to die.

When I closed my eyes, everything Tony Vale did to me appeared on the backs of my eyelids, as though I were watching a film. I stripped naked and rolled myself in a clean sheet and trembled for a half hour. Then I passed out, as though I was kept alive by an electric cord and God pulled it from the wall. When I woke up, Cody was sitting by me in my bed, wiping my hair with a towel.

"Who did this to you?" he said.

"Tony Vale."

"Where?"

"A house in New Jersey. Out in the country."

"I'm gonna get a cop."

"No, they're on the pad for the Mafia. I don't want them in here."

"I'm gonna get him," he said. "I'm gonna do it with a knife."

"You will not do any such thing."

"I brought you to New York, Bessie."

"Did you hear what I said?"

He put his head on my chest, as though I were the older sibling. His hair was curly and wet, and I kissed it, then hugged him. I could feel his breath on my skin. "I'm hurting inside, Cody. There're some things I'll need."

"You don't want a doctor?"

"No doctor in this city will enter this building," I said. "They think we're rats, and they treat us as such."

My anger was growing. I wanted to hurt someone. At the same time I knew that anger was a black box. I tried to stand, then had to grab the corner of the bed.

"I'm bleeding," I said.

"I don't know what to do, Bessie."

"Just stay with me."

"This isn't right," he said. "It's not right. This is America."

"Yes, and it's a man's America, too," I replied. "I'm nothing. Miz Banks is nothing. Aint Minnie's people are nothing."

He put a towel on the bed and laid me down and then lay beside me and pulled the bedcover over us, and then both of us went to sleep, like small children in a peaceful place far away, although I had no notion of where that could be.

On Monday I went both to class and to work, my face heavily made up, and spoke with few people. I limped and had to carry a cane and told my typing and shorthand instructor, Miss Wilkes, I had twisted my ankle and fallen down the stairs. She looked in my eyes and said, "Don't try to carry the world on your back, Bessie. It will break you for sure. I'll be here when you need me."

It's funny how the best people on earth, the most helpful certainly, are again and again the most unlikely. They're nondescript, as plain as mud, and appear out of nowhere, with the physical properties of a scarecrow standing in front of a tornado. But I determined I would not burden Miss Wilkes. The world I came from was one she would not understand. It was feral and founded on murderous policies, not molded by God out of clay but cut from rock and slag and peopled by maniacal preachers and gunmen and helpless women whose babies were rope-dragged to death through cactus by the Comanche. The state I came from was a necropolis, and its birthplace was a roofless church where 188 men and boys held out for thirteen days and were slaughtered to the last man, but not before they took fifteen hundred of the enemy with them.

I am descended from the Hollands and the Benbows. One of my ancestors in North Carolina was married to a woman of color. She was not his mistress; she was his wife, and he had three children by her. He was also a colonel in the Confederate cavalry. After the war, he ran for governor and was shocked when he was not elected. I think my ancestors were not the story of America. They *were* America, for good or bad, and it made me proud. I would not concede, nor reach out to corrupt men who governed a corrupt society. I would prevail, and no power on earth would stop me. And the man who would help me was not a man at all but my friend for life, the hoofed and meretricious spirit Mr. Slick.

I did odd things for the next few days. Mr. Slick and I brought food to the wife of Mr. O'Reilly, the degenerate man who shoved me in the face and died like the poor devils who were broken on the medieval wheel. Miz O'Reilly was obviously inside her own world and never looked directly in my face, but she held both my hands and seemed to see Mr. Slick. When we left, she was smiling. Just as I was about to shut the door behind us, I heard her say something.

"Ma'am?" I said.

"You," she answered. "You were a little girl in a woods a long time ago, weren't you? Somebody hurt you real bad."

"Say that again," I asked.

Her eyes were blank, as though all her motors had been cut, her words spoken by someone else.

I didn't know if Papa was in Mexico or Texas, but I sent a telegram to the house. It read:

HURT BUT OK NOW. NEED MONEY. NEED YOU.
DAUGHTER

This was the first time I had ever admitted my dependence upon my father. No, "dependence" is an improper if not a denigrating word. "Need" is in our chemistry; "need" was put there for a reason; "need" is love. The person who declares his independence of "need" sails a ship that has neither rudder nor oars.

Obviously my attitudes about the world were changing. I was witness to the attack of Miz Banks. I barely escaped being raped with her. I watched her fight inside herself for months. There is no darkness greater than the shadows of the heart. Every afternoon her eyes went somewhere else and a toxic vapor subsumed her soul. Then she began to heal. There was a sharpening of her features, a loss of weight, a cautionary light flickering in her face, perhaps a reckoning taking place inside her, an awareness that evil is consumed by its own flame. Better said, she had found hope.

And if she could, I could. Papa was back on our own property after having escaped from some of Pancho Villa's men. This was after he and others, all mercenaries, shot up one of Villa's trains. But I didn't care about any of that. I knew Papa was brave and loved me. I knew he would stand by me no matter what I had done, and I also knew he would never let the world hurt either of us again. Papa's great gift was his ability to accept people for what they were, not what they should be. It had taken a long time for me to make the same acceptance.

Through Miss Wilkes, my typewriting and shorthand instructor, Papa arranged a long-distance call at the college. I loved Miss Wilkes, just as I loved Miz Banks. They weren't just teachers; they gave of their souls to people whom they hardly knew. Did you ever see a mother rabbit run from her hole so the hunters wouldn't find her babies? That's what I'm talking about. That's what saints are.

Chapter Twenty-Eight

Miss Wilkes handed me the phone in her departmental office, and left the room and closed the door behind her. Through the window I could see an electric trolley on the tracks in the middle of the intersection. Passengers were getting on and off it, their day normal, their faces unperturbed.

"Hi, Papa," I said.

"Tell me all of it," he replied. "Leave nothing out."

I did. In a monotone, my words hardly more than a whisper. Every blow and penetration and pull of my hair. How Tony Vale threw me against the wall and kicked me in the stomach when I was on the floor and then spat in my face. I could see the long steel bar on the trolley's roof that was attached to the power line overhead, stiff and angular, sparks popping and showering from the tip. And I kept talking and talking and talking, and told Papa how Tony Vale twisted my arms when I refused to pick up his clothes, and how he flung me into the bathroom when I continued to disobey him, and how, when I had my clothes on, he put a blue-black Police Special to my head and marched me to his car and shoved me into the passenger seat, his face uncertain about what he would do next.

"Go on," Papa said.

"That's all. He drove me back to the city and left me on the sidewalk three blocks from my tenement."

He went silent, his breath echoing inside the phone's mouthpiece.

"Are you there?" I asked.

"What's Cody doing? Do not try to mislead me, either, Bessie."

"He wanted to go after Tony. I told him no."

"Go after him how?"

"With a knife."

"Has he got that out of his head?"

"Yes, sir."

"All right, this is what we're going to do," he said. "First, we do not confront Vale. Second, say nothing about him to other people. They will report you to him. Third, I will send you a money order today. Lastly, I'm going to talk to some friends of mine."

"Who?"

"I will give you no names. Down the track, you might be called upon to testify under oath. But you cannot testify about what you don't know."

"Are you coming up, Papa?"

"I don't wish to say. But do not go after that man on your own. Do you understand what I'm saying?"

"Yes, sir."

"There's another thing. Vale will be back."

"Pardon?"

"Rapists are all alike," he said. "They want to own the victim. They also want to convince the victim it was her fault. It's not hard to do. The jury and judges are all male. The woman doesn't have a chance. That's why a rope over a tree limb sometimes has its merits. I won't let you down, daughter."

I didn't try to tell Papa about the brain-damaged lady Mrs. O'Reilly, and the fact she associated me with a little girl who was hurt real bad in a woods many years ago. I had learned that stories about the spiritual aren't well received in modern times, even with Papa, who was dedicated in heart and soul to the past. I have a theory about all this. The material things we have substituted for the unseen world are mostly comprised of junk, or if not junk, technology that doesn't work or we cain't afford or is just flat boring to mess with. Think of it this way. Would you rather be around during the War between the States or owning a telephone that rings all the time?

The next week the money order arrived, but more trouble did as well. Papa was right. Tony Vale wasn't through with me. I stepped out one evening to buy some fruit and saw him standing across the street, in white trousers and a lavender shirt and shined shoes and a Panama hat, his coat hung with one finger over his shoulder. When he stepped off the curb onto the brick paving, I turned around as fast I could and ran up the stairs, then stopped, ashamed of myself, and walked back down again and took a breath and went outside. There was no one in the street. But Tony Vale had seen me run, and once more had degraded me.

I wasn't sure if I could keep my promises to my father. And the more I thought about it, the more grotesque my dreams became. Every night, Tony Vale came to my bedside and put his hands on places they shouldn't be. I would cover myself and roll into a ball, my knees pulled all the way to my chest, my breath foul even to myself. Then I would get up in my frustration and go down the hallway and use the community toilet and try to get back in my robe before a man saw my body.

I had accidently shot Jubal Fowler's father, and I had fired a pistol into the ceiling of Green Lantern Saloon, but those were melodramatic and even theatrical events compared to what I was thinking about now. I could not live as a ragged imitation of myself. I began to have fantasies that made me wet my lips and open and close my hands, and when a quiet voice inside me tried to lead me back into the sunlight, I would shush the voice and, hour by hour, construct a situation in the streets of the Lower East Side that no puppet show could equal.

Benny and Meyer and Frankie were always together, but they were not alike. Benny was the romantic, Meyer was the mathematician, and Frankie went to prison when he was eleven. When I knew them, I thought they were still at an age at which I could turn a little dial in the back of their heads and straighten them out. Benny was my favorite, though. The day after I saw Tony Vale on the curb, Benny knocked on my door, a tulip drooping from his hand. He was wearing what looked like an Easter suit, and he took off his cap before he spoke. "Hi, Bessie. Can I come inside?"

"If you like."

He looked up and down the hallway. "Is Cody here?"

"No."

He stepped inside and bolted the door, then handed me the tulip. The stem had been broken off. "I'm sorry for what happened to you," he said.

"What do you think happened to me?" I asked.

"Tony Vale is telling people you're nuts and went crazy in Hell's Kitchen and got beat up by some Gophers. I know better. Tony Vale is scary. You got to go somewhere else."

"Sit down," I said. "There. In the kitchen. I want to talk to you."

"About what?"

"Do what I say, Benny."

He sat down at the kitchen table, his cap in his hands. His blue eyes and Easter suit and little-boy features would never be believed by people who knew him only as an adult. "Did I do something wrong?" he asked.

"No, there's an innocence in your eyes your friends don't have. It comes from only one place. Tell me where that place is, Benny."

"I don't know," he said.

"Maybe one day you will. In the meantime, I want you to understand my relationship with Tony Vale. He's an evil man. Do you know why I say that to you?"

"No."

"I'm telling you something about myself. I'll never let a man like that defeat me. No matter what he does, I'll prevail. And I'll do so because I don't fear him. And my lack of fear comes from the same source the light in your eyes comes from. Do you understand me?"

"You mean like throwing a pipe bomb through somebody's windshield or something like that?"

I gazed idly at him for a long time. His eyes never blinked.

"What do you want to be when you grow up, Benny?"

"An actor. Out in Hollywood. Everybody is saying that's the place to be."

"I bet it is," I said. "You would be a good actor, Benny. Thank you for my tulip."

"You never understood what I was saying, did you?" he said. "Tony Vale kills people. He killed a rabbi. He kills people's pets. He's gonna kill you." He put his hand in his coat pocket and set a small semiautomatic on the table. "It's loaded. No serial numbers. Nothing in the chamber."

Then he grabbed my hand and held it to his cheek and ran out the door.

Ten days after Benny's visit, I was fired without explanation from the café where I was working, and the same night someone poured acid under our door. The slumlord who owned the building was furious. At Cody and me. He would have evicted us if Frankie Carbo hadn't hit him in the head with a sock full of sand.

My friends in the neighborhood were few. I was a target, and everyone knew it. Except for the instructors at the college, I had hardly anyone to talk with. Then two men broke into the typing room at the college and with either a hatchet or an ax chopped up every typewriter in the room. I had become Typhoid Mary.

Where had Papa gone, and what was he doing? This was the most desperate time in my life. Would my father leave me now? I thought about Jesus on the cross, and his last words, *My God, my God, why has Thou forsaken me?* Was his fate to be mine?

Then Mr. Slick tapped lightly on my door. I was a little mad at Mr. Slick. He had surely not helped out when Tony Vale attacked me. I was thinking about slapping Mr. Slick upside the head with a frying pan.

I eased the door open. "What do you want?" I said.

"I think I got news, but I ain't sure," he replied.

"Try to think about what you just said, Mr. Slick. You either have news or you don't have news. If you possess news, you tell others what it is. If you don't, you shut your mouth."

"You don't have to get grouchy about it."

"I am going to hit you, Mr. Slick. I swear."

"I think I saw your father."

I grabbed him by the arm and pulled him into the room and bolted the door. "Start over," I said.

"At the train depot. Him and two other men got off the Pullman. They were wearing Stetsons and cowboy boots. The redcap tried to carry your father's suitcase and your father almost pushed him off the platform."

"What were you doing in Pennsylvania Station?"

"Picking up tips where I can."

"Why didn't you speak to my father and confirm who he was?"

"He looked like he was in a bad mood, that's why. Them two others didn't look like no jokesters, either."

"Now you've got me in a quandary, Mr. Slick."

"About what?"

"Whether to pound on your head or throw you out the window."

"I know, Miss Bessie. I mess things up. It's just my way."

What could I say? Mr. Slick did his best, but his best was like someone else falling down an elevator shaft. "Are you hungry?" I said.

"Now that you speak of it. I've been hanging out at the mission. The soup tastes like the cooks boiled their socks in it."

"You said my father wouldn't let the redcap carry his suitcase?" I said.

"Yeah, there wasn't no doubt about that. Why?"

"It's nothing," I said. "There's some cheese and ham and bread in the cooler box. May I ask you a private question?"

"There ain't nothing much interesting about me, Miss Bessie. You know that."

"Did you know that Tony Vale took me to his bungalow in New Jersey?"

"I heard Vale had one," he replied. "I heard that bad things went on there."

"Why didn't you tell me?"

"I was jealous."

"Say that again?"

He dropped his head. "You run off with a man that's worsen than Indian Charlie, and wouldn't pay me no mind when I tried to warn you through the Italian restaurant window. I come up here to he'p, but it didn't mean nothing to you."

"You knew what was going to happen and said nothing?"

"I guess that says it."

He tried to look me in the face but couldn't. "Want me to leave?" he said.

I had no answer. I never thought Mr. Slick would ever betray me. I left him in the room and walked down to the Bay and watched a lightning storm building in the sky above the Statue of Liberty, then walked back to the tenement just as a raindrop struck the sidewalk.

Papa, where are you? I thought. *Why do you not call? Why do you always make things so hard?*

I stood in the middle of the street and watched the clouds darken. A wave of electricity rippled through the heavens, then a thundercloud burst overhead and poured down on the alley. I watched the lights go on in the windows above the stoops and let the rain beat down on my head until my clothes were soaked. When I went up to my tenement, Mr. Slick was gone.

Chapter Twenty-Nine

The sky was clear in the morning, the sunlight striping the alleyway with shadow and columns of light. I said my morning prayers before I dressed, then went downstairs and bought a cup of coffee and a roll from a vendor and sat on a stoop in the cool shade of the building and forgave Mr. Slick and tried not to be afraid and not to feel sorry for myself.

Children were beating a ball with sticks, all of them wearing caps. I wondered what would become of them. New York prisons were known as hellish places. Some waifs had already been there. Their heroes were people like Tony Vale. And I had walked with my hand on Tony Vale's arm, adding to his legitimacy.

It was hard to accept the possibility that Papa was close by, but deliberately not contacting me. I had another problem, too, one I described as a quandary to Mr. Slick. If the men Mr. Slick had seen at Pennsylvania Station were indeed my father and his friends, they were acting as vigilantes in my name, taking over my responsibilities, in effect assigning me the role of a coward and the instrument of an execution.

My head was throbbing. I went back upstairs and put on my best clothes and shoes and a Sunday straw hat, a big, floppy one with green and purple silk flowers piled on it, and no makeup. I had found out that Tony Vale owned the store from which his bouquets were sent, and that he came in every morning of the week.

I rode the trolley to Brooklyn and stepped down right in front of the store. A bell rang when I went inside. It was a large store, one with four or five young women behind the counters and displays, and seven or eight customers. I could see Tony Vale talking on the phone in an office, the door half open, one foot propped on the wastebasket. He was combing his hair with one hand. He did not see me.

"Could you ask Mr. Vale to step out here, please," I asked one of the clerks.

She was young and short and plump and had a round, Irish face. It was an innocent face, too. "I think he's busy now," she replied. "Can I help you?"

"Just tap a broom handle on his head and tell him Bessie is here."

"Pardon?"

"Or I can go back there and wrap the phone wire around his neck a couple of times."

"I'll be right back, ma'am," she said.

She went into his office, her back to me. He was still on the phone. He leaned sideways to see past her. He was wearing a long-sleeve black shirt with a tiny red heart on the pocket and a silver tie. He got up and came through the door. "What are you doin' here?" he said.

"I thought I would give you a chance to surrender yourself," I said.

"For what?"

"Raping me. Of course, there will be other charges, too. Kidnapping will probably be one. And assault and battery for hitting me in the face with your fist and throwing me against a wall. Since

I'm under eighteen, I'm sure you will also be charged with child molestation. By the way, my landlord saw one of your men pouring acid under my apartment door, and the police have said they are pretty sure your men vandalized the typewriters in the classroom where I study."

"Listen, everyone!" he said to the clerks and customers. "This girl has mental problems. I tried to help her. It was a mistake. I apologize for this scene you've had to watch."

In the corner of my eye, I saw Mr. Slick. He was writing in a notebook, his face absorbed. I had nothing to do with his coming there.

"I have contacted two newspapers, and may talk to others," I said to Tony Vale. "This journalist you see here works for William Randolph Hearst and will give you a chance to tell your side of the story, I'm sure."

Mr. Slick was nodding as I spoke.

Then I addressed the entire store. "My name is Bessie Mae Holland. I am sorry you had to hear the details of what Mr. Vale did to me. He's a criminal, a degenerate, and a sadist, and also a member of the Mafia. The fact that I put my trust in him will probably be the biggest regret in my life. However, if I did not tell you these things, I would have a greater regret, namely, to be party to the evil deeds he will continue to visit on others, people such as yourselves."

Then I walked out on the street, the buildings and traffic and noise of Brooklyn spinning around me, Mr. Slick at my heels.

Mr. Slick rode with me on the trolley all the way back to the Lower East Side. It was midmorning, and there were few people in the car.

"That's the bravest thing I ever seen, Miss Bessie," he said.

"Let's don't talk about it, Mr. Slick."

"You ain't mad at me no more?"

"No."

"Well, I am. I don't know what come over me. I didn't know Vale would do what he did at that bungalow, but that ain't no excuse."

"Will you shut up, Mr. Slick?"

"Yes, ma'am, I will," he replied.

I patted him on the top of his hand.

"But I got to say one more thing," he added. "Vale didn't have no gunsels with him at his store. But he's got them. And he's gonna use them. On both you and me."

"Thank you for the reassurance, Mr. Slick."

"No, you're not hearing me. I'll sleep on your fire escape. I'll sleep in your alley. I'll sleep in your trash cans. I will sleep in your toilet. I ain't gonna let them people hurt you. No. Sirree. Bobtail."

How could a body be afraid when she had a guardian angel like Mr. Slick? I immediately said a prayer for additional help.

My situation was not funny, though. It's easy to be brave in public. What if I were abducted by Tony Vale's gunmen and brought to a basement in Five Points? The thought of it made my knees go weak.

That night Cody and I put the kitchen table against the door. I slept with Benny's pistol under the mattress. I also had nightmares, this night and every night. I saw Mama getting out of her grave in order to protect me. She was wearing the dress she wore in her coffin. It was damp and pressed against her skin and stained with decomposition. I also saw the little girl in the woods who had watched her father snap the necks of her murderers. I saw Aint Minnie and Snowball's cabin at night, the lids of the woodstove rimmed with fire. I beat on the door, but they would not answer.

The same with Lancelot and Traveler. I wanted to pet and feed them apple chunks on my palm and hug and smell them and scratch their ears and kiss their noses. But they ran away, disappearing into the night, their eyes rolling. I saw Papa silhouetted in the hallway, wearing his Stetson and Peacemaker, but when I approached him he turned his back on me and walked loudly down the stairs.

I thought I was having a breakdown, although I was not sure what a breakdown was. My stomach felt sick, the muscles in my back tied in knots; a rash spread across my shoulder blades and wrapped itself under my left arm.

Cody shook me at 3:17 in the morning. "What is it?" I said.

"You're having a bad dream."

I tried to remember what it was. Then I said, "It wasn't a dream. Mama was here. So were Aint Minnie and everybody else."

"It was just a dream, Bessie."

"No, it wasn't. I'm going to die."

"Not as long as I'm here," he said.

Then I started to cry. He sat by me and rubbed my back.

"Papa was in the hallway," I said.

"No, he was not."

I clenched my fists. "You're right," I said. "He wasn't here. Just like always. When it counts, Papa's not here."

In the brightness of the morning, I experienced a terrible form of clarity. I was on my own, no matter what I did, no matter how many people knew I was raped by Tony Vale. If I wished to live, I would have to depend entirely on myself. Anything less would place me in the hands of a diabolic man. My death in all probability would be longer and more painful than the one Jesus suffered. Should I sit by and watch an anaconda wrap itself around me?

I stared down in the alley below. One man was leaning against a wall, his hands in his coat pockets, his cap shadowing his face, as though he had fallen asleep. Farther down the alley, a second man, one wearing a crumpled fedora, was flipping a coin and catching it. He looked up at me, then looked away. Both men were wearing suits. I had seen neither of them before.

For the first time in my life, I put a pistol in my purse, remembering Benny's words, "It's loaded. No serial numbers. Nothing in the chamber."

I looked at the date on the free calendar Cody had brought from a saloon. It was Tuesday, the night Tony Vale always played poker in a Harlem card parlor. I wanted to believe a divine hand was telling what to do. Then I saw a piece of yellow paper under the throw rug that Cody and I kept by the door. The paper was folded twice and pressed flat so that it was no larger than two square inches. I opened it gently with my fingers. I recognized the penmanship immediately.

Don't worry. Friends are with me. What has happened will never hap-pen again.

Love.

P.

I had no way of knowing how many hours or days the note had been there. We had cleaned the acid, but the note could have stuck under the throw rug before or after the acid was poured. But more importantly, what was I supposed to do with the information in the note? If Papa was trying to hide evidence of rough justice in the making, he was doing a masterful job.

And how about saying "Don't worry" to someone whose daily life was a nightmare? I wanted to break a ceramic pot over Papa's head.

Chapter Thirty

It was lovely riding up to Harlem in the trolley. The windows were down, the air fragrant after a short rain, a pinkish-red glow on the buildings, music coming from a rooftop or an open-air bar. I had no plan about Tony Vale. Or at least that is what I told myself. But what else could I do? Depend on Papa's note? Try to embarrass Tony Vale again in public? That didn't work very well. The only thing I got out of it was a terrible lesson: people believe what they need to believe; they change their minds when they're ready. Noah's neighbors probably dismissed the weather report.

I got off the trolley one block past the card parlor. A colored preacher stood on a shoeshine stand, waving a Bible at a small crowd. But he wasn't talking about the Bible. He was talking about Jim Crow. The things he was saying would have gotten him killed in San Antonio or Houston. I have never understood the attitude in either the North or the South about people of color. Northerners like them as an abstraction and fear them as individuals. Southerners are fond of them personally and hate them in groups.

How smart is that?

But I wasn't thinking about people of color or the preacher on the shoeshine stand. I wished he was giving a sermon based on Ecclesiastes. I wanted to hear and to believe that the earth would abide forever. I wanted to believe that God held me in His palm and that His children were all around me, that the music I heard from the rooftops or sidewalks was the music of the spheres, the music Shakespeare heard at the Globe or Socrates heard when he paused with his class at the Acropolis.

I was now standing in front of Tony Vale's favorite card parlor. There were many of them in Harlem, and another kind of gambling as well, what was called the "numbers game." Harlem was beautiful back then, but like all stories about Eden, its denouement was not long in coming, and my little friend Meyer had a lot to do with it, but that's another story.

I stood like a post in the twilight, fifteen years old, so frightened through the day I could not eat lunch or supper, a semiautomatic in my purse, a .32 round now in the chamber, wondering if I was about to make the worst mistake in my life.

Or if, in walking away, would I end up tied to a basement chair, blindfolded, a gag in my mouth, waiting for a pair of pliers to touch my body? I know that's an ugly image. But it's the one I lived with.

Should I have just depended on Papa? Maybe. But what if he were drunk? What if no "friends" were with him? What if Mr. Slick never saw Papa pushing away a redcap, which I interpreted to mean that Papa had his Peacemaker in his suitcase? Or what if my father was sentenced to a Yankee jail for the rest of his life?

I walked inside the card parlor. It was a strange environment. There was a dimly lit, short bar attended by a colored man in a starched white jacket, and at least two other rooms deep in the back of the building. The walls were covered with rolled red leather. One of the rooms had strings of beads hanging from the top of the doorway. There were eight or nine women behind the beads, women of all races, smoking and lounging on couches, creating a haze that was like the smoke and tiny blades of fire inside a charcoal burner. An Oriental woman in a dress that was as tight as snakeskin lit a cigarette in a gold cigarette holder while she looked at me. Her mouth was thick with purple lipstick, her teeth white and sharp when she smiled, her eyes glinting.

The door to the other back room was half opened. I could see men playing cards on a green, felt table inset with cups for poker chips.

"Is Mr. Vale here?" I asked the bartender.

He was shaking ice inside a chrome-plated mixer. "Who?" he grinned.

"Mr. Anthony Vale."

He squinted and shook his head and blew out his breath, as though I were a nuisance, then became more vigorous with the shaker. "The bar is open, but the back rooms is a membership club. We cain't give no names for the membership people."

"Would you please not talk to me like I'm stupid?"

He set down the shaker and looked both ways. "Where you from?"

"Texas."

He stared at the far end of the bar. I followed his eyes, my vision adjusting to the gloom. Three men were seated at a table in the corner. I could not see their faces. They were big and bareheaded, their hats crown-down on the empty table next to theirs.

"This must be peckerwood night," the bartender said.

"What?" I said.

"I'm from Miss'sippi. I got a good job here. I got a feeling something is going on."

"What are you talking about?"

"All of you wit' the same accent coming in at the same time. This is Harlem. Ain't ch'all caused enough grief down where you come from?"

"I'm not here to cause you grief."

"Who's them men back there? The ones you was just watching?"

"I don't know."

"They the law, ain't they? Goddamn it, I knew it."

"Don't use God's name in vain," I said.

He touched the heel of his hand to his head. "You listen——"
His anger was so great he couldn't finish his sentence.

"That may be my father back there," I said. "I'm trying to stop
something very bad from happening."

"*You're* gonna stop something? You got no idea what you're fooling wit'."

"I suggest you go down the street," I said.

"Me!" he said, pointing at his breastbone.

I had never spoken to a person of color in that fashion, and it
did not make me feel well. He propped his arms on the cool box,
then looked sideways at me. "I'm gonna fix you a cherry fizz wit'
ice, I'm gonna put some lemons and limes in it. I'm gonna be nice
to you. Then I'm gonna pretend you and them ofays ain't here. You
got that?"

"No," I replied. "And I don't know what an ofay is. But thank
you for your offer. I'm sorry if I have offended you."

Then I walked toward the back of the bar. The cigarette smoke
was eye-watering. I still could not make out the three men at the
table. They were drinking mug beer. One spat at a cuspidor. I hoped
Frank Hamer was there. But I knew that was not the case. Frank
Hamer stayed within the rules. Papa didn't have rules. Or at least
not the kind others would recognize.

The three men had not seen me and were rising from their
chairs, the chair legs scraping on the floor, their shoulders as wide
and horizontal as ax handles, their backs to me. One of them was
unshaved, his cheeks covered with stiff white whiskers, his profile
like the profile on an Indian penny.

The unshaved man took off his raincoat and hung it on the
back of his chair. A holstered pistol was buckled on his side, and
another one stuck behind his belt. He picked up a domed Stetson
hat and fitted it on his brow. I had no doubt who he was.

How did we all arrive there, in Harlem, at the same time? It may have been Kismet, but I doubted it. Papa was going to get Tony Vale, and may have been following him for days. That's how he wiped out Indian Charlie's gang south of the border. Papa was unrelenting. I was an adverb, and now he was about to commit an execution, a homicide, a murder, and I was going to be witness to it. I wished I had never told him of my troubles with Tony Vale.

I followed him and his companions into the card room.

Papa kicked the door shut with the heel of his boot and drew his Peacemaker. There were seven men around the card table. Except for Tony Vale, they all looked dumbfounded, their faces twisted out of shape with either indignation or shock or absolute terror.

"Which one of you is Vale?" Papa said, with no acknowledgment of my presence.

Tony stood up slowly, his fingertips touching the felt, his face composed. "What can I do for you, pal?" he said.

"Lay your piece on the table," Papa said.

"I don't carry firearms."

"I think you're a liar," Papa said.

"Why should I lie? I got no idea who you are."

Papa's knuckles whitened on the Peacemaker's grips. "I'm the father of the innocent girl you raped and beat with your fists."

There was a tremolo in his voice, like the tension in a guitar string about to pop.

"Yeah, I see her behind you," Tony said. "She's been telling people the same lies all over the city. I don't need to rape women, pops. So why don't you and your two friends roll up your act and get the fuck out of here?"

"Take off your clothes. You can keep underwear on."

"Are you crazy? Or a queer or something? I got news for you. You're not gonna make it out of here."

"I'll count to three," Papa said.

"You got wax? You're about to die, Homer."

"Homer?" Papa said.

"Yeah, Homer, as in 'hick.'"

Papa inverted the Peacemaker and clubbed Tony across the bridge of his nose. Blood splattered on his cheeks and hair and his lavender shirt. He bent over, his hands pressed on his nose, a muffled sound squeezing from his mouth.

"You son of a bitch," he said, straightening up, looking at his palms.

"Put the piece on the table or take off your clothes."

"I don't have a piece, and I don't take off my clothes in public. So fuck you. Take yourself and your daughter and your friends back to Shitsville, and be thankful you're not hanging from your rectum on a meat hook."

Papa looked at the other poker players, who were trying to shrink as small as they could.

"Get under the table," he said.

All of them got to their knees, knocking back their chairs, pushing against each other under the table. Papa pulled the revolver that was tucked in the back of his belt, and placed it on the felt in front of Tony Vale.

"It's a converted .44-40 Remington," he said. "It's a beaut, all chambers loaded, including the chamber under the hammer. I don't like carrying a revolver with a cartridge under the hammer, but I didn't want to cut you short."

"Are you nuts?" Tony said.

"I'm putting away my Colt in my holster. I'll count to five."

"I'm not gonna do this," Tony said.

"Yes, you will. It's not up for discussion."

"I don't think you're gonna do shit."

"You're wrong about that, partner," Papa said.

He hefted his Peacemaker out of its holster and swung it across Tony Vale's jaw. I heard it snap, and saw Tony's mouth open and the redness of his tongue. He cupped his hand and drained a mouthful of blood and teeth into his palm. His poker hand was turned up on the felt. He had been holding a heart flush. He wiped his mouth on his sleeve. "You're nothing," he said. "A dogcatcher. If you didn't have your niggers, you'd shoot yourselves."

I couldn't take it anymore.

"Papa, stop it! Now!" I said, grabbing his arm, getting between him and Tony Vale. "He's paid enough! Everything you're doing is turning you into him!"

But I was wrong, just as most fools are when they tamper with evil. Tony bent over, as though he were about to vomit, just as I tripped and knocked Papa off-balance. One of Papa's friends tried to steady him and now the two of them were tangled among the legs of the men under the table. Tony pulled up his trouser leg and reached into the sock on his right foot. A small semiautomatic pistol was strapped to his ankle. Someone under the table jerked Papa's Peacemaker from his hand, then fumbled it on the floor.

The light in Tony's broken face was demonic. That's the only way I can describe it. I was convinced he was one of those made different in the womb, a creature born from another tree. In three or four seconds the situation had turned completely around, and Papa was about to leave this earth. Why had I come here? What had I done? I felt helpless and contemptible. My father was going to die before my eyes, and he knew it. Both of his friends could not shoot without hitting me, provided they had weapons, which, knowing Papa's solitary ways, they probably didn't.

I pulled Benny's small pistol from my string purse just as Tony raised his hideaway. I don't remember squeezing the trigger. I felt the gun jump in my hand, but the report was not loud and more like a damp Chinese firecracker than the discharge of a firearm. Time seemed to stop, or better said, to drag, even the sounds around me, like someone yawning. Tony was looking straight at me. I thought I had missed. Then I saw a hole in the center of his forehead, like a black dot the circumference of a pencil. The muscles in his face collapsed one at a time, until his face was a bowl of porridge. As he went down, his chin banged on the table's edge, sprinkling a stack of poker chips on his clothes.

Chapter Thirty-One

We went out the back door. Papa hired a jitney for his two friends and sent them to Brooklyn, and hired another jitney for us. We drove all the way down to the little park on the bay not far from the Statue of Liberty. It was dark now, and the winos and the tramps and the deranged seemed to be everywhere around me. Perhaps I was traumatized. I felt as though there was no circulation in my hands and my legs. My hearing was gone, as though someone had clapped his hands on my ears. My fingers were still trembling on my thighs.

Papa wrapped his raincoat around me. The wind was cold, even though autumn was weeks away.

"You have to listen to me, Bessie, and never forget what I tell you," he said. "You saved the life of your father. It's that simple. It was me who planned this. It was me who messed it up. The man who ate the bullet had it coming. Had he prevailed, he would have turned your life into hell on earth. When you bury a bucket of shit, you bury a bucket of shit. End of story."

"I may go to prison, Papa."

"No, you're not. Nobody cares about this man. They'll put flowers all over his casket and weep and cry all the way to the graveyard, then the next day let their dogs piss on his tombstone."

The wind smelled like oil and kelp and dead fish that had washed in the rocks below. "I have something else on my mind, Papa. I'm not just me. I believe that somehow I'm an extension of the little girl who was killed in the woods. Whatever punishment I suffer, she will suffer, too."

"Maybe everything you say is true, Bessie, but you cain't mortgage your life on things you cain't see. It's not what's out there, it's how you address it."

I didn't want to hear it. "Can I go back home?"

"Our home in Texas?"

"Yes, sir."

"That would be the best news I ever had."

He helped me stand up from the bench, then smiled. "I bet your mama is mighty proud."

"You think so?"

"You two are the best goddamn women I've ever known."

"Don't take God's name in vain, Papa."

"I won't ever do it again," he replied. "I swear."

I waited for the police to bang on the door in the morning. It didn't happen. Instead, little Benny Siegel tapped on it that afternoon. "Can I come in?" he said.

"Yes, you may, Benny," I replied. "I want to talk to you."

He pulled off his cap and closed the door behind him. "Talk about what? I came here to help. You cooled out that bastard. Everybody is glad."

"I'm going away, Benny. I may never see you again. I want you to make me a promise."

"What?"

"This morning a vendor told me you and Meyer were selling protection."

"Me? Jeez, who would tell you that?"

"Look me in the eye, Benny."

His eyes were sky blue, with an ethereal light in them. He never blinked. He was the most innocent little boy I ever knew.

"It's the Irish and Italians who are selling the protection, Bessie. Me and Meyer don't do that. We just protect our own people. Come see in Williamsburg. I told my mother about you."

"I'm going to miss you, Benny," I said. "I think you'll be a famous man. But you'll have to get away from these gangsters."

"When Owney Madden gets out of jail, we'll all have jobs. That includes Cody. Cody is gonna box for him."

I shook my finger at him. "You forget about Owney Madden. He's a killer, Benny."

"They all are," he replied. "The cops, the Black Hand, the street-corner guys, the politicians. They're all in on it."

"In on what?" I asked.

"The world. It's a killing field. My family escaped the pogroms. Then the Irish tried to kill them."

"Come here," I said.

"What for?"

"This." I hugged him. His body was warm and smelled of soap. Then I released him and kissed the top of his head.

"Wow," he said, blowing out his breath, his cheeks red as apples. "You're making me feel kind of funny."

"Goodbye, Benny. You'll always be my favorite little boy."

Then I went into our small kitchen and began pulling food items off the shelves so he would not see my eyes. A few minutes later I heard the door close, and I wept out loud. That's a funny way to be, isn't it?

Papa and I rode the night train in a chair to Chicago, then transferred to a Pullman for the rest of our journey. I did not know where his friends went, nor did I want to know. Papa left an unsigned note for Cody, but did not see him again for many years. I think this was to protect Cody from the police, rather than a show of resentment because Cody had run away from home. Under Papa's knife and bullet scars and rowdy ways, he had a gentle heart. Actually we had a fine time on the train. We saw buffalo in Oklahoma and dry lightning in the Arbuckle Mountains and cowboys in chaps watering their cattle in a lake that was bloodred, all of this from the dining car while we spooned down ice cream and strawberries.

I thought I would grieve over the death of Tony Vale, or the way in which he died, but I didn't. We all die sooner or later. Tony Vale chose soon. Plus, I had invited him to the Baptist church down the street from the Grand Theater. You'd think he would have had a little gratitude. Some people's children.

The only person I asked forgiveness from was the colored bartender in the card parlor. So I sent up a prayer that Jesus could pass on to him. It went like this: "I hope I didn't seem mean or curt. I think you are a nice man. Bad things have been done to me, just as they have been done to you. Frankly, I don't know how our Lord puts up with us. I hope you're doing well and that you stay out of bars and other bad places and never return to Mississippi."

It was wonderful to be home. While I was gone Papa had built a new barn with a loft and stalls and a tack room. When our jitney arrived, the first two critters to come out the barn were Lancelot and Traveler, followed by a mess of chickens, a three-legged coon, a tiny shoat that had lost his mommy, and an orange cat as big as a pumpkin. Most human beings are not aware of the complexity of animals. Did you know a horse has two screens in his brain? A horse can meet another horse one time and remember that horse for twenty-five years. A Siamese cat will mourn the death of its owner. Isolate a buffalo and he'll break down a fence to join any kind of herd, even llamas.

I petted and picked up and hugged every critter I could get my hands on. It was a joyous day. The evening sky was ablaze, the tall grass bending in the fields, the smell of rain in the air. I vowed I would lead a better life and let trouble alone. But even as I thought those words, I knew a destiny had already been chosen for me. That destiny was connected to the little girl who had been murdered and buried in the woods north of us, a woods that had now been ground into splinters, its roots plowed up and dried and soaked with kerosene and burned.

As I stood on the porch, before entering the house, I looked to the north and at the darkening of the sky and knew that the kingdom of petroleum held sway over us all. The trenches in Europe, the atrocities in Arabia, and the freighters and passenger ships sinking to the bottom of the Atlantic were about oil. For just a brief moment, I felt a humming through the boards under my feet, as though the earth were alive, its heart pumping, blood coursing through its veins.

I knew my time had come. But come to what? Only God knew. I wasn't just fooling myself either.

Chapter Thirty-Two

At sunrise I looked from my upstairs window, and sure enough saw the elevated top half of Mr. Slick sliding through a blanket of fog that was as thick as cotton. I thought I was dreaming. Or losing my mind. Then I realized he was sitting on top of a Shetland pony. Thank heavens he was all right. I had felt guilty about leaving him in New York, but killing a Mafioso and trying to get out of town while trying to manage Mr. Slick was more than I could handle.

I put on my robe and a hat and my cowboy boots and went outside. "How did you get back, Mr. Slick?"

"I got special ways," he replied. "But I ain't supposed to talk about them."

"Really? Where'd you get the Shetland?"

He squinted as though in deep thought. "Found him wandering around. Thought I'd do a good deed."

"I see. Would you like some breakfast?"

"Yes, ma'am. I'm ready," he said. He slipped down from his horse. It had no saddle, only a bridle. It also had a brand, one used by a rich oil man in the vicinity.

"Are you sure you want to be riding that horse, Mr. Slick?"

A look of great wisdom came into his face. "I might donate it to some poor colored people. Yes, I think that's a good idea, Miss Bessie. Me and you are always on the same track."

I fixed buttermilk biscuits and gravy and eggs and bacon and coffee and put it on the table. I should have given Mr. Slick a shovel.

"Can you stop making all those noises?" I said.

"What noises?"

"And don't talk when you have food in your mouth."

"The food don't care where it's at. So why should people?"

How do you respond to a statement like that?

"I'm happy to see you, Mr. Slick, but I think you're here to tell me something."

"Them Atlas Oil people want to talk to you."

"They can talk to Papa anytime they want."

"They ain't interested in your daddy. They want to talk to you."

"About what?"

"It's what they call a dome. The dome sets on top of a lake of oil way-to-heck-down under the earth."

"I know what an oil dome is, Mr. Slick."

"Them Atlas people think y'all got most of the dome inside your fences. They're wee-weeing in their pants to punch into it before somebody else drains it off."

"The little girl who was murdered in the woods is still out there in a sludge pit," I said. "I don't want to have any truck with people who would violate a little girl's grave."

"How are they gonna find her remains, Miss Bessie?"

"I don't know. That's on them. And I don't want to talk about it anymore, Mr. Slick."

He stared down at his plate, a spoon in one hand, a butter knife in the other. "You sure fix a mean breakfast, Miss Bessie."

Three days later Papa left home. I didn't hold it against him. He had risked his life for me in New York, and in his way he had made up with Cody. He said he was going back to Mexico or Galveston or the Big Bend country. I think in his mind they were all one place—a mystical, geographic escape to a dimension where Creation had not quite cooled. There was something he told me, however, that made me wonder about his state of mind. I even feel embarrassed to mention it now. He said that down in Mexico, in a wasteland that had no name, after he killed several Mexican soldiers outside a brothel run by the woman who owned the House of the Rising Sun in New Orleans, he had found the cup Jesus had used at the Last Supper.

There. I said it. That was Papa. A little eccentric. I guess we all have our way of dealing with this world and the next. But Good Lord, why does everybody in my family have to be crazy?

The next morning I woke in an empty house. The only sound in it was the wind. But I did not become forlorn. Somehow, in a very short time, I felt a change in attitude about the world. I didn't know why. Maybe it was because of what happened in New York City, and the thing I had done to Tony Vale. But I don't think so. I believe coming back to Texas on my own volition set me free. When Papa and I crossed the Red River, I knew I had returned to a special place, one that should not be mocked. My ancestors and people like Jim Bowie and Davy Crockett and Susanna Dickinson and Sam Houston and the Angel of Goliad were not fictitious characters. They were unlikely heroes and heroines, born poor or uneducated or drunken or loose with their morals, yet they wrote their names on the sky and their names are still there.

Perhaps I was no different from any of them. I was tired of other people controlling my life and treating me like a fence post. Is there any law in the Bible or the Constitution that states a child has to accept the will of stupid or corrupt adults? When David was about twelve he slung a rock between Goliath's eyes and chopped off his head for good measure. That was always one of my favorite Biblical stories.

The next day I put on my mother's pink dress, one that touched my feet, and a frilly white blouse and Mama's patent leather shoes, and I have to say, when I looked in the mirror, I saw a right nice-looking girl.

I hitched Traveler to the buggy and went straight to Miz Banks's house. I had not seen her since I returned from New York. She had changed greatly, all for the better. "I'm going to see the people at the Atlas Oil office, Miz Banks," I said. "Would you give me the pleasure of your company?"

"I certainly will, and we'll take my car," she replied. "Provided you call me Ida."

Ida stayed in the car while I went inside the Atlas office. The same obnoxious city marshal in a gray uniform was sitting behind his desk, with one foot in the wastebasket and the other on his desk. His eyes went up and down my body. "He'p you?" he said.

"Probably not, but I suspect your employer can," I said.

"What was that?"

"Tell your superior that Miss Holland accepts his invitation to speak with him."

"My superior?"

At the end of the hallway, I saw a door with frosted glass and a brass plate. "Thank you for your 'he'p,'" I said.

"Come back here," he said.

I heard him trip over the wastebasket behind me. The brass plate under the office door was engraved with cursive rather than block letters. It read, *Mr. Jared Cohen.* I opened it without knocking and walked in. The man behind the desk was slim and of medium height and perhaps thirty years old. He wore a brown suit with a black silk vest and watch fob and a trimmed mustache. He was writing on stationery with a pen. He looked up at me, his eyes flat, never leaving my face. He put down his pen and rose from his chair. "May I help you, ma'am?"

"I'm Bessie Mae Holland," I said. "I understand you wish to speak about the possibility of drilling on our land."

"That is correct," he said. He walked past me and closed the door. "Please have a chair."

"Why is it that you would like to speak to me rather than my father?"

He sat back down behind his desk. "I respect your father, but he's a stubborn man. That's his choice. But I don't think it's a wise one. I thought you might speak to him."

"I don't need to. He has given me power of attorney. You can check with the county clerk if you wish. What is your offer, Mr. Cohen?"

"Right now we're just thinking about a test well. It's a bit premature to——"

"No, you are not thinking about test wells at all. You already know what's down there. It's a lake. I'll ask you again: What is your offer?"

"One-ninth of everything that comes out of the hole."

"No, we will take sixty percent."

"I beg your pardon?"

"But right now percentages are not the issue. Your company disturbed a child's grave. Her remains are close by a sludge pit. If you can find and validate her remains and provide her a decent grave, we will work out the details of your lease. And the word is 'lease,' not 'sale.'"

He touched at his chin and rolled the tips of his fingers on his ink blotter. "Has somebody coached you, young lady?"

"No, I do not go to people for 'coaching.' And please do not refer to me as 'young lady.'"

"I wouldn't dream of it."

"Thank you for your time," I said, and got up from the chair and began to walk out.

"I'll get on it," he said.

"Repeat that, please?"

"I have a friend who's an archaeologist at the university in Austin. I'll put in a request today. If he cannot do the job, I will get someone else. Within a week, I will have the best of the best working for us. You can observe the entire project. I give you my word."

"Then we have the beginnings of a deal, sir."

"The beginnings?"

"Maybe a little more than that," I said.

He smiled. "I've heard about you."

"There's one other concern. A man named Indian Charlie used to work for you. Is he still your employee?"

"His name is Charles Swan. He works security for us."

"He's a rapist and a killer. I want your word that he will never get near our property. If he puts a foot on it, his life will be in jeopardy."

The humor went out of his face. He rubbed his nose and huffed air out of his nostrils. On the back of his hand was a burn scar as thick as a rubber patch. "Agreed," he said.

"Then good day, sir," I said.

I was almost to the door now.

"Miss Holland?" he said.

"Yes?"

"I hope you don't get offended, but you're a very unusual young lady. It's a pleasure to know you."

Mr. Cohen kept his word. Two days later an archaeologist and three engineers and a dozen laborers began draining the sludge pits in what used to be the woods north of our property. However, I did not have much faith in their search. The area was too large, the damage to the subsurface too great, the constant grinding of the machinery and the total disregard for the habitat the worst I had ever seen. What had not been dug up had been burned. What had not been burned had been pushed in mounds and sold to vegetable farmers or the state highway department. Mr. Slick pointed out to the engineers the general area where he said he had seen the bones, then changed his mind two or three times.

Three weeks passed. I think Mr. Cohen spent a fortune on his search. But a fortune to an oil company and a fortune to ordinary people are quite different in substance. Regardless, I stopped thinking about my relationship with the Atlas Oil Company, and spent my time working with Miz Banks, or rather Ida, on the rental library she was building in the old firehouse. Then on a soft, autumnal evening, with the cicadas droning in the trees and the swallows circling our chimney, Mr. Cohen drove up our dirt road and parked in front of the porch and tapped on the door.

I was glad to see him, but I didn't know why.

"How do you do, Mr. Cohen?" I said, opening the door.

He removed his hat. "I'm well," he said. "But I need your help on a couple of matters. I'm afraid they're a bit macabre. Do you mind if I come in?"

Chapter Thirty-Three

He sat down in Papa's chair and looked at the encyclopedias on the bookshelves and the cats roaming through the house, but made no mention of them. I did not offer him anything to eat or drink.

"We found the skeletal remains of a female in her early teens," he said. "They were in soft dirt beneath the lip of a sludge pit. Ironically the leakage created a kind of cocoon, a bit like wet coffee grinds, that protected the bones. The archaeologist believes the child was killed by a blow from a hard object. There was no sign of a coffin or even a shroud, which probably means the remains were not from a formal cemetery, not even a family one."

"How long ago did she die?" I asked.

"Several decades."

"There's no clothing, no rings or bracelets or religious medals?"

"Nothing."

"So this could be an Indian grave?"

"That's possible."

"Then maybe this is all for naught," I said.

"Except for one thing. About four hundred yards away our engineers found the skeletons of two adult males. Their burial was not conventional. They looked like they were piled together. Their clothing and their boots had rotted on their bodies."

"The archaeologist believes the men went into the ground about the same time the little girl did?" I said.

"Yes."

"But that doesn't mean they were her killers?"

"No, it does not. However, this is the macabre element I mentioned. The girls' killers were hanged from a tree, correct? At least that's the legend?"

"Yes," I said. I had not told Mr. Cohen about the film footage Mr. Slick had shown me in Miz Banks's house.

"These men did not strangle to death," he said. "I always assumed that occurs in most lynchings."

"The father of the little girl was a preacher and put all his weight on their bodies and snapped their necks," I said.

His face went blank. "How did you know that?" he asked.

"The preacher wanted to put them out of their misery."

"That doesn't answer my question."

"I saw it."

"Did I hear you correctly?"

"Yes, you did."

His eyes crawled around the walls. "Could I have a glass of water, please. Maybe lemonade. I don't drink."

I still had coffee on the stove. I poured him a cup, my hands unsteady. I was about to give up a secret about myself. I guess you have done that, too. It's like standing on the edge of a cliff. You can burn the written word, but not the spoken one. Don't let anyone tell you different.

I went back in the living room and handed him the cup and saucer. "A friend had footage on a movie reel that showed the lynching of the two men. I watched them die."

"I'm having a hard time with this, Miss Holland."

"That's understandable. The images are still flickering inside my head. I dream about them at night. It's not pleasant."

He started to speak, but I raised my hand. "That little girl lives in me and I live in her," I said. "I don't care if anyone believes me or not. I know what I saw. I also know that Ida Banks was raped by Indian Charlie. I know that because I saw it happen. But almost everyone else in this community has chosen not to believe what was done to her. Are these people truthful? No, they're not. They're aiding a conspiracy of the worst kind. I don't lie. I saw what I saw."

"I think you have great wisdom."

"No, I don't," I said. "I have no wisdom at all. That's why I don't try to impose my way on others. And that's why I don't tell others what I see or don't see. I don't care what they think."

"You saw Mr. Swan, or Indian Charlie, attack your friend?"

"Yes, and I saw him burn down our barn as well."

"Nobody told me this, Miss Holland. But I've only been with Atlas for one year. I'm a geologist more than an administrator. That said, I'm going to investigate this man Swan. You know much about airplanes?"

"No."

"I'm an aviator." He lifted up the back of his left hand; the scar tissue on it looked like splattered cake batter. "I joined the Royal Flying Corps and five days later went down in flames on the Marne. I was dropping leaflets the Germans scooped up for sanitary purposes. Would you like to take a spin?"

"In an airplane?"

"I assume you've already driven around in automobiles."

"Maybe another time."

The issue was not airplanes. Mama always said business and friendship guaranteed suspicion and long nights with no sleep. Her example was the McCoys and the Hatfields. They killed one another over a pig that wandered into the other's cornfield. Also, one of them had the name Alafair.

But I was lonely at the house. It filled with the wind and reminded me over and over that I had no family and few friends. Ida Banks and I ate Mexican dinners in town, but that did not make us part of the community. The other problem was Ida. When she was tired, a shadow would creep into her face and I would have to wiggle the top of her hand to get her attention. Sometimes I wondered if I had overestimated her recovery or if she was slipping back into madness.

Two days after Mr. Cohen's visit to my house, I called his office and accepted his invitation. On the way to the airstrip, he told me more about himself, but in a humble way. In reality he talked more about the interesting people he knew and the historical events he had witnessed rather than about himself. He left Nova Scotia when he was twenty-two, and in 1908 drilled the first oil well in the Mideast, in the heart of Persia. From that day on, he said, England would be an oil empire. He also said to never make an enemy of an Arab. Because of the Arab's desert environment and the endless, cloudless sky above his head, he believes he has already been subsumed by God and consequently has no fear. He said a friend of his, a linguist named T. E. Lawrence, told him that.

We had to step on the wing of his biplane to get into the cockpit, which frightened me dearly, because I was sure the wing would break off. But it didn't, and we raced down the pasture, scattering jackrabbits in the sage, then lifted above the hangar and its red wind sock into the sky, my stomach dropping five hundred feet straight down.

Within minutes we were over the Alamo. It was a stunning experience. From the air you could reconstruct the stucco walls and roofless chapel and barracks and the water well and the 188 men and boys who held out for thirteen days against four thousand Mexican soldiers. You could also see the San Antonio River and the long, grassy plain that sloped back to Mexico, and the trenches dug by Santa Ana and the artillery pieces he fired intermittently so the Texans could not sleep, and the gully through which twenty volunteers from Gonzales worked their way in the dark so they could enter the walls and be with their friends, knowing they would never leave.

Mr. Cohen made a circle and went low over the roof of the chapel. I could see the people on the plaza looking up at us, their faces reflecting the light like tiny mirrors. I tried to wave at them, with a scarf in my hand, as though we were all friends, all on the same journey. Then I yelled, and felt stupid for my efforts.

In the next few days I talked business with Mr. Cohen. I liked him. He was a gentleman. From what he said, I guessed he was a bachelor or perhaps a widower, the kind who lets his deeds define himself. He did not misbehave, nor did he use coarse language. Except for his Canadian accent, I would have taken him for Southern gentility. I introduced him to Ida Banks, and she invited him to her rental library. In turn, he gave her fifty dollars to help with her inventory, and the name of a bibliophile friend of his in Houston's River Oaks, which at the time was becoming the richest neighborhood in the world. That is not an exaggeration.

In the meantime, he fired Indian Charlie and brought a drill rig and a crew to our property. They went to work immediately, and continued to work fourteen hours a day, and sometimes longer than that. The animals and poultry fled into the pasture, then one by one drifted back to the barn and watched the drill engine clanking, then gave up all interest. During this period Mr. Cohen came to the property three times a day. He could not be accused of lollygagging.

Two weeks later Bertha Lafleur, the madam of what Cody called "a straddle house," was at my door. The smell of money can work wonders on people.

I didn't ask her in. In fact, I latched the door and talked through the screen. Her two gunsels were standing by her car, a huge black one with hand-crank windows and rolled leather and a hand-cranked police siren on the driver's door. Notice I called them gunsels and not gunmen. Because that's what they are called in the North. And I wasn't afraid of them. Tony Vale's gunsels ended up with either a venereal disease of the brain or a bullet in the head and a shovel full of dirt in the face.

"Papa is down in Old Mexico," I said to her. "Or along the Gulf Coast someplace."

She looked over her shoulder at the drilling rig. It was late evening, and the stanchions were metal and silhouetted against a molten sun, the derrick men gone for the day. "I can't believe you actually talked your father into letting the oil industry on his land."

"He didn't. I did."

"*You* did?"

"He gave me power of attorney. Why are you here, Miss Lafleur?"

"May I come in?"

"No," I replied.

"I am having considerable trouble with Indian Charlie. He blames me for money he lost in his drug dealings. We have talked about this in the past. I tried to help your father, and instead I ended up with a debt to a man who branded my chest."

"That's none of my concern, so please leave," I said.

Her eyelids were fluttering. "Oh, that's just wonderful. Now Indian Charlie has lost his job, evidently thanks to you, but none of this is your concern?"

"Indian Charlie lost his job because he's a psychopath," I said. "Maybe he can work as a doorman at your brothel."

"You little brat. How would you like a good spanking?"

"I heard madams such as yourself do that sort of thing in brothels. Is that true?"

"Open this door," she said.

"Certainly. Just a moment."

I went into the kitchen and came back with a broom, then flipped the latch off the screen and went out on the porch and smacked Bertha Lafleur right across the fanny. Her mouth dropped open. "Fletcher!" she yelled.

Fletcher was the bodyguard who wore a derby hat and a German pistol in a shoulder holster, and had a face like a smoked ham. I jabbed the broom straws right in his snout.

"Wrong fella you picked on," he said.

"So what's to lose?" I replied, and belted him across the side of the head, knocking his derby hat in the flowerbed.

It was a brave thing for a young girl to do, I know. But I was in for a heap of trouble. Then I saw Mr. Cohen's sports car coming up the road, a rooster tail of dust behind him, a pair of goggles on his face and a smart golfing cap on his head. *Thank you, Lord*, I said silently.

"You contact your father immediately, Miss Sassy Pants," Bertha Lafleur said. "He owes me, and he knows it."

"What Papa *knows* is he saved you from being killed by Indian Charlie on the border years ago," I said.

She got in the back seat of her car, and got her two gunsels in the front, and the three of them motored past Mr. Cohen, looking straight ahead, like black cutouts against the sun, as though Mr. Cohen were not there.

I knew they would be back. But I didn't care. As Mama used to say, if you're afraid of risk, stay out of the game. Then see how you enjoy life in the bleachers with the other whiners.

Mr. Cohen got out of his sports car and pulled off his goggles with his thumb. "Who was that bunch?" he asked.

"A woman named Bertha Lafleur and her two underlings. She owns a brothel in San Antonio."

His eyes went sideways, then back at me. He had a half grin on his face. "They got lost and were asking for directions?"

"No, they're mixed up with Indian Charlie and narcotics."

"Does this have something to do with our drilling rig?"

"Yes, Bertha Lafleur would like to own it."

"What did you say to them?"

"Not much. I swatted Miss Lafleur across the rump with a broom and poked it up her bodyguard's nose for good measure."

"That's all?"

"No, I also slapped him upside the head with it."

"You hit a brothel owner and a gangster with a broom, and they just took it?"

"Not exactly. The gangster had a Mauser pistol in a shoulder holster. Had you not come along, I would have been in for it."

"There's no one in the house?" he said.

"No."

"This is wrong," he said. "I need to straighten this out."

"You've helped me just fine, Mr. Cohen. But I can take care of myself now."

"I thought you might like some ice cream. I also need to talk business with you."

"I'm awful tired, sir. Can we just sit on the glider?"

"I would love to," he replied. He did not put his cap back on, and waited for me to sit down first, then sat at an angle, his back straight, three feet from me.

"Before you talk finances, tell me when the little girl's bones will be buried in a proper cemetery," I said.

A stray bird dog named Major had just walked up on the porch and plunked his seat by my foot, his tail swishing.

"Next week," Mr. Cohen said. "But I must ask you something. You have never used the little girl's name. Why would you not speak her name?"

"Because she's me," I replied.

Major cocked his head at me, his tail dead still.

Chapter Thirty-Four

There was pity in Mr. Cohen's eyes. "Please don't look at me like that, sir," I said.

"I think you're a brave young woman, Bessie. But there are times when we shouldn't give way to our imaginings."

"The little girl is me because I'm intended to live the life that was stolen from her. The lives of many people are joined with the dead. I'm not the only one."

"How do you know all this?" he asked.

"A voice in my head."

The sun had become a lake of fire cupped inside a low cloud on the horizon. He rubbed on top of the scar tissue on his left hand. "I shot down two planes in my excursions over the Marne. We called it 'burning their kites.' Then I got my own kite burned. I think the fellows I killed have already stood by my bedside and will probably be with me a long time. They were fellows my age, and probably had living parents and siblings and sweethearts, but with a burst of my Vickers, I soaked their lives with gloom and loss. So I accept what you say, Bessie. You're truly a good young woman, and don't be lecturing me on what I should and should not call you."

I admit his words made me a bit breathless and that I experienced an emotional moment that I could not define, as though I were mixing up my feelings for my father with Mr. Cohen and the romantic stories of Sir Walter Scott. I'm sure my face was flushed.

"I would like to go for that ice cream," I said.

"That's a very good idea," he replied. "But if you don't mind, there's a special place I would like to take you."

He drove me to a geological fault called the Devil's Backbone, out in the Hill Country in a place that looks for miles and miles like the earth has collapsed and dwindled into the sunset. He got out of the car, opened the door, and escorted me inside a tavern. "Do you know why I brought you to the Backbone?"

"I'd hate to ask," I replied.

He pointed through the glass at the endlessness of the landscape. "I believe we're already in infinity. I believe the Indians knew that. Their shamans all say there are no fences on the Ghost Trail. That's why they don't understand ownership. You cannot own a handful of atoms."

The men at the bar could hear him. They looked at him, then turned away, but in a polite fashion, their faces vacant.

"I don't understand why you're telling me this," I said.

"I believe we often use geology for the wrong purposes," he said. "I do my best, but I did the same with a Vickers machine gun and learned you can't turn off the lights of your conscience in the darkness or your sleep."

Then Mr. Cohen stopped and ordered ice cream with cinnamon on it for both of us before he went on.

"I went to our headquarters in Houston and talked for two days with some gentlemen who were not in agreement with me regarding your property. Finally I got half of what I wanted. Now I need your blessing."

"On what?" I said.

"There will be no sixty percent given to the owner, which is you. However, you will receive forty-nine percent. Believe me,

Bessie, this can make you and your father rich people. Now here's the rest of it. We think there's a long ridge under your land, one that is filled with oil and natural gas but is serpentine in its contours and consequently unpredictable in terms of potential. Possibly you're sitting on a lake. But there is also a possibility the ridge can thin out like a centipede and, instead of punching through a huge pay sand, we'll end up with a string of dusters and a lot of debt."

"What does all that mean?"

"If we hit a lake, the gentlemen in Houston will want to carpet your ranch with drill rigs, literally, their stanchions crisscrossing each other."

"That doesn't sound good," I said.

"I was afraid you would say that."

"I also think it's dumb."

"Pardon?" he said.

"What happens when you punch holes all over the gas dome?"

"The same thing that happens if you drive spikes all over a dirigible," he said.

"The land caves in?" I said.

"Like cardboard."

"Why not space out the rigs and get my neighbors to do the same?"

"Greed doesn't work that way, Bessie."

"Papa and I will take less of a percentage and divide it up with our neighbors. No wells closer to each other than one hundred and fifty feet. Our cattle can graze and the oil can be pumped out in a pipeline and put in storage tanks somewhere else."

He sat back in his chair and placed his spoon in his saucer.

"What's wrong?" I said.

"Did you ever have an IQ test?"

"Ida Banks had me take one."

"What were the results?"

"The examiner said my intelligence was immeasurable. That's not true, though. The issue is vocabulary. Why?"

"Nothing," he said, and began eating his ice cream again. "Other than I think the wrong people are running the planet."

It was dark when we got back to the house. I turned on the living room lights and we sat on the porch in the cooling of the day. Again, I was having thoughts I shouldn't. I kept opening and closing my hands, and tucking my thumbs under my fingers. I knew I wanted to confess something to him, but told myself I didn't know what it was.

"Are you all right, Bessie?"

"I'm not sure."

"Is it something I did or said?"

"No."

"Do you want to tell me what it is?"

"I don't want to burden you, sir."

"You could never do that to me, Bessie. And you don't have to address me as 'sir' or 'mister.'"

"I shot and killed a man. He raped me and I killed him. He was in the Mafia. This was not long ago."

He gazed at the barn and the blades of the windmill ginning and the animals drinking from the tank in the moonlight. "Where did this happen?"

"In New York."

"Does your father know about this?"

"Leave my father out of it."

He nodded, then propped his hands on his knees. "Do you see anyone who condemns you?"

"What do you mean?"

"Just what I said. The world does not condemn you, and neither do I. That means you go your own way and put this behind you forever. You're a fine person, and don't you forget it."

My face was on fire, my eyes wet, a tic in both hands.

"When will your father be home?" he said.

"I don't know." For just a moment I thought he was making an advance. My heart sank like a rock.

"I want to put a couple of guards on your property," he said. "Don't argue about this. I have the right to put guards on the rig, if nothing else. Okay?"

"I guess," I replied, my voice a whisper.

"The earth is a grand place, Bessie. Don't let evil men spoil it for you. The bastards aren't worth the parings of your fingernails."

Then he picked up my hand and kissed it and got in his sports car and drove through the gate and over the cattle guard, his red taillights winking on a knoll.

Two days later Papa returned smelling like a barn. He had bought a bunch of sheep in Mexico and ridden home with them in the boxcar. The first thing he saw on arrival was the drilling rig. I thought he would have a fit. But he surprised me.

"How in the hell did you do all this?" he said, standing on the porch, his duffle bag on the steps, a Mexican saddle he bought with the sheep straddled on the banister.

"I told Mr. Cohen you had given me power of attorney, so his lawyers drew up the papers and I signed them."

"You got to be eighteen to get a power of attorney, don't you?" he said.

"The county clerk didn't care, the notary didn't care, I didn't care, you didn't care, and Atlas didn't care."

"This Cohen fella isn't a rounder?"

"No, but I don't know how long he's going to be in oil business," I said.

"Like your mama used to say, the best judges of people are children and dogs. You have anything to eat?"

"You need to take a bath, Papa."

"I'm fixing to."

"Not in the house. Either in the tank or the hog trough," I said. "Either will be an improvement."

"You surely know how to say it, daughter."

It was wonderful having Papa home again. He was fascinated with the workings of the drill, and walked down in the morning with a big tin cup of coffee and hot milk for himself and a bucketful for the drill crew. Supposedly some Wobblies, that's the Industrial Workers of the World, were trying to unionize the Texas oil fields, and I thought Papa and I might have a conflict with the Atlas office in Houston, but Mr. Cohen read our minds and said, "If you're willing to take a little less, we'll pay your crew union scale."

"What about the other crews?" Papa said.

"That's their business," Mr. Cohen said.

I began to realize that Papa and Mr. Cohen had much in common. They didn't lie; they didn't compromise their principles and they were not afraid. Even though one was much larger than the other, they had the same posture—with their shoulders pinned back and their chins up. But it was the way they wore their confidence that made me feel good. When trouble was brewing, they said nothing, as though it were not worth talking about. Few men know how important that is to a young girl.

We were getting down in the fall now, and on a couple of mornings the grass was stiff with frost and the stock tank filmed with ice. I thought that Bertha Lafleur and Indian Charlie might be out of our lives, but I should have known better. The trouble came in a way I never thought possible. And it involved Ida Banks, and a secret part of her life I would have never imagined, and believe it or not, the reemergence of Benny Siegel and his love of movies.

Chapter Thirty-Five

Evidently Benny had gotten my address from Cody. I was happy that Cody gave it to him, because I still had hope that Benny would find the sunny side of the street and not be shut away at Sing Sing, a place renowned for its use of the cat-o'-nine-tails and an electric chair that delivered pain and sorrow that could only be compared with the suffering of the damned.

I couldn't wait to read his letter, and took it from the mailbox on the road and tore it open with my thumb and unfolded the letter inside. His stationery was light purple and had roses in the corners and an angel at the top of the page. I suspected Benny had stolen it, but I didn't care. I was just happy to hear from him. He had written his words in blue ink with a fountain pen. His penmanship was lovely, and I suspected he had labored long in his letter.

Dear Bessie, we miss you a lot. I wish you had not left us, because other than our families we know no adults such as yourself. Cody is doing well with his night-school classes and his boxing at the gym. Jack Dempsey visited the gym and said Cody had the stuff of a champion. I think that's what it's all about in America. That's going to be my goal. You have to be somebody. It doesn't matter what.

There are some great westerns playing at the theaters. I saw "Knight of the Range" at the matinee yesterday. Harry Carrey starred and William Canfield played a guy named Gentleman Dick. This afternoon I saw "Stampede in the Night" with Hoot Gibson. It was really good, too. That's when I had an idea. Why are we up here trying to get into the fruit cart business when we can make cowboy pictures? Your family is the real thing, right? Your father was a rodeo cowboy with Tom Mix, right? You're smart, Bessie. So is Meyer. We could really do something.

The westerns all get made in California. What did California have to do with herding cows from Texas to Kansas? You told me yourself Oklahoma was a huge toilet for millions of longhorns or whatever. Why not make movies where they happened? Texas is probably even a bigger toilet than Oklahoma. Why not use it?

Don't forget me, little Bessie. I call you "little" because you're always going to be like us. We'll never grow up. Why grow up when you can make motion pictures?

Meyer and Frankie say hello.

Your friend forever,
Benny

I couldn't wait to share his letter. It was innocent and joyous and had ideas no one else had thought about. That was Benny, always thinking, with that blue glow in his eyes. And he was right. Dallas and Houston and Tulsa were saturated with money, and if it wasn't there yet, it was coming. Spindletop was just down the road. Improbable people and improbable ideas were making fortunes. The drill bit on our rig was invented by a man named Hughes in Houston. The rotaries didn't punch their way through the dome; instead, they were inset with diamonds and angled at each other so they could grind stone into grit. The richest wildcatter in the state started out as a waterboy who worked for fifty cents a day. Prostitutes, gamblers, and drunkards had found a new kind of Valhalla. And now a street kid in a New York slum was talking about bringing the film industry to Texas.

Oh, I know, it was just a dream. But it's the dreamers who lead us away from ourselves, and it's also they who rise with the sun and let go of yesterday's failures and sorrow. At least that's how I like to think about it.

I hitched up Traveler and went straight to Ida Banks's house. I never thought about calling in advance. That was not the way she and I did things. We had an age difference, but our souls and our experience in the world were the same. We would always be outsiders, reticent, distrustful of crowds, and out of step.

Traveler trotted me up to her front door, and I dropped his tether weight on the ground and twisted the bell under her mailbox. There was no answer. I twisted the bell again. No response. Her Model T was in the shed, and the windows in the house were open, the curtains blowing inside. I turned the doorknob slightly to see if it was locked. It wasn't. I hit the door with my fist, then walked around back, rattling the door in the jamb. Her wash was flapping on the clothesline. I touched my hand to one of her shirts. It was dry. That was unusual. Ida thought it unseemly to leave her wardrobe and undergarments for the public to see.

I went back on the porch and opened the door and leaned inside. "Ida?" I called. "It's Bessie! Are you okay?"

The wind was blowing through the house, the joists creaking in the ceiling. "Ida! You're scaring me!"

Then she walked out of her back bedroom, wearing pressed blue jeans and a pink shirt with a white collar, her hair brushed, her face made up. "I didn't know you were coming," she said.

"You're usually here this time of day. I hope I didn't interrupt you with something. I can come back."

"What is it you want, Bessie?"

Her tone was hurtful. I couldn't believe the way she was acting.

"I received a letter from one of the little boys I knew in the Lower East Side," I said. "He has ideas about making films with us. I thought you might be interested."

I said "us" to show her what was mine was also hers.

"I have some obligations to take care of, Bessie. You should have called."

"Then please take care of your obligations."

"You have to forgive me. I'm just a little agitated."

"Yes, that's a very good description of yourself," I said. "I hope you're pleased with it."

"You have to leave, Bessie. I'll explain later."

"There's no need. Traveler and I will be on our way."

"You don't know everything about me, so don't be so huffy," she said.

"I wouldn't be huffy for the world."

I walked down the hallway and through the living room and out on the porch. Guess who had just driven herself up the dirt road and was now driving herself into the yard. Yes, you guessed it, Bertha Lafleur, who was getting out from behind the steering wheel while putting lipstick on her nasty mouth. Her felt hat was of the new style, one with the angularity of a barber's razor, her skirt the color of iron and wrapped around her legs as tightly as tape. Her bodyguards were nowhere in sight.

"Starting to figure it out, are you?" she said.

"Figure out what?" I said, my voice weak.

Her eyes seemed filled with gloat. She looked down the road, then back at me. "Wake up, girl. None of us choose the world we're born in. Get that stupid expression off your face."

"You're a leech," I said. "You couldn't destroy my father, so you've gone after Ida."

"Get the fuck out of my way," she replied.

She plowed past me and went into the house. I was numb, my eyes swimming. Traveler was nickering. I scratched his ears and stared at nothing. I don't know how long I stood there. I really don't. Because I had never done what I was about to. Not even in the card room in New York. Both Ida's and Bertha Lafleur's faces looked as round and white as pie dough in a pan when they saw me coming.

Chapter Thirty-Six

Cane or no cane, I struck Bertha Lafleur in the face with my fist and knocked her over a chair on the floor in the hallway, and before she could get up I got on one knee and rained my fists on her face as hard and as long as I could. I heard Ida screaming behind me and felt her pulling at my shoulders, but I didn't care what Ida did or said, I was going to tear Bertha Lafleur apart.

When my mother died, I wanted to die. I think I would have done exactly that, take my own life, if I had not feared for my soul and had not substituted Ida Banks and Aint Minnie for Mama. Now what I considered a serpent had taken Ida from me. But a serpent was a poor symbol for the likes of women such as Bertha Lafleur. She turned poverty-stricken young women into carriers of sperm for the lowest lowlifes in Texas; she provided the heroin for the veins and the souls of the weak and the downtrodden and the desperate, then corrupted the police and the court and the politicians while living in a Victorian mansion among greenery that could have decorated Eden.

I wanted to kill her worse than I did Tony Vale. I had never felt rage like this, nor had I ever lost physical control of the murderous energies that obviously lived in my viscera and my unconscious and perhaps my soul.

I think Ida hit me with an object, but I knew not what and didn't care. I pinned Bertha Lafleur to the floor with my knees and tore open her blouse and her undergarments, and when she tried to fight back, I broke her lip on her teeth. Then I saw the brand marks on her breast, and other scars as well, the kind that barbed wire leaves, and hot cigars and cigarettes, and maybe a fishhook through a nipple.

I am sorry for the images I have described here, but this woman's body was tortured for years, probably as a child, certainly as a convict, and as a whore or just as a dance girl a drunken cowboy disapproved of.

Suddenly I heard the words Mr. Cohen had said to me after I told him I had shot Tony Vale to death: *The world does not condemn you, and neither do I.*

I began to cry, then to weep uncontrollably, my tears falling on Bertha Lafleur's breast and face. I wiped her hair out of her eyes and tried to cover her breasts with her torn blouse. I got to my feet and ran into the kitchen and wet a towel and came into the hallway and pushed Ida aside and got on my knees and kissed Bertha Lafleur's face and cleaned the blood out of her eyes and tried to hug her against my chest.

She could barely open her mouth. One of her eyes was sealed shut. Her cheeks were bloodless. "Don't fret, child," she whispered. "We're a tough bunch."

I wanted to take her to a physician, but she refused. Ida and I put her in the bathtub and, at her demand, wrapped her in a sheet. But I bathed her myself, all of her, and washed her hair and dried it and took off my own shirt and dressed her with it.

"If you wish to have me arrested, I will not deny any of the charges," I said.

"You're an innocent girl, Bessie," she said. "Believe it or not, policemen slouching around on my furniture are not good for my business."

"What can I do to make this up?"

"One, you can call me Bertha. Two, I could use some oatmeal and some hot tea."

"I have to ask you something else," I said.

"Yes?"

"About the narcotics. The tar or whatever they call it. It costs the users their souls."

"Yes, most of them. I used it on the prison farm. I also used it on the line. You know what the line is, don't you?"

"You mean the 'cribs'?" I said.

"Yes, indeed. Serving men who couldn't wait to tear up a fourteen-year-old girl."

"I want you to know how sorry I am, Bertha."

"I have a question for you," she said. "When you were hitting me, something happened inside you. What was it?"

"I killed a man."

"What?"

"In New York. As dead as hell. I told somebody about what I did and haven't worried about it since. He's a good man. He said I'm un-judged and un-condemned, and that I should go about my way. I believed him and still do."

She placed her hand on my forearm. "Don't say any more."

"That's what he was saying, Miss Bertha. Or just about."

She did not understand what I was saying. I put her hand in mine. "I have a friend in New York, a little boy named Benny Siegel. He's in love with the movies. He'd like to start up a production company here."

"A little boy?"

"He said you don't have to grow up if you can make movies."

Her eyes went sideways. "Does your father know you're talking about things like this?"

I didn't get home until late. I felt like I had aged twenty years. So did Traveler. I brushed him and kissed his nose and scratched his ears, as I always did with him and Lancelot when I put them out, then I went to say good night to the fellas on the rig, who were about to "go to the house." That's what they said when they shut down the rig: "We're goin' to the house!"

They were nice fellas, too. I knew they used profanity, but they didn't use it in front of me. They said "no, ma'am" and "yes, ma'am," and removed their hats when they came up to the house. That's the funny thing about Southerners, and particularly Texans: they have the dirtiest minds on the planet but the best manners. Anyway, I brought them a quart of lemonade and some tin cups and an angel food birthday cake I baked for the driller, whose name was Skeeter. There was no mystery about the origins of his name. The poor man's face reminded me immediately of an insect. Actually, not just his face; everything about him. He was grinning when I put the cake in his hands, a big Mexican straw hat shadowing his features. But I had the feeling he was grinning about something other than cake.

"You smell them rotten eggs, Miss Bessie?" he said.

The evening breeze was blowing across the drill floor into my face. "I guess you could call it that," I said.

"It ain't rotten eggs. It's gas."

I breathed the wind again. If there was an odor in it, I couldn't tell. Skeeter had been on the job since seven in the morning and needed to take a couple of dips in the cattle vat. In other words, he smelled worse than the drill. "I have hay fever," I said.

"See that big pipe running out of the wellhead? When you see it start sweating, run for the house and get on the phone. I'll be a-waiting."

"I surely will, Mr. Skeeter."

"Miss Bessie, do you know you are the only person in the world who has ever called me 'Mister' Skeeter?"

"You're a very nice gentleman, Mr. Skeeter."

"Thanks for the cake," he said. "Let's go to the house, boys!"

* * *

It happened in the middle of the night. I thought I was having a dream. I felt a vibration through the house, and heard a tinkling of pots and pans in the kitchen and a rattling of the windows. I got out of bed and put on my slippers and looked out the window at a cold moon over the pastures and the barn and the windmill and the oil rig. Most of our cows were bunched in a draw, the way cattle do when a storm is coming.

The tinkling and rattling stopped, and the interior of the house was quiet again. Papa never woke up. I was glad he didn't. I had not told him what I did to Bertha Lafleur. I knew he would not take me to task, but I did not want him to know the level of anger his daughter carried inside her, because most of it originated with him and his desertion of his family, which I still feel is the worst sin a man can commit.

Then the whole house shook, like it was jerked off its foundation. I ran down the stairs and out into the yard. Papa was behind me, turning on all the lights. The stanchions of the rig were trembling, a steel bolt popping here and there, a spar actually twisting, a stink like sulfur rising out of the hole.

"Good God, it's fixing to blow!" Papa yelled.

It blew, all right. About seventy feet and for three or four minutes. The flume even had some oil in it. But most of it was saltwater, enough to soak both of us and make us look like fools.

The flume wilted back into the hole and gurgled on the rig floor, then disappeared, leaving nothing but a black, greasy smear. Papa put his arm across my shoulders and wiped my hair out of my eyes. "It's just not meant to be, Bessie. We got along fine without the oil business, and we'll get along without it now."

"Why does God let you think one thing while He lets something else happen?" I said.

"Did you know the skin is off your knuckles?" he asked. "What the hell is going on, daughter?"

"Nothing," I said. "I've just been wanting too much."

"How about I fry some pork chops and eggs? Look at the horizon. The sun is rising and another generation is fixing to pass away. Let's be happy with what we have."

I didn't argue with him. We walked back toward the house, the air cool and fresh and smelling of salt and an odor like seaweed full of shellfish that has died on the beach.

Then the ground shook as though an invisible fist had struck it; the derrick began to shake again and an eruption broke loose and crashed upward with the weight of a wrecking ball in reverse and tore all the boards from the drill floor, followed by a gusher of pure, black oil that must have gone one hundred feet in the air, the derrick disintegrating, chains and spars clanging, the red sun breaking across the fields, like a magical light rippling from one horizon to the other. Within seconds Papa and I were drenched in oil, our eyes peeking out of shiny black masks.

"Oh, Lord God Almighty!" Papa said, twirling in a circle, his arms spread wide. "The eyes of Texas are upon you, daughter! Praise the Lord! I think Canaan land just hit us in the face!"

Chapter Thirty-Seven

In the drilling business there are two kinds of oil wells, gushers and dusters. The average is nine dusters for every gusher. During the next eighteen months we punched six gushers in a row. When I was born, farmland such as ours sold for ten dollars an acre. Now you couldn't buy it, at least not with the mineral rights. The irony was our neighbors hated our guts because we forced them to limit the number of wells they could drill on their property. Papa talked to them until he wrote off his efforts as "not worth diddly-squat on a rock, primarily because our neighbors are the stupidest people on earth."

Papa gave an interview to the local newspaper, ran for city council, and got three votes.

But our politics and financial concerns were small. It was 1918 now, and the Zimmermann telegram had been intercepted and passed on to us by the British, leaving no doubt that Germany was encouraging Mexico to invade Texas. I did not think our neighbors were the dumbest people on earth. I thought the Germans were. Zimmermann even made a speech confirming this was their handiwork. Is it any wonder they elected Hitler?

Bad things were done to the German immigrants in New Braunfels and Fredericksburg and other places in the Texas Hill Country. These were splendid farmers and carpenters and worked from cain't-see to cain't-see and kept their streets and yards the cleanest in the state. The vigilantes who terrorized them were mostly white trash looking for a cause. I think the white trash have proved themselves the one group on earth who should be rounded up and put on an ice floe to the Aleutian Islands.

Soldiers were all over the little towns. The trains were full of them, the windows down in the heat, all of them wearing campaign hats and long-sleeve khaki shirts, waving at the girls as they went through the station. I heard Bertha Lafleur's bordello had a waiting line night and day, which I did not like and considered disgusting, even though I now treated her as a friend and tried to make up for the beating I gave her. Two Baptist friends told me they saw her in their churches, dressed in a widow's veil and sitting on the mourner's bench. I asked her if that was true, but she did not have much to say on the subject. Well, that's not exactly accurate. What she said was "Mind your own damn business, Bessie."

Jubal Fowler volunteered for the army and went to France. His father hosted a going-away tribute in the Green Lantern Saloon. I was not invited. I hope everyone had a grand time. Four months later, Jubal came home. Or part of him came home. The rest of his mind was still in a trench. He was locked in jail twice, manacled with his hands behind his back in a solitary cell, and hit on his knees and on his bare feet with a baton. Our sheriff was not interested in war stories.

On a Friday evening in late August, I saw him sitting at a stone table under a Chinaberry tree in front of the courthouse. He was drinking from a bottle of wine wrapped in a paper bag. He seemed to see right through me when I walked by.

"You're not going to say hello, Jubal?" I said.

"Sure I am, Bessie," he replied. "I thought you didn't want to say hello to me."

I sat down at the stone table. It was cold and hard, even though the temperature was in the seventies. His hair was still as stiff as straw.

"I tried to visit you at the jail, but the sheriff wouldn't allow me in," I said.

"Yeah, I cain't say I'm proud of myself," he said.

I touched the bottom of the paper bag. "You have to take care of yourself, Jubal."

"I hear you're starting a movie company," he said.

"I'm trying to."

"With Bertha Lafleur?" he said.

"Who told you that?"

"My uncle's a cop. He works for her."

"Your uncle has his head up his butt," I said.

"When did you start talking like that?"

"Just now."

The cicadas were singing in the trees, and the sky was yellow and purple and red, like rain falling on a fire.

"I got to tell you something," he said. "You probably know what it is, but it's plumb eating me up. I was with Indian Charlie and them others when they did what they did to you and Miz Banks."

"But you saved me, Jubal. So don't forget that."

"No, it was them Jewish cowboys at the leper colony who saved y'all. I didn't have nothing to do with it."

"I don't think Miz Banks holds it against you, Jubal. So stop beating up on yourself."

He took a drink out of the bottle. "Indian Charlie is a son of a bitch."

"I've gotten that impression."

"He thinks you got him fired from Atlas."

"I'm going to the movies tonight," I said. "Want to come?"

"Listen to me, Bessie. Indian Charlie ain't the same Indian Charlie your father knew. He's much worse. He's smarted-up and is hurting people real bad and getting away with it."

"I am not interested in Indian Charlie. Do you want to go to the movie theater or not?"

"The manager don't allow me in."

"We'll see about that."

"I don't blame him. I smell bad and I start talking to myself when the lights go down."

"Where did you get hurt?"

"Nowhere, except inside my head. It was the artillery. It buried me alive. The funny thing is, the mustard gas went right over me. Everybody else in my trench got blinded or killed."

"Is there any way I can help?"

"You can give me a job."

"We're fixing to punch another hole next week. I can talk to the driller."

He nodded. "I always wanted to be a roughneck."

I may have told Jubal a fib when I said Miz Banks probably didn't hold a grievance against him for not coming forward as a witness against Indian Charlie and the others. In my opinion it would have made no difference. The juries were all male back then. In the eyes of the average male juror, Ida would have been categorized as a sexual degenerate, suffragette acid-thrower, socialist underminer of the Constitution, and a follower of Charles Darwin, which meant atheist. If you believe in what are called "the good old days," you must not have been there.

Actually I was afraid Jubal was going to ask for a job with our production company. We had already made a news film about Pancho Villa. Papa talked Villa into it. Not only that, Villa planned his battles to get the best lighting rather than think about his soldiers. The footage that became known as "Villa's Apple Tree" was shot by Ida Banks's crew. You don't want to know what was hanging from Villa's Apple Tree. They also tried to film George Patton driving into a village with dead Mexican soldiers tied on the fenders of his car.

*　*　*

Jubal said something, though, that bothered me, like a spider running up your sleeve. It was the remark about Indian Charlie smarting-up. I had seen him a couple of times around the Hill Country. He was well-dressed, his hair clipped, his nails manicured. I looked him straight in the face in a restaurant. He tipped his hat and glanced at my feet, a smile on his face, then went right past me, so close I could smell him. I didn't know what the glance at my feet meant, or why he would smile, and it bothered me all day. That's how men like him work. They turn you against yourself.

I had learned a lesson in the Lower East Side of New York. The bodies of the Irish immigrants buried in my tenement building decades ago were still there, in the same way the bodies of slaves lay in our corn and cotton fields. When the plow scattered the teeth of the slave along the row, the farmer looked the other way.

Many times I visited the grave of the little girl who was ravaged and murdered by outlaws, and put candles and flowers around her headstone. I also told her I would live my life as an extension of hers. And every chance I had I would seek justice for people such as herself. Of course, I had told that to Lancelot many times, although I don't know if a discussion with a mule about being a light-bearer would be considered the oath of a temporal knight.

It did not take me long to learn the culture of the oil and gas business. The people at the bottom were thankful for the good jobs they had. They were brave to a fault and were often hurt and sometimes killed. The people at the top did business with baseball bats.

Mr. Cohen was a kind and good man. He also had a classic education and was always gentlemanly in social as well as private occasions; he was also well-known for walking away from a conversation that contained profanity. Lastly, he was honest.

I talked to our driller Skeeter about a job for Jubal. He stuck his hands in his back pockets and began rotating his neck.

"Something wrong?" I said.

"That boy don't have the best history around here, Miss Bessie."

"He fought for his country, Mr. Skeeter. He ought to have a second chance, don't you think?"

"It ain't his past I'm worried about. There's a rumor a bunch called the 'Tarantulas' is about to get active. These are KKK and White Camelia people. It's run by this man who was an Indian killer back in the nineties."

"Indian Charlie?"

"That's him. He ran security at Atlas. Jubal Fowler worked for him. I ain't sure he's completely free of the association."

"Jubal has no association with Indian Charlie, Mr. Skeeter. I give you my word."

"I ain't arguing. Tell the boy it's hit-it-and-git-it and not to be talking like a crazy person, because that's what he does."

"I will certainly tell him that, Mr. Skeeter. Thank you."

"Don't be thanking me, Miss Bessie. I ain't sure I done you a favor."

I didn't forget Benny Siegel. I asked him to come down on the train and told him I would pay for his trip and he could stay at our house and bring his parents if he wished, and eventually we would try our best to make a Western movie. I was proud that Papa and Ida and Ida's friends, all of whom were IWWs, could film Villa and his soldiers and even try to film George Patton driving corpses around, but that was not making a movie.

Making a good movie was hard. Most of the people involved in it were defective. They are some who came to the house or stopped me on the street: cowboys who had been kicked too many times in the head, a door-to-door seller of shoe polish, prostitutes who had been patients at the asylum in Austin, carnival people and circus acrobats, and confidence men of every stripe. A local lady who had been an actress in California said that Hollywood was chosen as the location for the movie studios because it was close to the La Brea Tar

Pits, which is an underworld of pterodactyls and other monsters it's better not to think about.

Benny wrote back and said he was coming, Then I realized he and his family might have expectations I could not fulfill. We were dreamers, but ultimately wishful thinkers and amateurs. I had never met Benny's parents, but Cody said they came from Hungary and worked very hard and often had little food. An oil well is an icon no American disrespects. It should be on our currency. Literary art and movies are esteemed with the respect we give comic books. Our community didn't even give us that. Some people were now calling Ida Banks a Bolshevik, which was the latest enemy our neighbors could think up. I had the feeling South Texas would not treat the Siegel family kindly.

Two days after Jubal went to work on our new rig, the sheriff, Slim Millard, pulled up on our yard and got out and tapped with one knuckle on the door, his face pointed downward, fiddling in his mouth with a kitchen match.

Papa was in town. I opened the door. The sheriff kept sucking on his matchstick. I thought Jubal was in trouble. "What do you want?" I said.

"I got your nigra and her daughter in the back seat," he said. "Tell me what you want to do."

Chapter Thirty-Eight

I walked down to Sheriff Millard's vehicle. It was a Dodge touring car, the same kind Lieutenant George Patton drove in Mexico while killing people. Aint Minnie and Snowball were huddled in back.

"Has this man hurt y'all?" I said.

"Not with his hand," Aint Minnie said. "But with his mouth. In front of all them people in the grocery store."

I could hear the sheriff's boots crunching on the dirt behind me. "Watch it, Minnie."

I turned around. "If you threaten her again, I'll have charges filed against you," I said.

"Have it your way, Miss Holland," he replied. "Go ahead, Minnie. But if you lie, you can go to jail."

"I waited for the white people to get done at the cash register," Aint Minnie said. "I had all my purchases in my tote sack, 'cause colored people ain't allowed to use the baskets. When the last white lady was gone, I started taking my purchases out of the sack and putting them on the counter. Then I got a candy stick for Snowball and dropped my sack on my foot. There wasn't no one standing around, and I was kind of dreaming and I paid Mr. Jack and was goin' out the door when he hollered 'Get yourself back in here, woman!'"

The man who owned the store was Jack Fowler, Jubal's uncle. Aint Minnie wiped at her nose. Snowball got tighter under her mother's arm, as though she were burrowing into a tiny fortress.

"A whole bunch of ladies and children came in. I told Mr. Jack I wasn't doin' nothing but buying my groceries and leaving his store. He went around the counter and picked up my sack, and shook out some string beans on the flo'. I said I was sorry but I had went back for the candy and forgot to hang the tote bag on the pegs for colored people. He called Sheriff Millard and made me and Snowball stand there and wait in front of all them white people. Then Sheriff Millard shoved us in the back of his car and told me to keep my goddamn black mouth shut before I got a pop in the face."

I looked at the sheriff. He was a good eighteen inches taller than I, his striped britches tucked in his boots, his cheeks unshaved, his long body as thin as a whip, his stomach hanging over his belt like a water balloon. "Why are you doing this, Sheriff?" I said. "When did Aint Minnie ever harm anybody?"

"She's your nigra. I took her here instead of jail. Do you stand behind your nigra or not?" He took his matchstick from his teeth and examined it. "I'll tell Mr. Jack everything is okay out here, but we need to make an agreement. I hear your crews are gonna get hot meals. To show goodwill you need to buy your vittles from Mr. Jack's store. This ain't a bribe. It's just business."

"Papa's not here," I said.

"What does that have to do with anything?"

"If he was here, he would take an ax handle to your head."

"Get your hand off my car door," he said.

"I'm taking Aint Minnie and Snowball into my house, Sheriff. If you try to come inside, I'll shoot you and take my chances with the court."

He shook his matchstick at me, like a professor in front of his class. "Ever hear of a man named Tony Vale? I've talked to the New

York City Police Department. I've got you, girl. You sass me again and I'll hang you up to dry."

I felt my stomach flop, my heart seize in my chest. But I was surprised. My fear had gone away.

"Do your worst, Sheriff," I said. "No matter what happens, I'm going to heaven and you're going to hell."

I love being a Baptist.

As I look back over the years, none of the important events, either good or bad, were ever planned. Like lightning hitting the roof or black gold raining down on our heads. They just happened. In our case, the sunny side of the mountain was starting to get cloudy. The new well, the one we thought would be the seventh gusher in a row, turned out to be a duster. So did the next one. Also, Mr. Cohen's enemies at the Atlas office in Houston were trying to push him out. Some of them were now claiming that the agreements I signed were not valid, because I had lied about my age in order to receive power of attorney over Papa's property, and hence we owed a large amount of money to Atlas.

I also discovered the sheriff, White Trash Millard, was working in concert with some New York City detectives who would not let go of the shooting death of Tony Vale. Actually, I didn't care what they did. Maybe it was just my youth, but I concluded that the world can only do so much to you. Let the world break its fists on your face, Mama said. Life's a party. Laugh at your enemies. Or pity them. But give them no power. I loved my mama.

With those kinds of thoughts in mind, I decided to make a real movie. And I mean a real one. About the leper community and our friends the Hebrew cowboys Ezra and Ezekiel way down on the border. Of course, this was the place where Ida Banks and I were attacked by Indian Charlie and his entourage. When I suggested the project to Ida, her face clouded.

"You don't want to go back there?" I asked.

"I return there in my dreams at 4:30 every morning."

"We don't have to do it."

"Is our story going to be in there?"

"That's up to you."

"A story needs an ending," she said. Her eyes stayed on mine.

"What are you thinking about, Ida?"

"Bertha says you told her you killed somebody in New York. I cannot conceive of your doing that, except for one reason."

"Which one is that?" I replied.

"You were raped, weren't you?"

"Yes."

"I've thought about killing Indian Charlie, Bessie."

"The man I shot was about to kill my father. That's the only reason I killed him. Something is going to happen to Indian Charlie, Ida, and he'll never see it coming. And it will probably be worse than anything we could have done to him. Don't seek revenge on this worthless man."

"Have you suddenly become prescient?" she said.

"I wish you wouldn't talk to me like that. It's not like you."

We were in her kitchen, with coffee cups and pink grapefruit from the Rio Grande Valley in front of us. Out of nowhere, her face crumpled. She got down on her knees and sobbed in my lap. I don't think I ever knew anyone who silently bore so much pain.

"We're going to make a documentary, Ida," I said. "We're going to put ourselves in it. If the world doesn't like it, they can kiss our foot. One Big Union."

The latter was the mantra of Joe Hill and the International Workers of the World. She looked up at me, then nodded her head, her eyes red. "When do we start?" she said.

But there was something ominous occurring in our community. Maybe the suspicion and the anger I saw around me was simply a reflection of the fear and bloodshed that had spread around the world. I'll never be sure. I think we all want to be lovers of humanity, but sometimes it doesn't work out that way.

The Ku Klux Klan burned a cross on the high school yard. White boys shot Mexicans and colored people with BB guns and slingshots. It was against the law to criticize Wilson's war policies. Most people don't believe that today, but it's true. Federal authorities arrested people for exercising the First Amendment of the Constitution. Colored soldiers who were treated badly in Houston rioted and killed sixteen white people, firing at civilians with rifles. Nineteen colored soldiers were hanged and dozens went to jail, many who had gone up San Juan Hill with Theodore Roosevelt.

It wasn't a happy time. I think we lost our identity.

Early on a warm morning in November, Sheriff Slim Millard drove his touring car to Aint Minnie's house, kicked open the door, and handcuffed her and pushed Snowball down and wrestled Aint Minnie into the back seat of the car, then drove away and watched Snowball run after her mother in the rearview mirror.

Two hours later a bondsman called me and told me what little he knew about Aint Minnie's confinement or the charges against her.

"Is she hurt?" I asked.

"If she's not now, she will be," he answered.

"What did you say?"

"The sheriff don't abide getting a piss pot thrown at him through the bars in his own jail."

Papa was out of town, this time fishing with a friend on the Comal River.

"Stay with her," I said to the bondsman. "I'll pay whatever fee you want."

"I done the Christian thing," he said. "Now y'all are on your own, Miss Holland. If I were you, I'd get unstuck from this."

I hitched up Traveler and the two of us went to town as fast as we could, as though Traveler knew one of our best friends was in trouble. I tied Traveler to the iron tethering post at the courthouse and went straight into Slim Millard's office. He was eating his lunch on top of his desk blotter, his sandwich dripping lettuce, mayonnaise, and tomato on his fingers.

"Is she still in a cell?" I said.

"What do you think?"

"Where's Snowball?" I said.

"How the hell should I know?"

"What are the charges on Aint Minnie?"

"Disorderly conduct, destroying a police vehicle, destroying public property, theft, and—"

"Theft of what?"

"Food at the grocery store. Mr. Jack decided to pursue the issue."

"Why now?"

"You didn't buy your vittles from his store, Missy. That would have been the smart thing to do. But you didn't let me finish the charges. Minnie assaulted an officer of the law. That would be me." He shoved a chair at me with his boot. "Sit down."

"I don't care to, thank you."

"I can have you in a cell in five seconds."

"Then that's your prerogative."

"My what?"

"I know nothing about the purchases or non-purchases at Mr. Jack's grocery," I said. "But you can tell him I will take care of it immediately."

"That ain't gonna cut it. She hit a white man. In fact, she tried to gouge out my eye. I'm not gonna take shit like that from anybody, particularly from a nigra. Now sit down."

I could see no mark on his eye. "I said I'll stand. I do not like your tone of voice, nor your attitude toward colored people."

"You don't seem to know what's going on here," he said, dropping his sandwich in the waste can and wiping his hands on a towel. "I'm having daily talks with a detective in New York who can have you arrested and transported to his jurisdiction *like that*."

He snapped his fingers.

"I cain't even guess at what you are talking about," I replied. "It seems to be an obsession you have. Let me explain a couple of things to you. I lived in the Lower East Side of Manhattan Island. It's full of Irish and Jewish and Italian gangsters. They kill one another with regularity. The police are almost as bad as they are. There was one gangster in particular who was a friend of my brother Cody. His name is Owney Madden. He's what is called a 'stone killer.' He is also about to be released from Sing Sing. I will contact Mr. Madden and tell him you are harassing me because you and the New York Police Department want to send him back to prison or the electric chair."

The sheriff's eyes looked like marbles rolling in a saucer.

"Would you like me to get things started?" I asked.

He ran his tongue behind his teeth. "I'm just doing my job," he said.

"I'll be back in twenty minutes with my attorney. Please get Aint Minnie ready to leave."

"You think your shit don't stink, don't you?"

"You never disappoint, Sheriff."

"What the hell is that supposed to mean?"

"Sir, would you stop picking your teeth?" I said. "It's truly disgusting."

Chapter Thirty-Nine

I waited for Aint Minnie outside. When she came out of the jailhouse door, the sun shone brightly on her face; it was lopsided, half of it swollen, one eye closed, as though it had been stung by a wasp. I helped her into the buggy.

"Did you hit the sheriff?" I said.

"I sassed him. That's all he needed," she said.

"Wait here," I said.

"Don't do it, Bessie. That's what he wants."

She was right. But there is nothing lower than a man who deliberately strikes a woman, especially one whose race doesn't allow her to fight back. Looking at her made me think about the blows Tony Vale rained down on me. Aint Minnie's face looked as hard and mean as a rock.

"You're not thinking about getting even, are you, Aint Minnie?"

"I ain't made up my mind about anything," she said. "Where's Snowball at?"

"I called Miz Banks. She's at her house now. We'll pick her up on the way home."

"Thank you for what you done," she said. But her tone was lifeless, her good eye looking straight ahead. I had no doubt what was in her mind.

I gripped her wrist and squeezed to get her attention. "You get those thoughts out of your head," I said.

"I ain't got no thoughts," she replied. "I ain't got nothing. Just my li'l girl. He threw her in the dirt."

I didn't say any more. There are some forms of human behavior that cannot be explained or accepted. I'm talking about people like Tony Vale and Slim Millard. But the answer, the one we want to wreak on our enemy, takes us into the grave we have prepared for him.

I flicked the reins and headed toward home just as the clouds burst and hail began clicking like tap hammers on Traveler and the buggy and Aint Minnie and me. It was that way all the way to the house, as though the sun's heat was no longer ours.

At sunset Papa clanked open the chimney and started a fire. He was wearing his long underwear with suspenders and no shirt. The dust was blowing, the windmill spinning, our cows bunching up. Papa walked back and forth in the living room, opening and closing his hands.

"Are you restless, Papa?" I said.

What a foolish question.

"I've never known my own mind, Bessie," he said. "That's a painful admission at my age."

I told you about his pursuit of the Chalice. I did not want to get into that. He actually believed he had found it. I didn't want to tell him that he was using symbols for the father he never had and perhaps trying to deal with death.

"Don't run off on me, Papa," I said.

"You've got a fortune, Bessie. You could hire an army. You don't need me pestering you."

"We do not have a fortune," I said. "We're partners with the Atlas Company. Right now they're dumping all their drilling expenses on us. Now we've hit two dusters. Our business partners are sharpers."

"What about the six wells that are pumping out there?"

"This is what I'm trying to tell you. Atlas takes the oil out of the ground and claims it as a loss on their income tax, then lets us pay most of the drilling and maintenance costs. Know why the South lost the war?"

"Why?"

"The Yankees were smarter than we were. They cut off our food."

But I had already lost his attention. Papa was not keen on what he called "ciphering" and business talk. Out the window I could see a car coming up the dirt road, the sky layered with strips of purple clouds in the background, rain streaking across the car's headlights.

"It's Mr. Cohen," I said.

"Y'all going somewhere?" Papa asked.

"Not to my knowledge."

"He's not coming on to you, is he, Bessie?"

"He's not that kind of fella, Papa. And I resent your asking that."

"Men are men. It's the way we're made. It's in the Bible. Adam was lonely, so God took a rib from him and made Eve. That's why men have constant inclinations that get us in a mess."

"Do you realize how crazy that sounds?" I asked.

"I'll be in the kitchen," he replied.

I opened the door for Mr. Cohen. He was dressed in a tweed suit and a tie and a black vest, but he wore a beat-up fedora and low-topped, scuffed boots. That was Mr. Cohen: an elegant man, but one who understood the world of working people. And who also knew the human cost of war.

He removed his hat, but didn't speak.

"Is anything wrong?" I said.

"I've been let go, Bessie, and I wanted to tell you before someone else did. I also wanted to tell you what a pleasure it has been working with you and your father and knowing your other friends."

"I'm very sorry to hear that," I said.

"It's been coming, so I had already prepared myself and talked to a couple of academics looking for a professor." He was turning his hat with his fingers on the brim as he spoke. "To be frank, I think you and your father will need help in your dealings with Atlas. I have an attorney friend or two I can recommend."

"I don't want anyone else, Mr. Cohen."

"Don't try to deal with these men by yourself. They're like Roman imperialists. As long as you conform to their will, you'll be fine. The day you don't will be the day you'll have trouble. These men have no boundaries. Are you hearing me?"

"Yes, but you need to hear *me*, Mr. Cohen—"

"Please call me Jared."

"I want you as our partner, Mr. Jared. Papa thinks highly of you. Not many people can say that."

"I feel I'm taking advantage of you."

"The wrong people always feel bad about themselves. The people who are bad never feel guilty about anything."

He was smiling now.

"What's funny?" I said.

"Nothing. You're just a really nice young lady."

I felt a flush in my face and a weakness or urge inside me that I did not want to recognize.

"Papa!" I yelled. "Will you come out here! We need to talk business!"

And that's how the Holland Oil Company was born, for good or bad.

Sure enough, Papa left town and Jared Cohen and I took on the Atlas Company. It was a great learning experience. Corporations don't fight fair. In fact, they don't fight at all. They're like the Russians. They let proxies do it and bleed their enemies one cut at a time.

Who were their proxies? You name it. I think the sheriff was one of them. I think a detective or two from New York might have been working for them, also. But the one proxy I was sure about was Indian Charlie. I saw him on the street in town and also in Houston and also in San Antonio. I saw him at a beer fest in New Braunfels and at a Baptist church picnic on the banks of the Frio River. That's right, at a church picnic on one of the most beautiful rivers you have ever seen, as green as green can get, lined with big trees that were as green as the water, the trees on the bank swaying against a blue sky.

Indian Charlie was there for only one reason. He was proving to me that no matter where I went, he would be there, too. Simultaneously, he got a message to me, but in a way I could not prove. Outside of Beeville a female derelict was found mutilated in a ditch, barely alive, one leg taken off at the knee, her undergarments twisted into the tourniquet. She had once been a prostitute in Bertha Lafleur's brothel. A note by her side read, *Tell the traveling girl she's next.*

When I read the story in the newspaper, I remembered the way Indian Charlie had looked at my feet. I told the authorities in Beeville that the culprit was talking about my horse Traveler. They were not impolite; they were even paternal. But an investigation of Indian Charlie couldn't be opened because a note written by a maniac made what was a possible vague allusion to Robert E. Lee's horse. Plus, Indian Charlie had three friends who said he was at a bowling alley in Corpus Christi the night the former prostitute was butchered. Plus, the victim was so intoxicated with alcohol and laudanum she didn't know who took her out to the ditch.

But at the church picnic, he made sure I saw him. There was a brilliance in his eyes, a glow in his face, a suppressed laugh on his lips as he stared straight in my face across a buffet table. I wanted to kill him. On the spot. Instead, I did nothing and engaged in a worthless conversation with a minister about shutting down all the distilleries in America. He was definitely for it. Indian Charlie walked away, shooting me a vulgar sign over his shoulder.

I had another problem, too. Aint Minnie would not give up her grievance against the sheriff, for which I couldn't blame her. Sheriff Millard had struck her in the face, degraded her, and thrown her child in the dirt. He also had taken the side of the grocer, one of the Fowlers, and accused her of stealing a handful of snap beans. What I could not make her understand is that you do not fight on the territory or the terms of your enemy. My grandfather was in the Army of Northern Virginia during Jackson's Shenandoah campaign, and used to quote his famous line: "Always mystify, mislead, and surprise the enemy, if possible, and when you strike and overcome him, never let up."

Aint Minnie wasn't listening. There was a dulled-over look in her eyes, an agitated tic in her mannerisms, an angry flick of the hand when washing dishes, a cup throw in the bottom of the sink like a musket ball.

"You're letting the sheriff eat you up, Aint Minnie," I said on a Saturday after she had just shaken the litter box into the rose bed and it blew back in her face.

"Then let Mr. Hackberry come back and take care of his cats," she said. "Cats ain't supposed to be goin' to the bathroom in the house. They're supposed to dig a hole in the ground, squat down, do their bidness, then cover it up. It ain't a hard thing to understand."

"Why didn't you bring Snowball with you today, Aint Minnie?"

"Because she don't feel good. Because she ain't got rid of the way she was treated. Because she thinks y'all let us down."

"I'm sorry she feels that way," I said. "Is that the way you feel?"

"There's a time when you got to stand up. I'm talking about me. I'm tired of white people like the sheriff. Tired of their insults. Tired of going around the back of the house. Tired of not lookin' them in the eye."

"We don't treat you that way."

"I ain't stupid, Miss Bessie. The sheriff wants to cook you and your daddy in a iron pot. And he's gonna do it through me. But that don't mean I cain't fight back."

"You'll lose Snowball, Aint Minnie."

"I'll lose what I lose," she said.

"Don't you talk like that."

"Listen to yourself, Bessie. Just listen."

I think that conversation was the unhappiest one I ever had. I walked out of the house down to the barn. The wind was warm, out of the south, from either Mexico or the Gulf. Our six operative wells were clanking away, the ground humming, at least in my imagination, the smell of the animals probably the same as it was when Noah loaded God's critters two by two on the Ark, when the world was about to be reborn.

I wanted to be back in that ancient time, when God gave mankind a second chance, because I was not sure we would ever get one again.

I was so glad to have a film company in the works, even though it was a very modest and certainly idealistic one. But it allowed me to enter the world of artists and actors and writers and people who were dissatisfied with their beginnings and made a conscious choice to become someone else. Look at Papa. He went back to the eleventh century and became a Templar Knight. I just hoped he didn't get arrested on Friday the thirteenth and burned at the stake.

Ida Banks and Mr. Slick and I went down near the border and filmed the leper community and our friends the Hebrew cowboys. Both the geographical and cultural environment there were strange, not quite real, detached from all we knew about ourselves and our origins. The land was broken into huge slabs of rock that tilted toward the Rio Grande, but the sod was soft and black and moist and the grass like big patches of velvet among the stones that looked like they had been thrown there by giants.

The cruelty of leprosy had left its mark in many ways. At first glance its victims shocked your sensibilities. Perhaps your eyes watered and your fingernails bit into the heels of your hands. Then you looked at them again and simply saw a distortion or a blur rather than a disease daily consuming a human being. The log homes and dormitories in which they lived were carpentered by masters. The personnel were Mennonites and Maryknoll Sisters and of course our friends the Hebrew cowboys, Ezra and Ezekiel, and several long-bearded men like them, all of them armed and dressed in black.

I had the sense the latter group was more pragmatic in their view of the world.

It was wonderful to be among them. And it was wonderful to put them on film. I felt that something magical occurred when the images of the community were transferred into our cameras. We had caught what was best in human beings and animals and painted it on light, an event that is neither logical nor supposedly possible. It was like dipping your hand into infinity.

We had no formal scriptwriter. Not unless you count Mr. Slick. I had long accepted his spirituality, and I mean that in the meta-physical sense, because poor Mr. Slick was not a saint, but I think his uncurable behavior and unhinged view of normalcy had finally found a home. Mr. Slick was going to make movies. He even wore tall, lace-up boots and a snap-brim cap and britches a cavalry officer would wear, and smoked purple cigarettes with a gold holder.

Our storyline was brief. Two women went to a Sunday morning service and then on a picnic in a touring car and broke a wheel in a desolate area, and found themselves surrounded by Ku Kluxers. This did not coincide with D. W. Griffith's *The Birth of a Nation*. Ida Banks had lost weight and looked like Lillian Gish. I played myself. The Kluxers were mounted and wore black, conical hats and scarlet robes with white crosses. With an electric fan blowing, the dust filled the skies and the Kluxers circled us on their horses while we clung together, shaking in fear, our eyes lifted heavenward.

We also changed history a little bit. Guess who rescued us?

Elderly Confederate veterans. They were armed with Spencer rifles and ball-and-cap revolvers, and their uniforms were in rags, their goat beards lifting in the wind. They gave out the Rebel Yell, *woo, woo, woo,* which wasn't a yell but a fox call, and either blew the Kluxers out of their saddles or rope-drug them through the cactus, but of course we couldn't get any of the sound on the film, which was a big loss. I guess you cain't have it all, though.

Then it began to rain. I thought we'd wrap everything up and film another day. But Mr. Slick had other ideas. "Are you serious?" he said, rain peppering his face like hail on a cantaloupe. "This is a baptism. The world is being re-created. This ain't just happening. The Lord has got His hand in this. I ain't figured out what it is, but roll it just the same. I said, 'Action, y'all!' "

Chapter Forty

When I returned home that evening, there was a letter in our mailbox with no return address. But I knew the penmanship. It was from Benny. He had not acknowledged my invitation to visit and to bring his family, and had hurt my feelings, even though he was a child and I was a young adult, or thought I was. His message began:

> Dear Bessie, I can not come to Texas to help you make movies. My family has been hurt by the criminals in our neighborhood. Sometimes I will tell you about this. Frankie got thrown in the can, but the police have not bothered me or Meyer.
>
> Be careful about the bulls. They're everywhere and they're mean. A detective has been asking questions around the Lower East Side. None of us know anything. You get my drift?
>
> I will never go to the can. Meyer will not either. I hope things don't go too bad for Frankie.
>
> I love you, Bessie. You're the best girl there is.
>
> This is me signing off,
> B.

I didn't hear from or about Benny until 1926, when he was arrested for rape. The girl who went to the police was told by Benny's friends that she would either drop the charges or have acid flung in her face. She did what she was told.

There are wounds that time does not heal.

The next day our driller, Mr. Skeeter, came up to the house and knocked on the door. I opened it and asked if he wanted coffee. He was wearing a tin hat and strap overalls without a shirt; his body looked like leather stretched over a skeleton. "No, thank you, Miss Bessie," he said. "I got a problem with Jubal Fowler."

"What's wrong with Jubal?"

"The question should be what's right with him. He comes to work with liquor on his breath and talking to hisself and laughing about things nobody can see. That boy ain't right in the head, Miss Bessie."

"He was buried alive in a trench, Mr. Skeeter."

"I went up Kettle Hill. You don't have to tell me about war. Jubal showed up this morning with knots all over his head and face. I cain't have a man swinging them tongs when he cain't hardly see."

"Send him up here, would you please?" I said.

"Yes, ma'am," he replied.

Ten minutes later Jubal was on the porch, grinning at me, his hair sticking out from under his cap. I stepped out on the porch and did not ask him in. "What happened to your face, Jubal?" I asked.

"I was chopping brush and hit a nest of yellowjackets."

"Those are pretty big knots."

"That's because those were pretty big yellowjackets."

"You cain't bring last night's alcohol to the rig, Jubal."

"I won't do it no more."

"Can I count on you?"

He twisted his neck and looked at the windmill ginning in the breeze and the water pumping into the tank. It was a fine day. We had plowed under the thatch in the fields, and seagulls from the Gulf were cawing above them and picking in the rows.

"It's strange how things are made, ain't it, Bessie?" he said. "Birds that belong on the water fly miles to pick slugs from dirt that they ain't got any right to. That's what humans do, too. They don't just take part of things. They take it all."

"That's not a good way to think, Jubal."

He grinned at me again. "Probably not," he said. "But you know me. I didn't pay attention to Miz Banks when I should have, and instead listened to all them damn people in the Bog."

I put one hand on his upper arm. It felt like a firehose pumped full of water. "You're a hero, Jubal, and brave on many levels. You saved me from Indian Charlie. I'll always have a place for you in my heart."

He swallowed, his eyes widening. "I better get back on the rig. I ain't gonna drink no more, Bessie. I promise you with all my soul."

Then he turned and walked as fast as he could past the windmill and the cows drinking from the tank, and past the barn, and out into a plowed-under pasture dotted with seagulls, theirs beaks filled with slugs as fat as caterpillars.

The next day I received a phone call at 6:17 a.m. I thought it was Papa and an emergency was at hand. Back then we had our faults, but we respected one another, even those we didn't like, and we didn't wake them up in the early hours. "Hello?" I said.

"This is Sheriff Millard," the voice said. "Is your father there?"

"No, what do you want?"

"I've got two problems I thought you ought to know about. A welfare social worker has made a report on your nigra woman."

"On Aint Minnie?"

"That's what I said. The report is about the unfit nature of the child's home, what's-her-name, Snowball. I'm talking about the child's safety. And I'm also talking about nigra men coming in and out like they're in rut. I'm talking about turning tricks. Are you listening?"

"Aint Minnie works for us and always has. She has never been on welfare, and has no need of it. And what you say about her private life is a slanderous lie."

"Could be. But this welfare social worker has got her mind set."

"What do you want from me, Sheriff?"

"I don't want anything. I'm passing on information."

"No, tell me how *much* you want?" I said. "That's what your call is about, isn't it?"

"I knew I'd get into this. You're nothing but trouble, girl."

"I'm going to hang up now."

"This is the rest of it, darlin'," he said. "There's a detective from New York City in town. An Italian gangster named Anthony Vale got his brains splattered on a wall in Harlem. Guess what local person he's interested in."

"I wouldn't know, Sheriff. But it's so good of you to wake me up before seven a.m. and tell me these things. Thank you. Goodbye. And please never call here again, you ignorant peckerwood piece of trash."

I put the earpiece back on the hook and stared at the wall. I didn't care about the New York detective or what might happen to me because of Tony Vale's death. If I went to jail, I went to jail. I was a good Baptist, and a good Baptist never fears anybody or anything. But the thought of Aint Minnie's losing Snowball brought tears to my eyes.

Why did we have such evil in the world, I asked myself. Why were men like Slim Millard allowed to walk the earth? It wasn't right.

I got dressed and decided to accomplish two goals by two p.m. To talk with Aint Minnie and guarantee her that no one would take Snowball from her, and to buy a car and learn how to drive it so I could take care of all these problems. So that's what I did. The used-car salesman in town had a dozen vehicles parked on a lot next to the slaughterhouse where I shot Jubal Fowler's father. I picked out a fire-engine-red 1910 Maxwell Touring Car. The salesman started instructing me on how everything worked, but it was really boring to listen to and I wondered if contraptions such as automobiles were all they were stacked up to be. Actually I had early learned a little from Ida. In fact, they seemed made by simpletons for simpletons.

For example, as the salesman said, *you* had to start it, literally, because it couldn't start itself. You bent over in front of the bumper and whipped the crank with all your might, then jumped back so it didn't break your arm and then slap your face. Then you got in it, aimed at where you were going, moved the gas rod, and took off down the road. The engine sounded like a junkyard falling off a cliff.

Ida went with me and almost had a heart attack. She said I was on the wrong side of the street and that people were running away from me. I think they were running from a fire down the street, because I could hear the sirens. Besides, horse riders and carriages went everywhere they wanted. Why should automobiles be different? That garbage can that got stuck under my Maxwell Touring Car frame was thrown there by a notorious drunken prankster who had just stumbled out of an alley. He was a harmless man and I did not hold his prank against him. I loved Ida, but I never could understand why she had to make big drama out of little things.

When we got out in the country, I gave the engine all the gasoline it would take. Ida was bouncing up and down, hanging on to the passenger strap with her right hand while pressing her left hand on her chest. I declare, she should have been a thespian.

When we got to Aint Minnie's cabin, neither she nor Snowball was there. I drove Ida home, then returned to the ranch, dead tired, my Maxwell Touring Car coated with dust. A man in a suit and vest was sitting on our porch steps; he was bareheaded, his head shaved. I had seen him before, but I could not remember where. A square black car with all four windows down was parked on the grass. The man was chewing gum vigorously, snapping it between his teeth. He got up and spat out his gum and fitted a fedora on his head.

"Looks like we meet again, baby girl," he said.

I remembered now. He was the investigative policeman who went door-to-door in my tenement building when the downstairs neighbor was beaten to death with a baseball bat. He chewed gum and seemed to delight in giving people pet names. Mine was "lassie" and "baby girl." He was also keen on giving a young girl a lascivious wink.

What's the best way to deal with evil people? Shut them down before they're out of the chute.

"Get out of here," I said.

"It's not good to get your dander up, girlie. It'll spoil your looks."

"What if I go inside and get my shotgun and run you to the gate? This is Texas. We do it for fun here."

"You're a hot one, all right. Familiar with the name Tony Vale? An elegant dago who caught a round in the middle of his forehead? The niggers say a girl resembling you did it."

"I'm going inside now. If you're not gone in five minutes, I'll call the sheriff."

"Got news for you, lass. He swore me in. I'm here with his blessing. Let's talk inside. I'm not a bad fella."

The sun was red and low in the sky, the temperature dropping, a hint of rain in the air. The cretinous nature of the man was unmistakable. Skeeter and his crew had "gone to the house." I was on my own. I walked past the man from the Lower East Side and mounted the steps. I could feel his eyes undressing me.

"I got a bottle in my vehicle," he said. "We'll have some drinks and get all this straightened out. Your sheriff is a rodent you can buy with a campaign donation. The report I give in New York will exonerate you of any wrongdoing. You're a nice lass and you don't need this grief in your life. How about it?"

"How about what?"

"The drinks. Maybe a bite to eat. How about some cake? I'm keen on angel food."

He stepped closer to me, blocking my way. His collar was unbuttoned, his upper chest ruddy, his eyes wrinkled at the edges, like a turtle's. "Come on, doll," he said. "I'm trying to help. Be a little generous. Look at those oil wells. You've been blessed. But you have to give up something of some kind. You can't keep everything for yourself."

"Get out of my way."

"I know what Tony Vale did to you."

"You know what?"

"He took you to his place in the country and put you through the traces. I'm not like that."

"Don't you dare put your hand on me."

"What's wrong with you, baby girl? You don't know who your friends are."

I could feel his breath on me, and the heat and feral odor radiating from his body. He wet his lips and circled my wrist with his thumb and forefinger. I could not believe this was happening to me again. I should have carried a pistol or a knife or a barber's razor or a knitting needle. Instead I had believed that a person went only once to Golgotha.

Then in the distance I saw an open car coming across our north pasture. The driver was wearing goggles and a duster, coming hard, bending down the grass under the car's frame, passing the wells we called donkey pumpers or rocking horses. I had no idea who the driver was. I didn't recognize the vehicle, either. Perhaps it belonged to one of the surveyors. But why would a surveyor be in the pasture after working hours? And the only way to come into the pasture was through a narrow gate on the north fence, which was next to the woods where I believe the little girl was murdered.

I could not keep all these thoughts straight in my head. I believe in the presence of evil. Whether it is driven by an intelligent source, I do not know. But I have no doubt that it lives in the human breast. I could almost smell the sulfur on the clothes on the policeman from New York. For those who choose not to believe these things, I say gather the angels around you, because you will need them.

The policeman worked his hand up my arm and squeezed it so tightly I thought the bone would break.

Then he saw the car coming and released me, stepping back as though he had touched an electric wire. "Nothing happened here," he said. "You got me, lass? You fucking got me?"

I ran inside the house and loaded one of Papa's guns. When I came back on the porch, the New York policeman was gone. But so was the car. It made no sense. I walked out to the pasture and took Lancelot and Traveler and Papa's Shetland pony Shorty with me. (When Papa rode Shorty through the high grass, he looked like he was gliding through the field without a bottom half.) The sun was almost down and the wind was blowing and the grass was swaying, and I could not distinguish the shadows from the grass pressed into the ground by the weight of the car's wheels.

I felt like a fool. I had a house full of weapons, yet I had almost allowed an evil man to have his way. I could not bear the cavalier fashion in which I had put myself in danger. I cannot say this vehemently enough. My anger was such that I wanted to die. I washed my hands and arms in the sink with a detergent powder that turned my skin the color of a boiled crab. Pardon me for not telling you the other thoughts I had, and how much I wanted them to become a reality. They were not the thoughts of either a reasonable or Christian person. But I could not help it. If God could send Joshua to wipe out the Canaanites, why should I be denied?

Chapter Forty-One

T he social welfare department, with the cooperation of the sheriff's department, came to pick up Snowball one day after the visit of the New York policeman to my house. Aint Minnie fought physically against the welfare woman and the two sheriff's deputies, at first slapping at them, then using her fists. Had I not gotten there in time, the welfare woman and the two sheriff's deputies would have beaten her to the death, I was sure. One deputy had already thrown her against the corner of her iron cookstove and split the side of her head. There was blood splatter on the other side of the room, and a butcher knife on the floor. Both deputies were opening and clenching their fists when I walked in.

"What in God's name are y'all doing?" I said.

I knew the woman. She had been a matron in an Oklahoma prison and was fired as a security officer from the state asylum in Austin. Her body was a figure eight and all fat, with a small head and not a glimmer of humanity in her face.

"Minnie is running a crib, Miss Holland," she said.

I had become "Miss Holland" since oil was found on our land. "Her name is Aint Minnie," I said.

"You're interfering with an officer of the law," one of the deputies said.

"I'll do worse than that," I said. "I'll have the three of y'all in jail."

"She pulled a knife on us," he said.

"That man's lying, Bessie," Aint Minnie said. "I was peeling potatoes when they come in. And I ain't had no men in here except my cousin visiting from Beaumont and the preacher in our church."

"What do you say to that?" I asked the welfare worker.

"I'm acting on Sheriff Millard's orders," she said.

"Some journalists from New York are in town," I said. "I think they're connected with a New York detective who is meddling in our business. I will give them your names so he can interview y'all."

Neither the woman nor the deputies could follow what I was saying, because what I was saying was nonsense. But like all bullies, they were afraid of power. She glanced at the deputies, then back at me. "I'll confer with the sheriff," she said. "We don't want to see an injustice done to anyone."

"Where's Snowball, Aint Minnie?" I said.

"Hiding under the bed," she said.

I picked up a towel from the drain and put my arm around her shoulders and pressed the towel to the wound on the side of her head. I looked at the deputies and the welfare woman, and wondered what drove them. Did they despise humankind or just themselves? Were they like the creature in William Blake's poem when he asks, "What the anvil, what the chain, in what furnace was thy brain?"

"Shame on y'all, each one of you," I said. "Just flat shame on you."

They looked askance and walked out in silence. It was a strange moment. The only fuel a candle has is itself. And that's what they were. People consumed by their own flame. Regardless, I had no more time for white people such as these. They weren't worth the dustpan it takes to dump them in a wastebasket. But believe it or not, thoughts like that will make you one of them. It's guaranteed.

I bandaged Aint Minnie's head and cleaned her kitchen, and went home. Then I loaded not one gun but three. One went under my bed, one went in my purse, and one went under the seat of my Maxwell Touring Car. Then I drove to town, with no plan in mind. At least I thought I had none. It was Sunday and the house was lonely. I overslept and missed church and could not get the images of the policeman from New York out of my mind. Nor could I rid myself of his smell and his forefinger and thumb curling around my wrist and his casual attitude about raping me in my own home. I drove to town and found myself banging over the ruts and potholes in the road without feeling them, the engine clattering and grinding as though it wanted to tear living tissue into shreds.

On Monday morning Skeeter and the crew were back on the job, then Jared Cohen drove up at noon with a watermelon for the "boys," as we called them. Oil field roughnecks are usually carefree and afraid of nothing, particularly the ones out on the water. We had a bunch of them working for us. They didn't have a teaspoon of fat on them and were as sunbrowned as coconuts. One of them had a guitar and was singing a song while Jared sliced up the melon.

> *Ten days on,*
> *Five days off,*
> *I reckon my blood is oil crude now,*
> *I reckon I'll never lose*
> *Them mean old roughnecking blues.*

I liked to be among them. They were uneducated but well-mannered and usually shy. Their piney-woods twangs were probably part of a seventeenth-century British dialect, although they had no such knowledge about such things. They were the kind of men who would always remain boys. The sun was bright, the wind cool, the sky blue, and I didn't want to think about the policeman from New York. I wanted to be a little girl again and believe that all of humankind had crossed the Jordan and had made up for the all the Canaanites Moses and Joshua had killed. I wanted to see the human race as it was supposed to be, not what we have become. I wished Papa and Mama were here, dressed in finery, and proud of their children. I cannot describe the loneliness and sense of loss I was experiencing.

"Is everything all right, Bessie?" Jared said, putting a slice of melon in my hand.

"Oh, I was daydreaming a little bit," I said.

But I didn't fool him. So I tried again and added a bit more, which is always a mistake. "I think I ate too much pie before I went to bed. It gets me to tingling."

"If I can help in any way," he said.

"There's nothing wrong with me, Jared."

"Sorry," he said.

I pressed my hands to the sides of my head. "I fear what the sheriff is going to do to Aint Minnie and Snowball."

"He's not going to do anything."

"You don't know that," I said. "You don't know what goes on in Huntsville and Eastham. It's sickening."

"I'm sure it is," he said. "I didn't mean to argue with you."

"Were you driving an open car in the north pasture on Saturday?"

He blinked. "Was I in your pasture on Saturday? Without your permission?"

"We're business partners," I replied. "You don't need my permission."

He lowered both his eyes and his voice. "No, it was not I."

Once again I had made a mess of things. "That's a mighty nice melon you brought the boys," I said.

"Well, as you say down here, they're right nice boys."

But there was no way to undo the damage I had just done, and I had done it to the kindest man I had ever known.

At 2:17 the same day, the sheriff himself was at my door. With four deputies behind him. All of them looking at the crews on our rigs or laying pipe to a storage tank or constructing a donkey pumper that makes money twenty-four hours a day, and wondering why they ever put themselves in the sway of a man like our sheriff.

"Am I under arrest?" I asked.

"No," the sheriff said. "Not unless you want to do something real stupid. I want you to do an identification."

"Of what or whom?"

"Don't be cute," he said.

"Sir, you are either an idiot or the most offensive public official I've ever met."

"It might have to do with your brother Cody."

I felt my heart come to a stop. "What?"

"You can follow me in your car," he said. "What's it gonna be, Miss Holland?"

The sky had filled with rain clouds. I went inside and got my hat and left behind my purse, the one with the gun inside it.

Two deputies rode in front of my Maxwell Touring Car, and the sheriff and the other two deputies rode behind me. The sky was splintering with electricity, the dirt road empty of other cars, rolling over a bare hill that seemed to drop into nowhere.

Our three-car caravan pulled to a stop at an isolated adobe building outside of town. The mud bricks were cracked, the cedar poles in the roof eaten into balsa wood by termites. The New York policeman's car was parked outside, all four windows still down. The building was sometimes used as a crib by some Mexican brothers who ran a bar and gas pump down the road.

"Take my key and open it up," the sheriff said. "I want to get my camera."

"What does this have to do with Cody?" I said.

"You tell me. I hear he's making a name for himself in New York. Hanging around with gangsters."

"You lied to get me here, didn't you?" I said. "It seems that every time you open your mouth, a lie comes out. I've never seen the like."

He stuck a key into a large padlock and opened the door. I wondered where he got his key. Answer: he had his thumb in every pie in the county.

"Step inside, please," he said.

I was not going to let him frighten me, and I walked inside. But a fall always follows pride. The room was dank and smelled of feces; beer bottles were broken on the floor; a stained mattress was rolled up on the far side of an army bunk bed.

"Go look at it," he said.

"At what?"

"You know what."

"I do not."

He pushed me forward with the points of his fingers, causing me to lose balance and grab the back of a chair.

"I said look at your handiwork, you little bitch." He shoved me deeper into the room, past the foot of the bed. "That's a human being there. How does it make you feel?"

He shoved me down on the floor. It was made of concrete. My knees and hands were painted with rat feces.

"Hey, Sheriff, maybe hold off there—" a deputy said.

"Mind your business," the sheriff said.

I got up, shaking with anger. I wanted to kill him. A body lay on the floor, a newspaper splayed over its face.

"Here, I'll let you have a good look," the sheriff said.

"I don't want to see this," I said. I was so angry my teeth were chattering. "It has nothing to do with me. You damn trash, if you touch me, I'll cut your hand off."

"Yell if you want, but you're not getting out of this," he said. He removed the newspaper from the face of the corpse. "You really gave it to him, didn't you?"

In the dimness of the light, both eyes of the dead man were nothing but black holes. The third round had gone straight into the mouth. The imprints of small animals were crisscrossed on his chest. I tried to turn around and get out of the building. The sheriff knotted my sleeve in his fist. "You'll leave when I tell you to. Confess now and get ahead of this. And don't give me your shit."

Then I realized why Slim Millard had taken me there. My fingerprints were now all over the interior of the room where the policeman from New York had drawn his last breath.

"Did you hear me?" the sheriff said. "Why are you staring at me?"

"I thought you were simply ignorant and greedy. But I think you work for the devil."

"You should know, you twat," he said.

"I'm driving to the newspaper office now. You are one of those people God has put on earth to prove there is no such thing as white supremacy. So get out of my way or shoot me. You're a sad creature, Sheriff. And you smell bad."

I walked out of the adobe, the ground shifting under my feet, and got into my Maxwell Touring Car and drove to our small-town newspaper. The publisher interviewed me for twenty minutes in his private office, then shook hands and said how sorry he was for the ordeal I had just experienced. I looked back through his office window as I was leaving. He was bent over a file drawer, stuffing my interview deep inside it, up to his elbow, leaning on it.

Chapter Forty-Two

I went home and stayed in the bathtub for a half hour. We had a water heater now, as well as a telephone and electricity and plumbing and a commode, all those modern things that are hard to give up once you've had them. I would like to tell you how I felt about the passing of the policeman from New York. The truth is I didn't know. I have to say something else, too. My family is a strange breed, as you have probably guessed. We have blackouts. The son I would have later had them all his life. Or maybe the Hollands just don't like to remember what they have done. I believe sometimes it's better not to study on your thoughts too much. It can flat flummox your head, that's for sure.

I called Jared Cohen and told him what happened. "I'll be there in twenty-five minutes," he said.

"No, I want you to forget it," I said. "I got myself into this, and I'll get myself out of it. I want to talk to you about Midland."

"Midland, Texas?"

"Yes, Skeeter was poking around over there," I said. "He says there's some interesting geological things we should look at."

"We've got our hands full here, Bessie."

"Then we'd better take our hands someplace else."

The receiver went silent.

"Are you still with me?" I said.

"Nobody will ever own you, Bessie. With your permission I'm going to hang up and drive to your house. Then I'm going to take you to the best dinner you have ever had. Then we'll talk about Midland. Is that acceptable to you?"

I put on my best dress and waited for him in the living room. I wished I could talk to Papa, but I had no idea where he was. He didn't mean to, but he left a big hollow place in me when he took off and didn't have the common decency to tell me where he was going. I would rather he simply go away and tell me he was never coming back. Then I would be rid of him, as bad as that sounds. Leaving me guessing all the time was a torment, and even worse was the pain and self-degradation I experienced when I tried to explain the suffering he caused me. Sometimes I wanted to shoot Papa.

Everybody dies. Why shouldn't some people do it earlier than others? Oh, I didn't mean that. I just got so exasperated I wanted to pick up a thunder mug and pound some people in the head until it was a stump.

I was so deep in my thoughts, I barely heard the knock on the door. Nor did I hear the sound of a car. I put the chain lock on the door before I opened it.

"What are you doing here, Mr. Slick?"

"Worried about you, Miss Bessie. That son of a bitch Slim Millard is spreading rumors all over town you're being investigated in the murder of that bucket of beer-piss from New York City that probably had it coming."

"Mr. Slick, you will have to stop that language."

"I fret about you, Miss Bessie. I ain't got the smarts other men has got, but I just plain love you to death. Can I come in? It's getting right chilly. You don't have some pastries or jelly sandwiches handy, do you?"

How do you deal with a spirit such as Mr. Slick? What if heaven is filled with a few million like him? Have you ever thought about that? Anyway, I fixed him a snack. I also kept looking at my little pocket watch. But he paid it no attention.

"Mr. Slick, were you driving around in our north pasture three days ago?"

He looked studiously into space. "I don't own a car."

"Did you borrow one three days ago?"

"To borrow it I'd have to drive it. I ain't quite mastered that yet. Someone was driving around in your pasture?"

"Forget I mentioned it."

"No, ma'am, I ain't forgetting nothing. Bad people is aiming to kill you. I ain't gonna let that happen, Miss Bessie. I'm gonna get them first. You betcha."

"No, you are not!"

"One sure got his ticket stamped, didn't he?"

"Say that again?"

"The bucket of beer-piss—"

"What did I say about your language, Mr. Slick?"

"Excuse me, the gentleman from New York City is being dumped in a potter's field because nobody in New York City wants to pay for the embalmment and shipping in a train car. Also, the coroner don't want him stinking up the county garage, where he's at now, along with a couple of rats that got inside his clothes. I say we chalk up a few others."

"No," I said. "You do not 'chalk up a few others.'"

"I know. If you said otherwise, it wouldn't be you talking, Miss Bessie. You're a kindhearted woman, and that ain't ever gonna change." He took a deep breath.

"What is it, Mr. Slick?"

"I just wish I wasn't me."

"Don't say that."

"Well, I'm stuck with what I am. That's all I was saying. It's a terrible fate."

But that was not all he was saying. Mr. Slick was lonely and homely, like a balloon in the wind, and probably would never find safe harbor. He finished his strawberry-jam sandwich and sucked his thumbs and all his fingers. He seemed to read my mind. "It's just good to have a friend like you, Miss Bessie. Spirits like me don't usually get assigned to intellectuals."

Through the side window I saw Jared Cohen's sports car coming up the road. Mr. Slick saw it, too. "I didn't know you was having company," he said. "You should have told me."

"You don't have to go. Have dinner with us."

"I know my betters," he said. "I'm gone."

"Don't leave with your temper up, Mr. Slick. Don't commit a crime on my behalf."

He went out the back door without answering, his eyes glassy, his profile as sharp as tin.

I opened the front door for Jared.

"Ready to go?" he said.

"I'm not sure. Did you see Mr. Slick?"

"The spirit who visits you sometimes? No, I didn't."

"He doesn't let everyone see him," I said.

"I gathered that."

"You don't believe he's real, do you?"

"I don't challenge the beliefs of others, Bessie. The people who deny a greater reality than the physical one take the easy way out. They destroy the great mystery, and with it the incremental discovery of art and science."

This was why I was falling in love with Jared Cohen. I did not want to go out to eat, and I did not want to take a drive. I longed for my father and mother, who were not there. And my brother

Cody, who was not there. I was tired of being alone. To this day I believe a rejected child is the saddest person on earth, and I want to kill the people who made them orphans. Years later from the time about which I have written, I heard a quotation from a child who died in one of Adolf Hitler's extermination camps. Her last words were "I want my mommy." Those words have never left me, not for one day.

I'm sorry for digressing. But sometimes I just cain't help it.

"Jared?"

"What is it?"

"I don't know how to say this?"

"Don't think about this policeman from New York or the sheriff or any of their minions. They're not worthy to breathe the same air as you."

"I don't want to go to dinner. I've got things inside me that are really bad."

"How about I fix something from your icebox?"

"No."

"Oh, Bessie, I hate to see you hurting like this."

"I'm all right. On occasion I have spells. That's all."

"No, you are not all right. The world has not treated you fairly. You know what Thomas Jefferson said? 'I tremble for my country when I reflect that God is just.'"

He put his hands on my shoulders and tried to look into my face, but I wouldn't let him. I ran upstairs and closed my bedroom door, and curled into a ball and stayed like that for at least an hour, then fell asleep and didn't wake until dawn. I guess you could say I acted like a child.

I could hear my slippers flapping and echoing in the emptiness of the house as I walked down the stairs. The woodstove was dead and there was frost on the windows, the front door unlocked. I stepped out on the porch without a coat or hat. I could see steam rising from our cattle in the pasture, and the sun glittering coldly on Jared's sports car. I walked down the steps, the dust blowing in the wind. He was sleeping behind the wheel, a blanket draped over his head. He opened his eyes, although I had made no sound.

"Oh, there you are, you sleepyhead," he said. "Look at the sun. It's a grand day. Let me fix us some eggs."

Chapter Forty-Three

I guess I have learned a lesson or two. But what I have learned is pretty depressing. The big lesson? Don't plan. No matter what it is, good or bad, it's not going to happen. I never dreamed I would live in a New York slum, nor would I have a corrupt Northern police officer chasing me in Texas. Or see that same police officer get his comeuppance in a harsh fashion.

On top of that, we were just getting started. Do you remember the man named Tater Dog or Mr. Dog? The one who had a head that looked like a ball of yellow wax someone had tamped with a ball-peen hammer, and a face that had been splattered with bird shot? Indian Charlie's friend? The one who tried to assault me and whose foot I spiked with Ida Banks's knitting needle?

Four days after the body of the New York police officer was found, a hobo in the early hours climbed into a deserted boxcar not far from the school where all this had its origins, where Ida was fired and Cody was almost blinded with a slingshot and where I said goodbye to the Texas educational system. The hobo had just relaxed on some grain sacks and moldy hay and was about to enjoy his bottle of wine when he discovered he was not alone.

A body was resting on its side two feet from the hobo. Because the temperature was fairly cool, serious decomposition had not begun. Although the tissue was discolored, it was still rubbery and the coroner with just the naked eye could tell how Tater Dog or Mr. Dog had died.

I was in the open-air market only a few blocks away when I heard about it. Some of Mr. Dog's friends at the Green Lantern Saloon were indignant, and said their friend was "a good ole boy" and did not deserve his fate. So I drove to the boxcar to see what they meant by "his fate."

The sheriff was not there, and neither was the press or the publisher I trusted after Sheriff Millard maligned me and tried to charge me with a homicide. But his friends knew what they were talking about.

I took no joy in the death of Mr. Dog, even though he had wrestled me to the ground while Ida Banks was being raped by Indian Charlie. Whoever killed Mr. Dog hated the world. I was not far from the boxcar when the body was removed. The coroner was talking to an assistant. He was a retired military man, and had been in Cuba in 1898 and later in the Philippines. The stories that came back from the Philippines were not proud ones.

"The bastard who did this was delivering a blow with a blade and probably brass knuckles simultaneously," the coroner said. "And bloody well enjoying it."

Then he saw me listening. "May I help you, Miss Holland?" he said.

"Yes, where is Sheriff Millard?"

"Out of town, I think."

"I'm shocked," I replied. "Am I still a suspect in the killing of the New York policeman?"

"Only an idiot would think you a suspect in a crime of any kind, Miss Holland."

"Thank you, sir," I said.

I started to walk back to my Maxwell Touring Car, then stopped. "I knew the dead man in the boxcar," I said to the coroner.

"He's a friend of Indian Charlie. He tried to rape me. He also watched while Indian Charlie raped Miss Ida Banks."

His face turned to stone. "I didn't know that," he said. "But it enrages me. Is your father back in town?"

"No, sir, he is not. Why do you ask?"

He looked at the body in the boxcar. The blood had turned black, the skin blue. "Because you shouldn't be alone," he replied.

A pall fell on the town for the next few days and nights. People locked their doors, and turned off their lights early so they could not be seen through their windows, even in the Bog. A preacher held an open-air prayer service near the old stucco water well left by Spanish missionaries. The drunkards that hung around the Green Lantern Saloon were gone from the street. The hardware store on Main had a run on guns and ammunition. The newspaper printed an editorial written by the president of our Chamber of Commerce advocating calm, although there was no lack of calm but rather the opposite—the town had the vibrance of a corpse.

On an early morning I drove in my Maxwell Touring Car to Bertha Lafleur's lavish Victorian home in San Antonio. I went deliberately in the morning so I could catch her at her residence rather than her place of business. And I told no one where I was going, not even Jared Cohen or Aint Minnie or Ida Banks.

The gunsel named Fletcher opened the door. He had a facial expression that reminded me of wet concrete. He was wearing his Mauser pistol, the strap tight across his white shirt. "Good morning," I said. "Would you tell Miss Bertha that Miss Bessie would like to speak to her?"

"You got an appointment?"

"I don't remember," I said. "You can ask her that after you deliver my message."

I couldn't blame him for his hostility. The last time I saw him, I poked him in the snout and swatted him on the side of the head with a broom. But manners are manners, and this man had none. He continued to stare at me, breathing through his mouth. "Would you just not stand there, sir?"

"Wait here," he said, and closed the door in my face.

I immediately opened the door and went into the foyer. "Sir, your station in life is not your fault. If you could do another kind of work, you probably would. However, that does not give you license to abuse others."

The light in his eyes was of a kind I never wanted to see again. I wasn't afraid of him, but neither did I wish to act foolishly with a dangerous man. I knew why I had taken issue with someone whose hostility I should have ignored. I was punishing myself for the way I acted with Jared Cohen. I had run up to my bedroom like a spoiled child. And I had another problem, too. I had thoughts and desires about Jared that I should not have allowed myself. I know I dwell on being a good Baptist. But that's the way I have always been. Sometimes it really makes me angry.

Fletcher was still staring at me.

"Sir, I apologize for seeming sharp," I said. "I have bad days."

His eyes went away from me, then came back. He nodded, then went into the kitchen. A moment later, Bertha came out. "What a lovely surprise," she said. "Join me for coffee, will you?"

We sat at her kitchen, with a view of her backyard. The frost had killed or damaged many of her tropical flowers, like an affliction. I was never good at symbology, but it was very disturbing, and I didn't know why.

"I've come to you out of need, Miss Bertha," I said. "I cain't find my father and am terribly worried about him. I am also hurt by his behavior."

"His indifference, you mean?"

"Yes, his indifference," I said.

"Your feelings are understandable, Bessie. Your father is probably in Mexico and in a brothel, a saloon, or jail. Or maybe he's dead. He will never change."

"That's not helpful," I said.

"It's what he is. Don't torture yourself. And stop calling me 'Miss.'"

"You're still angry at him, aren't you?" I said.

She looked like I slapped her. "For what?" she said.

"Not marrying you."

She started fiddling with her coffee spoon, then hit on her temples with the heels of her hands and went to the window. "We get one life. I chose what I am. Look at the flowers. The petals are turning gray, almost overnight. Is this some kind of awakening? If so, it's not a pleasant one."

"Maybe you're a better person than you think you are, Bertha."

"Don't fool yourself," she said.

Mama always said never to touch a bruise on the soul of another. But I did not know how to speak of Bertha Lafleur's life without doing just that.

"A prostitute in Beeville was mutilated outside a saloon," I said. "At one time she worked in one of your cribs."

Her chest was rising and falling, her face heating. "Go on," she said.

"Was it Indian Charlie?"

"What do you think? There's nothing he's not capable of."

"He would amputate my leg?"

"You act like I'm to blame," she said.

"I don't have bodyguards, Bertha."

She sat back down and swallowed. "Do you carry a weapon?"

"Yes."

"What kind?" she said.

I told her.

"That's too small. Fletcher, come here!"

Fletcher came to the kitchen door. "Yes, ma'am?" he said.

"Would you give your Mauser to Miss Bessie? I'll reimburse you or buy you another one."

His eyes were flat, his face insentient. "I prefer to keep it, ma'am," he said.

"I don't want the property of other people, Miss Bertha," I said. "Thank you just the same. And pardon me for calling you 'Miss.' It's the way I was raised."

"Thank you, Fletcher," she said.

He disappeared from the doorway. Bertha's face was red. "You came here for advice. I'm not the one to give it. The day does not pass without something pulling loose in my life. Each day seems shorter and a little cooler. Do you know the song 'Red River Valley'?"

"Yes," I said.

"That's where I wanted to live. The Red River Valley seemed like the most beautiful place in the world. I wanted to spend my life as a ranch girl with Hackberry Holland, the man who plumb broke my heart."

I guess you never know what's on the other side of a coin, I thought. I got up from the table and thanked her for her time, then walked back down the driveway to my Maxwell Touring Car. On the seat was the German Mauser 1896 broomhandle pistol. It was unloaded, but a box of cartridges lay next to it.

Go figure.

The big irony of my trip to San Antonio was waiting for me in our mailbox out on the road. It was a letter from Papa written on the back of a pamphlet promoting a surgeon in Kansas who transferred goat glands into impotent men. It read:

Dear Daughter,

After getting stirrup-drug and kicked in the face, I was stuck seventeen days in a Coahuila jail with some of the nastiest varmints you have ever seen. The good news is I've found your half-brother Ismael. He's a fine young fellow and has fought in France alongside colored troops from New York.

I will be home in two or three days after you receive this letter. I think maybe I should hang up my spurs.

Love,
Papa

I had heard it before, and I didn't want to hear it again. He hunted for a son who didn't want him, and left his daughter to dream of jackals and piranhas in an empty house. I tore up his letter and stuck it back in the box, and hoped he saw it when he returned.

Then I learned the mechanisms of the Mauser semiautomatic pistol Fletcher had given me, and shot the whole box of cartridges at tin cans behind the house, and drove back to town and bought another box of bullets and practiced some more.

Two days later Papa telegrammed and asked me to pick him up at the train station the following afternoon. It was a strange request. He had many faults, but he didn't like people waiting on him. He thought it was a reverse form of servitude and control. Anyway, I went to the station in my Maxwell Touring Car. I couldn't believe what he looked like when he stepped down from the Pullman, a colored porter steading him with one hand.

Papa was a skeleton. I had heard about dysentery in Mexican jails. He always said Mexico wasn't a country. It was a rip in the firmament where pain and human sacrifice were written in the stone and generational poverty was a given and the beauty of the land belonged to whoever owned the most guns. The kind of place Papa loved.

When I saw him on the train platform, I wanted to cry. He was not only emaciated, his face was webbed with scabs and abrasions that ran into his hair. His Stetson and his favorite Western coat were gone.

"Is that your automobile?" he said. "Heavens, that's a vehicle for swells, Bessie. Who taught you how to drive?"

"Myself."

I thought another insult was coming.

"I should have known. There's not a dadburn you cain't do. I've never seen the like of it. Let's go in the station and get some ice cream. You look wonderful."

That was Papa, mercurial as quicksilver always on the sunny side, never conceding to the Great Shade. "Why are you looking at me, daughter?"

"What did they do to you, Papa?"

"Hit me with a telephone book and a few other things."

"What did you do to get in jail?"

"Tried to join up with Zapata. I think they're going to kill him. Anyway, I'm done."

I'd heard that before. But I was happy to have him home. We stopped by the ice cream stand in the station, then put his suitcase in the back of my Maxwell Touring Car and headed home. He fell asleep, with his chin on his chest, then woke up just as we were approaching the mailbox on the dirt road.

"Aren't you going to pick up the mail?" he said.

"I forgot," I said.

But I never forgot the mail or the newspaper and the little notes from neighbors who couldn't afford telephones.

I parked my car and got out and scraped the mail out of the box, letting the pieces of his letter drift down the road.

"What's all that paper blowing in the ditch?" he said.

"An advertisement or something," I said.

"You got my letter, didn't you?"

"Oh, yes," I said. "It's mighty good to have you back, Papa."

"Thank you," he said. "Did you know you've got more twitches than a frog on a woodstove?"

I said nothing to him about the death of the New York policeman. He had closed the book on what had occurred in Harlem and I did not want to revisit it, either. I do not know if there's a hell, but if there is, Tony Vale earned a job shoveling coal, so I say let him enjoy his new career, and the heck with the rest of it.

But I had another problem when it came to sharing with Papa. His father the preacher was a violent and drunken and dangerous man, and left many an emotional scar on his son. The consequence was Papa would belittle my injuries, which increased them tenfold.

However, he had one gift I could count on, and it came to him from his long experience as a Texas Ranger with gunmen such as Deacon Jim Miller and Wes Hardin and King Fisher: he understood bad people and could smell them from a mile away, and look at the scene of a crime and figure it out in five minutes. He used to say, "I am not omniscient. Stupid people are stupid, and all criminals are stupid. The short version is, you cain't scrub the stink out of shit."

I fixed a steak for him his first night back and tomato soup and mashed potatoes and fried eggplant for myself, and ate in the kitchen and watched the sun go down.

"I probably shouldn't talk about this at the table, but while you were gone that fella named Tater Dog was killed," I said.

He stopped eating, his eyes in neutral space. "The one that tried to assault you?"

"Yes, he died in a boxcar by the school. I heard the coroner talking to his assistant. He said the killer used a knife and brass knuckles at the same time. Unless I heard wrong."

Papa went back to eating. "He's talking about a trench knife. The blade is sharp and pointed and thin, like a razor is. The handle is actually a set of brass knuckles. You can get them in any pawnshop. What did the sheriff have to say?"

"He wasn't around."

"Yep, Millard is good at not being around. Is Aint Minnie all right?"

"No, he's given her a terrible time."

"He'll get one between the eyes directly," he said.

"How do you know that?"

He rubbed at his forehead. "That man's got death painted all over him. He knows it's coming, and he's scared out of his britches. That's why he's cruel. That's why all of them are cruel."

Chapter Forty-Four

Peculiar things began happening. Our neighbors were not happy with us. Maybe some of them felt we were more prosperous than they, and simultaneously were drawing off the reservoir of oil we had punched into. One of our pumps was blown up, probably by a stick of dynamite. The pressure coming out of the hole was like an ocean bursting though the neck of a soda bottle. The wellhead ignited, and the flame blew at least two hundred feet into a black sky, the pasture jittering with light. The specialists from Dallas who handled blowouts charged us a fortune.

I wanted to blame my neighbors, in part because I could understand their resentment. We had four hundred acres. Most of them had twenty or thirty. But I believed then and I believe now that Indian Charlie had decided to declare war on Papa and me and the Holland Oil Company. But we could not prove that. Nor could we prove that Atlas Oil might be encouraging the evil ways of Indian Charlie, a man who delighted in the pain and degradation of his victims.

Think I am exaggerating? Ask your United States senator to criticize the Arabian degradation of women and girls and the beheadings of their criminals and the crucifixion of their bodies.

Slim Millard, our sheriff, said there was no evidence of an explosion, and if there was, he would bet on the Industrial Workers of the World as the saboteurs.

"Our workers are IWW," I said.

"I'll believe that when I see it."

"I'll show you our books."

"They may get union wages, but they ain't in the union," he replied, picking his teeth, looking at the hump of concrete poured on one of our most productive wells. "Got you, girlie."

"You're a vile man," I said. "Please don't come here again."

He picked up a stray chunk of dried cement and bounced it off the top of the sealed well. "I'm gonna be around to haunt your little ass until the day you die. You can tell your father that, too. If he ain't drunk."

That night the war news was bad and it influenced our lives in an irrational way, maybe because we sent off our boys with grand parades, then discovered that some of them would not be coming home. Maybe we wanted to prove we were part of their sacrifice. I don't know. The only lesson I've learned in life is that people in groups do not think very well.

The Germans had used dirigibles to drop bombs on British cities. They blew apart civilian homes and burned and mutilated and buried alive hundreds of innocent people. We had blackouts three nights in a row, with a single searchlight in a cornfield sweeping the skies. Ironically, on the third night we experienced a dry electric storm that was so bright the searchlight was useless. Then we had hail that pounded like hammers all over the county. I had never heard so much racket. My ears were ringing. Then it stopped.

I had gone to church that night. In the silence all of us went outside to see the damage. The stars were winking among the clouds, and the air wet and fresh, and fog was puffing along the ground. It felt like spring, and perhaps a new beginning, perhaps like the baptismal moment Mr. Slick talked about when he lectured the rest of us on the metaphysics of making movies.

The downtown area was dark. The only light burning was in a window on the corner of the courthouse, the office of Sheriff Slim Millard.

The lighted window was not unusual, nor the lack of movement inside the office. The sheriff came and went at odd hours. The broken window glass was explainable, too. The courthouse lawn was covered with hailstones. It was a smear on a tall shard of glass protruding from the window frame that brought the attention of a passerby. It glittered darkly against a lamp on the sheriff's desk. The passerby walked gingerly across the lawn and peered into the office, then cupped his mouth and ran into the town square, shouting, "Help! Somebody has hurt the sheriff! Oh, who could have done this? Please help! Maybe there's time!"

I had just left the church a half block away, and was about to start my Maxwell. (I had stopped calling it my Touring Car, lest I become a snob and become prideful about material possessions, which in fact I was.) A few people had already started running toward the courthouse. Most of the electorate liked Slim Millard because he enforced Jim Crow, and did it without making them watch his handiwork. Or course, they would not admit that, and would be indignant if someone raised the possibility. In my case, I did not want to see any more of Slim Millard, and tried to keep in mind Jesus's admonition in Matthew 5:25 to settle our differences with our adversaries quickly and be done with them.

Then an ambulance came out of nowhere while somebody was trying to cut the chain on the front door with bolt cutters. I didn't believe Jesus would want me to flee an emergency, regardless of the disgusting and depraved subhuman who was in the middle of the emergency. Plus, I had Girl Scouts of America medical training.

I followed a solitary ambulance attendant who was running down the corridor with a stretcher collapsed on his shoulder. Other people were behind me, a deputy trying to hold them back. The sheriff lay in the middle of his office, his face jerking, his arms outstretched. There were four or five punctures in his chest. He was wearing a checkered flannel shirt and his striped britches and his stovepipe boots and a big silver belt buckle with longhorns on it. A bubble of blood and saliva fluttered on his lips. Empty cartridges were scattered all over the floor. One eye had rolled back in his head. The other was staring straight at me.

"I just got back from France," the attendant said. "I ain't got no training for this."

"We need to turn him on his side," I said.

"Yeah, shit, what am I thinking?" the attendant said. He started to roll the sheriff over.

Then the sheriff spoke. He was gasping, the bubble on his mouth broken. "Her."

"What?" the attendant said.

"Her," the sheriff repeated.

The attendant got down on one knee. "Who did this to you, Sheriff?"

The sheriff was swallowing, trying to twist his head and clear his throat, trying to keep his good eye on me. "Her," he said.

I got down on my knees and turned my head and leaned down over his mouth. "What is it, Sheriff?" I said.

His voice was like a feather inside my ear: "I ain't ready," he whispered.

"For what?" I said, although I knew.

He breathed through his mouth, in and out, his good eye on the ceiling. "I'm scared."

I picked up his left hand and held it with both my hands. "Say what I say."

"Say what?" he replied.

"Just repeat my words, sir," I said, and tried to smile. "Don't be afraid."

I put my mouth to his ear and said some words he repeated slowly one at a time. Then I held his hand in mine until the light went out of his eye and he stopped breathing and his mouth locked open. His fingernails had broken my skin.

"What was y'all talking about?" the attendant asked.

I got to my feet, my knees aching.

"Did you hear me?" he said. "Who did this? Some maniac?"

"He didn't say," I replied.

"That don't make no sense. You ain't hiding something, are you?"

I had not paid much attention to the shells. There were nine or ten of them on the floor. All of them 7.63 rounds.

"It has been nice meeting you," I said.

"What do you mean?" he said. "What's going on?"

I didn't reply. I wanted to leave the courthouse and never return. No one else had entered the room, but a crowd had formed in the corridor. All of them were waiting for me to say something, but I didn't. I walked through the crowd without speaking and went out the door into the cold cleanness of the night and the starry dustiness of the heavens, and pretended I was rising into the constellations, that I was set loose from the world and would never touch its surface again.

Be my light, my sword, and my shield, I said inside my head. *Let me be as brave as Joan of Arc and Boudicca and Perpetua and Felicity and Sacajawea and Sojourner Truth. Let me be more than I am.*

In the early morning I saw Mr. Slick drive up to the front of the house in a Model T and get out. It had just started to rain. He was wearing an Australian diggers' hat and looked right handsome in it. I opened the door before he could knock. Papa was still asleep.

"I got to do some serious talking to you," he said.

"I was fixing to say the same thing," I replied. That was the truth. I hadn't slept all night, even with my pillow clamped around my head. I had one of the biggest burdens my conscience ever had to carry. I felt like pouring a quart of castor oil in my brain.

"It can wait, Miss Bessie. I been holding back on something for a long time. I was a criminal with Indian Charlie. I never hurt nobody physically, but I was always in the background and I knowed that he was evil through and through and capable of doing things I don't want to ever talk about. Are you hearing me or am I scaring your socks off?"

"That was back then, Mr. Slick. That's not now."

"No, I got to come clean and say it all, rain or shine or whether you slap me cross-eyed or not."

"Sit down," I said.

He took off his hat and wiped his face with his hand. I thought he was fixing to cry.

"Sit down!" I repeated, and shoved him on the couch. "I need your help, Mr. Slick, and I don't want to hear anything about Indian Charlie. You know about the sheriff?"

"Yeah, the son of a bitch ate a shitload of lead pistol balls," he said, then made a face at what he'd said.

I started to lecture him on his profanity, but didn't. Why not? Since last night I had the heart-dropping sense that I had no moral authority to judge anyone. Why? I was pretty sure who shot the sheriff. Maybe I even heard the name come from the sheriff's lips and paid it no mind and deliberately concentrated on his theological situation as a better option than anything else. But it lay heavily on my soul, like a chain wrapped around my chest.

"You ain't gonna fuss at me for using bad language?" Mr. Slick said.

"I might have to inform on someone," I said.

"What?" he said.

I repeated myself.

"No, you ain't got to do no such thing, Miss Bessie. Stay away from them people."

"What people?"

"The law. They ain't no good. At least the ones here'bouts."

But that was not the subject on his mind. His face was tilted up, his mouth puckered, his eyes bursting with something he wanted to say. His small hands opened and closed in his lap.

"You know about the woman that got her leg cut off?" he said.

"Yes," I said, my voice hoarse.

"Indian Charlie done it. But it ain't the only time."

"Pardon?" My heart felt like it was eaten by threadworms.

"Eight or nine years ago. He told me when he was drunk. That's when I run off from him and his gang. I ain't never told you that because I was ashamed."

"Well, you've told me now, so I forgive you, Mr. Slick."

"That ain't all. I saw Jubal Fowler's father on the street yesterday. He said, 'Tell the Holland girl she's fixing to walk like me. Dragging one leg or none at all.'"

There were tears in his eyes.

"Mr. Fowler is a woebegone man," I said. "He beat and demeaned his son and ruined his young life, and was crippled by a young girl, namely me, and probably wakes up every day despising himself."

"Indian Charlie come into my house last night. At first I thought it was a dream. But it was him. He said, 'I got the green light, Slick. I'm taking y'all apart piece by piece.'"

"Why would he want to warn us?" I said. "I think you had a dream, Mr. Slick."

"It wasn't no dream. He threw a dead bat on my chest, then walked out the back door into the rain."

I heard Papa moving around upstairs. Mr. Slick looked up at the ceiling. I thought he was going to bolt and run.

"I'll fix us some breakfast," I said.

"I'd really like that," he replied.

⋆   ⋆   ⋆

I went to the office Jared Cohen had rented in town and told him everything Mr. Slick had said. But I didn't mention the knowledge I possessed about the possible killer of Sheriff Slim Millard. Jared listened quietly, his gaze drifting casually a few times out the window at the wagons and horses and motorized vehicles passing by, some of the wagons and trucks stacked with drill pipe.

After I finished, he knitted his fingers and said, "Mr. Slick is a good fella, I'm sure, but an imaginative one, also. I'm more worried about your experience with the sheriff's last moments. I think you acted with great courage and humanity. Yet you say nothing about that."

"What's to say, Jared? He died, the poor thing."

"It is hard to think of this man as a 'poor thing.' He tried to file charges against you for the murder of a New York policeman. Did he renounce that? Did he apologize?"

"No."

"So what did he say?"

"He feared for his soul."

"I see. Well, his fear was probably justified. But I think you're not being square with me, Bessie."

Nothing got past Jared Cohen.

"There were cartridges all over the floor," I said. "They were 7.63 rounds. I know because I was given a Mauser broomhandle. I bought cartridges for it just recently. In town. I have already gotten a call from the state attorney general's office in Austin. They would like to talk to me."

"Who cares? You tried to help a dying man. You can't be a killer and a savior at the same time."

"I'm not a 'savior,' Jared. People believe whatever they need to. The Austin people could build a case against me in five minutes."

"The sheriff didn't try to tell you who shot him?"

I let my eyes go empty.

"This isn't a time to protect someone, Bessie."

"Sheriff Millard uttered a name."

"You want to tell me whose?"

"He said it out of context. He was dying. It could mean anything. He thought he was going to hell. If I give out this person's name, this person will be eaten alive."

"You will not even give the gender?"

"You are not listening to me, Jared. I'm not going to say any more."

"That's all right."

"What do you mean 'it's all right'? I feel like I have broken glass in my head."

"No, no, you misunderstood me, Bessie. If you're holding back, you have a valid reason."

I was full of fear and confusion and conflicting voices inside my head. I had to do something, but I did not know what.

"Thank you, Jared," I said. Then I got up and left.

"Come back," he said.

But I didn't.

I started the Maxwell and drove straight home and did not stop at the house but kept going past the windmill and the barn into the north pasture, Traveler and Lancelot looking curiously at me, my Maxwell vibrating like a fissure was opening under my wheels, all the way to the equipment sheds where Skeeter and his crew were racking pipe.

The rain had quit, and the sun was out, and there was a gentle breeze blowing through the grass.

"Howdy, Miss Bessie," Skeeter said. "Could I he'p you?"

"Good morning, Mr. Skeeter," I replied. "Do you know where Jubal Fowler is?"

"Over yonder in the shed," he replied. "Something wrong?"

"How is he doing?"

"You mean about drinking and all?"

"Yes."

"Fine. The boy has really shaped up since you talked to him. Carrie Nation couldn't have done no better."

"Carrie Nation?" I said.

"I'll get him right now, Miss Bessie."

Chapter Forty-Five

Jubal walked to my car window, shading his eyes with one hand. "You finally gonna go to the picture show with me?" he said.

"I wanted to see how you're doing," I said. "Mr. Skeeter says you're doing real good."

He looked at the horizon, where the trees were blowing and leaves were churning in the air. "You know me. If I stay away from the saloon, I'm right as rain. How are *you* doing?"

"Fine," I said. "You heard about Sheriff Millard?"

"I sure did."

"Who do you think would do something like that?"

"Every darkie in the county?"

"That's not funny."

"Probably not. But Slim was mean as spit to colored people. There isn't no question about it, Bessie."

"You used to call your slingshot a nigger-shooter."

"I don't talk like that no more. Not since I was in the reformatory and seen what the colored boys had to go through."

But I knew he wasn't thinking about the reformatory or colored people. He hung his hands over the windowsill, his head hanging half down. "You reckon there's a chance for you and me?"

"Chance for what?"

"Don't act dumb, Bessie."

"We're longtime friends, Jubal."

"There's friends and then there's friends," he said.

"You have a lot of qualities, Jubal. You didn't wait for the Selective Service. You volunteered and came home a hero. I admire you. I always did."

He grinned. "Yeah, 'admire.' I like that word. I declare, I never thought I would be 'admired.'"

"Don't make fun of me," I said.

"I'd cut out my tongue before I'd do that. I just don't know why you—" His words caught in his throat. "I think I'm coming down with a cold. I'd better get back on it. Skeeter don't look kindly on loafing around."

He bounced the cup of his hand on the windowsill and walked away.

"Jubal?" I said.

He pretended not to hear.

I drove to the house and went inside and sat in the gloom by myself. I had no idea where Papa was. I didn't know anyone could feel this alone.

I did something unusual early next morning, just at sunrise, when the only lights burning in town were at the Green Lantern and the funeral parlor, which I never understood. I drove to the old school and parked in back and got out and walked onto the playground. The building was smoking with dew, the dirt in the playground damp and gray and packed as smooth as soaprock. The school had plumbing now, but the outhouse was still there. The outhouse where all this started. The outhouse where I tempted Jubal Fowler and got him into a fight with Cody, one that almost blinded him.

I pulled open the door, the hinges squeaking. The two holes sawed in the planks where we squatted looked hand carved and rubbed free of splinters, the earth down below no longer smelling of chemicals, no longer a fecal threat, no longer an undefined connection to the seminal urgencies we carried inside us without understanding what they meant.

But as I stood in the doorway, I was not alone. A tiny cottontail rabbit was hunkered down on the dirt, probably trapped inside, its ears pinned back, its nose twitching, its warm brown eyes bright with fear.

"Hi, little fella," I said, stepping aside. "Run along now and find your mommy. She's probably back in the woods. And don't be coming to the schoolground. It's nothing but trouble."

He took off, just like I said, running the way cottontails run, in S's and circles, then finding a hole or another place to hunker down.

I went back to my Maxwell and started the engine. It coughed and backfired and rattled, and I drove through the town and made all the racket I could make, wanting to get even with whatever people get even at.

What am I saying here? I'll tell you. Living on this planet is a serious matter if you think about what you and your cohorts do on a daily basis and stop pretending what's going on around us.

I felt a dark time was at hand. Spanish influenza had struck the nation and had begun killing hundreds of thousands of people. President Wilson let a patriotic parade go forward in Philadelphia, no matter what the attrition, claiming that the war effort would be impaired if the parade was cancelled, and twenty-seven thousand people died. Meanness is meanness, whether in the form of a germ or a Princeton professor in the White House jailing those who criticize his policies.

Most people might say the discordance and struggles in a defeated Southland were of a different kind, but I think they would be wrong. We had stepped through the door at the bottom of the century and found our agrarian world suddenly shrunken, a skyline of smokestacks more common than a forest or limestone fences and red barns and Holstein cows grazing all on a green knoll. Plus we were beset with guilt. We put our fellow human beings up for sale.

The influenza pandemic would become most ravenous in San Antonio. That's where it would also die. And the oil industry and the Rockefellers would obtain power and wealth that had no precedent. The Sundance Kid and Butch Cassidy were already undone by the telephone, and the violence of the plains would shrink inside poisonous seed bearers like Indian Charlie, who would scorch his name on the sky or on the bodies of his victims, in the same way the Harpe brothers did. The lesson is: history doesn't repeat itself, it metastasizes.

Six days after the death of Sheriff Millard, burglars broke into an armory in San Antonio. The theft was of such serious concern, the army would not say what was stolen, other than "weapons."

On the seventh day after the sheriff's death, another one of our pumping wells was dynamited. Later that night someone slipped a note under our front door that read, *Hope you have read up on the lake of fire. If you have not, it is in the Book of Revelation. Night-night and sleep tight, you fucking bitch.*

Two detectives came down from Austin with a search warrant and went all over the house and the backyard and found the Mauser broomhandle pistol given me by Fletcher, and the spent cartridges and bullets I had fired at tin cans on a stump, one on which we used to butcher chickens, until I told Papa we were done killing critters of any kind.

The detectives seemed right proud of their work. "While y'all are here, why don't you inspect the pump well somebody blew into junk and a few thousand barrels of oil smoke?"

"Really?" one of them said. "That must have been pretty nasty. Remind us to come back and check that out."

They put the broomhandle pistol and the 7.63 bullets and empty cartridges in a canvas bag and tied the hand straps together, then wrapped a raincoat around the canvas bag and knotted a rope around the coat.

Now they could do whatever they wanted with the evidence, both the bullets in the sheriff's body and the spent shells on the floor of his office, the shells I bought from a vendor and the bullets I had fired in the backyard. Back then women were not allowed on a jury. If you were a girl my age, how would you like taking your chances with the system?

Then I had a funny dream, the kind that tells you what you're really thinking about during the day. My grandfather was in the Army of Northern Virginia and went up Cemetery Ridge, where in an hour's time eight thousand Confederates lay dead or dying on the slope in ninety-degree heat. My grandfather survived but just barely. As he lay in an ambulance wagon on the retreat, he heard two voices through the canvas flap. One of the men talking was General Lee.

"Sir?" my grandfather said.

"What is it, son?" the general asked.

"I have no water, general, and I fear I may die."

"Take my canteen. And don't die, either. I want you to come see me after the war."

Grandfather said the other soldier was A. P. Hill. But that's not the point of the story. My grandfather was released from a Yankee jail after the surrender and, with some other former prisoners of war, camped on the lawn at Washington College in Lexington, where General Lee was president. He invited my grandfather and his friends to attend Sunday Mass at the High Episcopalian church close by. My grandfather was very uncomfortable because he was a Baptist and thought Henry the Eighth was a washtub of whale sperm. Nonetheless, he could not offend the general.

After the consecration, an emancipated slave woman walked from the back of the church up the aisle and knelt at the Communion rail. The congregation was shocked and began murmuring and looking at each other; perhaps a couple of ushers headed up the sides of the congregation. General Lee immediately rose from his pew and walked quickly to the front of the church and knelt at the colored woman's side.

The inside of the church became as still as a broken clock. Then the other communicants lined up behind him, their hands folded in prayer.

I believed I understood what my dream meant. I think the general must have carried great guilt for the mistakes he made. They were not minor ones. He killed civilians as an artillery officer in the Mexican War of 1846, and sent fifty thousand men up Malvern Hill into Yankee artillery, and went up Cemetery Ridge after delaying an earlier and much better opportunity. His dreams must have reeked of death.

When he died in a fever, he supposedly said, "Strike the tent and call for Hill!"

I believe he said that; I don't think he was talking about the war, either. I believe he was talking about leaving the war forever, letting go of all the human folly that binds us to our vices and blinds us to the fruits of the earth.

That's what I wanted to do. I had made many serious mistakes, beginning with the moment I stepped in the school privy on that particular morning on the playground, when I knew Jubal Fowler would peek inside.

When I woke from my dream about General Lee, I decided I was through with worry and shame and guilt and all the other dross with which those emotions clutter the day. Let the world do its worst. Why fear the Veil? It's just the veil. Ask Stephen Crane.

Chapter Forty-Six

That evening, in the gloaming of the day, I made a bucket of hand-crank ice cream without letting Papa see me, then piled it in two bowls and took it into the living room, where he was reading his encyclopedias, his glasses perched on his nose, his cats all over the couch.

"That looks mighty good," he said. "You'd better get some more bowls."

"They're on the kitchen table," I said. "Just give me a minute."

"I wasn't fussing at you."

"Yes, you were, but don't worry about it," I said. Then I put his bowl on his stomach, almost dropping it, and went back in the kitchen, closing the swinging door, and filled the pet bowls and brought them in the living room and almost started a cat riot. Papa was laughing.

"Why do you enjoy chaos?" I asked.

"It beats dullness?"

"What are you reading?"

"An essay on 'The Miller's Tale' by Chaucer. That story sure sticks in your mind, doesn't it?"

I am not going to tell you why the word "sticks" is the last word in the English vocabulary you should use when discussing "The Miller's Tale."

"How's the ice cream?"

"Cain't beat it. Got a confession, daughter."

"What's that?"

"I could have popped a cap on Indian Charlie back before the turn of the century. And I could have gotten away with it, particularly down on the border. But I never dropped a man unless he pulled on me first. Although there's one exception, and it's plumb near driving me crazy. I never told you about the specifics of the attack on Pancho Villa's train. It had two locomotives, with a long string of boxcars and flatcars behind. The flatcars had sandbags and Maxim machine guns on them. The boxcars were loaded with peasants, the poorest of the poor. My horse went down under me, but the captain pulled me up behind his saddle and we started firing. Oh, Lordy, did we fire. Right into a car loaded with children and women and old men."

He set down his bowl. "You don't have to die to go to hell, daughter. It can catch you in your sleep and not let go."

"It was an accident, Papa."

"In your eyes. Or even mine. But not the families of those people who died. I spared Indian Charlie and murdered innocent people. There's something wrong with that equation."

I sat down by his side and put my hand on his shoulder. "You stop whipping yourself. You didn't do it on purpose. I don't want you ever blaming yourself like that again. Do you hear me?"

He bent his wrist downward and rubbed his eye with it. "You sound just like your mother," he said, and blew out his breath. "I declare."

The weather took a turn the next two days, in a way I had rarely seen. We were approaching winter, but the sky was stormy, threaded with lightning, sometimes splintering the clouds with thunderbolts that sounded like the earth was about to rip apart. All our friends came to see us, carrying stuffed eggs and salads and fruit cakes, acting like it was Thanksgiving or Christmas, or the way people do at a wake. I suspect you already know this, but you only find out who your friends are when you experience difficulty. You can have all the friends you want when you bring your checkbook. Your real friends back you up when your cotton has burned and the roof blown off your house.

Our friends didn't just go the long mile, they pestered us to death: Jared Cohen, Aint Minnie and Snowball, Ida Banks, Mr. Slick, Bertha Lafleur, the postman, the Mexicans and colored people who had been with us so long we couldn't remember their names. The darkness and lightning creaking in the clouds were scary, like a Good Friday painting, like a warning that forces greater than us were in play.

But Jubal Fowler, who should have been a friend, was not around, except to report for work and jump on the truck and go wherever the crew was going. He also had a habit of dropping from the back of the truck at the end of the day and walking home to the Bog. So that's where I went in my Maxwell, whether it was smart or not, and knocked on the Fowlers' door. Mr. Fowler opened it, his face lighting like a kitchen match.

"Well, lookee here," he said. "Miss Prima Donna."

He was still walking on crutches, his face still like rubber that kept flexing as though he couldn't control it, one eye lower than the other, a string of spittle dripping from the corner of his mouth. But his biceps had grown and looked as hard as oak from the amount of weight he had to press on his crutches.

"Hello, Mr. Fowler. May I speak to Jubal?"

"Trying to mess him up more than you have?"

"I thought Jubal liked working for us," I said.

"Tell your father to get himself a better brand of rubbers," Mr. Fowler said. Then shouted over his shoulder, "Get your ass out here, Jubal! It's Miss Outhouse of 1914."

"That's interesting, Mr. Fowler," I said. "The sheriff has said the same kind of insults to me. They're always anal. I'd forgotten y'all are in-laws."

Jubal came to the door. The sky was dark, the barometer dropping, a single flash of lightning in the clouds that made no sound. I could hear rain tinkling on the roof. "Maybe you ought to go, Bessie," he said through the screen.

"No, you have to talk to me."

He stepped outside and pulled the door behind him. "What's going on?" he said.

"Why have you been avoiding me?"

"I ain't. I get to work early. That's all."

"But you manage not to see me."

"I don't know what to say. I thought I was doing good work for y'all."

"You are, Jubal. But I'm troubled."

"About what?"

"Did you bring a German broomhandle from France?"

"I might have."

"Did you shoot Sheriff Millard with it?"

"Them things are all over the place," he said. "Don't be making up stories."

"Did you bring home a trench knife?"

"Same answer."

He wore a green cloth cap and his hair looked freshly cut and washed and dried; it made me think of the day Jubal Fowler might have become my Valentine rather than a source of constant trouble for me and himself.

"I know you want to take care of me," I said. "But I cain't let you make me an instrument of harm."

"I'm going inside now," he replied. "My father ain't the best person to live with. I'll keep in mind the things you said. Good night, Bessie."

He stepped inside and closed the door quietly.

I got in my Maxwell and drove home in the rain, the clouds lighting at the top of the sky. I felt I had just driven into a foreign country, but I didn't know how or where or why.

The storm hit two nights later. The thunder shook our house and the electricity lit the countryside and the rain flooded the roads, washing out the bridge where we used to throw wildflowers into the creek. Remember when I mentioned our postman as one of the friends who brought us gifts and such? He also owned the general store at the crossroads and sometimes delivered for the telegrapher at the train station. About ten o'clock the telephone rang. I picked it up from the coffee table in the living room. The electricity was out, and once again we were using kerosene lamps and candles plugged in soda bottles. Papa was half asleep on the couch.

"Hello?" I said.

"This is Herbert Volker, Miss Bessie. Sorry to bother you."

"It's no bother, Mr. Volker."

"I had a telegram for you, but my car slipped into the ditch. I can bring it to you tomorrow."

"It's for me, not my father?"

"Yes, it's for you."

"Do you know who's it from?"

"I cain't tell without opening it."

"Go ahead."

"Well, just a moment."

I heard him put down the telephone, then pick it up again.

"It's from Cody."

"Would you read it? You have my permission."

"I ain't supposed to do that, Miss Bessie. I'll lose my job."

"I understand."

I could hear him breathing against the telephone's surface. "So you'll pick it up tomorrow? That's what I'd do."

I wondered if Cody was in trouble.

"No, I'll drive down there now," I said. "It won't take more than ten minutes."

"Miss Bessie—"

His voice was full of phlegm.

"Are you all right, Mr. Volker?" I said.

"I think I got pneumonia," he said. "The front door will be unlocked. We'll be in back."

The connection went dead.

I woke up Papa and told him Cody had sent us a telegram that Mr. Volker was holding for us.

"He told you it's from Cody?"

"Yes."

He wiped the sleepiness out of his face with his sleeve. "I hope he's not in trouble. I just had a dream about him. I ran him off. My own son. God forgive me."

"You didn't aim to," I replied. "You've made it right in every way you can."

"I'll go down there with you."

"No, you'll end up with the Spanish flu. I've got my slicker."

"Take a pistol."

"It's under the seat of my Maxwell."

"I never saw anyone so proud of a traveling junk pile."

I started to verbally smack him. But I was premature in my judgment. "That's the poet in you," he said. "Just like your mother. I always loved that name. Alafair. I loved her name before I loved her. That's a funny way to be, isn't it?"

My Maxwell splashed through the holes on the way to the cross-roads, drenching the windshield, jarring my teeth. Up ahead I could see the general store and the small porch where people sat and talked and played checkers and dominoes and smoked and drank soda pop because Mr. Volker was a member of the Assemblies of

God and didn't believe in drinking alcohol. A candle or a lamp was burning in the back room. I parked the Maxwell and got down and went inside fast because the rain was flying and felt like it had BBs in it. Mrs. Volker was an invalid and in dementia, and her husband often read to her late at night. Mr. Volker was a very nice man.

I pushed the door shut and stamped my feet and pulled the slicker's hood off my head. I could see two figures in rocking chairs silhouetted against a kerosene lamp.

"Hello!" I called.

There was no answer. I was almost deaf from the wind and rain. "Mr. Volker? It's Bessie Holland."

Both figures seemed asleep, slumped forward, their faces in shadow. There was a Bible on a table and a cupcake with a single tiny candle stuck in it, one that was still pink and white and had never been lit.

I walked past the counter and into the room. I wished I had run. I could see their faces plainly now. Mrs. Volker had been shot behind her head; her hair was thick, iron-gray, a thin stream of blood running down her neck into her collar. Mr. Volker had been shot three times, all of them badly aimed. I couldn't move, as though I were caught inside a photograph. Mr. Volker probably tried to fight when he knew what was about to happen. He was brave and kind and was probably forced to make the call about the telegram to my house. Mrs. Volker, in her dementia, had to watch what was done to her husband. And I couldn't move, just like I was in a nightmare, my shoes glued to the floor.

"Gotcha, girl," Indian Charlie said, stepping out of a clothes closet. "You hear about them flamethrowers that was liberated from the armory in San Antonio? We're gonna have fun. You betcha."

He wasn't alone. Behind the store was a truck with a tarpaulin over the back and three men in the front seat, and two mounted, unshaved men in cowboy hats and shiny black slickers. Indian

Charlie tied my hands behind me, then twisted my hair in a knot around his fist and pushed me out in the rain and into the back of the truck, then climbed in after me.

"Why did you have to kill the old people?" I asked.

"I felt like it," he said, and grinned. He was seated across from me on a wood bench, with no hat, his scalp bony, his hair combed in streaks, his skin a waxy yellow, like the color of urine. Someone in front started the engine and turned onto the road, the floor rocking under us, some equipment vibrating under a tarp.

"I'll make you a deal," Indian Charlie said.

"You're evil, and you're going to hell where you belong. I don't talk to people who are going to hell."

"Well, you little shit," he said.

"Untie my wrists and say that to me."

"Is your father at home? Or out on a drunk?"

"Wouldn't you like to know?"

"You got a lot of money, girl. You can get yourself out of this. What I'm asking for ain't much, and it's also mine, so you ain't really losing nothing."

"The devil tried to tempt Jesus in the desert. It didn't do any good. I think you're probably worse than the devil. Plus, like all your kind, you stink."

"You see them two cowboys coming up behind us? Why do you think they're here."

"I don't care why."

"You will. I'm gonna take your animals."

"What?" I said.

"I got a particular interest in that horse that stomped me. What's his name? Traveler? I got you where it hurts, girl, and screaming ain't gonna do you no good."

Through the canvas flap I could see the two horsemen following us. I wondered what kind of men they were. I wondered why they would join forces with a man like Indian Charlie. But I knew the reason. My father had told me long ago. Like moths, they're drawn to the candle because the flame is the only light they know.

I got up, my wrists still tied, and tried to jump through the flap into the rain and mud, even under the horses' feet if necessary; I wanted to die there rather than be used against my father or the animals. Indian Charlie hit me in the jaw and knocked me to my knees, then dragged me to the rear of the truck's cab and put a second rope through the one on my wrists and looped it to an iron hook.

Suddenly the truck stopped, throwing me against the cab again. For a moment I thought another vehicle was coming on the road or the other outlaws had decided not to go up against my father or his friends, ones such as Frank Hamer. I heard the cab door squeak open, then a chopping sound, followed by a plummeting crash that brought down the only telephone lines that served our part of the county.

Indian Charlie winked at me. "Ain't no sleep for the wicked," he said.

A moment later the truck engine started again and the tires rumbled across a cattle guard.

Our cattle guard.

Chapter Forty-Seven

The truck stopped again. I thought Indian Charlie and his fellow degenerates were about to decide how to catch my father unawares and invade our home. But that wasn't it. Through the canvas I could see someone at a distance with a battery light. The three men in the cab got out and walked to the back of the truck. A ripple of lightning shone on their faces. I recognized only one of them—Winthrop Fowler, Jubal's father.

Indian Charlie was angry at him. "When are you gonna take control of that boy?" he said.

"Forget about him," Mr. Fowler said. "I'll talk to him later. You ain't even sure that's him."

"Oh, it's him all right. He cain't get that girl out of his mind. I ain't gonna have this, Winthrop."

"You tote your own end of the log," Mr. Fowler said. "I'll take care of mine."

"You ain't been taking care of anything, Winthrop," Indian Charlie said. "He killed a New York Peeler and my beloved friend Tater Dog, and then you went to clean up the mess by killing a goddamn sheriff. It makes me mad every time I think of it."

"You're not gonna talk to me like that, Charlie."

The wind had dropped and the rain had thinned, although the sky was still black, the moon erased from the heavens. I think

Mr. Fowler had made a mistake. Papa always said don't let your enemy know what you're thinking. Grin, look at your watch, yawn, open up the newspaper, but don't show one of your brain cells at work.

I could still see the battery light in the distance. It was bouncing as though someone were floating over the rows in the cornfield.

"I'm sorry, Winthrop," Indian Charlie said. "I'm getting old. Let's try to make a little money, tidy up the place, and find a café and have us some steaks and eggs."

"That suits me," Mr. Fowler said.

I knew then that Indian Charlie would not leave a soul alive on our property, not the animals, not the poultry, not me or Papa, and certainly not Winthrop Fowler. And if he had time, he would plow the ground with salt.

"What about my boy?" Mr. Fowler said.

"Jubal's just young," Indian Charlie said. "He'll learn. Just tell him to stop killing people for a while. Or at least without consulting."

"Sure, Charlie," Mr. Fowler said. "What about the girl and her father? You said if we get the money, we leave and all sins forgiven. That stands, right?"

Indian Charlie stuck a cheroot cigar in his jaw but didn't light it. His head was lowered, his neck like a long stick. "No reason that cain't happen. You know me. I go with the tide."

Then he stared in the distance.

"What's wrong?" Mr. Fowler said.

The horses were nickering, the two riders looking over their shoulders.

"That light in the field just went out," Indian Charlie said.

"Don't give it no never-mind," Mr. Fowler said.

"No never-mind?" Indian Charlie said. "That consoles me. It certainly does. Where in the hell did you learn English?"

Then a band of electricity pulsed in a cloud and leaped across the heavens, lighting the entire countryside.

"Spread out!" Indian Charlie said.

"What is it?" Mr. Fowler said, his crutches stiffening up.

"On the porch. It's that son of a bitch Hackberry Holland," Indian Charlie said.

I was never prouder or gladder to hear someone speak of my father in that fashion.

Indian Charlie got in the back of the truck with me, flinging the flap shut. Then he flung it again because he didn't tie it. Like Papa said, stupid is as stupid does. He continued to stand while the truck was moving, his body as lithe and balanced as a gymnast, his face deep in thought.

"What are you looking at?" he said.

"Not much," I said.

"You want me to break your face?"

"Go ahead. It will still look better than yours."

"Listen, girlie, I'm a businessman. Your father has put poison about me in your head for years. I work for a company. Not no different from the soldiers that got sent to the Philippines and were told to kill everybody in sight. Or the mercenaries like your father down in Mexico."

"You mutilated a prostitute."

"I did not."

"You left a note. It was a warning to me."

"It was Tater Dog who did that. Now listen to me. Everybody knows your father ain't a supporter of bankers or banks or greenbacks and buries as many gold and silver dollars as he can."

Some of that was true, but I wasn't going to let on. "That's silly."

"Y'all hit serious oil. Give me fifty thousand dollars and I'm gone."

"How about these men with you?"

DON'T FORGET ME, LITTLE BESSIE

"I'll take care of them."

"You'll take care of me, too, Mr. Charlie. I'll be dead. I can smell the sulfur on you. You're the real thing."

"What do you mean 'real thing'?"

"I'm not going to speak any more."

"You'll do what I tell you."

He waited for me to speak. When I didn't, he hit me in the face and knocked me against the cab again, my hands and arms tied behind me. Both my knees landed without any protection on the rough-hewed planks that made up the floor.

He grabbed my shirt and shook me. "Did you hear me? You'll do everything I say."

I lowered my face, expecting him to hit me again. But he didn't. He walked up and down, then tore the tarp off the device bouncing around on the floor. I had seen ones like it in the newsreels in the movie theater. There was no synchronized sound then, so a man from our church played the piano in an orchestra pit while on the screen French soldiers arced streams of flame into the concertina wire and the German trenches and watched the young men in bucket helmets wilt inside the fire.

"Like it?" said Indian Charlie. "You still deaf? Want me to beat you up? Hey!"

But I kept my vow and did not speak.

The driver of the truck circled behind the barn and stopped, then got out and came around and lowered the tailgate and helped me down while Indian Charlie held one of my arms, because my wrists were still tied. The driver kept his eyes askance. The horsemen were in the barn with Traveler and Lancelot. I heard Traveler's back feet smacking against the wall. I knew it was he because he didn't like or trust strangers, especially rounders and bounders like the trash who would ride for Indian Charlie and Winthrop Fowler.

Indian Charlie walked me into the barn. Traveler was rearing, flinging his front hooves high in the air, the two horsemen trying to get a rope around his neck.

I had to speak out, vow or no vow. I couldn't leave the animals to the mercy of these men.

"What are you going to do to my animals?" I said to Indian Charlie.

He had dragged the flamethrower by the tarp into the barn. He looked at it, his unlit cheroot still in his mouth, the tobacco wet and soft. "What you already know," he said.

"Mr. Charlie, don't do this," I said. "I'll get you the money that I can."

"How much?"

"What you said. Fifty thousand."

"Where's it at?"

"Spread around. My father will help me dig it up if I ask him."

"But you don't know where it's at?"

"I have an inkling."

"Why is it I think you're full of it?"

Mr. Fowler came into the barn on his crutches, his upper arms swelling. He had been watching the house. "You saw Hack Holland on the porch, Charlie?" he said.

"I have to repeat it for you?" Indian Charlie said.

"I ain't seen anybody anywhere. Not inside or outside. Not at the window. Or up on the balcony. I don't think there's anybody in there."

"You think I got the willies and I'm seeing things?"

"You just didn't see what you thought you did," Mr. Fowler said. "The lighting and all."

"Could it be that he's upstairs?" Indian Charlie said. "With that .44 Henry he's known for?"

"I guess," Mr. Fowler said.

DON'T FORGET ME, LITTLE BESSIE

"Ain't nobody getting the jump on you, Winthrop," Indian Charlie said. He lifted the flamethrower from the floor and dipped his arms inside the straps and swung the tanks snugly in place. "All right, all y'all stop what you're doing and follow me."

Then he gripped me around the bicep and began walking me toward the house. The rain was like black and silver thread spinning in the air, the windmill out of control, the blades whirring and vibrating so fast they rattled the whole structure, the windowpanes in the house shining like obsidian, and the paint on the wood was the color of lead, and the broken pots and scattered dirt and flowers on the porch were like an image taken from a Nathaniel Hawthorne story, one that did not end well, one that was Americana and lived and relived without knowing it.

Chapter Forty-Eight

Indian Charlie walked me to the front of the house, his fingers biting into my upper arm.

"Come out, Mr. Holland!" he shouted. "Your daughter wants to tell you something!"

There was no response, and I wondered if Papa had gone to bed. Papa could sleep through the apocalypse. Indian Charlie released my arm and took a small revolver from his pocket, cocked it with his thumb, aimed with one eye, and shot a single round through the living room window. I could hear it pinging and breaking glass throughout the house.

"I'm fixing to burn you down, Mr. Holland!" he shouted. "Cain't we talk in a businessman way?"

Papa opened the front door and stepped out on the porch, wearing a new Stetson but no coat, the barrel of his lever-action Henry propped on his shoulder. His gaze lingered on me, then back at Indian Charlie. "Say what you got to say, Charlie."

"This has been a long time coming, ain't it?" Indian Charlie said.

"Not for me," Papa said. "I hardly gave you much thought."

"You killed my people, Mr. Holland. An unkind man would have sought revenge. But I let it go."

"That was not my impression," Papa said.

"Let's cut the cow flop here, Mr. Holland. Your daughter says you got fifty thousand dollars buried around your property. Dig it up and give me what's mine and we'll be gone with no hard feelings."

"Has he hurt you, Bessie?" Papa said.

"No, Papa. I'm all right," I said.

"Turn her loose and I'll give you what you want, Charlie," Papa said.

"It don't work that way," Indian Charlie said.

Papa didn't answer.

"You got a hearing problem," Indian Charlie said.

"In a few hours the sun's going to rise," Papa said. "You cain't change that. My advice is you go back to Mexico, Charlie. Maybe get you a vegetable farm and sell tortillas for a living."

"I'm leaving here with my money, or you're gonna have one less member in the family, Mr. Holland."

Papa showed no reaction.

"You know me, Mr. Holland. There ain't nothing I ain't done in emergency situations."

Papa nodded, but didn't speak. Indian Charlie pressed the muzzle of his revolver against the side of my head, then cocked the hammer. I heard the cylinder lock in the frame, and closed my eyes, my breath gone. I thought I would faint.

Mr. Fowler suddenly came to life. "Hackberry, I hate your guts, but I ain't part of this."

"You could fool me," Papa said, his body as still as cardboard, his right hand hooked through the lever of the Henry, his forefinger on the trigger. I could feel the muzzle of Indian Charlie's revolver against my scalp. Each second was like falling through space.

"I'll take you on, Hackberry," Mr. Fowler said. "Pistols or rifles or knives. I ain't choicy."

But he was talking and performing for Indian Charlie and the other men, not my father, and Indian Charlie knew it. He removed the muzzle of the revolver from my head and eased down the hammer.

"You don't think I'm a man of my word, do you?" he said to Papa.

Then Mr. Fowler realized he had stepped in it. "Hold on now, Charlie," he said.

"I'm sick of your babbling, Winthrop," Indian Charlie said.

He shot Mr. Fowler through the kneecap. Mr. Fowler's crutches and both of his legs collapsed under him, and he went down in a pool of water, moaning and gripping his knee, his eyes tightly shut.

"Hurts, don't it?" Indian Charlie said.

"I'll do it," Papa said.

"Do what?" Indian Charlie asked.

"Dig it up. It's by the outhouse. All in gold coins."

"How much?"

"More than I can guess. Most of them are collectibles. They never stop rising in value."

"Good man, Mr. Holland," Indian Charlie said. "And if you think I have limitations on the way I do business, watch this."

He shot Mr. Fowler through the top of his cranium, splattering his brains on his face. But he wasn't finished. He stuck his pistol back in his britches and pointed the fuel tube of the flamethrower at the sky and pulled the trigger, blowing a balloon of flame and heat and petrol smoke that was like a clothes iron pressed on my cheek.

"Flip the Henry into the rose bed or Miss Bessie is gonna be a chitlin," he said.

I suspect it was one of the most difficult things Papa ever did. Back then no Texas Ranger would ever give up his weapon, but Papa did and he did it for me, chucking the Henry over the porch rail into the flower bed. "I'll need some help," he said. "There's two or three shovels in the barn. A pick and a mattock, too."

"That's no problem," Indian Charlie said.

He turned around and nodded to two of his men, who made a face and dropped their heads and began walking toward the barn, obviously unhappy with their job. Steam was rising from the ground and the stock tank, the windmill still whirring. I had never seen the sky so dark. Nor had I ever been so afraid. I had heard former Confederate soldiers talk about walking uphill into cannon fire at Shiloh, their fear so great it set them free, as though they stepped on the other side of a wall. But that did not happen to me. I felt as though we were at the bottom of an ocean, one that was so deep it would daunt a whale.

The rain had stopped. Papa and I walked ahead of Indian Charlie to the privy in back. It was a very old one, cold in the winter and full of wasps and fecal odors in the summer. "Funny thing, daughter," Papa said. "All this started with the privy at the schoolhouse, and now it's going to end at the privy in our yard."

"What are y'all talking about?" Indian Charlie said.

"Just the way things turn out, Charlie," Papa said. "Nothing I planned ever came to anything. You know, like a snipe hunt. Standing at a fence in the dark with a battery light in front of a gunnysack, hoping you catch a bunch of snipe."

"What the hell is all that supposed to mean?" Indian Charlie said.

I knew Papa was talking to me, not to Indian Charlie. But I wasn't quite sure what he was trying to say.

"I was just trying to pass the time, Charlie," Papa said. "You're making me awful nervous with that hot-prod or whatever you call it. Jesus Christ, where'd you get that thing?"

Papa knew dadburn well where he got it, but he was doing everything he could to distract Indian Charlie and get a message to me. I just didn't know what it was.

"Charlie, I got to relieve myself," Papa said. "Be a gentleman, okay?"

"You'll have to hold it," Indian Charlie said.

"I'm talking about heavy-duty relief," Papa said. "I cain't dig or concentrate with my pipes plugged up, much less with a bucketload of organic matter sagging in my britches."

"Go inside. I'll give you five minutes," Indian Charlie said.

"Thank you, sir," Papa said.

He went inside the privy and pushed the door shut. I could hear him dropping his suspenders. The two men Indian Charlie had sent to the barn were returning with an armful of tools. A sliver of moonlight had just shone in a cloud. Then I saw a battery light again, this time behind the first well we dug. The well was pumping, clanking up and down. Then I saw a figure next to it, just for a second.

"I need some paper," Papa said inside the privy.

"Use your shirt," Indian Charlie said.

"I'm not coming out till I get some paper," Papa said. "You can shoot me through the wall if you want."

"There's a Sears, Roebuck catalog in the kitchen," I said to Indian Charlie. "I'll run in and out. But you have to untie me."

I could see him thinking. He knew my father. Papa was the most stubborn man in Texas, and often about things of no consequence. Indian Charlie looked at one of his men, a man who was either a halfwit or what people back then called a mute. "Take her to the house, Tom, but don't untie her," Indian Charlie said. "You got it?"

The man named Tom nodded.

"All right," Indian Charlie said to me. "You got two minutes."

I didn't know what Papa was doing, nor could I think of a way out of our situation. The man who escorted me to the kitchen didn't say a word. His eyes were hostile, suspicious, and cruel. People can be handicapped and mean. This was one of them.

"You go to church?" I asked. "Does your family know what you're doing? Do you want to live the rest of your life with a man like Indian Charlie?"

The look he gave me made me shiver. I thought about the guards in the tower where Joan of Arc spent her last days. I think they were cruel and morally demented men. I think they violated her before her death, also. I told Tom the Halfwit where the Sears, Roebuck catalog was and let him walk me down the steps again and back to the privy. I knew our time on earth was running out. My heart was beating, my stomach sick, and I began to pray.

Tom gave the catalog to Indian Charlie.

"I have to do it for him," I said.

"What?" Indian Charlie said.

"He has a pinched nerve in his back."

"You wipe your father?"

"You're a disgusting man," I said.

Indian Charlie chewed on his cigar, his face thoughtful. "Cut her loose, Tom."

Suddenly my wrists were free. Indian Charlie put the catalog in my hand. "Go on, do it," he said.

I stepped inside the privy and shut the door behind me. Papa was seated, his britches down on his ankles. He motioned me to lower my ear to his mouth. "Mystify, mislead, and surprise. Stonewall Jackson," he whispered. "When I say go, you run and keep running. Don't you dare argue with me, either. You run like you've never run in your life. It's the only chance either one of us has. Nod if you understand."

"No, I cain't leave you, Papa——"

He stuck a stiffened forefinger in my face. "It's the only option. Otherwise we both die at the hands of that man. You're brave. You don't have to prove it."

"What the hell you doing in there?" Indian Charlie said outside the door.

"What do you think, you dumb bastard?" Papa said. "Give me thirty seconds."

Papa stood up from the hole in the wood planks and pulled up his suspenders with his thumbs, then shoved the door open with the heel of his hand. "Find the tools, all right? I'm fixing to make y'all plutocrats."

"What's a plutocrat?" Indian Charlie said.

"You ought to investigate one of those correspondence colleges, Charlie," Papa said. "With your smarts, you could go somewhere. Anyway, let's get to work."

"I thought you had a bad back," Indian Charlie said.

"I do," Papa replied. "But stretching my muscles gets the damaged nerve off my spine. Keep in mind what I said about that correspondence college."

Papa took a shovel from the hand of one of Indian Charlie's men and inserted his boot on the blade and sunk it into the ground about ten feet from the privy, then began digging.

"You have to pardon me about the exact location," he said, breathing heavily as he spoke. "For sanitary reasons we've moved the outhouse eight or nine times, but I think I'm pretty close to the right spot. Anyway, y'all have any battery lanterns?"

"You need to shut up, Mr. Holland," Indian Charlie said.

"I think you're right," Papa said. "Let's get everybody to working. No lollygagging. No messing around. I mean let's just flat rip the yard apart. Get on it, boys. Y'all are going to be wealthy men. You might be able to pay your way out of hell. Oh, I forgot to ask if Charlie is paying y'all union wages and that sort of thing."

"I said to shut your mouth, Mr. Holland."

"Well, can these fellas work or not?" Papa said. "A couple of them look like they've got sleeping sickness."

"All right, boys, do what the man says," Indian Charlie said. "We need to get out of here."

But my father's words were sinking into these fellas. And it was not good for Indian Charlie. I could see the doubt in their faces, the lack of energy when they pushed a shovel into the dirt, the discomfort and hesitation when the man next to them swung a mattock.

Papa was the strongest man there, and out-digging the whole bunch, reaching down to a level that was past the rainwater and dampness and into dry dirt and a mixture of lime and feces that was like ground-up pecan shells. Then it hit me. He said we started at the privy, and would end at it. I knew what was coming next and prepared myself for it.

Except it didn't happen.

Jubal Fowler walked toward us out of the dark, from the windmill and into the yard. He may have been drunk. I couldn't tell. He didn't seem armed. He carried an unlit battery light in one hand; his other hand was thumb-hooked in his jeans. He could have been a high school boy taking a stroll.

"What are y'all doing?" he said. "Where's Daddy?"

The digging stopped. The only sound was the house and pecan tree dripping.

"What's going on, Charlie?" he said. "Where's my old man?"

Chapter Forty-Nine

"You don't have no business here," Indian Charlie said.

"You picked up Daddy tonight. That makes it my business, Charlie," Jubal said. "Where is he?"

"Go home, Jubal," I said.

"Where's my father, Bessie?"

I lowered my eyes and put my hand on Papa's arm. Jubal scanned the faces of Indian Charlie's men. "Where's Mr. Winthrop, boys?"

They weren't good actors. They glanced at each other or at the ground and then in the direction of the front yard. I could see Jubal's features sharpen, his eyes narrow, an unwanted knowledge growing inside them. He began to breathe hard, then harder. He turned and walked fast back to the front yard.

"Hit and git it, boys!" Papa shouted out. "Show me what you got! Come on, you boys have busted rock and been on the hard road, dug rice fields in Sugar Land, ate beans on the hard road in Eastham! That's it, boys! Fling it in the air! Dig all the way to China! A Georgia chain gang ain't got nothing on Texas boys! I'm proud as heck to be among you!"

Papa should have been a psychologist. It worked. They actually did what he said. This was probably the first time in their lives someone gave them a compliment. The air was full of dust and powdered lime and fecal matter that was like breathing tiny bits of wire. Indian Charlie's fellas were coughing and choking and swearing and perhaps scared to death, but they preferred the chaos of their labor to whatever was about to happen.

Then Jubal returned from the front yard. He looked stupefied.

"What did you do to my father, Charlie?" Jubal said. He was forty feet from Indian Charlie. "What did you do to him?"

"He did it to himself, Jubal," Indian Charlie said.

"He trusted you."

"I didn't have no selection, son. He went crazy. This little bitch yonder ruined his life and his brain."

"Don't you dare call me 'son,' you son of a bitch."

Indian Charlie was lifting the fuel tube on the flamethrower.

"You murdered my father," Jubal said. "For no gain. For nothing. Just for meanness."

"Not so, boy," Indian Charlie said. "I'll cut you in on the money we're digging up. After that, there won't be no stopping you. You can have women, automobiles, all the liquor and drugs you want, servants waiting on you. Or I can get you an office job in Houston. But I got to take care of the Hollands first. Starting with the girl. You know what's got to be done. Some people ain't learners."

Then I heard the loud clank of a shovel and a man grunt and bounce off the side of the privy. Papa was swinging his shovel, hitting anything he could.

"Run, Bessie, run!" he yelled.

Now I knew what he had planned all along. He was trading his life for mine. He had been right. There was no way both of us could survive. But one of us could, and that one was me.

But I would honor his wish and not argue. I would run and run and run. That was my decision, and I would have to live with it until I went to the grave, which would probably be a blessing. I ran past the pecan tree that shaded the side yard, and past Indian Charlie. At the same time Indian Charlie's men were running in every direction, because he had ignited the tip of the fuel tube again and was about to spray flame on either Papa or Jubal or maybe both of them.

Or at least that's what I thought. Vanity, vanity. What does that mean? I twisted my ankle and fell among the pecan husks. I raised myself on my elbows and looked at the backyard. Indian Charlie was walking toward me, squeezing short spurts of flame from the end of the tube.

Indian Charlie was going to burn me alive. Papa's knowledge about the hidden money was too valuable to lose. I was dispensable. Then I saw Jubal in silhouette, coming after Charlie and me. "Try me, Charlie," he said. "I ain't a cripple."

Indian Charlie turned around, his back to me, the two tanks strapped to it wet with dew. "I'll do it to you, kid," he said. "You know me. I ain't got no mercy."

"Then do it," Jubal said.

Indian Charlie squeezed the trigger on the fuel tube and a huge flame blossomed through the pecan limbs, but simultaneously Jubal pulled an object from the back of his leather belt and threw it at Indian Charlie. I had no doubt about what he had been carrying. He knew how to blow stumps when he was thirteen. He might have blown wells for one of the wildcatters or for Atlas. A half stick could work wonders.

The explosion of the half stick of dynamite and Indian Charlie's tanks was of a strange kind. It generated a brilliant orange and red light that surrounded Indian Charlie's body, as though he had become a withering seed, a soul that was not only being blackened but reduced to cinders.

I got to my feet, the leaves from the pecan tree drifting into my hair, the moon rising above the clouds, the sounds of animals on the wind. I could see Papa coming toward me, his arms open. All of Indian Charlie's men were running in different directions. I couldn't see them in their midst, and then I realized Jubal was gone, and I mean gone, like a character is gone when you close a book, as though all the pain he caused had been lost forever.

But I will tell you who was there, even though others would probably deny my account of events after the immolation of Indian Charlie. Papa put his arms around me and pulled me to his chest and squeezed so hard I thought my bones would crack. I loved his smell. It smelled like the earth, like smoke and sweat, like love and goodness, like courage.

I never wanted to leave Papa again. I knew I would, but not now. Papa was the conduit to another world, one of tinkling pianos and saloon dance girls who had their own kind of innocence, and Texas drovers who went to the ice cream parlor when they first hit Abilene, and saddle preachers who indeed saw the glory of God beyond the Cimarron.

I lost sense of time under the pecan tree. And I think Papa did, too. But neither of us cared. The dawn was here. Friends began to arrive in buggies or on saddles or in wagons or in Model T Fords. As the sunlight streaked across the land, almost like an entranceway to an ancient pantheon, I saw Aint Minnie and Snowball and Mr. Slick and Ida Banks and Bertha Lafleur and Jared Cohen and Skeeter and my brother Cody and the two Hebrew cowboys who took care of Christian lepers and our Mexican helpers whose names we no longer knew, and also some others, the mist rising around them, the Tennessean and his twenty-two men on their way to the Alamo, and Susanna Dickinson and my mother Alafair Holland and the little girl who was murdered in the woods.

"Daughter?" Papa said.

"Yes?" he said.

He waited a long time, then took a breath and said, "We've got to fix breakfast for a whole lot of people and take care of the critters too."

Epilogue

I did not marry Mr. Cohen. But I did marry a man who was very much like him, a classically educated gentleman from Louisiana who was an engineer and a kind and principled soul.

So I was conflicted, and I hate that word, with myself when I received the telephone call from Benny Siegel, who told me he was at the Shamrock Hotel with his sweetheart and they would love to see me.

Oh my heavens, I thought. What do I do now? Benny's reputation was notorious, and so were Meyer's and Frankie's. After Owney Madden got out of prison, he created the segregationist Cotton Club in Harlem out of Jack Johnson's former supper club, which served everyone. Cody became a professional boxer and Mr. Madden's bouncer and personal bodyguard, until he returned to Texas permanently and wildcatted and hit oil in the Permian Basin and became a rich man living with his family in River Oaks.

If you do not know what the contemporary River Oaks is like, I will tell you. The people who live there can buy New York City with their credit cards.

My husband was a good man. But he was a proper one, too, and the idea of his and my having dinner with Benny and his sweetheart was not tenable. No, that is an understatement. My husband would move to Mars before he would be in the same room with either Benny or Miss Virginia.

So I accepted Benny's invitation and took my son on the bus to the Shamrock Hotel on a lovely evening, the hotel that Glenn McCarthy built. And if you don't know who he was, he was the man who became Jett Rink in *Giant*.

We ate on the terrace, not far from the swimming pool, with a view across South Main of the oil wells that clanked and pumped night and day, while cattle grazed between the stanchions. Benny's hair was a little thin, but otherwise he looked youthful and handsome, his light-blue eyes merry, his brow free of worry. He talked about Jack Warner and George Raft and people whose names I didn't recognize. Our silent film company was eventually a bust, as well as the Holland Oil Company, although I have no regrets about my experience in either industry.

My little family was a happy one. We had a brick bungalow covered with English ivy on Hawthorne Street in Southwest Houston, when Houston was still semirural, in a neighborhood filled with flowers and bamboo and elephant ears and live oak trees hung with Spanish moss, which my husband especially loved. I would never change the way things worked out. I told this to Benny, maybe indicating to him that money and power are not everything. Sadly, I don't think my dear friend Benny learned very much. I wanted him to tell me the rape charge against him in the early 1920s was specious, although I knew Benny could not speak of this in front of his sweetheart, Miss Virginia, who was a beautiful, red-haired Georgia girl with probably the same upbringing I had.

So my little boy and I rode home on the bus, and I never told my husband what I had done. I hope he will forgive me, although he has been gone for decades. As I write these words, I am just short of one hundred and two years old. I hear Papa in the other room, believe it or not. He's calling now, and y'all know how Papa is, a dadburn mess. My son became a writer and wrote down a number of these stories. I think he's right good at it. I hope he gives me a credit or two. Anyway, I'd better go now.

Acknowledgments

Don't Forget Me, Little Bessie is obviously a different kind of book for me because the narrator is a young girl about to become a woman, in a time when the shadow of the Great War was about to touch all of America and not recede from its presence. In fact, T. E. Lawrence might have wanted to say a thing or two about it, all good, I hope. But all that aside, I think this is one of my best books. The Hollands are back, and none of them could be better to introduce a new reader to this pioneer family. She's a grand person, intelligent and kind, beautiful in spirit and body, and able to hide her heart lest it be shattered.

I'm old. But I'm glad I'm old. I remember Pearl Harbor and how cold and dark it was at my grandfather's desiccated house, the wind blowing, a small fire in the cookstove. In that part of Texas, the Dust Bowl had never gone away. The sky was hung with soot, the cotton killed by drought, the corn stalks feathering by dust devils so sharp they could stick a pin in you. Even though I was very little, I knew one day I would write a story about this place and the people who lived in it, and the kerosene lamps that burned inside their shacks, and the coldness that had actually shrunk the stars.

The people who were there are not gone. They are still there because we are. That's why I have always felt that art is collective in its creativeness and its making. And that's why I want to thank a number of people who one way or another are part of this fine book.

Thanks to my publisher Grove Atlantic and Morgan Entrekin, Zoe Harris, Deb Seager, Justina Batchelor, Natalie Church, Rachael Richardson, Judy Hottensen, and JT Green for the splendid editing and typography and artwork. I think there is none better. Also thanks to the Spitzer Agency, my guardians of forty-seven years, which includes Anne-Lise Spitzer, Mary Spitzer, Lukas Ortiz, and Kim Lombardini. Also thanks to my entertainment attorney Penelope Glass and my sidekick and Pamala's Erin Mitchell, who, like Pamala, can fix anything.

Last have been the team at home, Pearl, Jimmie, Andree, Alafair, and Pamala, who I always believe is out there.

I was a friend of Leicester Hemingway. When he read one of my books, he always called it a "whammeroo." I want to call it the same. I hope you do, too.

Thanks for listening,
James Lee Burke